in your dreams

Center Point
Large Print

Also by Kristan Higgins and available from Center Point Large Print:

Perfect Match
Waiting on You

in your dreams

WITHDRAWN

KRISTAN HIGGINS

CENTER POINT LARGE PRINT
THORNDIKE, MAINE

The text of this Large Print edition is unabridged.
In other aspects, this book may vary
from the original edition.
Printed in the United States of America
on permanent paper.
Set in 16-point Times New Roman type.

ISBN: 978-1-62899-428-5

Library of Congress Cataloging-in-Publication Data

Higgins, Kristan.
 In your dreams : a blue heron novel / Kristan Higgins. —
    Center Point Large Print edition.
    pages ; cm
    Summary: "Emmaline Neal asks the perfectly handsome Jack Holland to be her weekend date for her ex-fiancé's wedding. After one unexpected night together, will they start believing in their own happily-ever-after?"—Provided by publisher.
    ISBN 978-1-62899-428-5 (library binding : alk. paper)
    1. Large type books. I. Title.
 PS3608.I365715 2015
 813'.6—dc23
                                                        2014044845

This book is dedicated to my great friend—
the wonderful, the generous, the mighty
Robyn Carr.

in your dreams

Prologue

Well, now, it goes without saying that we all love Jack Holland. Especially us women.

But the Midwinter Miracle . . . Oh, gosh, can you even imagine? Not that we were surprised that Jack was wonderful—of course he was! First of all, he's John Holland's son, the only boy in the family, though I guess we'd have to say "man" now, of course. And he was in the navy, too, just in case he hadn't already won us over by being the nicest thing ever. Not to mention handsome! Those blue eyes . . . Even Cathy and Louise were talking about those eyes the other day!

Jack's just about royalty around here, since the Hollands are a founding family of Manningsport, and Jack's the head winemaker at Blue Heron, the Hollands' vineyard. Guess we won't have to worry about them selling their land to a developer, not with all those kids in the family business. And then there's the way Jack treats those three sisters of his, and his stepmother! A prince, that's what he is! Don't get us started on that ex-wife of his. She never deserved him.

Anyway, what we were saying? Oh, yes, the Midwinter Miracle! Well now, sure, it was a group effort. Levi Cooper, our police chief, he was wonderful (no relation to Anderson, and don't think we didn't ask). Levi and his deputy, Luanne Macomb's granddaughter, what's her name again? Emily? Emmaline? Anyway, they did the CPR. And that handsome Gerard Chartier, him, too.

But mostly, it was Jack.

Which was no surprise to us.

It was quite . . . well, *exciting* isn't quite the right word, is it? But it was remarkable, no disrespect meant to that poor family, of course. Manningsport just about shuts down in the winter, just us year-rounders left, no tourists until spring when the wine tastings start up again. So the Midwinter Miracle brought all sorts of media celebrities here—Brian Williams stayed at the Black Swan; did you know? So charming! And just about every-one and their brother had to drop by O'Rourke's when Anderson Cooper was in there.

That night put our little lakeside town on the map, and given that it happened in January, well, we could all use the distraction. Laney Hughes even opened up the gift shop off-season, there were so many people flocking to town. Unloaded plenty of Keuka Lake T-shirts, she sure did. Lorelei's Sunrise Bakery sold out of everything by 8:00 a.m. that entire week.

What's that? How's Jack doing? He's fine! He's wonderful! A true hero. Anyone will tell you that.

Why would you even ask?

Chapter One

Nothing kicked off Emmaline Neal's weekend like using a Taser.

Okay, okay, she hadn't used the Taser yet and she probably wouldn't get to *(dang),* but the tiny thrill of anticipation didn't lie. If indeed there was an intruder in the McIntosh house, it would be deeply satisfying to apprehend him. Barb McIntosh suspected a sex offender, and, if she was right, Em knew exactly where she'd target the electrodes.

Granted, Barb had already admitted to being addicted to *Law & Order: Special Victims Unit* ("That Christopher Meloni! So handsome!"). But she'd heard strange noises in the utility part of her basement, and her grandson, the notoriously creepy Bobby, wasn't home.

"Approaching cellar stairs," Everett Field whispered.

"Yeah, I can tell that, Ev, since I'm right behind you," Emmaline said. "And there's no need to whisper."

"Roger that," Everett whispered.

Despite the fact that Emmaline had only been on the job for nine months and Everett was more senior, they both knew she was a better cop. Ev wasn't the crunchiest chip in the bag.

"You sure Bobby's not here?" Em asked Barb over her shoulder.

"No. I called him on the phone and yelled down there, so . . ."

"Roger that," Everett said, reaching for his holster. "Alert for incoming hostiles."

"Get your hand off that gun, Everett," Emmaline said. "And where do you get this language?"

"Call of Duty."

"Great. Just calm down. We're not shooting any-one." Taser at most, and only then if there was a struggle.

The crime rate was pretty low in Manningsport, New York, population 715, a tiny town at the base of Keuka Lake. Everett and Em made up two-thirds of the police department; their boss, Levi Cooper, was the other third. Traffic patrol, the occasional DUI, vandalism, parking tickets . . . That was about as exciting as it got around here. Em ran a group for at-risk teenagers, of whom there were four. In the summer and fall, when the tourists came to taste wine and swim and boat on Keuka Lake, they were busier, but this was January, and things were quiet. In fact, this was their first call in three days.

Something thumped, and Everett squeaked. Chances were that it was a malfunctioning furnace. Possibly a raccoon. Levi always said if you heard hoofbeats, expect to see horses, not zebras.

They were in the cellar now; in front of them was Bobby's apartment; to the right was the door to the other half of the cellar, which housed the furnace and water heater and, Barb had told them, several dozen jars of pickled vegetables she'd put up this summer.

Thud.

Okay, something was in there.

"It's probably an animal," Em murmured, taking the Maglite off her belt. The utility room wasn't accessible from the outside, so a person would've had to come in through the house. And Barb always locked up (again, the mighty influence of *Law & Order*).

Everett put his hand on the doorknob and looked at Em, who nodded. Then he flung open the door, and Em flashed the light, and something moved inside, and Everett screamed and, before she could stop him, drew and fired.

Damn! The noise slapped her eardrums hard.

"It's a cat! Everett, it's a cat!" she yelled. "Holster your weapon!"

Everett obeyed. As he did, a ball of black and white leaped on him, hissing, and sank its teeth into his thigh. Apparently Puss in Boots didn't appreciate being shot at.

"Officer down, officer down!" Ev yelled, swatting at it. "Ten double zero, officer down!"

"Shut up," Em ordered. "You deserve it." He'd missed the kitty, of course. The guy was a terrible shot.

She lifted the cat gently by the scruff of the neck and pulled it off Everett's leg. All of a sudden, Everett was grabbed around the throat by Bobby McIntosh, who apparently *was* home after all.

"Why did you shoot my cat?" he yelled.

"Bobby! Let go of him!" Emmaline said.

"We don't have a cat!" Barb said from upstairs. "Bobby, did you bring a cat home?"

Everett was sputtering and red-faced. Em sighed. "Let him go, or I'll have to use this," she said, taking her Taser off her belt. "It hurts."

He hesitated. She cocked an eyebrow, and, with a sigh, he released her partner.

Drat. "Thank you, Bobby," she said. *So close.*

"Bobby! What were you doing down there?" Barb said. "I called you and you didn't answer! Where did you get that thing, anyway? I hate cats."

"I love them," Bobby said. "I got it from the shelter."

"Okay, so we're good here," Emmaline said. Everett's eyes were wide. "Come on, Ev—let's go. You're gonna have to file a report for discharging your firearm, you know."

"I thought it was a sex offender," Everett said, his hands shaking.

"It wasn't. You're safe now, buddy," she said, patting his arm. "Come on. Back to the station."

14

• • •

"You shot a cat?" Chief Cooper said fifteen minutes later, staring at Everett.

"I'm sorry." Ev stood there like a chastened kid.

"He missed," Emmaline said. Now that the ringing in her ears had faded, it was hard not to laugh. "The suspect was quite fast." Levi gave her a look.

"File the report, Everett. The incident is under review, which means you just increased my workload."

"Sorry, Chief. Um, Bobby McIntosh attacked me."

"Because you shot at his pet."

"In self-defense."

"Not really," Emmaline said. "The cat was the one acting in self-defense."

Levi bit down on a grin. "Your mother won't be happy about this, Ev."

"Do you have to tell her?"

"She's the mayor. So, yes."

"Shit." Everett heaved a sigh. "Anything else, Chief?"

"No. Fill out the report and get out of here."

Everett left the office and swiped a cookie from the desk of Carol Robinson, their newly hired administrative assistant, who'd been shamelessly eavesdropping.

"Thanks for not letting Bobby kill Everett," Levi said to Emmaline.

"I was kind of hoping to use the Taser."

"Could've used it on Everett," he said. "But good to see cooler heads prevailed."

It was about as high praise as the police chief gave, and Emmaline felt a small rush of pride. Granted, it had been an idiotic call in the first place, but still.

Levi, who'd been a year behind her in high school, stood and picked up a bouquet of red roses wrapped in green florist paper and tied with a white ribbon. His look warned her not to say anything.

"Aw," she said. "Flowers for the wife? You're such a snuggly teddy bear, Levi."

"Inappropriate, Officer Neal," he said, giving her his famous "I tolerate you because I have to" look. "By the way, about that crisis negotiations class. I got you a grant. You start in two weeks."

"You did? Oh, you're the best! I take back every complaint I ever filed about you."

"Very funny," her boss said. "I'm going home. Maybe I'll see you at O'Rourke's later."

"Maybe. Tell Pregnita I said hi."

He smiled and left the office, stopping to say something to Carol before he left the station.

It was hard not to feel a little jealous. Levi and Faith had been married a little over a year and had a baby on the way. Seemed like everyone was getting married these days; Em had been to three weddings over the summer. In fact, she was

16

considering marrying herself, just so she could register for the fun housewares.

Well. Time for her to go home, too. The O'Keefe Emergency Services Building, which housed the fire, police and ambulance departments, was about five minutes from town. Em drove past Hastings Farm, past the high school and into the Village part of Manningsport, three blocks around a small green at the edge of Keuka Lake.

Emmaline lived on Water Street, right next to the library, and often parked the cruiser along the green where the good people of Manningsport could see it and reconsider any bad decisions, like driving under the influence. O'Rourke's Tavern, the only place in town open year-round, glowed warm and bright. Maybe she'd eat there tonight, since she didn't have any plans. But first, home to the Wonder Pup—Sarge, her recently acquired German shepherd puppy, who'd need a walk and some exercise, despite his doggy door to the backyard.

She got out of the cruiser, her breath fogging in the cold, clean air.

"Hey, Em!" called a voice. Lorelei Buzzetta and Gerard Chartier waved as they went into O'Rourke's, and Em waved back. Gerard was a firefighter and paramedic. Em saw him nearly every day at work (and also saw Lorelei, who owned the bakery and could make the angels

17

weep with her chocolate croissants). The two had started dating a while back.

Through the windows, she could see Colleen O'Rourke, now Colleen Campbell, kissing her gorgeous husband, Lucas. There was Honor Holland and her husband, the lovely Tom Barlow. Paulie Petrosinsky and Bryce, who ran the animal shelter and had fixed her up with her puppy just two weeks ago.

Seemed like couples' night at the pub.

Maybe she'd stay in tonight. She and Sarge could watch YouTube videos of hostage negotiators, eat Kraft Mac & Cheese (don't judge, it was delicious). Maybe binge-watch *The Walking Dead.* She had a stack of books from the library, too. Or she could call around the Bitter Betrayeds, the name her book club had given itself, and see who else was climbing the walls.

Suddenly, the weekend spread vast and empty in front of her. No shifts till Monday. No plans other than a hockey game on Sunday—she played in the town league. She could do laundry and clean. Um . . . maybe buy some new towels. Go to the shooting range. That'd be fun, if solitary.

Her feet were getting numb. Time to get moving. Still, she stood there on the tiny town green, looking into the cheerful pub.

Maybe she'd drive to Penn Yan and see a movie, but it was a half an hour away, and there was more snow in the forecast. And after the big accident, everyone was feeling a little wary about winter driving.

Speaking of that, there was Jack Holland.

He stood outside O'Rourke's, staring at the building as if he'd never seen it before. Maybe she should check on him. They played hockey together, and he was her boss's brother-in-law and an EMT, so it wasn't as though she didn't know him.

He didn't move, seeming to be trying to decide whether or not to go inside the bar.

Em crossed the street. "Hey, Jack," she said.

He didn't answer.

"Hi, Jack," she said again. He jerked, then looked at her.

"Hey, Emmaline," he said, forcing a smile.

"How you doing?"

"Great."

He was so *not* great that her heart ached, looking at him stalled there, dead in the water.

Poor choice of words.

But he was clearly not great.

"You going in?" he asked, aware perhaps that too long a pause had elapsed.

"No. I'm headed home. I just got a puppy. Sarge. He's a German shepherd. Very cute. Hopefully he hasn't pooped on the floor."

Oh, yeah, the babbling thing. See, in addition to all the above, Jack Holland was ridiculously gorgeous. As in, *Hi, I've just dropped down from*

19

Mount Olympus. How you doin'? Tall and blond with eyes that were so clear and perfect and pure that they made a person think of all sorts of ridiculous synonyms for blue—azure and cerulean and aqua. His smile stopped traffic and made trees burst into flower and all that crap.

So yes, he rendered women stupid. Even women who were slightly prejudiced against very, very good-looking men. But everyone, including Emmaline, also knew that Jack was a tremendously nice guy.

"Jack? You okay?"

"Yeah!" he said too quickly. "Sorry. Just a little tired. You take care, Emma."

No one called her that. More than likely, Jack Holland had just forgotten her name. He opened the door to the pub. There was a roar of "Jack!" and "Hey! The hero!" and general cheering. The iron bell behind the bar clanged; the O'Rourke twins rang it in times of celebration.

Poor guy.

Emmaline knew that the good folks of Manningsport—and America—had been quite dazzled with what Jack Holland had done. So had she. How many people could have done what he did, after all? It *was* dazzling.

Which didn't explain the look on Jack's face.

Well. He had a big family and a lot of friends. Everyone loved the Hollands. He'd be well taken care of.

With a deep breath of the frigid air, Emmaline went around the corner to her house, a little bungalow. She'd left a couple of lights on for the puppy, and her little house fairly glowed with welcome.

Emmaline wasn't a Manningsport native, but she'd gone to high school here, living with her grandmother in this very house. Nana had died four years ago and left the house to Em and her sister, Angela, who lived in California. But to Em, the bungalow meant more than just home—it was where she'd found refuge and normalcy back in the day . . . and again when she'd moved here three years ago. She'd kept a lot of Nana's furniture, bought some of her own, painted here and there, and the result was a pleasing mix of old and new, no real style per se, but comfortable and cheery, and it never failed to make her smile.

She scooped her mail from the little brass mailbox, unlocked the door and got down on all fours. "Mommy's home," she said.

The scrabbling of paws and yips of joy were happy music of the soul.

Sarge ran to her, Squeaky Chicken, his favorite toy, in his jaws as an offering.

Emmaline gathered the puppy into her arms and kissed his furry head. "Hello, puppy," she said. She resisted the strong urge to indulge in baby talk to the dog to preserve his dignity and her own, but she couldn't help laughing as he licked her face, wriggling like a little otter.

She stood up, did a few twirls, since he loved that, then encouraged him to go outside before he peed on the floor from excitement. He galloped out, chasing a leaf across the small, fenced-in backyard.

Em flipped through her mail. A flyer for a discount on heart-shaped cookies and cupcakes at Lorelei's Sunrise Bakery—Valentine's Day preorders now accepted. No need to save that, unless she wanted to buy herself some goodies (which she did, though her uniform pants seemed a little hostile these days). A bill from the cable company. A postcard from her sister. *Saluti da Milano!* Right. Flawless Angela had been in Italy at, yes, an astrophysicists' convention.

Em flipped the card over. "Hello, sis! Hope you're doing well. I haven't been able to see much of Milan yet, but I hope to squeeze a few days of holiday after the convention. Hope to catch up soon! Love and kisses, Angela."

That was nice. Her sister, younger by four years, was incredibly thoughtful. She was Daughter 2.0, adopted from Ethiopia when Em went away to high school. The kind of daughter Dr. and Dr. Neal hoped to have, though they never said anything like that. Angela was brilliant, kind, cheerful and also stunningly beautiful with her glowing brown skin and enormous, expressive eyes. She'd modeled in college, even. If Emmaline didn't love her so much, it'd be really easy to hate her.

Sarge came back in through his doggy door, a clot of snow right on his nose. Ridiculously cute. She gave him his supper, then poured herself a Blue Point Toasted Lager. Yeah, yeah, the Finger Lakes were known for their vineyards, but there were plenty of great microbreweries, too.

Oops. There was one more piece of mail on the kitchen floor. She leaped for it, snatching it up just before Sarge pounced. He loved paper.

It was a wedding invitation, from the look of it. Thick ivory envelope, red calligraphy, a flower stamp.

It was postmarked "Malibu, CA," her hometown.

Her knees gave a warning tingle.

She sat down at the little enamel-topped kitchen table. Opened the envelope to find another envelope inside. "Miss Emmaline Neal & Guest," it said. She opened that, as well.

"Together with their parents, Naomi Norman and Kevin Bates joyfully request the honor of your company at their marriage ceremony."

Sarge put his paws against her knee, and she scooped him onto her lap. "So," she said to her dog, her mouth dry. "Looks like my fiancé is getting married."

Chapter Two

On Saturday afternoon, Jack Holland drove from the hospital in Corning back to Blue Heron, the vineyard owned and run by his family. The radio was tuned to a talk show, though what the topic was, Jack didn't quite know. Still, the voices were comforting.

It occurred to him that he was probably alone too much these days. That a battered cat was insufficient company. That he should be with people. But last night at O'Rourke's had been a circle of hell, all those people clapping him on the back and offering to buy him beers. Asking how he was doing. How Josh was doing. Thanking him. Telling him he was one brave son of a bitch and the town wouldn't stop talking about this for years, which made Jack's hands sweaty.

Still, he'd smiled and thanked people for whatever it was they were saying, because he knew in one corner of his mind that they were saying nice things, or what they thought were nice things, and he knew that the longer he stayed away from regular things, the harder it would be. He was fine. It was all fine. It was okay.

He'd stayed as long as he could take it. Colleen O'Rourke, who was like yet another sister in addition to the three Jack already had, gave him a hug, and so far as he could tell, he'd returned it. But once he'd gotten home, he just sat on the couch, Lazarus next to him, not touching but still there.

So being with his family, doing normal things, that was a good thing. He loved his family. They weren't a circle of hell. Well, not completely.

He put on his turn signal even though he was alone on the country road. Ever the cautious driver.

If only he could see Josh. Go when the parents weren't around. Just to see him.

Shit. He might have to pull over.

Once, when Jack was building his house, a bobcat had wandered in, lured by the smell of Jack's meatball sub there on the sawhorse. Jack came into the great room, and the animal panicked, ran straight for the closed slider and hurled itself against it again and again.

That's what Jack's heart was doing right now. Smacking and thudding against his ribs. His hands were slick on the steering wheel, but it was okay; it was fine—he didn't have to pull over. He was fine.

There looked to be a thousand cars at Honor's house. Jack and his sisters, Prudence, Honor and Faith, had grown up here in the New House, built in the 1800s. His middle sister, Honor, now lived with her husband, Tom, and Charlie, the teenager they'd sort of adopted. Jack's father and step-mother, Mrs. Johnson (technically Mrs. Holland, though no one called her that), lived in a spacious apartment over the garage.

Today was Faith's baby shower.

"Hey, Uncle Jack." Pru's son, Ned, approached Jack as he got out of the truck. "Why are we here again?"

"I have no idea," Jack said. "Solidarity for Levi, I guess."

Sure enough, the men of the family—Jack, his father and grandfather, his three brothers-in-law, and unofficial nephew, Charlie—were manfully hiding in the kitchen as a wave of feminine laughter came from the living room.

"Jack!" said his father. "Wine?"

"Thanks, Dad. Hey, Levi. How you doing?"

Levi looked pained. "They were just talking about nipple infections," he said, nodding toward the living room, which was hung with blue streamers.

"I call them the Coven for a reason," Jack said.

"Levi!" called Faith. "Come see this, honey. It's a Diaper Genie!"

"Ooh. A Diaper Genie," said Ned. "Grandpa, can I have some wine, too? Please? Quickly?"

"Are you old enough?"

"I am. Hurry."

"Levi!"

"They're calling for you, mate," said Tom, slapping Levi on the shoulder. "Best not keep the pregnant wife waiting."

"Your turn will come," Levi muttered darkly.

"The baby, I'm all for. It's the . . . stuff . . . that's making me nervous." He sighed and went into the living room to admire the diaper thing.

"A new baby," Dad said contentedly. "About time. Right, Jack? Another nephew for you."

"We can only hope he'll be as cool as Charlie and I are," Ned said.

Jack smiled. His wine was gone, he noticed. Funny. He didn't remember tasting it.

Mrs. Johnson bustled in, a towering plate of food in her hands. "I thought I heard your voice, Jackie, my darling boy! Would you like something to eat? You look thin."

"Mrs. J.," Jack said to his stepmother, "you look beautiful today. And every day, now that I think of it." His voice was pretty normal, he thought.

"Oh, you terrible liar!" She cuffed his head and beamed. "Come. See your sister. Make haste, and then you can eat."

Jack allowed himself to be led into the living room, where Faith sat, a plate of cake balanced on her baby bump, pastel-colored wrapping paper and tiny outfits strewn around her.

A dozen or so women talked at once, sounding like a slew of metal trash cans bouncing down a brick staircase. "Jack, how are you? Jack, you were amazing! Jack, thank God you were there! Jack, Jack, Jack!"

"Ladies," he said. The bobcat started ramming the door again, over and over and over. "Hey, sis."

He bent down and dropped an obligatory kiss on his sister's head.

"Jack!" Faith said, reaching up to pat his arm. "Thanks for coming, buddy."

"Sure. Which sister are you again?"

"The pregnant one. The queen."

He smiled. *See? Perfectly normal.* Faith was funny, and he reacted appropriately. Honor flashed him a smile, telling him he was doing okay.

"Well, I hope your labor will be better than mine, Faith," their grandmother said grandly. "Three days. No painkillers back then, either. It was the ether, or you toughed it out. Sometimes you died. John! Where are you, son?" Dad appeared in the kitchen doorway, already looking guilty. "Three days of labor with you."

"I'm sorry, Mom," he said. "Still." He sent Jack a pained look.

"I *loved* giving birth," Prudence said. "Ned slid out like a little otter, and with Abby, I didn't even have time to get to the car. She was born on the kitchen floor. Ass-first, no less."

"Thanks, Mom," Abby said. "I'm so glad everyone got to hear that."

"It explains a lot," her brother yelled from the kitchen.

"Make sure you get an episiotomy, Faith," said another woman. "Otherwise, you tear, and you wouldn't believe how much. Anyone else have stitches in their butts?"

Sadly, Jack had heard it all before. Three sisters who took no prisoners when it came to "sharing." It was like comparing war stories, he guessed, though his own stint in the navy hadn't resulted in any; he'd been in research down in D.C.

It was a little weird being in the New House— so called because it was newer than the original house built on the property, which had burned down last year. Honor had overhauled the New House this past summer, and while it was still the same friendly, sprawling old place Jack had grown up in, it took some getting used to. More power to her, but still a little disconcerting.

Or maybe that was just how everything was these days. The same, but off.

Levi came over and sat down next to him. "You hear some of those stories? Good God."

"Yeah, well, I grew up with three sisters. They can't be in the same room without talking about blood and ovaries. And then there was the crying and snarling when they were teenagers. Terrifying."

"Makes me glad I was in Afghanistan when my sister went through puberty," Levi said. "Probably a lot safer there." He was quiet for a minute. "You doing okay, Jack?"

"Oh, sure."

"Sleeping all right?"

"Pretty much," he lied. Levi shouldn't have to worry about him.

"Well, even with a good outcome, sometimes these things can be . . . traumatic."

"Yep. Sure."

"If you ever want to talk, just say the word."

"Thanks, pal. I appreciate it." The bobcat was back. *Thud. Thud. Thudthud. Thud.* He wondered if Levi could see the pulse in his neck.

Jack stood up as another peal of laughter came from the living room. "All right, I've had my estrogen dose of the day." He paused. "Have you heard anything about the Deiner kid?"

Levi looked up. "No change."

"Okay. Thanks." He tried to take a deep breath, but the air wouldn't fit in. Nodded at Levi, waved to the women, then made his way into the kitchen, where the other guys were now playing poker.

"Pull up a chair, Jack," said his grandfather. "We can deal you in."

"I have some stuff to do at home," he said, squeezing Pops's shoulder. "Dad, we should check the pinot tomorrow, okay?"

"Whatever you say, son." His father smiled at him, and Jack made sure he smiled back.

He went out to his truck. The sky was nearly dark. Another day past, so that was good. Not that the nights were easier. Just the opposite, in fact.

The door closed behind him. Tom this time.

"Hang on, mate," he said. "Just wanted a word. How are things?"

30

"Thanks, Tom. Things are fine."

His sister's husband was a good guy. In fact, all his sisters' husbands were good guys. They were even his friends, though he hadn't known Tom, a transplanted Brit, as long as he'd known Carl and Levi.

"If you need anything, say the word, yeah? You're always welcome here, of course. Honor's hoping you'll come watch one of those disgusting medical shows with her." Tom smiled, his eyes kind.

"I definitely will," Jack said. He probably wouldn't. "Thanks, Tom."

He got into his truck and headed down the driveway.

The road crew still hadn't repaired the guardrail, and a makeshift memorial had sprung up there the first night. Now the flowers were dead, rotting in their plastic florist wraps. A sodden teddy bear holding a heart had tipped over in the snow.

Don't look.

The truth was, he thought as he drove up the road, turning onto the long driveway that wound through the woods to Rose Ridge, he didn't want all the concern and attention and questions and hugs. He wanted not to think. He wanted Josh to get better. He wanted to have a do-over.

He put his key in the door and stopped dead in his tracks.

The house smelled like perfume.

Candles were burning on the table, and a fire flickered in the fireplace.

A beautiful woman unfolded herself from the couch. "Jack. Oh, baby, how are you? I've been so worried."

Shit.

The very last person on earth he needed.

"Hadley," he said, and with that, his ex-wife wrapped her arms around him.

She was here, she said, because of *course* she'd seen the coverage on TV and come as soon as she could. What a wonderful, *amazing* thing he'd done! The Midwinter Miracle indeed! Daddy was *so* proud, all of them were, of course it was just like Jack to—

"Hadley, what are you doing here? Really?" he interrupted.

She settled back on the couch, wrapping the throw around her. He'd have bet that she'd checked herself out in the mirror before he got home. *Blanket on or off? Do I want to look waifish and lost, or confident and strong? Hair up or down?*

She sipped her wine (which she'd helped herself to, he noticed). "I just had to come," she said. "And I don't want you to worry about a single thing. I took a leave of absence from my job, and I'm here for as long as it takes."

"As long as what takes?"

She took a deep breath. "Jack, I know how hard this all must've been for you, and I know we've had our problems—"

He laughed. That was one way of spinning it.

"And I want to be here for you. Take care of you." She paused, looking him directly in the eye. "Make things up to you."

"I haven't seen you for two years, Hadley."

"I know exactly how long it's been. I can't tell you how much I've regretted what happened between us. I've done some serious growing up these past couple of years, and I want to show you I'm not that person anymore."

It was a pretty good speech, he thought. "That's nice, but I'm not interested."

She looked down at her hands. "Can't say I blame you one bit."

She'd always had a way of making everything she did look beautiful.

"You need to leave now," he said. "Thanks for coming by."

"I understand," she said, and her voice was husky. She stood up and folded the throw. "Well, I'm staying in town for a little while, at any rate."

"Why?"

"Because even if you don't see it yet, I know we have unfinished business. And I want to help, Jack. I do."

"I don't need help. But thank you and good luck in the future and all that crap."

"You're angry. I don't blame you. Be that as it may, I'm here for the duration. Besides, it'll give me a chance to be closer to my sister."

Right. Frankie Boudreau, the youngest of the four Boudreau sisters, was in her final year at Cornell, getting her veterinary degree, which Jack knew quite well, since he still had the occasional dinner with his former sister-in-law.

"Well, don't let me keep you," he said. "Have a good night."

"That's fine. I . . . I just need to call a cab. I haven't rented a car just yet."

He closed his eyes briefly. Manningsport didn't have cab service in the winter. She'd have to wait a half hour, maybe more, for one to get here from Penn Yan. "I'll drive you. Where are you staying?"

"The Black Swan. Oh, Jack, thank you. You're such a gentleman."

Her suitcases were by the front door. Four in all, enough for her to stay for months. He grabbed them and went back to the truck. Hadley followed, shivering delicately. He held the door for her, the politeness ingrained.

"Thanks." She gave him a soft smile as she climbed into the passenger seat.

Jack had a feeling his life had just gotten considerably more complicated.

Chapter Three

"What the hell are those?" Emmaline looked in horror at the . . . the . . . the things in Shelayne's hands.

"Trust me," Shelayne said. "They're gross, but they work."

The Bitter Betrayeds had taken her clothes shopping, because, yes, she was going to the Wedding of the Damned. Every time she thought of it, she was tempted to channel Edvard Munch's painting *The Scream*, but she was going.

It would be worse to stay away. Kevin would think that she still wasn't over him. Naomi would gloat.

The thing was, way back when Emmaline and Kevin had first become friends, so had their parents, both sets so relieved their kids had found someone. When Em's parents had divorced ten years ago (yet remained in the same house, how was that for Dysfunction with a capital *D?*), the Bateses and the Neals would have dinner every third Saturday of the month. They went to Alaska together and, a few years later, to Paris.

So Emmaline's parents would be going to the wedding, as well as Angela. And if Em didn't go, there was a strong chance that both psychologist parents would analyze her motives in front of anyone who asked, saying that Em hadn't mustered the emotional fortitude to undertake this painful journey and find closure. Mom had already called three times this week to share her thoughts, and that would break the strongest resolve.

Allison Whitaker, unofficial leader of the Bitter Betrayeds, had leaped on the chance to avoid discussing another book no one had read and arranged an en masse shopping trip to the mall.

The Bitter Betrayed Book Club wasn't really about reading. As the name implied, you had to have been dumped. Allison, a Southern transplant and pediatrician, had divorced her husband after he became consumed with a passion for collecting antique cookie jars "and didn't even have the decency to turn gay, the way that hot Jeremy Lyon did." Shelayne Schanta, the head nurse at the E.R., had been thrown over for her own aunt. Jeanette O'Rourke's husband had impregnated a much younger woman some years back. Grace Knapton, who ran the community theater group and directed the school play, had been tricked into giving five grand to a Pakistani man she'd met online who professed to be in love with her, never to hear from him again. Granted, Grace wasn't really bitter—she laughed about the experience more than anything. But she was gifted in the art of cocktails (her Peach Sunrises were the stuff of legend) as well as cheese puffs, so they let her join.

Clearly, going to the wedding of the man who'd made Emmaline's membership possible was going to be discussed.

"You know what I think you should do," Allison drawled in her glorious Louisiana accent as she fondled a black lace bra. "Put some high-test laxatives in their drinks. I can prescribe you a little something on that front, darlin'. Or, even better, cut up a jalapeño right before the reception, see, and then rub it all over your hands—" she pantomimed this action "—and then touch their eyes. Hellfire and damnation, y'all!"

"How is she gonna touch their eyes?" Shelayne asked. "But actually, Em, if you *could* do what Allison said, then grab his junk, *that* would be fantastic. We had a case in the E.R. for that last year. It was hilarious. Well, to us nurses, anyway."

"Yeah. So tempting," Em said, unable to tear her eyes off the package in Shelayne's hands. "But I probably won't."

"Try those on, Emmaline," Jeanette said. "I might get a pair myself."

"Isn't it bad enough that I had to buy a bathing suit?" Em asked.

"Mandatory water sports." Grace clucked. "Who ever heard of such a thing at a wedding?"

"Exactly," Emmaline said.

"Shush, child," Allison said. "We showed you

mercy by letting you get a one-piece. Now get in there and show us your boobies."

"This is so humiliating," Emmaline said. But she obeyed, slinking into the dressing room with her bathing suit in one hand, and the . . . things . . . in the other.

Emmaline yanked her MPD sweatshirt over her head and took off her jeans. Put on the bathing suit, which was one of those "look ten pounds lighter" types, praise Jesus. But when she'd tried it on the first time, the Bitter Betrayeds had deemed her boobage to be unremarkable. All the squeezing and squishing from the miraculous fabric apparently minimized her bust as well as her stomach.

Enter Ta-Ta Ta-Dahs.

The Ta-Ta Ta-Dahs looked like raw chicken fillets. Their purpose: to boost the girls. The breasts. *Yeah.*

Em opened the package and grimaced. They *felt* like raw chicken, too. Em sighed, then hefted her left breast and stuck the thing underneath. Flinched. It was cold. Silicone, the package said. Maybe Em would just buy regular chicken breasts. It would cost less than these. She slid the right one in and looked.

Well, well. They worked. Ta-dah indeed.

She went out to show the group.

"Hello!" Allison said. "We have liftoff, people."

"How do they feel, Emmaline?" Grace asked.

"Disgusting. I'm changing back into my clothes now. You people have had your fun."

A little while later, seated around a table at the Olive Garden and sucking down Peach Sunrises that weren't nearly as good as Grace's, Em took a deep breath. "So, guys, I'd like to bring a date," she admitted. "You know anyone?"

"Jack Holland," came the chorus.

"Wow," Em said. "Is he for sale or something?"

"No, no," Jeanette said. She worked at Blue Heron and was therefore the resident expert on the Hollands. "He just does that kind of thing. You need a date, he'll go."

"Not Jack," Emmaline said.

"Why? He's *so* handsome! If I was twenty years younger . . . And he saved all those kids! I mean, he was gorgeous before, but now, I swear, things *pulsate* when I think about him. *Lady* things." This was from Grace, who was on her third drink. At least she wasn't driving.

"Jack took me to my sister's wedding," Shelayne said. "He's a perfect date. Gorgeous, we all know that, but he can also hold a conversation, he smells fantastic, he's not embarrassing on the dance floor. When we got home, he kissed me on the cheek. I offered sex, but he turned me down. Nicely, though, you know? My feelings weren't even hurt."

"His ex-wife is back in town," Allison said. Em already knew this—Faith had stopped by the

39

police station, presumably so Levi could kiss her and put his hand on her stomach and offer other married gestures of devotion, and spilled the news.

"His wife?" Grace asked. "The Southern belle? The blonde? When we did *Sound of Music*, I begged her to play Liesl, but she was . . . well. You know." She dropped her voice to a stage whisper. "Not friendly." This was about as mean as Grace got.

"Her name is Hadley," Jeanette said. "And, yes, she's gorgeous. She came in the gift shop at Blue Heron the other day. So stylish."

Emmaline remembered Jack's wife—tiny and blonde, as helpless and adorable as a newborn bunny. Once, they'd been at the grocery store at the same time, and Em had realized it was Mrs. Jack Holland because of the accent (small town, nothing else to talk about). Em had had her arms full of overpacked grocery bags, her Ben & Jerry's threatening to topple out. Gerard Chartier had seen Em struggling, said an amiable hello, then practically trampled her to offer to carry Hadley's one underfilled string bag, which seemed to contain an entire apple.

"Let's just say it got really chilly, and fast," Jeanette added with great relish. "Honor froze her out with that stare of hers, and Hadley got the point. She practically ran out the door."

"Who in her right mind would cheat on Jack Holland?" Allison asked.

"If Jack had a vagina," Grace said, "he could belong to our book club."

"No more Sunrises for you," Emmaline said. "Back to my problem, I don't think Jack is up for it. He's got enough on his mind." Also, he was too beautiful for a mere mortal such as herself. "You guys know anyone else?"

"I'll ask Charles's cousin," Allison said. The cookie jar–inspired divorce had not stopped Allison and Charles from talking every day. "He's a man. He must know other men."

Talk turned to what Emmaline should wear, if she should go on a crash diet beforehand, if she should color her hair and slut it up or, just to make Kevin feel guilty, wear smelly clothes and stop washing her hair a week beforehand.

"No, no," Jeanette said. "You have to be extra beautiful." She gave Em a hard stare. "Want me to send my daughter over? She knows about these things." In fact, Colleen used to make the occasional appearance at the Bitter Betrayeds, mixing her fabulous cocktails, but she was back with the guy who'd dumped her and rosy with love and hormones, so they'd kicked her out.

"You know what?" Emmaline said. "I'll just go alone and hang out with my family." She paused, picturing that. "Actually, if anyone can come up with a guy willing to fly to California for a few days, I'd make all those parking tickets go away."

And so it was that two nights later, Emmaline kissed Sarge seven times, made sure Squeaky Chicken was with him and walked around the corner to O'Rourke's to meet the man known to Allison's ex-husband's cousin. Mason Maynard.

According to Allison and the quick background check Emmaline had run, Mason was employed (score!) in marketing and didn't live with his mother (double score!). Never married, forty-one and fairly nice-looking in an unthreatening way. "He likes dogs, eating out and French films," Allison had said.

Emmaline had winced. "That's a red flag. And why 'films'? Why not 'movies'?"

"Attitude, Em. I have to go. I want to sext someone I met online."

"That's how serial killers—Allison? Hello?" Her friend had hung up.

But Allison had a point. Em would forgive the French films and even sit through one or two if Mason Maynard would be so kind as to go with her to the Wedding of the Damned.

Em took a deep breath and went into O'Rourke's, which was warm and quiet tonight, the gentle lights glowing with just the right amount of flattering ambiance. The usual suspects were here—the Iskins, Bryce and Paulie, Jessica Dunn and Big Frankie Pepitone. Lucas was smiling at his wife as she shook a martini shaker.

"Hey, Emmaline," Bryce said. "How's Sarge?"

"He's so great, Bryce," Em said. "I owe you."

"Aw, no, you don't. Just make sure he's happy."

"Hey, girl!" Colleen called. "Want to sit at the bar?"

"I'll take a booth, if that's okay. I'm meeting someone." She grimaced.

"A blind date?" Colleen was psychic about these things, as everyone knew. "You looking for someone, Em? Why didn't you ask me? I'm hurt."

Colleen was noted for many wonderful qualities; discretion was not one of them. "I'm not looking. I just need a date for a wedding." She took off her parka and hung it on the hook.

"Did you ask Jack Holland? He's always good for that. Except with me, come to think of it."

"Well, you're married now."

"True. But if you just want a date, ask Jack. He loves women in distress."

"He's got a lot on his mind these days, I'd think."

Colleen nodded. "He looks tired, poor guy." She handed Emmaline a menu. "Who's getting married?"

"My ex-fiancé."

"Holy Saint Patrick! Okay, we need someone *extremely* good-looking. When's the wedding and where?"

"Ten days. Malibu." Em had frittered away the two weeks since she got the invitation, debating whether or not to go, whether or not to scare up a date, whether or not to simply move to Alaska and date a crab fisherman.

Colleen gave her an odd look. "Uh . . . is this Naomi Norman's wedding?"

"Yes. How did you know?"

"I'm going, too. Naomi and I went to college together. Same sorority."

"Ah. Well, she was the other woman back when I was engaged." Might as well tell her up front.

"No! You know, I never liked her. I think she asked me to be a bridesmaid because she doesn't have any other friends."

"You're a bridesmaid?"

Colleen grimaced. "Sorry. I said yes because I thought it'd be nice to get out of this snowy hell with my husband before I'm too pregnant to travel. Well, we can hang out, anyway. The resort looks great."

"Sure does."

"So you have a date tonight, and you never know, he might be great. I mean, they never are, but let's keep a good thought. Wait, hang on!" She slapped her forehead. "You could go with Connor. Pregnancy brain. I'm forgetting every-thing, even my twin. Connor!" she bellowed toward the kitchen. "You have to go to that wedding in California with Emmaline Neal!"

"No, I don't!" came the answering shout. "Sorry, Em."

"No worries." Em felt her cheeks ignite.

"Yes, you do!" Colleen shouted. "Her ex-fiancé is the groom!" And hey, why *not* announce her romantic woes to half the town? But it was too bad, because Connor *was* nice and attractive and manfully gruff.

"Stop trying to hire me out," Connor said, appearing in the door to the kitchen.

"Fine!" Colleen said. "You're a jerk, Con." She turned back to Emmaline. "Want a drink?"

"Sure. Blue Point Lager, I guess."

"Or maybe a nice glass of pinot noir?" Colleen suggested. "Sends the right message. Sensuous, but not too self-absorbed, and not too butch, either."

"I'll stick with beer." She paused. "I'm not gay, you know."

"I know that. You just look it."

Em sighed. "Great."

"Put your hair down. It's pretty." Colleen reached over and took out the clip that was holding up Emmaline's hair. "There. Very hetero. I'm a whiz with makeup. Just putting it out there."

"Thanks. You must have things to do."

"Message received. I'll keep an eye out for your guy." Colleen smiled and bustled away.

Colleen's pushiness aside, Em was hugely relieved. Colleen would be at the wedding, and Lucas, too. Angela, as well. She'd have allies, in other words. Her parents were in the neutral column. It depended on their moods.

Hannah O'Rourke brought her the beer, and Em took a sip. Jerked her chin at the Manningsport Fire Department, who'd trickled in for their weekly meeting, which consisted of poker and dirty jokes.

So. What was she supposed to do at this very moment? She hadn't been on many dates since the breakup. She'd been on, oh, let's see now . . . two.

It had taken a while to get over Kevin, of course, the only man she'd ever dated, slept with, kissed or even held hands with. And those two dates had been pretty terrible. One guy had had to go to the hospital to pass a kidney stone; Emmaline was going to wait with him, but he told her to leave before his wife got there. The other guy had asked her to pick him up, then invited her in, flopped onto a couch, picked up his bong and asked if she wanted to get high and watch *SpongeBob.* "You have the right to remain silent," she'd said, and so the evening had ended in his arrest.

Also, men weren't really beating a path to her door. She'd read the books, the ones that instructed her to feign idiocy and let the man do all the work and be feminine and unavailable and all that, and she was more than willing to try. It was just that not many guys asked.

Em got it. She was a police officer who played hockey and had a smart mouth. Not unattractive, not drop-dead gorgeous, either, not like Colleen or Faith or anything. Shoulder-length brown hair. Blue eyes that were not sapphire, ultramarine, cobalt, turquoise or cerulean. Just ordinary blue. Her body was average, she guessed. She was in good shape in that she ran and took a kickboxing class from time to time. Then again, she'd eaten an entire Pepperidge Farm coconut cake just last night.

Kevin's parting words to her had been about her weight.

Sigh. Mason Maynard was forty-seven seconds late. Not that she was counting.

She'd been clear in her email to him that she was looking for a wedding date and nothing more. She'd pay for his flight and hotel for the weekend, of course, and all she wanted was an amiable companion. Someone to talk to and sit with and, when interrogated by her parents, to simply say they were friends.

She'd been to weddings without a date before, of course. But those had been the weddings of nice people. Tom Barlow and Honor Holland, Faith and Levi last year.

She looked at her watch again. Allison's ex-husband's cousin's friend was now three minutes and fourteen seconds late. She took a sip of beer, but not too much, because she didn't want Mason Maynard to think she'd been waiting too long or was the type to chug like a frat boy.

It was possible that Mason would be lovely. That at the age of forty-one, eight years her senior, he'd have a heartbreak story, too. That he'd completely understand why she needed a date, and, at the wedding, he'd be charming and self-deprecating. That they'd come back to Mannings-port and he'd say, "You know, I had a great time. Want to have dinner sometime?"

Because, yes. Emmaline had always wanted to get married.

It's just that she'd always wanted to get married to Kevin.

That's what happened when you met the love of your life when you were in eighth grade.

"Emmaline?"

She looked up so suddenly she practically dislocated her neck. "Hey! Hi! Yes. That's me."

Mason Maynard was better-looking than his photo.

Much better-looking.

Now *there* was something that didn't happen every day. He looked like Michael Fassbender. Hopefully in every way.

"Nice to meet you," he said with a faint smile. Emmaline's stomach did a flip, and she felt the start of a dopey grin.

He had beautiful dark eyes and graying hair, and he looked . . . he looked like a husband. Not that she was getting ahead of herself.

"Yeah. You, too," she breathed.

His grin widened. *Yep. Husband.*

"This is my sister," he said, stepping aside. A thin, similarly graying woman stood there, hatchet-faced and grim. "Patricia, this is Emmaline."

"Hello," Patricia said in a toneless voice.

"Hi," Em said.

Crap.

But no, no, this didn't mean anything. After all, it wasn't weird that a guy would bring his sister on a date, right?

Fine. It was freaky. But maybe there was a good reason. Maybe her car had broken down, or she had dropped by unexpectedly. Or, from the look of her, she needed a keeper.

"She wanted to meet you," Mason said, winking.

"No, sure. That's . . . that's great."

Colleen came over. "Hello! What can I get you?" she asked merrily.

"I'll have a vodka tonic," Mason said. "And my sister will have water with a very, very thin slice of lemon, please."

"You bet," Colleen said, shooting Em a look. "Anything to eat?"

"No, thank you," Mason said, as he and his sister sat down. "We're just here for drinks."

Emmaline wavered. On the one hand, *weird* already shimmered in the air. On the other, she was so hungry her stomach was growling. "I'll have the nachos," she said, food slut that she was. Patricia slid lower in her seat. "You can share, if you like," Em added.

Mason smiled. Emmaline smiled. Patricia didn't smile. Colleen walked back to the kitchen.

"So," said Em. "This is great, meeting you both."

"I have a small phobia about being alone with women," he said smoothly.

"So I always come with him," Patricia said. "Always. Every time."

"Ah." *Dear God, where do You hide the normal people? Love, Emmaline.*

Mason laughed warmly. "No, she doesn't."

"Yes, I *do*."

"No. She doesn't." Mason smiled again. "Only the first time. I realize it's a little strange."

"It's because of our mother," Patricia said.

"Let's not discuss it," Mason said.

"You should *tell* her, Mase," Patricia barked. "Keeping things bottled up is dangerous! It's dangerous!"

The fire department was now staring openly. The firefighters loved this kind of thing.

"It's fine," Em said. "Some things are too personal to discuss with strangers."

"He has boundary issues," Patricia said urgently. "We both do. Boundaries become very fluid in communes."

"Did you say commune?" Em asked.

50

"And the cats. Jesus." Patricia shuddered.

"So many cats." Mason's voice broke. He took a steadying breath, then tried to smile at Emmaline. She tried to smile back.

"I'm more of a dog person myself," she said.

"Thank you," he said, reaching over to grip her hand. That was a little uncomfortable, given that he was staring intently into her eyes . . . and that his sister was now trying to get something out of her back molar. "You're very kind. So! About this wedding. Difficult circumstances, I'd say."

"You know, I'll probably just go alone. I mean, it's fine. But thank you."

"He was your first love, you said in your email."

Shit. Why did she tell him that? "Yeah."

Patricia finished digging around in her teeth. "Mase, tell her about *your* first love. Do it. Tell her."

"You don't have to," Em said. "Really."

"No, no, I'd love to share the story. It's actually quite beautiful." He was still gripping her hand. "Lisbeth. She was so lovely, so very lovely. A friend of my grandmother's—"

"It was the commune. We should've run away from there long before we did, Mase."

"As I was saying," Mason continued, "Lisbeth was a beautiful woman. Oh, sure, maybe a little mature for a seventeen-year-old boy, but—"

"She was seventy-four," Patricia said, waggling a shaggy eyebrow at Emmaline. "Seventy. Four."

"Here are your nachos!" Colleen said, setting down the veritable trough of food. Why had Em been so gluttonous and ordered them? Because now she had to at least pretend to eat.

Hang on. She was a cop. She always had an excuse.

"You know what?" she said. "I forgot to mention that I'm on call tonight. Just in case I'm needed. Patricia, I'm a police officer, and it's such a small town that—"

"Actually, Levi's on tonight," Colleen said.

Dear God, could You please throw me a bone? Love, Emmaline. "No, I am." She gave Colleen a pointed look.

"No, I'm sure of it. Faith came in for dinner because Levi's working. So you're off—oh." Colleen seemed to realize she'd just bludgeoned a hole in *Titanic*'s last lifeboat. "Sorry."

"No! That's . . . that's great. I thought I was on call. But I guess I'm not. Good! Fine. That's good."

"Eat your dinner," Mason said with that broad, easy grin. Creepy, really. "Go ahead—enjoy while it's still hot. We never had hot food in the commune, so I love it now."

"Uh, would you like some? Feel free." *Do not. Do not feel free.*

"We're vegetarians," Patricia said, taking a nacho and examining it. "Though I order ham from time to time. Did you know the French for

52

ham is *jambon*? I find that fascinating." She put the chip back on the plate. "*Jambon. Jambon. Jambon.*"

"Back to Lisbeth," Mason said. "She and I were soul mates. It was so refreshing, not having to hide who I was anymore, not being blinded by what was traditionally considered beautiful. Which is one reason I think you and I will work out just fine, by the way."

"Uh, thanks."

"You're welcome. So Lisbeth's age was no concern. You see, at the commune, we didn't believe in aging."

Em took a nacho. "Really. How did that work out for you?"

"She died!" Mason cried. "Lisbeth died, dropped stone-cold dead when she was weeding the basil plants!" He burst into tears. "I never saw it coming!"

"Oh, Mase," his sister said, wrapping her arms around his neck. "Don't cry!" Apparently, her brother's tears were too much for her, because she began sobbing, as well.

Emmaline glanced over to the bar. Colleen had her hand over her eyes, her shoulders shaking with laughter.

"Coll?" she called. "Can I get these to go, please?"

Chapter Four

When Hadley wanted something, as Jack well knew, nothing could sway her. Not the opinions of other people, not common sense, nothing. And right now, she wanted Jack.

Which was an utter waste of her time.

"Marry in haste, repent in leisure," Jack's grandmother had intoned when he'd told her he was getting married.

"What's wrong with being a bachelor?" his grandfather had asked. "I wish *I* was a bachelor. I've been wishing that for six decades."

"So call a lawyer," Goggy had replied. "I'm ready when you are, old man."

In hindsight, they both had a point.

But Jack had been thunderstruck by love, and Hadley Belle Boudreau was unlike any woman he had ever met.

She was soft-spoken and smart and funny, and though Jack's three sisters would bludgeon him to death if they heard him say it, she had manners the likes of which Yankee women—or at least Holland women—just didn't have. Pru wore men's clothes and smelled like grapes and dirt, same as their father did, and had enjoyed tormenting Jack with gory, detail-filled talk of periods and ovarian cysts for the past several decades. Honor was brisk and unsentimental. Faith, the youngest, liked to punch him (still, even though she was pushing thirty).

But Hadley was—how could he put this?— refined. Southern. She was, God forgive him, a *lady,* the kind they didn't seem to make in the farming regions of western New York. And again, his death would be long, drawn-out and extremely bloody if his sisters (or grandmother, for that matter) heard him say that, which basically proved his point.

There was a vulnerability about Hadley; she was a tiny thing, five-foot-two, delicate frame, silken blond hair and big brown eyes, and her smile lit up a room. But she also had an occasionally bawdy sense of humor, which kept her from being too sticky-sweet.

They'd met at a wine tasting in New York City at a noisy, swanky restaurant near Wall Street populated by lean, fiercely fashionable women and loud, confident men, all aggressively eating hors d'oeuvres and trying to top each other's stories of that week's ballsy successes. But the restaurant was one of Blue Heron's best accounts in Manhattan, and the owners were quite nice.

Honor usually handled these things, but she'd asked him to go, and he was happy to. Tastings (and schmoozing restaurant owners) were part of the family business, and Jack wanted to do his part. He'd joined the navy's Reserve Officers Training Corps in college, and after he'd gotten his master's in chemistry (because wine making was all about chemistry), he spent his time in the navy in a lab outside D.C., studying the potential effects and treatment of chemical contamination in large bodies of water. Then he came back to Manningsport and assumed the position of winemaker alongside his father and grandfather.

That had always been the plan: education, military service and a return home, and the plan had been working just fine. He loved his family, loved making wine, loved western New York. While he was exceedingly popular with the fairer sex, he was getting a little tired of dating. He wanted to settle down, have a couple of kids.

He just had to meet the right woman, and given that he knew virtually everyone in Manningsport, he was fairly sure she wasn't there. He'd had his heart broken twice, once in college, once by a congressional aide, but since then, he hadn't had a relationship with staying power.

So that night, he poured wine and described what people were tasting (if they were interested). In the eyes of the Wall Street men, Jack was just a bartender, and if they were threatened by the way some of the women were eyeing him, they countered by ignoring him. Which was fine. He was only there to represent Blue Heron.

The women weren't his type, anyway—they all seemed to be dressed in stark, narrow black dresses and wore twisted pieces of wire for jewelry. Must be the trend that year, because they could've passed for clones, aside from variations in skin, hair and eye color.

"So what am I drinking?" one such clone asked, leaning forward to make sure he could admire the view (not that it was hard; her bra was an architectural wonder that presented her breasts as if on a platter).

"This is a sauvignon blanc," he said, "with notes of tangerine and apricot and some great limestone elements."

"Mmm," she said, letting her eyes trail down his torso.

"It's got a firm acidity and a long, clean finish. Great with any kind of fish or poultry."

"Want to come to my place after this?" she asked. "I'm Renee, by the way. Associate over at Goldman."

"Unfortunately, it's against company policy," he lied.

Another Wall Street clone sidled up to the bar and gave Jack the same speculative look as the first woman. He suppressed a sigh and forced a smile, poured some wine and delivered the shtick.

A male Wall Streeter stuck out his glass without even looking at Jack, and Jack poured obediently.

"Not that one! The cabernet!" the guy barked. Jack cocked an eyebrow and obeyed.

Then Jack saw her.

She was the only woman in the place not dressed in dark colors, which made her seem as if she'd just wandered off a Disney set. Her dress was bright pink, her blond hair was caught up in a twist with a few loose tendrils escaping and she looked a little lost.

A lot lost, actually. She glanced around, standing on tiptoe. Then, taking pains to say "excuse me" to the loud stockbrokers (who ignored her as if judging her to be inferior to their female counterparts), she made her way to the bar.

"Hello," he said. "How are you tonight?" He could smell her perfume.

"Hi there," she said. "I'm a little . . . overwhelmed, it seems. I'm supposed to meet my old college roommate, but she's not here just yet. Guess I feel like a fish outta water."

She had a Southern accent and a husky voice. It worked. Hell yes.

"Jack Holland," he said, extending his hand.

"Hadley Boudreau." Her hand was smooth and soft. "It's awfully nice to meet you. You're the first person who's smiled at me all day, I swear. I've never been to New York before, and my goodness, it's a whole different country, isn't it?"

Before she'd finished speaking, he was in love. She didn't fit into this loud, overconfident crowd, and Jack had the sense that if someone bumped into her or stepped on her foot, she'd burst into tears. You didn't grow up with three sisters and not know how women thought.

And Jack's sisters had always told him he had a thing for a woman in distress.

"Where are you from?" Jack asked.

"Savannah."

"Beautiful city," he said, smiling.

"Have you been there?" she exclaimed. "It *is* beautiful, isn't it?"

He told her how he'd presented a paper down there a few years ago, and her eyes grew wide with the mention of the U.S. Navy (the hottest branch, Jack always thought). She actually squealed when he mentioned a restaurant she knew, and she was so sweet and energetic and easy to please, she stuck out like a flower growing in an abandoned parking lot.

She kept sipping wine and seemed to get a little tipsy, which was cute, given that she'd had maybe a half a glass. Then again, she couldn't weigh more than a hundred pounds.

She was beautiful. Flawless skin, perfect nose, full, pink lips and a dimple in one cheek. She had a husky laugh that Jack found himself getting a little drunk on. Whenever he had to pour for someone else, he found himself looking back at her with a little wink or smile, and, each time, she blushed and smiled back.

When her friend came in (dressed in black, of course), Hadley introduced him, said how pleased she was to have met him and how grateful she was for the conversation. She extended her hand, and he took it, and held on to it for a long minute.

"I'm staying in the city for a few days," he said. "Would you like to have dinner with me?"

Hadley smiled. "I think I'd love that, Jack Holland."

They had dinner the next night at a gorgeous, expensive restaurant in South Street Seaport with a killer view of the Brooklyn Bridge. Was he trying to impress her? Absolutely. He walked her back to her friend's apartment, and when he went to kiss her, she blushed and offered her cheek. "I guess I'm old-fashioned," she said. "Hope you don't mind, but I don't kiss on the first date."

Somehow, that kiss on the cheek was more special than anything he'd experienced to date.

The next day, Jack called his dad and said he'd be staying in the city for a few extra days. He called on some accounts, but mostly he saw Hadley. Her friend was working; Hadley had been planning to do some sightseeing before their girls' weekend officially started. So Jack took her around and showed her the city—New York's most famous places—Greenwich Village, the Metropolitan, the Empire State Building and Times Square, but also the High Line, the Cloisters and a bike tour of Governors Island.

They shared a pretzel in Bryant Park, rode the Staten Island Ferry, bought a cupcake from a street vendor in SoHo. In Central Park, Jack hired one of those hokey carriages, and Hadley was over the moon. She let him kiss her on the lips, and she was sweet and soft and lovely. But she also had a quick sense of humor and an earthiness to her that Jack found incredibly hot. The sight of her eating a hot dog had almost brought him to his knees, and she grinned as she chewed, well aware of the effect she had.

She was an interior decorator and loved popping into hotels to see the lobbies. On their way out of one building, a man held the door for them, and Hadley practically had a kitten. "Did you see that? That was Neil Patrick Harris! Oh, I had the worst crush on him! Think he'd turn straight for me, just for an hour?" Then she stood on her tiptoes and kissed Jack's cheek. "This has been the best week of my entire life, Jack Holland."

For him, too.

What followed was a very old-fashioned courtship. Letters (not just emails, either). Long phone calls into the night. He sent her flowers and a snow globe of Manhattan. She sent him cookies and a scarf she knitted herself. After three weeks, he went down south to visit her.

Hadley lived in a sweet neighborhood, not too far from her parents and two older sisters. Her house was a tiny bungalow, the yard filled with flowers. When Jack knocked, she answered the door (wearing a dress and heels and smelling incredible), took his coat, hung it up in a closet and poured homemade iced tea into a tall glass filled with ice. She added a couple of mint leaves picked from her garden. She'd baked sugar cookies for him and served them on a porcelain plate, first inviting him to sit down and relax.

They had dinner with her entire family that night, and everyone seemed like wonderful, upbeat, intelligent people. Mr. Boudreau was a lawyer; Mrs. Boudreau had been a college English professor. Hadley had three sisters—Ruthie was a pediatric surgeon, and Rachel was a state representative. Both older sisters were married, and each had a son and a daughter. Hadley's younger sister, Frances-Lynne, better known as Frankie, was a senior in college, wanted to be a veterinarian and was looking at Cornell, Jack's own alma mater.

Clearly, the Boudreaus were a wonderful family, and, even more clearly, Hadley Belle would make an incredible wife.

That night, he took her back to the Bohemian Hotel, and they slept together for the first time.

Afterward, Hadley said that being with him had felt different, not that she was too experienced. But she knew it had been special. Meaningful.

He flew her to New York a few weeks later. It was a great time to visit Manningsport; the trees were in bloom, the weather clear and warm, and it was the weekend of the Black-and-White Ball, a fund-raiser his family supported every year. That year, it was held at McMurtry Vineyard, another operation on Keuka Lake. Hadley loved it, charmed everyone and practically shimmered in a white sequin gown.

"What do you think?" Jack asked Honor. "Isn't she fantastic?"

"She's *very* pretty," she answered, and it was only later that Jack realized Honor had dodged the question.

Hadley loved Blue Heron, loved Jack's family, loved the house he'd built high on Rose Ridge, tucked in the woods at the west end of the fields. "I can't imagine anything nicer than sitting on this here deck and watching the sunrise," she said.

Nine weeks after they'd met, Jack flew down to Savannah for the third time and knocked on the Boudreaus' front door. Mr. Boudreau ushered him into his study, poured him a glass of an excellent smoky bourbon and another for himself. "I think I probably know what's on your mind, son," he said, sitting behind his desk.

"I'd like to ask Hadley to marry me, sir," Jack answered. "And I wanted your blessing first."

"And they say Yankees have no manners," Mr. Boudreau said with a faint smile. He took a sip of his drink and considered Jack. "Well, now. I appreciate you coming to talk to me, I do. Let me ask you this, though, son. You sure you've thought this through?"

"I know it's fast," he said. "But yes, sir."

"And you don't think a little more time might be a good thing?"

Initially, Jack just thought Bill Boudreau was trying to keep his third daughter closer to home, or was just being protective, doing what fathers did. Later, it would make more sense.

"I think I know what I need to, sir. She's everything I could ever ask for."

Bill sighed. "She has her charms, doesn't she?" He slapped the desk. "Well, all right, then. Best of luck to you, Jack. I think you'll be good for her."

Jack took Hadley to dinner that night at 700 Drayton in the Forsyth mansion, her favorite restaurant. Afterward, they walked through the park, and, in front of the fountain, Jack took her hand, knelt down and pulled a little turquoise box from his pocket. "Hadley, make me the happiest—"

"Yes! Yes, Jack, yes, let me see that ring! Oh, my land, it's beautiful! Oh, Jack!" She let him slide it on her finger and practically danced in a circle around him she was so happy.

He'd definitely scored with the ring.

Originally, Jack was going to give her his mother's engagement ring, which his dad had given to him years ago for just such a purpose. But something told him Hadley would want something that had been bought just for her, so he'd checked with Faith, then visited Tiffany's and bought her an elaborate platinum-and-diamond ring that cost about as much as a new tractor.

He wanted to marry her fast and get her up to Manningsport, and she was all for it. Despite the rushed nature of the wedding, it was a huge affair. Hadley had an enormous binder she'd begun at age seven, complete with spreadsheets and thousands of pictures on her computer, organized by file—flower arrangements, bouquets, cakes, bridesmaid dresses, invitations, place settings. The only thing she didn't need was a gown; she'd bought her wedding dress when she was twenty-one, she told him, which struck Jack as slightly terrifying. Then again, things were different in the South.

Jack learned that at the ripe old age of twenty-seven, Hadley viewed herself as an old maid. Most of her friends had gotten engaged (or lavaliered, whatever that was) in college. The summer after she'd graduated, Hadley had been in eight weddings, and she'd thought her day would never come. When he mentioned he had two unmarried sisters older than she was, she shrugged. "Southern women can't wait to settle down and start a family. It's more of a priority for us."

She became a bit of a monster about the wedding, growing furious when the caterer didn't have the right shade of ivory for the napkins. Her eyes narrowed at the mention of a cousin who'd "stolen" her idea for a bridal bouquet last summer—everyone knew that Hadley's heart had always and forever been set on a bouquet of gardenias and bluebonnet, and then *That Vanna* had gone in and swooped up the idea, and now everyone would compare, and Hadley wanted to be completely unique yet traditional and have the most beautiful wedding ever held.

Jack was so, so glad to be a guy. But as he was one thousand miles away, he thought her bride-zilla antics were kind of cute.

"Of course it's going to be the most beautiful," he said into the phone. "Because you're the bride, baby."

"Oh, Jack! You always know what to say! But dang it all, I'm going to just kill That Vanna when I see her at my bachelorette party!"

Speaking of parties, there were many. The traditional engagement party, for which Jack flew down with his father so the parents could meet, and so Jack could meet Hadley's extended family. That had been very nice. Southerners really did know how to socialize, and Dad liked Mr. and Mrs. Boudreau very much. There were no fewer than three showers, and Hadley was a little hurt that Jack's sisters didn't come to each one. There was the bachelorette party, a party the night before the rehearsal dinner, the rehearsal dinner and a brunch for wedding guests the day after the wedding. Not to mention the wedding itself.

Finally, the big day came, which was a relief, because Jack just wanted to be married so Hadley could go back to being her sweet self and not some Martha Stewart–obsessed monster.

The wedding was held at her parents' lovely home, in the vast backyard. Hadley had what seemed like thousands of bridesmaids—her three sisters, his three and his niece, her sorority sisters and many cousins, even That Vanna, all clad in pale pink. Jack had a couple of friends from college, Connor O'Rourke, a buddy from the navy, and his father as his best man, as well as Hadley's brothers-in-law. Biggest wedding party he'd ever seen, frankly, and a little embarrassing that it was his.

But Hadley was radiant and happy, seeming to float on a huge, cloudlike dress. If she occasionally leveled a steely-eyed gaze at a bridesmaid who laughed too loudly or a kid who spilled juice on a table, well, she just wanted her day to be perfect.

Seemed pretty close to Jack. It was Southern hospitality at its finest.

White-covered tables held elaborate flower arrangements in blue mason jars. Half a dozen copper tubs filled with ice and glass bottles of Coke were left at strategic points (Jack had been schooled that Pepsi was viewed as a sin against humanity down here). Mint juleps and neat bourbons were served at the bar, and pitchers of sweet tea instead of water sat on every table. There was a groom's cake decorated to look like it was covered in grape leaves. The buffet had shrimp and grits, mac and cheese, fried chicken and roasted oysters. The wedding cake had twelve layers.

"Jesus, would you look at this?" Prudence said, fanning herself. "I feel like I'm at friggin' Tara."

The word *Southern* was tossed around endlessly, as if the guests needed to remind themselves where they lived—Hadley was from a good Southern family, it was a real Southern wedding, Hadley was such a Southern beauty, what a wonderful Southern tradition, the Southern food was Southern delicious, Barb was such a Southern mama, didja see Bill cry, of course, he's a Southern daddy, sure is hot, you can count on this Southern weather, oh, look at that beautiful Southern smile!

Jack lost count of the times he was told that for a Yankee, he was all right. Apparently, the War of Northern Aggression, as it was called down here, was still a sore spot.

The dancing went on into the wee hours before Jack could finally carry his bride over the threshold of their suite.

Their honeymoon was in the Outer Banks, a

perfect week of walking on the beach and making love, swimming and sailing, eating and drinking wine, opening gifts and talking (a lot) about the wedding. Hadley thought it had been magical and perfect and wanted to go over every minute, again and again.

They flew back to Manhattan for one more night away to break up the travel, and, yes, stayed in one of the posh hotels they'd looked at when they'd just met (a suite, though not the penthouse suite, which caused the briefest pout).

And then, finally, they drove to Manningsport, and Jack felt himself relax as they got closer to home. The wedding had been great (if exhausting), the honeymoon idyllic, but this was what he'd really been looking forward to. Not getting married . . . *being* married. Eating at home instead of restaurants. Sleeping in his own bed without the unfamiliar sounds of away.

And, Jack had to admit, he wanted to get back to work, because he loved his job. Two solid weeks of not working had made him a little itchy. He missed home, the morning fog that so often hung over Crooked Lake, the fields in the mist, the long, quiet afternoons with his father and grandfather, experimenting with techniques, listening to Pops's traditions, adding his own more scientific methodology, running things by Dad. He loved the smell of the grapes in the fields, the twisting vines and miraculous clumps of gold, green and purple fruit, the cool damp of the barns and cellars where Blue Heron wine was stored and aged.

But almost as soon as they got home, the troubles began.

Chapter Five

On Thursday, with a knifelike winter wind slicing off the lake, Jack went into the Cask Room, the stone basement where they stored the oak barrels filled with the red wines of Blue Heron. The cool walls, the distinctive smell of fieldstone, the dim lighting all spoke to the centuries-old art of wine making.

Time was the most important factor. In most things, he supposed. Too little time, and the wine wouldn't have the chance to mature and develop all the levels of taste and texture. Too much time, and the color would muddy and the flavor would fade.

Like Josh Deiner. Too much time without air. Too much time underwater.

One of the victims sustained a head injury and possible anoxic brain damage. He was the last one rescued.

That had been the report on the news. Jack had watched every minute of the coverage; he'd programmed his DVR to catch every story, every mention, hoping for a hint of something positive for Josh. The kid wasn't dead. That was it.

He wasn't dead *yet,* that was. Nor had he improved.

Jack realized he was sweating, despite the coolness of the cellar. He really needed to get some sleep.

Two nights ago, he'd come home from work to find his front door wide open and every light on; yet he had a clear memory of locking the door, as he did every morning, a leftover from living in Washington, D.C. When the hell had he gone upstairs and turned lights on up there? He had no clue, and it was unnerving. Jeremy Lyon, who was a family friend and a doctor, had called Jack to check on him; maybe Jack would ask for a prescription for a sleeping pill.

His phone buzzed with a text.

Thinking of u.

Hadley. Frankie had caved and given her sister the number, then called to apologize.

Hadley was the wine that hadn't aged enough— bright and beautiful in color, vibrant and lively at first taste, and then the lingering tannin, the cottony, unpleasant feeling. Too much, too soon.

Dinner w/ me & Frankie this week?

Playing the Frankie card so soon? Frankie sometimes came out to have dinner with Jack, sharing stories about school and herself and not mentioning her sister. She'd called right after the news of the accident hit and sent him a few texts since then. Jack had always liked her.

He shoved the phone back in his pocket, pulled the plug on the side of the barrel and inserted the sampling tube. He let it fill and then poured the wine into the glass. Swirled and inhaled the scent, getting notes of blackberry, tobacco and leather. *Nice.* He took a sip. *Nope, not ready yet. Too cottony.*

The door at the top of the stairs opened, and his youngest sister came waddling down the stairs. Her giant golden retriever, Blue, followed, making a beeline for Jack's leg.

"Hello, you horny bastard," he said. The dog smiled up at him, happy dope that he was.

"Hey, Jack," Faith said.

"Hey. Should you be down here in your delicate condition?"

"I have at least seven weeks to go. Also, Goggy brought in half a ton of grapes the day she went into labor with Dad, and Pru drove the grape harvester the day Ned was born, so I think I can handle the stairs." She handed him a foil-wrapped package. "Lemon cake from Mrs. Johnson. I was told not to eat any. It's so unfair, you being her favorite."

"I can't help being perfect," he said in a pale imitation of his usual back-and-forth with his sisters. The cake was still warm. He'd eat some later, maybe. Then again, his appetite hadn't been so good.

Faith sat at the old wooden table. "Can I smell the wine, at least?"

He handed her the glass, and she took a deep sniff of the wine. "Oh, nice. Leather and plum. This'll be great in a few months, don't you think?"

"I do."

She settled back in her chair and rested her hands on her bulging stomach. "So how are you doing these days, buddy?"

"Good. Fine."

"Yeah?"

"Yep. Thanks." He wasn't about to burden her with tales of limp, lifeless teenagers. "I'm fine, Faithie."

"Good. You know, we all love you, even if you're a little prince."

"Please. I'm head winemaker for our family dynasty. You, on the other hand, plant pretty flowers." Faith was a landscape architect, and while he completely respected what she did, he wasn't about to tell her. It would throw off his big-brother coolness.

"I'll ignore that. So, Jack."

"Yes, what's-your-name?"

"You know Emmaline, right?"

"Sure."

"She needs a date for her ex-fiancé's wedding."

"Okay."

"It's—wow, that was easy." Her dog came over and sat next to her, putting his cinder-block-size head on her knee, and Faith scratched his ears. "It's in California—that's the thing. It'd be the whole weekend. Colleen's going, too. She knew the bride in college."

"No problem." It was winter, things were slow and, man, it'd be fantastic to get out of town, somewhere warm where people didn't want to ask what it was like to save those kids. "Who am I going with again?"

"Emmaline, dummy. The cop."

"Right. Tell her yes."

"Hooray! And here we thought you had no purpose in life." Faith grinned. "Would you tell her, so this doesn't feel so eighth grade?"

"But it *is* so eighth grade, Faithie. That's what you love about it."

"Just obey me, okay? I'm brewing you a nephew." She stood up and rubbed her lower back. "You like her, right? I mean, you'll be a good date and all that?"

"Sure. She's the best right wing on the hockey team."

"Women love to hear that kind of thing."

"I'll mention it, then." He opened another barrel. "Anything else, whoever you are?"

74

"Yes. Will you be the baby's godfather?"

He did a double take. "Sure. Thanks, Faith." He went over and kissed her head. "I guess I figured it would be Jeremy. Or Tom."

"Jeremy and Tom aren't my beloved, much-worshiped older brothers."

Jack smiled, and this time, it felt genuine. "Don't think I've forgotten how you told Megan Delgado that I had roundworm."

"Hey, I did you a favor," she retorted.

"Did you? Because last time I looked, she was still incredibly gorgeous."

"And speaking of gorgeous women—"

"Smooth."

"I know. Speaking of gorgeous, I hear Hadley's back in town."

"Yep."

"Is she looking to reconcile?" Faith asked.

"Yep."

"You interested?"

"Nope."

"Why now?" Faith asked. "Did she see the rescue coverage or something?"

"Yes." He removed Blue from his leg. The dog looked a little blurry. That wasn't a good sign.

"Jack, come on! I get enough one-word answers from Levi when he's grumpy."

"Uh, yeah. She saw something on the news and thought I might need her."

"Do you?"

"Like I need roundworm." His inner ear ached.

Faith smiled. "So you want Pru and Honor and me to go beat her up? We could bring Mrs. Johnson. She never liked her."

"I'll let you know."

The water had been cold like he'd never felt before. Cold enough that his bones hurt.

"So this wedding comes at a great time, then," Faith said.

Jack gave his head a little shake. "What wedding?"

"Jack! Jeesh! The wedding you just said you'd go to. Emmaline's fiancé."

"Right, right. I'll stop by the station. Now get out of here and go plan your next garden. I have wine to check." He paused. "Thanks for godfather. That means a lot, Faith. Tell Levi, okay?"

"I love you," she said, giving him a hug.

"Love you, too." She always smelled like vanilla cookies or something, his youngest sister, and Jack hugged her back, the blurry, floating feeling fading a little.

Faith pulled back. "Oh! The baby just kicked. He knows his uncle Jack is here." She put his hand on her stomach, and Jack felt a strange, firm, wavelike motion.

His nephew. A little boy who'd dig in the dirt and play with trucks and learn to drive the harvester years before he could drive a car, and when he did drive a car, his uncle Jack would put the fear of *God* in him, and that kid would never, ever, *ever* drink and drive and crash—

He removed his hand and cleared his throat. "Got any names picked out yet?"

"No," she sighed. "Levi says whatever I want is fine, which makes me insane."

"Heartless bastard."

"I know. It won't be John . . . I'm saving that for you, so you can have John the Fifth. *If* you ever get married and produce the Holland grandchild. Not that Mrs. J. has been complaining about that or anything. Or Goggy. I was over at Rushing Creek today, and she said, 'Oh, sure, it's wonderful that you're having a baby, Faith, but I want a *Holland* baby to carry on the family name.' "

"Let's not forget my superior gene pool," Jack said. He paused. "But if you want to name the little guy John, go ahead, Faith. Dad would love it."

"Nope," she said. "You're John Noble Holland the Fourth. You get to have Number Five if you want. If you can trick some woman into marrying you, that is." Then, realizing that perhaps his marital state was a sore subject with his ex-wife in town, she added, "Sorry."

His heart was beating way, way too fast. "Don't worry about it. Actually, do worry about it. Make me a cake or something, and I'll forgive you. Now get out of here. I mean it."

Because a flashback was coming, and Jack wanted to be alone when it hit.

•••

On the day the car went into the lake, Jack had been waiting twenty years to save a life.

For twenty years, he'd never been in quite the right spot at quite the right moment. For twenty years, it seemed like he'd always been five minutes too late or five minutes too early, just missing the chance to help.

For twenty years, he'd had to live with the image of his youngest sister trapped in the crumpled wreck with their mother's body, and for twenty years, he'd been waiting for the chance to make up for that. Not that the thought made sense—he'd been away in college when his mother had died, but the thought that his little sis had been alone, in shock, with no one to help for more than an *hour* . . . that his mother had had no one to hold her hand in her last moment . . . that no one had come to help for far too long . . . Of course it left a mark.

From that day on, Jack had been on alert. He joined the navy thinking he might try to become a SEAL, but Uncle Sam had other plans after seeing his test scores, so to the lab he went. It was fine; he still had to train, improved his swimming skills, get advanced scuba licenses—open water diving and specialized rescue, black water search, whatever he could.

But that feeling never went away, even after his service was done.

Every time a car raced past him on the highway at ninety miles an hour, every time he saw a motorcyclist tearing around town without a helmet, the pictures would unfold. The accident. The victims. What he would do, how he would help, how he'd make sure his own pickup truck was pulled safely off the road, how he'd call 911 as he ran, how he'd pull the driver from the car or out of the road and put pressure on the wounds until help came. He had a fire extinguisher in his car (didn't everyone?) and a window-breaking tool on his key chain, as well as a hammer in the glove box. Flares. A first aid kit, a really good flashlight (batteries changed twice a year), a seat-belt cutter and a blanket.

In the summer if he was down at the lake, he'd count the kids in the water and check to make sure parents were alert and not too engrossed in their books or conversations or phone games. When the flight attendants went over safety procedures, Jack listened, then looked at his fellow passengers and noted who would need help should their plane land on the Hudson or in an Iowa cornfield.

As Honor said, a hobby was a hobby.

Jack put his training to work and became a volunteer rescue diver for the Manningsport Fire Department. He was certified for ice rescue and as a lifeguard. He was an EMT.

And still, he'd never saved a soul. Last

spring, when his grandparents' house had burned down, it was Honor who'd done the heroics; Jack's house was way up on the ridge, about as far away from the Old House as you could get on Blue Heron land. By the time he'd gotten down there, Honor had already saved their grandmother's life, with a little help from her fiancé.

But on January 12, Jack had gone down to the dock to take photos. He loved winter, loved the brilliant red sunsets at dusk and the cold wash of the Milky Way at midnight. From here, he could see the Crooked Lake to the east and all the way up to Blue Heron to the west. So around 4:30 p.m., he was taking photos of the fields where the snow and dormant vines stood in stark contrast to each other. The sky over Rose Ridge deepened, promising one of western New York's famous sunsets. There might even be the aurora borealis later on.

At times like this, the power of the land spoke to him. It wasn't just the fact that the Holland family had helped found this town, that his ancestors and grandparents and parents had worked this land. It was the area itself: the cold, deep lakes, the gorges and waterfalls, the fertile, rocky soil.

This kind of thing reminded him of how much he had. A family—three married sisters, a niece and a nephew and another on the way. His father and stepmother. A job he loved. His, uh . . . his cat. His health. All that good stuff.

It was just that lately, Jack had been feeling a little . . . unfinished.

After twenty years of being a widower, Dad had gotten married last spring. Which was great, because Mrs. Johnson was the world's finest woman and had been like a surrogate mother since Jack's mom had died. Pru and Carl had been together for nearly twenty-five years. Honor and Faith both married recently. Goggy and Pops had recently fallen in love after sixty-five cantankerous years of marriage, thanks to the fire.

Jack . . . Jack had gotten divorced after eight months of marriage.

And then he heard the car. Judging from the sound of the engine, it seemed as if the car was going at least sixty miles an hour in a thirty-five-mile-an-hour zone.

He turned away from the water and waited, oddly calm. The car would crash. How could it not, going that fast?

Then again, he'd had that same thought hundreds of times. Maybe thousands.

None of that ever happened, but the instinct—to watch over, pay attention, be alert, be ready—was a reflex. His rational brain knew how unlikely it was that what he feared and watched for would come to pass.

But he looked up the hill anyway. In another few

seconds, he'd be able to see the car as it came down the curve on Lake Shore Road, thirty feet up the hill from Keuka.

Later, when people heard about the accident, how Jack of all people happened to be there at that exact moment, they said the usual things— everything happens for a reason, it was a miracle, God works in mysterious ways.

To Jack, however, it was more of a statistics thing. All these years *not* being there had to end eventually.

Almost automatically, he processed what might happen: the car swerving off the road as the driver tried to handle the curving road, the vehicle rolling over and over into Blue Heron's chardonnay vines, which were closest to the road. Or the car would smash into the same telephone pole he himself had scraped when he was sixteen.

Worse, the car would hit the big maple at the base of the entrance to Blue Heron. The driver was a teenage boy, Jack guessed, because there was no one on earth who believed in his driving skill and immortality more than a teenage boy.

Hopefully, everyone in the car was wearing a seat belt. The windows would be closed, since it was January, so no one would be thrown from the car. Going that fast, though, even with air bags . . .

The engine screamed with a downshift as the hotdogging kid played with his life.

And here it was. The screech of brakes applied too late. Jack tensed for the crunch of metal as the car rolled or hit a tree, the subsequent, constant blare of a horn.

The sound came, but it wasn't what Jack expected.

Instead, there was a sharp, oddly clean noise, and Jack felt his mouth drop open as the car burst through the guardrail, snapping off the topmost branches of the hillside trees. It sailed over his head, its engine still revving, tires spinning. Jack had a detailed view of the chassis.

And then there was a tremendous *whoosh* as the car hit the water nose-first—the lake wasn't frozen; it was too deep for that. There was a massive slosh, and a crow screeched from a tree and Jack saw the white, terrified faces of two boys. Yep, teenagers.

The car was a silver coupe. An Audi. The nose started to sink almost immediately, the headlights shining down into the lake. The sky was red and purple, helluva sunset, his boots were off and he was diving. He much would've preferred to do this in August, and holy mother of *God,* the water was cold.

For a second, the frigid shock slammed all other thoughts from his head as every muscle in his body contracted in shock even as he was cutting through the water (*thank you, United States Navy;* they'd trained him to act first and think later).

His bones already hurt from the cold.

The boys were screaming, their voices muffled by the closed windows. *Damn.* The best thing would've been if the windows were already open, giving them an exit. One boy was pounding it with his fist. Pointless, since that wouldn't break anything except a bone in his hand. The electrical must've already gone out, if they couldn't get the windows down by pushing the button. Or they were just panicking and not thinking of it.

Now the boy was hitting the door with his shoulder. Also pointless with several tons of water pressing against the doors. No, they'd have to break the windows and get out that way, or let enough water in to equalize the pressure and then open the door.

But they don't teach that in high school, and, yes, Jack thought he recognized one of the boys as a classmate of his niece, Abby. Seniors or thereabouts.

The thoughts shot through his head rapid-fire.

The water would be flooding in through the front of the car.

They maybe had five minutes before the car was submerged. Maybe eight, but that'd be pushing it. That is, eight for hypothermia. Obviously less time if they couldn't breathe.

Jack's arms already felt heavy and dead. Not good. No, strike that, no negative thoughts permitted. Just move. He made it to the car, which was now halfway into the lake at a forty-five degree angle, the water up to the middle of the windows. Four boys, two in front, two in back, one with blood on his face. The driver was slumped over the wheel.

"Help us! Help!" the bleeding boy pleaded, and it wasn't like Jack wasn't trying.

He fumbled in his jeans pocket for the window breaker he had on his key chain. Ten bucks on Amazon, and not only did he have one, but every member of his family did, too. His dexterity was off, thanks to the cold, his fingers clumsy and slow.

One of the kids had his iPhone out. *Good.* Help would be on the way. Then again, by the time the fire department got here, the boys would be drowned. They'd *all* drown, Jack included, or die of hypothermia. How many minutes had he been in the water? One? Two?

The car was slipping deeper.

There. His numb fingers closed around the little device. Pressed it against the window, his hands shaking hard, and it slipped right off.

"Hurry! Hurry!" the bleeding boy screamed.

"You can do this," said another, oddly calm, voice muffled behind the glass.

Jack positioned the tool again, pushed hard and the window shattered, water rushing in.

The car immediately began sinking faster, but already, one boy was wriggling through the window. Jack grabbed the collar of his coat and hauled him out. Did the same with the second, the calm one, Sam Miller, that was his name. "Get to the dock," he said. They were already swimming. They'd make it.

The driver, on the other hand, wasn't moving, which was not good, and the bleeding boy was screaming. Should've been out by now.

The tail of the car slipped underwater with a gurgling sound.

And then it was quiet.

Jack grabbed on to the roof and went with the car, the water gripping his face and head with a fist of ice. Through the window, the boy grabbed on to his arms. Jack pulled him free, but it was hard, the car was tipping in the water, nose down, the headlights shining into the eerie dark water.

The boy was free, and Jack kicked his numb legs, hoping they were moving upward. His lungs burned; the rest of him was dead. Then they surfaced, and the air was so cold it hurt, but damn. The kid choked and gasped, still clutching Jack.

"Relax and kick," Jack said, his lips hard with the cold, his breath clouding the air. The boy just grabbed Jack harder, so Jack looped his arm around the boy's neck and swam.

The dock was sixteen, twenty feet away, maybe. He could make it.

How many minutes had it been? Three? Five? More?

Sam was on the ladder of the dock, reaching out for them. He and the other boy grabbed their friend by the arm, silent with shock and shivering with cold.

Jack was already swimming away.

"I can help!" Sam called.

"Stay there," Jack ordered.

He was also shivering. No, shuddering. This wasn't good. This was *Hypothermia: Stop Fucking Around* edition.

Still . . . what was the word? Still . . . survivable.

The last boy, the driver—probably dead. Drowned, if not killed on impact. Jack himself would probably . . . what did they call it? Oh, yeah. Die trying.

It was getting hard to think. Advanced hypothermia.

So quiet now, the red sky above, the frigid water all around.

The cold didn't hurt so much.

The car's headlights were still on. Jack wasn't sure why.

A deep breath, a hard exhale, a deeper breath, and he was under again, swimming as hard as he could and still too slowly.

The car rested on the driver's side on the bottom of the lake. Ten feet deep, give or take. A fish swam in front of the headlights, then was gone into the darkness.

Jack tried to open the passenger door, but it was locked or jammed. But the window was smashed. The dashboard was still lit up. The clock said 4:41.

He reached in for the driver, who looked oddly peaceful, arms drifting, hair waving in the current. Eyes closed. Almost certainly dead. Not wearing a seat belt, a huge gash visible on his forehead, black against the white of his skin, blood trickling up in a dark, lazy swirl.

No bubbles, meaning he wasn't breathing.

Jack reached for the boy's arm and pulled.

The kid didn't budge.

Soon Jack would have to surface again or die down here. Which maybe wouldn't be so bad. Nice that he could see. Deep blue all around.

He pulled again. A little movement now, but Jack's chest was working, wanting to breathe, and if he didn't go up now, *now,* he'd drown, navy or no navy.

His niece was eighteen, too.

He'd want someone to try one more time for Abby.

He pulled as hard as he could, bracing his legs against the car, all the air in his lungs leaving in a bubbling rush.

And then they were moving, heading up, and how they were doing it, Jack didn't know because he couldn't think anymore, but they were making it, a centimeter at a time, and then there was the sky, red and purple and violently beautiful, and full of air, like icy needles in his lungs, but so, so good, the sound of his gasps tearing through the cold.

His gasps. Not the kid's.

He held on to the boy and tried to keep going. It wasn't pretty. It was hard and sloppy and weak.

A siren screamed, then another. Police and firefighters, on their way.

The dock was still so far away. Jack closed his eyes, his head slipping again under the water. *Shit.* Kicked harder, his legs really just flailing now.

The boy was still and quiet. No breath, no coughing. No resistance.

Jack's labored panting rasped in and out of his aching lungs.

The water splashed, over and over, a hopeless, wet sound as his arm smacked lifelessly in a sorry imitation of swimming. He held on to the boy with his other arm, and God, it was hard.

Still not there. Still not there. In between each stroke, Jack's face dipped a little lower in the water. He choked on some water.

Still not there.

Then someone grabbed his arm. Sam Miller, clinging to the dock ladder, reaching out for him. God bless Sam Miller.

The other boys reached down and grabbed on to

their unconscious (dead) friend, hauling him up the ladder, ice in their hair now. One of the boys was sobbing.

Sam reached down for Jack, pulling him up, which was good because Jack was not going to be able to make it out himself. Water streamed off him, and he fell onto his knees. "On his side," he managed, and they obeyed, turning the limp boy onto his left.

"Oh, shit, Josh," the sobbing boy said. "Josh, please."

Josh. Right. Josh Deiner. A troublemaker.

It was now too dark to see if any water had come out of Josh's mouth, up from his lungs. Jack pushed him on his back and started chest compressions. He couldn't feel his hands, but this was a brutish job, just push, push, push, elbows locked, fast and hard.

The sirens were louder.

Sam breathed into Josh's mouth.

One . . . two . . . three . . . four . . . five . . .

God, he was tired.

And then there were red-and-blue flashes, and footsteps thudded down the dock.

"Jack, we got this," said a voice. Levi. Emmaline Neal was there, too, another cop, a good hockey player. They knelt down and took over compressions.

There was a clattering, and Jessica Dunn and Gerard Chartier were running with the stretcher.

"Dry him off!" someone ordered. "He has to be dry if we're gonna shock him."

There was a whole crowd now. The three boys were being wrapped in blankets and hustled away, their faces white in the gloom.

The sun was still setting. How could that be? It seemed as though hours had passed.

Someone put a blanket around Jack, too, then led him down the dock, arm around his waist, holding him when he staggered. The three boys climbed into the back of one of the town's two ambulances.

The other would be for Josh.

"Let's get you out of the cold," said the person at his side. It was Emmaline. *Huh.* He thought she was back with Josh. She opened the door of her cruiser and gently pushed him in.

"Is he dead?" Jack asked.

She glanced down the dock. "He's not dead till he's warm and dead. You know that. Let's worry about you right now, okay?"

She was about to close the door when Sam Miller came over. His face was ruddy now—he was warming up. "You saved us," he said, his voice cracking. "You saved us all."

But Jack hadn't, because Josh Deiner's body was still on the dock, Levi and Gerard on their knees next to him as if in prayer.

The media called it the Midwinter Miracle, going for alliteration over accuracy. And for a few days,

91

it was big news. Anderson Cooper, among others, came to town and interviewed the three boys— Sam Miller, Garrett Baines and Nick Bankowski, who were tremulous and fine, save for a broken nose on Nick. Their parents wept and called Jack a hero, an angel, the hand of God. A former navy SEAL was interviewed and attested that it was a "helluva rescue."

As police spokesperson, Levi gave a statement, as well, and when Anderson asked if Jack was indeed his brother-in-law, Levi said, yes, he was. When asked to characterize Jack, Levi said, "He's a good guy." That was it, and Jack was grateful.

He himself was asked for interviews by fifty-seven media outlets. He didn't give any.

That night in the E.R., Jack's father hugged him for a long, long time. Pops's voice broke as he told Jack how proud he was. His sisters fussed over him and his niece wept, and his nephew got teary-eyed, as well. Mrs. Johnson made him his favorite dinners every night for the next week, as did his grandmother, not to be outdone. So there was a lot of food. Jack tried to eat it.

Josh Deiner was unavailable for comment, since he was in a coma. There was brain damage. He was on a ventilator.

At night, when Jack couldn't sleep, it was Josh Deiner's still, limp body he saw, lying on the wooden dock, ice forming on his eyelids since there was no heartbeat to keep him warm. The face of Josh's girlfriend as she sobbed on Anderson Cooper's shoulder. And the words Josh's mother had spat at him in the E.R. ran through his brain, over and over and over.

You left him for last. The one who needed you the most, and you left him for last.

Chapter Six

Emmaline sat in front of the computer with Carol Robinson, who tapped the screen. "That one's cute. He has beautiful eyes."

It was true. "Yeah, but look. Aggravated assault."

"That rules him out?"

"It does, Carol."

"You're so fussy. All right, who's next?"

They both flinched at the next photo—no teeth.

"This is so much fun," Carol said. "So much more interesting than real estate. Oh, that one's a hottie."

Emmaline clicked for more information. "Currently in federal prison. Damn! All the good-looking ones are behind bars."

"What are you doing?" Levi asked. Both women glanced at him, then looked back at the screen.

"We're looking for a man for Em to take to the wedding," Carol said.

"Did you input that report like I asked you to?"

"Not yet," Carol said blithely. "And don't give me that look, Levi. I changed your diapers."

"No, you didn't."

"But I could have. I'm old enough to be your mother."

"Grandmother, even."

"How dare you!"

Levi gave them a tolerant look. "Em? Is Manningsport so free of crime that you have time for this?"

"It's after five, and yes," Emmaline pointed out. "This hellish wedding is in eight days, and I still don't—"

"Feel free to keep your personal life private, Em," he said. "Like I do."

"Yeah, right. You call Faith twenty times a day—"

"I call Faith three or four times a day, as she's my wife and expecting a baby and it's the middle of winter and I want to make sure she—"

"This one! This one," Carol exclaimed. "If you don't go out with him, I will."

Em looked. Yep, the guy was gorgeous, all black hair and green eyes opened a trifle too wide.

"He looks a little psychotic," Em said.

"Yeah, well, who looks good in a mug shot?" Carol asked. "Don't be so picky. Even Robert Downey Jr. didn't look so hot, and please. That man could be eating a can of cat food and I'd still want to sleep with him."

"Inappropriate talk for the workplace, Carol," Levi said. "Besides, Officer Neal, I thought my brother-in-law was going with you."

"Who? Jack? No."

"Faith said she was asking."

"Why?" Emmaline yelped. "How did she even know?"

Levi gave her a martyred look. "It was announced at O'Rourke's the other night. And it's all you talk about."

"No, it's not!"

"Sure it is. Also, I may have mentioned it in the hope that you'd get your mind back on work."

"Oh, please. Who went on seven calls yesterday, huh? It wasn't Everett, let me tell you, Chief." Levi raised an eyebrow and waited. "Besides," she added, "I don't want to go with Jack."

"Why not?" Carol asked. "I'd go with Jack. Jack's adorable. Those eyes!"

"Thanks, Carol," came a new voice, and, shit, it was Jack himself. "Hey, Em."

"Hi," she grumbled.

Sure, he spoke to her. Of course he did. He was nice. They played hockey together (along with ten or twelve other people). When he came into the station, which he did every once in a while to talk to Levi, he always said hello (and goodbye). If she saw him at O'Rourke's he'd say hello (and goodbye).

And, of course, the day of the Midwinter Miracle, he'd asked if Josh was dead.

But now, as her potential date, it was different.

Jack folded his arms and looked down at her. "Faith said you were looking for a date for a wedding."

"Yep."

"Don't just sit there like a lump," Carol hissed. "Smile at him. Who else are you going to take? A convict?"

"You didn't have a problem with that ten seconds ago."

"Smile!"

Emmaline tried to obey. Carol waited. Levi waited. Jack waited.

Had she mentioned he was extremely gorgeous?

"Okay," Em said. "Maybe we could discuss this over a beer."

"Sure."

"Meet you at O'Rourke's around six?" That way she could get home, walk the puppy and give herself a pep talk.

"Sounds good," he said. "See you, guys."

"Go!" Carol said. "Change into something feminine. Wear perfume. Men love that. Don't they, Levi?"

Emmaline left, glad for the brief drive home, which gave her time to think. She rolled down the window and let the frigid air cool her cheeks.

Yeah, fine. She'd take Jack. Of course she

would. When a Greek god said he'd go to a wedding with you, a wedding where you desperately needed to appear over the groom, you didn't say no.

Even if it meant the loss of your dignity. Even if this was one cash transaction short of prostitution. The truth was, she'd rather take a stranger, because, for some reason, that seemed like it'd be easier to tolerate than a person who was so . . . nice. Who might (perish the thought) pity her.

She wondered why Jack was game. He sure as hell never asked her out. She wasn't even sure he knew she was female, for all the interest he'd ever shown before.

But the day she'd moved back to Manningsport, her heart raw and scraped by Kevin, a floating, terrified feeling enveloped her as she lugged boxes into her little house. The whole thing was surreal. Could this really be happening? She was moving here? Instead of getting married? It had been a wet day in April, cold rain pelting her, mocking the brave little pink buds on Nana's magnolia, and Em felt like she'd never be warm again. She'd never have Kevin next to her in bed again.

It was shocking.

No crying, she told herself. *Just buck up. Big deal. You were dumped. Happens all the time.*

Didn't stop the hot tears from sliding down her cheeks.

Then a pickup truck stopped, and a man got out.

"Need some help?" he asked, and without waiting for an answer, he grabbed a box and carried it inside the little bungalow. "I'm Jack Holland," he said. "My family owns Blue Heron Vineyard."

"Emmaline Neal," she said, wiping her eyes with her sleeve.

"Welcome to town." He smiled, kindly ignoring her tears (because if he was a serial killer, he wouldn't care about that—he'd just kill her and wouldn't *that* serve Kevin right), and went back to her Subaru for another box.

She remembered the Hollands; she'd been a year ahead of Faith in school. Jack probably wasn't a serial killer. She would've told him that she'd lived here for four years, that she once played at his house as a kid. But heartbreak was swallowing her whole, and it was all she could do not to sob. She wasn't supposed to be here. She was supposed to be in Michigan with the love of her life. Her wedding was supposed to be in seven weeks.

Jack and she unloaded the rest of the boxes in silence. "Take care," he said, then drove off.

Every time she saw him from then on, Jack Holland said hello. She briefly entertained a revenge fantasy in which he fell for her, and Kevin would be wild with jealousy and dump that horrible Naomi. But no. Jack got engaged shortly after Em moved to town, and then married.

He stayed nice. His wife was very friendly, too; Jack introduced them once at O'Rourke's. Hadley seemed to be the epitome of girlie-girl—she bought foamy coffee drinks, always wore a skirt or dress. When she was in O'Rourke's she drank pink cocktails and nibbled lettuce leaves.

The town gossip said she wasn't good enough for Jack.

Turned out, it was true. When his marriage imploded, the gossip machine ran red-hot. Hadley had cheated on him, people said. Took up with the stockbroker who owned Dandelion Hill, who died (in the saddle, according to the rumors) shortly thereafter.

Even so, Jack stayed Mr. Nice Guy. Didn't get drunk, didn't pick up the many women who hit on him, didn't put his fist through a window.

As for Em, she just thought he was . . . nice. And, yes, beautiful. She checked him at hockey one night, a full-body slam, and for a second, they were tangled together, and it had been *so* long since Kevin, a full year and a half, that Emmaline had forgotten how it felt to be pressed up against a man, even if they were both clad in bulky protective gear and fighting for a puck. Then she was free, sailing down the ice again, wondering if Jack had felt anything, too.

He didn't. Or if he did, he treated her as romantically as he treated Levi or Jeremy or Gerard, which was to say, nada.

Em walked the dog, smooched his cheeks, fed him and then walked to O'Rourke's.

This was so embarrassing.

Jack was waiting just outside. "Hey," he said, opening the door for her.

The pub was about half-full: Colleen was kissing her husband; the Iskins were there, Lorena as loud as ever, Victor silent. The Meerings ignored each other, as usual. Cathy Kennedy and Louise Casco were deep in conversation. There were Bryce and Paulie, arm-wrestling at a table. The Knoxes waved—Em had been out to round up their chickens from the road just that morning.

Emmaline went to a booth in the back and took off her coat. *Crap.* She'd forgotten to change. Most nights, she went from her uniform to her pj's. Well, it didn't matter. Besides, she loved her uniform. Especially her weapon. And Taser.

"Hey, guys. What can I get you?" Hannah O'Rourke asked.

"I'll have a beer. Cooper's Cave IPA?" Em said.

"Same for me," Jack said.

"You got it, kids." Hannah waltzed away.

Jack didn't say anything. Smiled at her, which made her stomach hurt. "Um, do you want dinner?" she asked. "I'm buying."

"I'm fine, thanks."

"Great," she said.

Hannah returned with their drinks. "Anything to eat tonight?" she asked.

"Nope, we're good," Jack said with a friendly smile. "Thanks, Hannah."

"Great. Let me know if you need a refill." The waitress went to check on another table. She was pretty. Maybe Jack and she should hook up.

Get to it, Emmaline.

"Okay, so here's the deal," she said. She drained half her beer, then wiped her mouth with a napkin. "My ex-fiancé is getting married, and I don't *want* to go alone, but I certainly *can* go alone. My sister and parents will be there, and, actually, Colleen and Lucas, too, and it's not like I'll be a pariah or a laughingstock, and I'm not going to set myself on fire or burst out sobbing during the ceremony or anything like that. I just would like to have a date, sort of a human shield. But I can take a friend if you don't want to go."

"I thought we were friends," Jack said mildly.

"Oh. Yeah. Sure." She paused. "But listen, Jack. You don't have to go. I imagine it's been a pretty rough couple of weeks for you—"

"I'd love to go. Thank you for asking."

"I actually *didn't* ask. You offered." And now she sounded like a shrew. "Or your sister asked, but I didn't ask her to ask you." *Stop talking,* her brain advised. Her mouth didn't obey. "My point is, you don't have to come. I mean, yeah, it'd be nice to go with a guy who looks like a Greek god—" here he smiled "—but I'm not one of those women who—"

"Hi, Jack."

Oh, shit on corned beef. It was Hadley. The beautiful ex-wife with the wicked cool name.

"I saw you sitting here and just thought I'd come over and say hey."

She was *gorgeous.* Em had forgotten just how much. *Crikey.* Emmaline practically had a crush on her, she was so flippin' beautiful. She smelled fantastic, too. Huge brown eyes, silky blond hair, pink cheeks, heart-shaped face, full, soft lips. She wore a soft green knit dress, tan leggings and cool suede ankle boots on her tiny little feet. Em guessed that her own hips were about twice the width of Hadley's. In fact, if Hadley turned around, Em wouldn't have been surprised to see wings sprouting from her shoulders, the better for her to flutter away to sprinkle fairy dust.

"Hadley." Jack stood up, towering over her. "This is my friend, Emmaline Neal. Emmaline, you might remember my ex-wife."

The blonde gave her a sunny smile that didn't reach her eyes. "Hadley Holland. So nice to meet you."

So she hadn't dropped the last name. *Interesting.* "We've met, actually."

"Have we? I'm so sorry. I see you're a police officer?"

"Yes," Emmaline said.

"I always admire women who can go into a

male-dominated field. Me, I'd never last! I guess I'm just not tough enough. I can't imagine having to run after a criminal and tackle him. My goodness! You must be so strong."

"Are you hitting on me?" Em asked.

"Oh, bless your heart, no!" Hadley laughed merrily. "It's just that I'm an interior decorator. No guns or tackling involved in that! More like painting and fabric choices, making a house into a home."

Em had to admire the skill with which Hadley had just drawn the line. Hadley—delicate and artistic. Emmaline—manly and brutish.

"What can I do for you, Hadley?" Jack asked.

"I was just . . . checking in, I guess," Tinkerbell said now. "How've you been, Jack?" She gave his arm a squeeze. *Nice manicure.*

"I'm great." His face was completely neutral.

"I'm so glad to hear that." Hadley smiled (beautifully, tragically). A Yankee would've recognized Jack's response as the cold shoulder, but Hadley was Southern, and Southerners could make conversation with a block of wood, it seemed. "Jack, I talked to Frankie today. You know how she just adores you. Even more now, after your big save. Why, she was bragging to all her friends that you're her brother-in-law!"

"Ex-brother-in-law," Jack said.

"Well, now, she doesn't think of you as an ex anything," Hadley said smoothly. "But shoot, I didn't mean to interrupt y'all's evening. Jack, I'll call you about having dinner. Bye, Evelyn! So nice to meet you!"

With that, Hadley fluttered her fingers and floated away. Jack sat back down and took a sip of beer. Emmaline noted he hadn't turned down the dinner invitation.

"So," he said. "When do we leave?"

"Right. That's another thing. The wedding's Saturday. It's in Malibu, so of course I'll pay for your plane fare and hotel and stuff."

"No, you won't."

"Yes. I will."

"Not necessary."

"I'm paying for your flight, Jack, or you're not going."

He shrugged. "Fine. So we'll go, I'll pretend to be your boyfriend—"

"No, no," Emmaline said. "No. Like I said, I just want a pal." She sighed, then rubbed her eyes. "You really don't have to come, Jack. Allison Whitaker would love nothing more than to leave her kids and come with me."

"But you want to go with a guy, or else you wouldn't have been looking at mug shots with Carol."

"Well, yes. If I take Allison, my parents will never believe I'm straight."

"Are you?"

"Yes! I was engaged to the groom, okay? I'm

straight!" *Must use inside voice.* "It's just . . . they think I'm not."

Jack wasn't looking at her. His gaze was on Hadley, who was perched alone at the bar, trying to get Colleen's attention. "Excuse me a second," he said and got up from the table. He went over to Colleen, said something and then came back. Colleen sighed hugely, then pulled out a menu, went to Hadley and handed it to her.

Based on her excellent powers of deduction, Emmaline would guess that Colleen was ignoring the former Mrs. Jack Holland, and Jack had just asked her to knock it off.

So. The Princess of Beautiful Land was back in town and sprinkling her fairy dust on Jack. And while everyone knew Hadley had cheated on him, men were generally stupid about things like this. People who looked like Hadley (and Naomi Norman, for that matter) got away with some very stinky crap.

"So when do we leave?" Jack asked, sliding back into his seat.

"Thursday?"

"Thursday's great."

She paused. "Okay. Thank you, Jack."

"My pleasure. It'll be nice to go somewhere warm."

"Malibu is beautiful. Every day of the year, more or less."

He finished his beer. "Send me the info on the

flight and hotel so I can make a reservation, okay?"

"I'll make it for you. You're not spending one thin dime on this trip."

He smiled at her so suddenly that it was like being wrapped in a warm, soft blanket. "And blah blah blah blah," he said. Well, he probably said actual words, but Em couldn't quite hear at the moment, as she was rendered close to death by the beauty of that smile, those crinkling, pure blue eyes, the tousled blond hair, the . . . the . . . the glory that was Jack Holland.

Then he stood up, squeezed her shoulder and left, waving at the O'Rourke twins and nodding at his ex-wife, who positively beamed and fluttered, butterfly-like, back at him.

Which took away some of the glow.

Even so, it was a good five minutes before Emmaline trusted herself to stand up.

Do not fall for this guy, she warned herself. Very sternly.

But her shoulder still buzzed from the warmth of his hand.

This was a disaster waiting to happen.

Chapter Seven

"Let me do that for you." Jack gave his date his very best stern big-brother stare. It didn't work. It never did, now that he thought about it.

"I'm fine. I can put my own stupid suitcase away." Someone was in a foul mood, but he couldn't blame her, given their destination. There was a pause. "No, thanks, I mean."

"I'll get that," said a flight attendant, wrestling the bag away from Emmaline. "Have a seat, and I'll be right back with some champagne."

"Why did you do this?" Emmaline hissed.

"Because I'm six-three and the seats in coach only fit very skinny dwarves," he said, sinking into the leather seat.

"Fine. But why did you upgrade *me?*"

"Because you're not a skinny dwarf."

"Is that an insult?"

"Is it? Would you *like* to be a skinny dwarf? Because even though you're acting like Grumpy—"

"Okay, okay. Fine. I'll sit here. But I don't like it."

"Of course you do. It's first class. Relax, Emmaline."

She flopped into the seat, and Jack had to smile.

She was so far from relaxed it was almost funny.

For himself, he was downright thrilled about this wedding. He *loved* Kevin and the bride for having a wedding, for inviting Emmaline to bring a date, loved that it was across the entire continent. He hadn't felt this good since before the accident. He'd be away from people wanting to shake his hand and buy him beers, from the food that Sam Miller's mom kept bringing over, from the hospital parking lot, from his well-meaning but omnipresent family, from Hadley popping up every other day. If his seatmate was grumpy, that was a small price to pay.

The flight attendant came by with two glasses of champagne. "Thanks," Jack said.

"You're very welcome." She smiled at both of them. "Are you a nervous flyer?" she asked Em.

"I am today," she answered, chugging her champagne. "Oh, shit! I forgot my hair slime!"

"Surely they have stores in L.A.," Jack murmured.

"Not this stuff. I order it online. From Sicily. It's hard-core. Sicily understands hair frizz. You can't even buy it in America."

"Made with angel wings and freckles?"

She took his champagne and drained that, too. "And the blood of infant fairies, yes."

The flight attendant kept up with her unflagging, slightly creepy smile. "Let me know if there's anything else I can get you." She moved down the row.

Emmaline fiddled with her phone and rebuckled her seat belt a few times. Pulled out her hair elastic and then put her ponytail back in. Opened the shade. Closed the shade. Tried to put her champagne flute in the seat pocket. Put it on her tray. Took it off her tray.

"Will you stop fidgeting, please?" he said, taking the glass from her. "Just calm down. Your hair will be fine. We'll have fun."

"My hair will not be fine, Jack. And this is my ex-fiancé's wedding. It will be as fun as a hanging."

"The food will be better, though."

"Hardly. They're vegans."

"Now you tell me. When I'm trapped on a plane."

Emmaline was pretty enough when she smiled, Jack thought. Granted, she looked a little on the homeless side at the moment—scraggly hair and no makeup, gray sweats that screamed *don't look at me—I'm sexless.*

He wondered if she was. She always seemed pretty sparky to him. Granted, his contact with her had been limited to "Hi, Em/Bye, Em" at the police station or O'Rourke's and the occasional body check during a hockey game (much more fun than checking Gerard Chartier), but she seemed to have a little something going on.

"We don't know each other that well, do we?" he asked.

"I guess not." She started fiddling with the tray back again, so he took her hand.

"Relax," he said. "It's not like we're flying off to face the firing squad."

"That would be a cakewalk compared to this."

The plane began taxiing down the runway. Emmaline took her hand away so she could clench the armrests. "So do you like having sisters?" she asked.

"No. You want some?"

"I already have one. Angela. You'll like her. She's very beautiful." Her knuckles were white.

"Tell me about the bride and groom," he said.

She took a deep breath. "Right. Kevin Bates and Naomi Norman."

"The Norman-Bates wedding?"

Another smile tugged at her lips. She had a pretty mouth, pink and full and sweet.

Ah. She was talking, her words rapid-fire. "Yeah. So, he was my boyfriend from eighth grade on. We went to the same college and lived together and seemed pretty happy, more or less. I was, anyway. Then he fell for someone else and . . . that was that." She shrugged and looked out the window.

Jack had grown up around females. He'd been the date for a lot of women in the past few years. Actually, he'd always been good for that sort of thing. He'd asked Eve Mikkes to the prom many years ago because Eve was nice and funny and had been in a fire when she was younger, which had left some pretty severe scars on her face and hands. He'd gone to five high school reunions in the past few years, three weddings and a fiftieth wedding anniversary. He had the aforementioned sisters.

So he recognized a woman who'd had her heart broken.

"The love of your life, huh?" he asked.

She glanced at him, then returned her gaze to the clouds. "Yep."

He took her hand once more and squeezed it. "Stick with me, kid. I promise you we'll have fun."

Emmaline met The One in eighth grade during dodgeball, a game that further proved that gym teachers hated children. A few years before, someone's parents had sued the school to eliminate dodgeball, but then someone else's countersued to have it reinstated, and while there was currently a lawsuit to have it banned once more, the dreaded sport was still allowed, apparently, because Ms. Goldberg was smiling her snakelike evil grin and fondling her whistle.

Bad enough that Emmaline was already a target of her classmates. She didn't need to be pelted with red rubber balls. But worse than that, as everyone knew, was the choosing of the teams.

She tried to look nonchalant and unconcerned,

even as her palms sweated and her heart thudded, as the horrible ritual began. Lyric Adams (daughter of a middle-aged rock star and his fourth wife) and Seven Finlay (son of an award-winning British actress and her third husband) were the popular kids, and anointed by Ms. Goldberg to do the honors of bolstering or destroying the egos of their classmates, one by one.

"Ireland," Lyric called, and Ireland, who was the daughter of big-deal producers, bowed her head graciously as if accepting her own statue and cantered over to her best friend's side.

"Milan," Seven countered.

Most of Emmaline's classmates were named for a place—in addition to Milan, there were two Parises, three Londons, a York, a Dallas and a Boston. It sounded more as if Lyric and Seven were in a geography bee than gym class, but hey. Emmaline wasn't kidding herself. She would've loved a cool name. Would've loved to have been one of the popular kids, even though she recognized their cruelty. She would've settled for less, even . . . would've loved to have been able to turn to the new boy and make a joke about all the map names and how the two of them were out-casts because of it.

That wasn't possible, however.

"Jupiter!" Lyric called with a hair toss.

"Diesel," Seven countered.

Her fellow pariah had moved from a town that most of Em's classmates had never heard of . . . Tacoma or something. His parents didn't work in the entertainment industry, and he was therefore already marked as an undesirable. Also, he had a human name, which didn't help.

Kevin. Kevin Bates.

Kevin was also—insert dramatic pause—*fat.*

In Malibu, it was far more socially acceptable to be a heroin addict or murderer than to be overweight. When he walked into Algebra, Emmaline's classmates stared at him as if he had a nipple growing out of his chin. To be fair, many of them had never seen a fat person in real life. Not in Malibu. Not on the pristine beaches or exclusive mountains where their families cavorted. Being fat? Who would've dared?

Why hadn't his parents sent him in for gastric bypass? A tummy tuck or lipo? At the very least, why not a fat camp? Surely if there had been a surgery to fix Em's problem, her parents would have jumped on it. Why *not* fix something that made life so hard? In Malibu, it seemed that imperfect children were tossed into the ocean, or sent to live in a more normal state.

On his first day, the teacher asked Kevin to tell the class about himself and the other kids had peppered him with questions . . . Granted, he was fat, but that would be tolerated if he was, say, Steven Spielberg's son.

Kevin's mother was an accountant; his father was a computer programmer.

The death knell. It wouldn't have mattered if Kevin's mom won the Nobel in economics or his father invented time travel; it didn't matter that his parents happened to make a very comfortable living. Kevin didn't have dinner with movie stars, he didn't come to school in a limo and he was fat. He was no one, buh-bye.

Em knew the feeling. She wasn't fat. She wasn't tiny, either, by SoCal standards; she was solid, lacking mouselike bone structure or an eating disorder. But her problem wasn't her size.

It was her stutter.

Words had always fought her. Years and years of speech therapy hadn't done much. The only way she got past it was if she was relaxed or spontaneous or had a patient audience, and even then it was a struggle.

And patience wasn't a quality associated with children. Not being able to get out an answer, not being sure if her throat would lock and the horrible sounds would start and stop, start and stop as her classmates watched in gleeful horror . . . It made her an easy target.

It didn't matter that Emmaline got her black belt in aikido at the age of eleven. That she was great at sports. That she was tall and smart and, except for class participation, got really good grades. Her classmates were led by the mean popular kids, vampires who only seemed happy if they were feeding off someone else's misery.

When they were smaller, Em got into a lot of fights, back in the good old days when "acting out" was more acceptable. In fifth grade, however, Asia Redding's parents had threatened to sue the Neals after Emmaline had pushed Asia at recess. Never mind that Asia had been mercilessly mocking Em's stutter for years.

Emmaline's defense had been to pretend (miserably) not to care. She mastered the dead-eyed stare and wore Doc Martens and black clothes. She learned sign language for the rude phrases her stutter wouldn't let her say.

Her parents told her to laugh it off or ignore it. But her parents were child psychologists, so they had no idea how kids really acted. At least pretending to be tough protected her from having the mean kids know how much it hurt.

Next to her, Kevin heaved a sigh. Emmaline sneaked a look. His expression was amused and tolerant. He glanced at her, and his mouth pulled up in a smile. "Sucks to be us, huh?" he said.

Us. That had a nice sound to it.

"Chord," Seven called.

"Birch," Lyric said.

"Guess *his* parents hated kids," Kevin murmured. "Birch? Seriously?"

A smile started in Emmaline's chest. There was something about Kevin. He had . . . swagger. Here he was, fat in the land where sixteen-year-old girls got breast implants for their birthdays, where boys had personal trainers and professionally done highlights before they started high school. Fat? *Fat?* It was a rejection of the very fabric of society. Almost James Dean in terms of rebellion.

Kind of thrilling, really.

"Journey." This was said with a sigh, as Journey was the product of a first marriage whose parents were still together, and therefore not nearly as cool as the other kids. Not on Emmaline's and Kevin's level, but still pretty far down. Also, he was named after a band and not a place, so . . .

Now there were only two of them left.

Emmaline sneaked another look at Kevin.

He looked back. Rolled his eyes. Not at her . . . at *this,* the horrible ritual of crushing the human spirit. She smiled.

"Kevin, I guess," Lyric said. "Whatever."

"Great," Seven said. "I'm stuck with Eh-eh-eh-Emmaline."

Em glanced toward Ms. Goldberg, who was jotting notes on her clipboard, pretending not to have heard. She wouldn't chastise Seven, Em knew. And Em wouldn't be able to tell her about it.

"Asshole," Kevin muttered, then sighed and walked over to join his teammates, Gulliver among the Lilliputians.

That day at recess, Kevin waited for her by the door. "Want a Twinkie?" he asked.

She took the strange, tubular cake in wonder. Her parents were on a macrobiotic kick these days, tragically. "Th-thanks," she said.

"So you stutter?" he asked.

"S-s-somet-t-t-times." Most times.

"I'm fat," Kevin said.

He had beautiful dark eyes—amazing eyelashes—and curly black hair. If you looked closely, he wasn't really *that* fat. Husky, that was the word. And, yes, soft. But he was tall, about the same height as she was, and the truth was, he was kind of . . . handsome.

"Want to be friends?" he asked, so of course she fell for him.

Around Kevin, her stutter wasn't quite so pronounced, and when it did come up, he waited. Not like her parents, who stared at her, waiting, waiting, *waiting.* Maybe if they hadn't been riddled with PhDs and gurgling with words like *transference* and *empowerment* and *self-actualization,* Em would've felt a little less freakish.

Mom and Dad knew exactly what the recommended method was for dealing with a stutterer (or a *nonfluent speaker,* as they liked to call her). "We have all the time in the world," Mom would say. That was another thing. There was always a *we.* There was never *I.* "Don't feel pressured. We'll wait as long as it takes."

Which made the stutter even worse. Their take on her speech impediment was relentless reframing (Em knew all the terms). "We *love* your stutter, because we love you!" Dad said once, which was just ridiculous.

She *hated* the stutter. She pictured it as a skeleton dressed in a black suit, rising up, wrapping its sharp, hard fingers around her vocal cords and squeezing, smiling as it did.

Kevin got it. He liked himself; he didn't like being fat. He liked her; he didn't like her stutter.

They kissed for the first time in April of eighth grade, when they'd been friends for months. His lips were soft, and he didn't do anything more than just kiss her . . . no tongue, no groping. It was lovely. He smiled afterward. "Want to go to the movies this weekend?" he asked.

"Sure," she said. "What do you want to see?"

Not one stutter.

Unfortunately, the idea that the two freaks of eighth grade were dating was deeply offensive to their beautiful, oddly named classmates. The bullying got worse. Emmaline found a used condom in her locker, such a disgusting sight that her throat locked for the entire day. One day when she went into music class, all the other girls burst out laughing for no apparent reason. Someone put a pregnancy test in her backpack, which caused her mother to deliver a lecture on sex and readiness, ignoring Emmaline's protest that she and Kevin had kissed and that was it.

But it was when Lyric threw a lit match at her in science class that shit got serious, as the saying went. The match went out before it landed in her hair, thankfully, and Emmaline shoved Lyric, who then screamed as if she were being chased by cannibals. Em was suspended for a week. Worse, she had to apologize to her bully, and, no, a note wouldn't do.

But she had Kevin.

Then came the news. Kevin got into his dad's alma mater boarding school. In Connecticut. Kevin was wise beyond his years, it seemed; he knew they were only fourteen. Of course he'd be going.

Her only true friend. The boy she loved.

She sat down at her computer at home and wrote her parents a letter. She wanted to go live with Nana and go to high school there, because she just couldn't keep fighting the good fight.

Nana, her mother's mother, lived in Mannings-port, New York, a lovely little town on a big lake where Em spent each summer. Nana was the epitome of a grandmother—she cooked, she clucked, she cuddled. Those summer weeks were fantastic, filled with plenty of gluten and red meat and sugary desserts. Bike rides and morning swims in the chilly lake, hikes and waterfalls and visits to the candy store. Nana even invited a couple of other girls over to play, and, unlike the

Malibu crowd, these girls seemed nice. When one heard her stutter the first time, she put her hand on Em's arm and said, "Don't worry. I have epilepsy, so I'm different, too."

Em stuttered less there. Still stuttered a lot, but not as much.

Her parents were all too supportive of the idea of her moving.

"Very empowering," Mom said, pretending she had something in her eye.

Dad cleared his throat. "This is a healthy decision. We support you."

All three of them knew they couldn't fix her or her problems.

In a sense, she was running away, but the idea of leaving her mean-spirited peers filled her with such relief and excitement that she didn't care.

The kids in Manningsport viewed a native Californian as exotic and fascinating, not minding that she didn't talk a lot and, when she did, viewing her stutter as a little bit glamorous.

Em's relationship with her parents improved, too; she had more to say, not having to look into their faces; the phone and email made communicating a lot easier. And telling them that she, who had never joined any school club before, was now on the hockey team and in chorus, because singing didn't awaken the stutter like talking did . . . Well, she could hear their relief.

Nana's house was a cozy bungalow with clever

little cupboards and wide windowsills, and a stained glass window on the way up the stairs. In the nice weather, Nana sat on the sweet little front porch, chatting with passersby (which just didn't happen where Em was from), sometimes inviting a neighbor to come up and have a glass of wine or iced tea. Em's grandfather had died when she was small, and Nana had the occasional date, which Emmaline thought was adorable.

And it was nice being useful to Nana, shoveling the sidewalk and scraping the car, running to the grocery store three blocks away. Em was needed. It was a great feeling. Sometimes schoolmates would come over to hang out and study and eat Nana's fabulous desserts.

Another benefit of living in New York—she could be closer to Kevin.

They were still hours apart, but they planned it carefully; if her grandmother would drive her down to Connecticut once in October and once in February (and Nana would—she was a big believer in romance), and Kevin and Em both went home for Thanksgiving, Christmas and spring break, then they could see each other almost every month. They wrote, emailed, talked on the phone, and it was always the same, always great. Kevin was funny and nice and . . . safe. He would never make fun of her. Never reject her.

In February of that first school year, Em got a call from her mom.

"We have a wonderful, wonderful surprise for you," she said. "You're a big sister! Here. Want to talk to her?"

"W-w-what?"

"Hello?" came a voice. "It's Angela."

And so she had a sister. Angela Amarache Demeku Neal, adopted from Ethiopia. Her name, roughly translated, meant *angelic, beautiful, brightly shining champion.*

Emmaline meant *little rival.* Also *laborious.* Her middle name was Mara, which meant *bitter.*

Only child psychologists could mess with their kid's head like this.

Angela was ten years old. Her biological parents had died long ago, and she'd been raised in an orphanage. She was very nice. And smart—she could speak three languages. And beautiful, even at ten, big exotic eyes and long graceful limbs. She was extraordinarily polite and called their parents *Mama* and *Papa,* with the emphasis on the second syllable, so much more aesthetically pleasing than plain old *Mom* and *Dad.*

It was hard not to feel a little . . . replaced. Her parents would call to list Angela's accomplishments and qualities. Sometimes, Em wondered if they were punishing her for living with Nana, but they did seem to genuinely adore Flawless Angela. Who wouldn't? Angela loved nothing more than the times Em was home on break. She'd leave bouquets of flowers on Em's pillow, tuck little notes into her suitcase. For that first Christmas with the Neals, she made Emmaline a beautiful scarf she'd woven herself in the Ethiopian tradition.

So sure, Emmaline loved her little sister. She didn't get to see her much, and it took some getting used to, but Angela was great.

In the meantime, she and Kevin stayed together. With him, Emmaline felt most like herself—her wisecracking jokes didn't get so strangled by the stutter. With him, she could drop the tough act and relax a little. Even though the kids in Mannings-port were nicer, Em was still on guard. She had trust issues, according to her parents.

But with Kevin, she was normal. All through high school, their romance continued. They both went to the University of Michigan. And then, one day during her sophomore year, something miraculous happened.

In Shakespearean Tragedy, the professor told the students they'd be reading aloud, just a few lines each.

Emmaline's heart sank. Her stutter had quieted down over the years, but it was still there, especially when she was forced to perform. Her heart thudded, and she could barely see the passage from *King Lear.* Morgan, the boy who sat in front of her, was a drama major, and he read in a beautiful British accent, quite embracing the part of Bad Guy Edmund.

Then came Em's turn—King Lear with the body of his beloved daughter. The most important part of the play. The stutter rubbed its bone hands together in glee. Her classmates waited.

She closed her eyes, imagined herself as Sir Ian McKellen, then looked at her book and read.

"Howl, howl, howl, howl! O, you are men of stones:

Had I your tongues and eyes, I'd use them so

That heaven's vault should crack. She's gone for ever!"

The stutter's jawbone dropped in shock.

Her words had come out with a British accent, too, and she hadn't stuttered once.

"Nice, Emmaline," the professor said. "Meggie, take it up."

Em noticed that her hands were shaking, and a strange sensation filled her chest.

It was joy.

From then on, if she felt her throat lock up, she'd imagine the words in an accent, and her brain and throat detoured around the stuck sounds like a car veering around a roadblock. After all those years, her problem, which had made her so miserable, such an outcast, was gone. When she told her parents, they were quiet for a minute. Stunned.

"That's wonderful!" Mom said. "You must feel very empowered."

"We're glad for you," Dad said from the other phone (they always talked jointly).

"We're getting a divorce, by the way," Mom said. "But we'll be living together. Nothing will change for Angela. Or you, for that matter."

One day about a month later, she and Kevin were at his off-campus apartment, lying in his queen-size bed. He was quiet.

"Everything okay?" she asked.

After a long minute, he said, "You don't stutter anymore."

She didn't answer, not wanting to jinx it.

"It's a little weird," he said. "I don't know. We both had a . . . thing . . . when we first met. And now yours is gone."

"Well. You never know." She paused, feeling almost guilty. "I feel it there. Like it's lurking, waiting to come back."

He sighed. "Well. It's good, I guess."

It would've been nice, she thought later as she walked through the bitter wind to her dorm, if he'd been thrilled. After all, few knew better than Kevin how the stutter had paralyzed her, marked her, locked her in an invisible prison.

But she understood. He was afraid.

Kevin, you see, *hadn't* lost the thing that had made him an outcast. He was still fat. He was, in fact, obese. When she'd met him, he was perhaps thirty pounds overweight. He'd gained possibly fifty more pounds at Choate.

The weight kept on coming in college.

Though he never told her what he weighed, she

guessed he was at least a hundred pounds above where he should be.

Maybe more.

They never talked about him losing it. With other people, Kevin cheerfully acknowledged that he was fat, or "a big guy." He loved food, loved to eat, and he didn't just eat junk food and pizza (though he didn't abstain from those, either). He'd cook for her, and, yes, his portion would be huge. But Em loved to eat, too, and the last thing she wanted to do was pass judgment or make him feel unattractive. Kevin knew he was heavy. It wasn't a secret.

Besides, she loved him. Truly was attracted to him. His dark eyes were so beautiful, his smile and laugh were totally infectious and he was a great kisser.

But as college passed and he started law school and continued to gain weight, she worried.

They both went home to Malibu for the holidays that year, and Kevin had to buy an extra seat on the plane. His face was fiery with embarrassment, but the thing was, he really did take up two seats.

He didn't speak the entire flight.

"I'm gonna join a gym when we get back," he said in the car.

"Great," she answered calmly. "I'll join, too, if you want. It'd be good for both of us."

He grunted.

And join they did. Kevin went once. Em went five times, then stopped, worried that it wasn't helping. Besides, she ran five miles a few times a week, even in the winter. As ever, she was a strapping woman; she'd topped out at five-ten and had muscles and an ass and some padding. Here in a normal state, her size ten (and sometimes twelve) was deemed quite average. In Malibu, the size "Large" didn't fit her.

Kevin graduated from law school and accepted a very decent offer from a big firm. They both stayed in Ann Arbor, that lovely little city. Em had a pleasant job at a newspaper, trying to put her English major to work by writing obituaries, checking movie schedules and, later, doing some features.

It was oddly thrilling to be able to order a drink and pay bills, talk about coworkers and go shopping for a couch. Both of them liked their jobs and got promoted, moved to a nicer apartment and seemed well on their way to becoming full-fledged adults.

Kevin proposed at an Italian restaurant over eggplant parm and garlic bread, getting down on one knee and presenting her the ring. She said yes instantly and kissed him. Had to give him a hand getting up, but she covered well, pulling him into a hug. The other restaurant patrons clapped politely, but Em saw a few puzzled looks.

He's wonderful, you jerks, she thought even as

she smiled. *He's the sweetest man I've ever known.*

And he was.

He was also lazy, unhealthy and could easily leave her a widow.

So Emmaline made the mistake that changed her life.

She joined SweatWorld, the gym nearest their apartment. She'd never liked gyms, preferring to run. But Kevin hated running (not that he'd tried it in the past decade).

So SweatWorld it was, one of those horrible places with too-loud music and mirrors and complicated machines.

Her plan was to learn what she could and then gently suggest that he give it a try, using the wedding as motivation. They'd set their wedding date for June, and it was August now. Almost a year to get healthy, and then to stay healthy, because Emmaline had loved this guy since she was in eighth grade, and she wasn't about to lose him.

But boy, she hated going to the gym. All that sweat, the smell of bleach-soaked wipes that people used to swab down their machines, the clack of weights and the grunts of humans, the whirring of spin class, the shouts of the staff.

There was one woman in particular Emmaline avoided. A hard-muscled trainer named Naomi Norman who stared as Em ran on the treadmill. Naomi's modus operandi was to scream at her clients, using words of encouragement such as, "Don't be such a fucking pussy! Get your fat ass in gear!"

Rumor had it that Naomi had been a marine, a convict, a gym teacher and raised by wolves. All seemed true. Em did her best to pretend to be in the zone, earbuds firmly in place. When she did ask a SweatWorld employee for help with a machine, she made sure it was one of the nice people.

After a month, Em broached the idea of Kevin coming with her, and she used Naomi. "Babe, you have to come with me. You know that woman on *The Biggest Loser*?"

"Not really, no," Kevin said, not looking up from the paper.

"Well, Naomi is like her, except with very large hemorrhoids. She's evil. I'm scared of her."

"So find another gym." He got up to pour more coffee (adding half-and-half, not the nonfat creamer she'd bought).

"Well, this one's two blocks from here. You should come one day, honey. To protect me from Naomi."

He smiled at that.

It was a start.

She knew Kevin didn't like being overweight. She knew his blood pressure and cholesterol were high. She also knew he was aware of how to lose weight and why he should.

And she knew that her telling him to do it wasn't going to do the trick.

A week or two later, on a quiet Sunday morning, she bit the bullet. They were finishing breakfast (pancakes and bacon . . . a lot of bacon). "Hon, why don't you come to the gym with me today?"

"I'm really busy," he answered instantly. And it was true; his job as a corporate tax attorney kept him at the firm till late in the evening, and he did work at least for a few hours each weekend.

She covered his hand with hers. "Kev, I love you. You know that. And I'm so excited to be married and have kids and all that good stuff. But I want us to have a long and happy life, and . . . well . . . I'm worried that we won't if you don't get healthier."

She knew not to use words like *diet* or *portion control* or *exercise more* and the like. *Focus on health and love,* the literature had said. She'd read dozens of articles on the subject. Obesity interventions, they called them, and she cringed a little at the phrase.

Kevin looked at her for a long minute. There was hurt in his eyes, and her own welled with tears.

"I just don't want anything bad to happen to you, babe," she whispered.

"I could get hit by a bus crossing the street," he said, a defensive edge creeping into his voice.

"I know. So could I. But—"

"Fine. I'll go."

"Really? That's great!"

"I'm not making any promises. I'll go once."

"Thank you." She kissed him, and he smiled. Her sweet Kevin, the nicest guy in the world. She took him to bed first, to show him how she felt. Yes, he was a big man, but she felt so safe with him, her head on his chest afterward, his heavy arm around her.

They had to stop to buy gym shorts that fit, and Emmaline was horrified at how big they were. The weight had crept on, ten pounds here, another ten there, and somehow or another, Kevin had become immense.

He was quiet on the way to the gym. "You okay?" she asked.

"I'm disgusting."

"Oh, Kevin! You're not!" She squeezed his arm. "Honey, you have a big frame, and, yeah, you're heavy. But we're doing something about it. Okay?"

He gave a dejected nod.

Em held the door for him, chattering away, hoping to God Naomi wasn't there. Her goal was just to get him to walk a little on one of the treadmills, make it fun, chat about the wedding, try to keep him distracted, because Kevin hated exercise (obviously). The more painless this could be, the better it could work.

Kevin registered as Em's guest, signing the

waiver they made people sign if they topped the scales at more than 30 percent of their ideal weight.

Kevin weighed almost twice what he should, the skinny, muscular man with bleached teeth told them. His ideal body weight was 188; he weighed 354.

"It's fantastic that you're here," the man said. "Congratulations."

Kevin mumbled in response. He didn't make eye contact with Em as they walked to the treadmills, past the weight machines and the muscleheads screaming with exertion. Kevin was out of breath by the time they got there.

He was dying inside, Em knew. She smiled at him and set the treadmill at the lowest speed. Set hers at the same.

"This was probably the hardest part," she said in a low voice. "Just walking in the doors."

Kevin didn't answer. He bumped up the speed a little higher and started jogging.

Em knew he wouldn't be able to keep that up. Too much, too soon.

Sure enough, he had to lower the speed a minute later. She pretended not to notice and kept walking, though if she were alone, she'd be running at her usual seven miles an hour.

Then she saw Naomi.

The trainer was wearing microshorts and a sports bra. Her arms curved with perfectly defined, elegant muscle, and her stomach was flat and lean but not ripped. Long, tanned, beautiful legs. Her body was perfect. Not unappealingly muscular . . . just perfect. There was no other word for it.

And evil personified, because her face changed as her gaze stopped on Kevin. Her hands went to her hips, and she sauntered over, slowly, her eyes narrowing.

"What are you doing in my gym?" she asked Kevin, her voice just shy of yelling. "Really. What the *fuck* are you doing in my gym?"

All around them, people grew quiet.

"How *dare* you," Emmaline said. "Back off, Naomi."

"Is this your *man?* Are you here to be *supportive?* Huh?"

Kevin's face flushed even redder.

"As a matter of fact, yes," Emmaline bit out. "He's here. He's taken the first step, so shut up."

"Oh, how sweet." Naomi sneered. "Guess she has the balls in the family, huh, fatty?"

It was nearly dead silent now.

"I'm reporting you," Em said. "You can't talk to us this way."

"Is that right? We'll see, won't we?"

"Be quiet," Kevin muttered.

"Yeah," Em echoed. "Shut up, Naomi."

"I was talking to you," he said.

Emmaline stopped walking, then jerked to a

run to avoid being thrown off the treadmill.

"You're disgusting," Naomi said, her eyes on Kevin. "You know how much fat you're carrying right now? Slick, yellow, nasty-ass slabs of fat? Oh, wait, you have a big frame, right? You're a big guy. Is that what you tell people? Is that what *she* tells you? You have a slow metabolism? Thyroid problem? Bullshit."

"I do have a thyroid problem," he mumbled.

"Right. You're a fat, lazy food addict, and you make me *sick*. You've done this to yourself. You *made* yourself disgusting."

"I have an eating disorder," Kevin said, his voice meek.

"I have an eating disorder," she mimicked. "No, you don't. You have no self-control, no self-respect, and you're lying to yourself. I bet she lies to you, too. 'I love you just the way you are, honey!' Right?" Naomi looked around at the other gym members, who were unabashedly staring. "Well, guess what? Everyone here looks at you and thinks you're grotesque. No one cares about your great sense of humor and beautiful mind."

"That's not true! Stop it!" Emmaline yelped.

"Shut *up*," Kevin ground out.

He had never said anything like that to her. Ever.

Naomi reached over and pushed the stop button on Kevin's treadmill. He was drenched in sweat; the seven minutes they'd spent walking just now was more exercise than he'd had in a long time.

"Get out," she said. "Go home, lard-ass. Order a pizza. Bet you have Domino's on speed dial."

Just last night, Em had made a big salad with grilled chicken; Kevin had a huge serving, then called for a pizza. Extra cheese.

Now he just stood there, his head hanging.

"You want to lose weight, lard-ass? It's not gonna happen from climbing on a treadmill twice a week. You think just walking in this door is enough? It's not. You may as well not even try."

"Jesus," Emmaline breathed. "Honey, let's go. There are plenty of other—"

"What do I have to do?" Kevin asked.

Naomi smiled. "Every fucking thing I say."

It went against all the literature. It went against everything her parents had said. Bullying wasn't supposed to work. Humiliation wasn't supposed to motivate.

Kevin signed up for a six-month membership with two hours of personal training a day.

"Why?" Emmaline asked as they went to the car. "I don't get it, Kevin."

"She told me the truth," he said. He wouldn't look at her.

When they got home, he went straight to the bathroom and turned on the shower. A minute later, she heard him crying. It broke her heart, but he wouldn't unlock the door when she knocked.

He didn't eat for the rest of the day.

The next day, he wasn't there when she got

home from work. She texted him; he didn't answer. Around nine, he came in, sweaty and red-faced, a stiff new SweatWorld gym bag in his hand.

"Hey!" she said. "How was it?"

"Good."

"Um . . . honey, I'm so glad you're doing this, but do you think Naomi is the best person to—"

"Yeah. I do. Thanks."

Three days later, he came home from the gym with a list in his hand and, without further ado, opened their cupboards and began tossing everything into the trash, making disgusted noises as he read labels.

"What are you doing?" she asked, retrieving a can of chicken stock. "Come on! That's not even opened!"

"It's poison," he said. "Look at the sodium count." He gave her a condemning look. She did the grocery shopping, after all. He picked up a packet of pad thai sauce and tossed it in the trash.

"Okay, hon, we can donate this to the food pantry. But can you tell me what's going on?" He tossed an unopened box of Special K, which she snatched. She loved cereal. "Are we going gluten-free or something?"

"Yeah. And sugar-free and dairy-free."

"What's left?" she asked, trying to make a joke.

He turned on her. "Do you think this is funny? Look at me. I'm sickening."

"No, Kevin, you're not."

He rolled his eyes and went back to the purge.

That weekend, he was so sore he could barely put on his pants. But he went to the gym, anyway. "Naomi says pain is weakness leaving the body," he told her.

She went with him, but Naomi ignored her, preferring instead to screech at Kevin, calling him lazy, a quitter, a slug. Twice Em had to go to the ladies' room to cry.

"I think it would be best if you and I went to the gym at different times," he told her on the way home. "I appreciate the support, but I need to focus."

"But . . . well, sure. Whatever you need, babe. Whatever works."

"Thanks," he said, squeezing her hand.

Naomi took Kevin grocery shopping, and when Em saw the receipt, she yelped; two bags of gluten-free, dairy-free, sugar-free, organic food cost more than she spent in a month.

All through the fall, he kept it up. He ate only lean protein and hard-to-digest vegetables and lumpy shakes made from green powder and soy milk. Quinoa and flax and wheatgrass. Egg-white omelets and raw broccoli, grilled fish and re peppers. He did fasts and cleanses and purges. Th bathroom smelled ghastly. His sex drive dropp

And all he could talk about was working c "Naomi says" became the two words that be

most of his sentences. Caloric load, adipose, anaerobic, layered eating . . . It was all they ever talked about. Well. All Kevin ever talked about.

He did, however, start to lose weight.

Nine pounds the first month. Eleven the second. In December, they had a big fight over her wanting to bake Christmas cookies to send to her parents and Angela. Kevin said they "couldn't afford the risk" of her baking something not in his diet plan.

She baked the cookies anyway when he was at work, boxed them up, sealed them with packing tape and addressed them, then went for a run. When she came home, she found Angela's package ripped open and a furious Kevin. He'd eaten at least a dozen cookies, he said, and it was her fault. She threw temptation in his path when he was at a vulnerable point, and how was that being supportive?

"See, I thought I was baking cookies for my family," Em said frostily. "I didn't realize I was such a temptress."

"Laugh it up. You'll be crying over my coffin if you can't support me."

"I do support you! And, my God, I'm so sick of that word!"

"I have to go to the gym," he said with a martyred air. "And I'll have to fast now for three days. Please have the rest of the cookies removed from our apartment when I get back."

"For God's sake," she muttered. "Fine." She sighed, then hugged him. "I'm sorry. I love you, and I'm really proud of you, okay? I just didn't realize I wasn't supposed to bake for anyone anymore."

"I'm an addict," he said. "Please be more respectful of my issues."

He only lost four pounds that month. Her fault again, he said, for bringing him to her office party and letting Angela and her mother make Christmas breakfast.

The gym became his favorite place. Those long hours at the law firm weren't as carved in stone as they'd seemed. In fact, the partners were all thrilled he was taking better care of himself.

So was Emmaline.

Except she barely saw him anymore, and, when she did, all he could talk about was food and exercise.

They couldn't go out to eat with friends because the temptation was too great. If Emmaline went out with friends from college or coworkers, Kevin asked her not to bring home the leftovers. They couldn't go to the movies. Night after night, they stayed home, Kevin falling asleep in the chair, exhausted from his workout.

Occasionally, they'd go for a run together, but Kevin mapped their route with painstaking care because God forbid they pass a bakery or hot dog vendor. "Naomi says it will take an entire year for my resistance to strengthen," Kevin said as they ran through a deserted industrial park at seven o'clock one Saturday morning. "Until then, I have to be really careful."

Emmaline went along with it, eating what Kevin ate, not buying anything that wasn't listed on the Naomi-approved list, not smuggling in Ben & Jerry's, no matter how much she missed it.

Kevin had taped Naomi clichés on the fridge, which made eating at home a guilt-riddled affair. *Whatever you eat in private, you wear in public. Abs are made in the kitchen. Don't kill your workout with food. The question isn't can you, it's will you. Nothing tastes as good as being thin feels.* Em had to dispute that last one. Ben & Jerry's definitely tasted better than being thin was. Not that she was thin. But she wasn't fat.

Not yet.

As Kevin lost weight, food became more seductive than ever to Emmaline. It was all she could think about. Time became measured in the hours until she could eat. She fell asleep thinking about food, and as soon as she was done with one meal, she started imagining the next.

While once she'd brought a yogurt and an apple for lunch, she now started eating a huge meal at work. Philly cheesesteaks and burgers and nachos, clam chowder and the Scrammy Hammy at Big Boy. She craved cherry pie, a Michigan specialty.

One day, she came home from work to find Kevin there, a rarity since he'd discovered the gym. "Hi, babe!" she said happily, dropping her bag on the floor.

"Hey, gorgeous," he said, hugging her close, and for a second, she felt such a surge of love and longing it nearly made her stagger. She hugged him back, noting that her hands could now touch. He really was melting away.

Suddenly, Kevin stepped back. "Are you trying to kill me?" he said.

"What?"

"You! You smell like . . . yes! You went to Ray's Red Hots today, didn't you?"

He made it sound as if she'd just kicked a baby panda in the stomach. "Guilty, Your Honor."

"It's not funny, Emmaline," he said, sounding like a sulky kindergartener. "You *reek* of Diablo Dogs."

"Well, I had two, Kevin. Okay? Sue me." The hot dog stand was an icon in Ann Arbor, and, back in the good old days, she and Kevin had stopped there often.

He glared at her, then grabbed his gym bag and left.

"Oh, for crying out loud, Kevin!" she yelled down the stairs. "*I'm* not on a diet! You are! I think I'm allowed to go out for lunch."

He didn't come home that night.

First time ever.

She didn't want to speculate about where he might be.

Instead, she went to the store and bought a pint of Ben & Jerry's and ate the entire thing. Peanut Brittle. It was flippin' delicious.

When Kevin came back the next night, they made up. Sort of.

By March, he'd lost seventy-seven pounds, and Emmaline noticed something one night as he dozed in the chair, exhausted from the fresh gym hell Naomi had invented for him.

Kevin was *gorgeous.*

Oh, she'd always thought he was good-looking. But now his face was emerging from the chubbiness of jowls and chins. He had beautiful cheekbones and a square jaw. His eyes, now closed, seemed bigger, his lashes a dark smudge on his cheeks.

If only she liked him the way she used to.

It had been a long time since they'd had fun. Or sex. Or fun sex. *It's just a stage,* her conscience told her. *He's still your Kevin.*

Except he wasn't.

Once, Kevin had been easygoing, funny, mellow and kind. These days, he was vain, obsessive and . . . *mean.* There was no other word for it.

He *hated* fat people. Stared in disgust. Clucked in disapproval. He also hated people who got gastric bypass. "Cheater," he said one night when they were watching the news about a person who'd lost three hundred pounds. "He'll gain it back. Health is like marriage. You can't cheat on it and expect it to work." One of Naomi's quotes.

"Speaking of marriage, hon," she began, but the phone rang, and it was Naomi, who was also watching the "cheater" on TV.

One day, when they were standing in line to get into a concert at the university, he saw a chubby little boy, about eight or nine years old. "You don't have to be this way," he said. "I was fat once, too."

"Kevin!" she admonished. "Stop it!"

"You're not doing him any favors, letting him eat junk," he said to the boy's mother, who gave him the finger.

"Honey, you can't be so judgmental," she told him later. "I know you just want to help, but that was mean."

"What's mean is his mother setting him up for diabetes," he said.

He had a point. But his point wasn't backed by kindness.

When Naomi gave him the green light to eat out in public, Emmaline almost cried with relief. Finally, she thought, they'd return to their regular lives. Sure, they were eating a lot healthier (except for her secret lunch binges). But not eating out or going to friends' houses for dinner . . . it was hard! Finally, she thought, they could be normal. Go out for dinner, see a movie. Talk.

That night, Em was thrilled. Wore a dress, did her makeup with care, left her hair down because Kevin liked it that way. The restaurant was French and romantic, candles flickering, their server soft-spoken and attractive.

"Would mademoiselle care for a drink?" he asked.

"I'll have a glass of pinot noir," she said. Kevin glanced at her, and she hoped he'd order one, too. He was edgy, poor thing, in a restaurant for the first time in months and months.

"And you, monsieur?"

From the table behind her, someone cleared her throat. Twice. Three times. Emmaline turned around and looked.

It was Naomi, her glittering eyes fixed on Kevin.

"Ice water," Kevin said tersely. "And don't bring any bread."

"Please," Emmaline added. She looked back at Naomi. "Hi. Want to join us?"

"You passed your first test, Kev," Naomi said, ignoring her. "You're doing great. What do you see on the menu that you can have?"

Em sighed.

Thus went dinner. Naomi would cough or hack at each wrong answer. Green salad? And what type of dressing would monsieur care for? (Hack.) No dressing? Very well. Grilled salmon? (Cough.) Make that haddock. Brussels sprouts (cough) no salt, no oil. No potatoes.

"I'll have what he's having." Em sighed. It wouldn't be fair to order the roasted duck with Gruyere bread pudding and butter-glazed asparagus. Forget the chocolate soufflé that was already calling to her from the dessert menu. Anyway, she'd gained a few pounds over the winter, and her jeans had been a little tight last time she'd worn them. That being said, the woman at the next table was cooing over something cheesy and delicious smelling. Em's stomach rumbled.

Naomi came over and bent down to murmur to Kevin, her ass practically in Emmaline's face. "Look around, Kev," she said. "You wanna be like those heart attacks waiting to happen?"

Emmaline looked past Naomi's perfect ass. Didn't see anyone abnormal. Her eyes stopped on a middle-aged couple, normal enough in build. The server was bringing them dessert.

"One piece of cheesecake? Five *hundred* calories. Seventy grams of fat," Naomi said. "Picture your heart, Kev, slimed up with that shit, the muscles pumping slower and slower, clogged with cheesecake." Kevin stared as if hypnotized.

"That's not really how it works," Em murmured. They both ignored her.

"Champagne on the house," the server said to the older couple. "Happy anniversary, and thank you for sharing it with us. How many years?"

"Twenty-five," the woman answered, smiling.

They were a nice-looking couple and clearly very happy together, holding hands, smiling.

"All those two have to do is get off their lard-asses and move and stop indulging themselves at every turn," Naomi went on. "But no. They're here instead, stuffing their fat faces—"

"Okay, thanks, Naomi! Nice seeing you," Emmaline interrupted.

"She's right, Em," Kevin said.

"What's life without cheesecake, though?" Em said with a smile. "Just once in a while, of course."

"See, *that's* the attitude that will keep you fat, Kevin. The attitude that will keep people staring at you, wondering why that lard-ass doesn't look in the mirror once in a while and see how repulsive—"

"Stop," Emmaline said. "Just . . . Naomi, Kevin and I are out to dinner, and I appreciate you helping him get healthy, but please. You're just being cruel."

"She's being honest," Kevin said hotly.

"Well, she's also being mean and nasty and hateful!" she snapped. "Who wants to live the way she does, in the gym all day long, never able to enjoy a meal, drinking those disgusting shakes! I'd rather be like them over there!" Em pointed to the couple. "They don't look like lard-asses to me!"

Whoops.

The restaurant had gone silent, and the anniversary couple sat frozen, the man with a forkful of cheesecake halfway to his mouth.

Naomi lifted an eyebrow and went back to her prison rations.

Kevin asked for the check. He didn't speak to her in the car, even when she tried to make light of the night. When they got home, he went into their bedroom and closed the door. A second later, she heard his voice as he talked on the phone. "Hey, Naomi. It's me."

When Kevin had lost a hundred pounds, he asked to speak with Emmaline.

"I think we should break up," he said calmly. "My life is taking a different direction, and I need to focus on that." He didn't meet her eyes.

"We're getting married in two months," she whispered.

Nothing she said made a difference. She tried not to cry and failed. Tried not to beg and failed there, too.

"You don't support me," he said, the accusation dripping like melted butter.

"I *do* support you," she said. "You know I do."

"No, you don't. You keep talking about the old me."

"I *miss* the old you! You were happier, Kevin! I'm not talking about being fat. You were funnier and happier and enjoyed everything more. Now all you do is go to the gym and count calories. That's no life!"

"Naomi says—"

"Please! Not another one of Naomi's famous quotes. Not when you're breaking up with me!" She started to sob. "Kevin, I've loved you since I was thirteen."

"You don't know me."

"How can you say that?"

"Em, you'll never understand. I'm finally someone I like. I'm sorry you don't, but Jesus! Don't tell me to go back."

"Can't you be healthy and still be sweet, Kevin? Because you were the nicest, best person I ever—"

"Yeah. I had to be, so people wouldn't hate me."

"No one hated you, Kevin. No one hates a person for being overweight."

He rolled his eyes. "Right. Look. I'm sorry, okay? But I can't be the true *me* while I'm with you. You're holding me back."

She wiped her eyes with the back of her hand. "K-K-Kevin, p-p-please."

The stutter bolted upright, a delighted rictus grin on its face.

It was back. Kevin's fat was disappearing, but after all these clean years, her stutter was back.

Kevin looked at her, his face gentling. "I'm going to say this for your own good, Emmaline," he said tenderly. "You've gained weight this year. You might want to watch what you eat."

And that was that. The Kevin she'd loved, who'd made being picked last for teams tolerable, who'd loved her when her words were stuck, was gone, shed like a snake skin.

He moved in with Naomi.

She wrote him a letter, unable to stop herself. It was filled with phrases such as "never stop loving you" and "don't understand" and "please give us another chance" and all those wretched, horrible, debasing phrases that your friends tell you never to say. He didn't answer.

When it seemed truly final, she went home to Malibu to break the news to her family.

"Kevin and I broke up," she said that night around the kitchen table with her parents (who no longer spoke directly to each other, yet still lived together) and Angela, who was visiting from Stanford, where she was getting her PhD in astrophysics.

"We figured that was coming," her mother said smoothly. "*I* accept you exactly as you are."

"And *I* love you unconditionally," Dad said, not to be outdone.

"Um . . . thanks," Emmaline said. "What do you mean?"

"We always knew," her father said.

"Knew what?"

Mom patted her hand. "That you're gay, honey."

Emmaline blinked. "No, I'm not."

"You don't need to pretend, Emmaline. Your *father* and I don't care what your sexual orientation is." She handed Em a tissue.

"Your *mother* and I had dinner with the Bateses the other night," Dad said. "They told us about Kevin's weight loss. It's wonderful, isn't it?" Good old Dad, ever clueless.

"I liked Kevin better when he was fat," Angela said. "And I'm so very sorry about this, Emmaline." Flawless Angela always said exactly the right thing.

Em went back to Ann Arbor, only to find that the paper was downsizing, and she was out of a job.

Nana had left Angela and Em her little house in her will. They'd planned on renting it, but now, it was a godsend.

The newspaper in Manningsport had one paid employee. Even if there was an opening, Em had her fill of covering town meetings and school concerts.

There was a job advertised for administrative assistant at the police department, which had all of one full-time cop and one part-timer. Levi Cooper, the chief, had been a year behind her in high school, a bit of a toughie, on the football team. All grown-up now, a veteran, somewhat grumpy and good at his job.

Em found that people confided in her as they

called with their problems. "Oh, Emmaline, hi, honey. My husband is late coming home, and I hate to be neurotic, but you think Levi would swing by Suzette Minor's house and see if Bill's car is there? You know Bill. You don't? Well, he's not the most faithful dog on the sled team."

One day, a woman came into the station and introduced herself. Shelayne Schanta, looking to start a book club. Could she put up a notice on the bulletin board? "My fiancé dumped me for my aunt, can you believe that?" she said. "Gotta find something to do in my free time."

"My fiancé left me six months ago," Em heard herself saying.

"Did he cheat on you?"

He had claimed no, but even if hadn't slept with Naomi before he dumped her, he'd been emotionally unfaithful, putting all his trust and attention and time into that shrew. Also, *People* magazine's "Half Their Size" edition had just come out, and Em (and the rest of the world) got to hear what Kevin really thought of her. That was infidelity enough.

"I think so."

"Welcome to the club," Shelayne said. "The bitter betrayed."

The name stuck, and the Bitter Betrayeds became her refuge. There wasn't much reading, but there were martinis and venting. They hung out at O'Rourke's from time to time. Emmaline joined the town hockey league, having become a pretty good skater during high school. She kept up her grandmother's flower garden; the smell of lilacs and irises reminded her of happy memories.

As it had been in school, her attitude became her armor. If she was a tough, mouthy jock, then she wasn't a woman who'd been tossed over for a mean girl.

But God, she missed Kevin.

She kept a button-down shirt of his from when he'd been at his heaviest. It was massive; she could wrap it around herself twice. It reminded her of the man who would make her macaroni and cheese on the second day of her period each month. Who had cut out *Dilbert* cartoons for her all through high school. Who sent her the complete set of *Buffy the Vampire Slayer* when she had her appendix out.

Whenever she felt lonely, or whenever she felt that maybe the time had come to register on eCommitment or Match.com, she found herself staring into her closet at that old soft blue shirt. She'd take it out and sleep in it, and even though the old Kevin was no more, she couldn't help remembering the boy who'd befriended her when she'd had no one else.

Chapter Eight

The drive from LAX to Rancho de la Luna was not going to be long enough.

Emmaline's plan was to get to the resort, check in as quickly as possible, then hide in her room, kill half a bottle of wine and fall asleep watching TV.

Jack fell asleep within seconds of getting into the passenger seat of the rental car, though he did run a hand over the hood as they got in. Because, yes, she'd rented a tricked-out Mustang convertible. She wasn't going to pull up at Rancho de la Luna in an economy car.

She pulled onto the 405, flipped off the driver who laid on his horn behind her and tried to unclench.

Jack didn't stir. His head was tipped back, blond hair shining in the sun. His sunglasses were on, and he looked like he belonged here in the land of the beautiful people. Faith had been right about her brother; he was a fantastic date. So far, anyway. Cheerful, reassuring, gorgeous. This wasn't a surprise as much as a concern, because Emmaline could definitely see herself becoming a slutty cliché and sleeping with her wedding date to prove she wasn't a dried-up, rejected hag.

Inglewood. Culver City. Santa Monica. The familiar names flashed past alongside the speeding cars. It was a bit of culture shock, driving on L.A. highways again, the sunlight glaring and the smell of exhaust all around her.

Yesterday, the five-year-old Cabrera triplets had come up to her in the park to play with Sarge, and they'd all ended up rolling around in the fresh snow and pretending to be snakes (Lucia's idea). Then all three kids climbed on Em and told her to be a pony, and she crawled around in the snow, whinnying, much to their delight (and Sarge's).

Twenty minutes in SoCal, and she was already homesick.

Relentless golden sunshine beat down. It was in the mid-sixties, maybe hotter here on the highway. She took the Santa Monica Freeway and headed for the Pacific Coast Highway.

Mom had told her a while ago that Kevin and Naomi had moved back to Malibu. That was before her parents had moved to Stanford to be closer to Angela.

Weird, picturing Kevin back here. In her mind, she saw the chubby, pale boy she'd first met, and a bittersweet ache swelled in her chest.

There was the ocean, glittering blue and calm. The scruffy hills of Southern California formed a wall on the eastern side of the road, the Pacific on the other.

"This is beautiful," Jack said, sitting up and taking off his sunglasses.

Not to her, it wasn't. Em had forgotten how dry it could get. Sure, the ocean was gorgeous, a shimmering, sparkling expanse today. But the landscape was scrubby and sandy, unless it had been gardened into an unnaturally lush oasis. Hotels and houses were plopped gracelessly along the highway—anything for a water view.

If she'd had better memories, it probably would've looked prettier. After all, Malibu was considered one of the most beautiful places in America.

As they came into the city proper, Em's heart rate kicked up. Okay, it *was* beautiful, perfectly kept houses dotting the hills, the yards bursting with gardens. Palm trees and flowering bushes grew in lush clumps.

"Lots of celebrities live out here?" Jack said.

"Oh, yeah. Bruce Willis, Courteney Cox, Leonardo DiCaprio."

"You ever see anyone famous in town?"

Em smiled at the question. "Sure. A lot of actors stay here if they have an event in Hollywood. Morgan Freeman held the door for me once."

"Cool."

She turned off the PCH and headed up toward the ranch. The sun was starting to set, and her stomach grumbled. Despite being fed in first class, she was starving.

"What's the plan for tonight?" Jack asked.

"I'm hoping to hide in my room and order dinner and drink wine," she said. "You can do whatever you want." Then, realizing how rude that sounded, she added, "I mean, see the sights. It's a beautiful ranch. Used to be a rehab place for the wealthy."

"I'll do whatever you want," he said.

Don't tempt me, Jack. She turned onto White Horse Canyon Road. Her heart was twanging with nervousness now. There was the sign— "Welcome to Rancho de la Luna, America's #1 Luxury Boot Camp."

"Luxury Boot Camp?" Jack said. "Kind of an oxymoron."

"It's like the place on *The Biggest Loser*," Em said. "Naomi is a fitness guru."

"How fun for the rest of us."

Without warning, Em pulled over onto the side of the road, getting an enraged honk and some curse words from the car behind her. She flipped them off—it was the California way, after all—and looked at Jack. "Okay, here's the deal. He was fat, she made him her project, they fell in love. My parents think I'm gay. And did I mention I have a very perfect and beautiful sister?"

"You did."

"Also, my parents are divorced but still live together and don't speak directly to each other. They may analyze you. They're psychologists."

"Ah. And anything else?"

"I'm probably forgetting something, but for now, no."

He smiled. "You want to stop and change first?"

She twitched. "Excuse me?"

He shrugged. "Three sisters. I figured you wouldn't want to face your ex looking like—"

"Like what, Jack?"

"Like you've just flown across the country and forgot your miracle drug for hair."

"I didn't bring you along for snark." She threw the car back in gear. "I'm not one of those people who's fixated on looks."

"I can tell."

"Jack, if you don't want me to stab you in the neck, shut it. Your publicity team said you were the perfect date. Act like it."

He grinned. *Ah.* He was joking. She felt the tug of a small smile. "Sorry," she said.

Rancho de la Luna—Ranch of the Moon—was gorgeous. White stucco with red clay tile roofs, beautiful plantings, a fountain. Orange and lemon trees were in bloom, competing with the soft white of ornamental pear trees, and the scent of jasmine was thick in the air.

Very romantic.

"Welcome," said the valet as she pulled up to the huge wooden doors. "Are you here for the Norman-Bates wedding?"

"We sure are," she said, getting out and handing

him the keys. "I'm Janet Leigh, and this is Anthony Perkins."

"Nice to meet you!" he said, flashing a smile so brilliant Em almost shielded her eyes. "Head on in, and make yourselves at home here at Rancho de la Luna!"

Jack retrieved their bags from the trunk. "Showtime," he said, reaching for her hand.

"No, no. None of that," she said. But damn, she was glad he was here, a tall, handsome date. Really, he should start charging. He'd make a fortune.

The lobby of the resort featured Mexican tile floors and clean white walls. Some lurid religious art hung on the walls; Em had read that the place had been modeled after a Spanish mission. She glanced around. Nobody she knew.

"Emmaline Neal," she said to the clerk.

"Welcome," the woman said, clicking some keys. "And your name, sir?"

"Jack Holland. Can our rooms be adjoining?"

"Not necessary," Em said.

"It's no trouble," the clerk replied cheerfully. "I can put you in rooms 112 and 114. Just go down this hall and take a right. Both rooms have ocean views." She smiled again at Jack and handed them both keys.

"Thank you," Emmaline said. She picked up her bag, turned and nearly bumped into an *extremely* beautiful man. Dark hair. Dark eyes. Broad shoulders, chiseled bone structure, and electric attraction buzzed in her stomach.

"Emmaline!" the man said. And holy bleepity-bleeping bleep, it was Kevin.

Her face went hot immediately, and her knees felt sick and weak.

He looked like the love child of Johnny Depp and Orlando Bloom. Square jaw, perfect nose, lovely mouth and those eyes . . . The eyes were the same.

"You made it," he said.

"What?" She cleared her throat. "Yeah, I did. Um, we did. Yes. Thank you for inviting me. You look . . . you look great, Kevin."

Almost three years since she'd seen him last. He'd been very handsome, yes, and strong and solid.

Now, though . . . now he was a sculpted wonder of science and divinity. His T-shirt, which read Trample the Weak, Hurdle the Dead, clung to his pecs, and his arms . . . his arms were a thing of beauty. Those were Daryl-from-*The-Walking-Dead* arms. Jeremy Renner arms.

Em closed her mouth. Presumably, Jack was nearby and hadn't burst into flames, but even if he had, it might've been hard for Emmaline to look away from Kevin.

Her ex grinned. "That's right. You've never seen the end result. Pretty amazing, huh?" he said, and with that, he took off his shirt and flexed.

Such a . . . such a . . . such a jerk.

But holy bleep.

He was tan and hairless (he used to have chest hair, but the landscape was smooth and golden now). Perfectly defined muscles, no trace of fat anywhere. It was as if New Kevin had killed Old Kevin, melted down his fat and used it for lamp oil or something, because even though she'd slept with this guy for years, she didn't recognize one thing on that beautiful panorama of skin and muscle and beauty.

Then Naomi came jogging up, wearing workout gear smaller than any bathing suit Em had ever owned. Emmaline tore her eyes off Kevin's eight-pack (was there such a thing?) and blinked.

"Babe. There you are." Naomi slid a tanned arm around Kevin's perfect waist and smirked at Emmaline. "Emily. Long time no see."

"It's Emmaline."

"Right." Naomi hefted up a liter of bile-colored sports drink and guzzled.

"Hi. Jack Holland," came a voice. "The bride and groom, I take it?"

"Sorry," Em said. "Jack, these are Kevin Bates and Naomi Norman. This is my friend, Jack Holland."

Naomi scanned him up and down. "What's your BMI?"

"I have no idea," he said patiently.

"How much can you bench?" Kevin asked.

"I'm not really a gym kind of person," he said, smiling. He took her hand. She didn't remove it. She might've even been squeezing it very hard.

She should've hugged Kevin to show she was over him. She should've smiled. She should've said, *Kevin, hey! Look at you, gorgeous!* and been all casual and happy and not frozen and stupid.

"This is a beautiful spot," Jack said. "We were so happy to get out of the weather back home."

Neither Naomi nor Kevin answered.

"Emmaline, why don't we get settled?" Jack said.

She stared at him mutely. Better than looking at Kevin, that was for sure. Let alone Naomi.

"Good idea," she said, and hooray for her, she was speaking at long last. "We'll see you guys later. Of course. Because it's your wedding! Yay!" *Oh, Lord.* Where was her gun? She *had* packed it, right? It would be so great to shoot herself right now.

Jack laughed, angels bless him, and put his arm around her shoulders. "Long flight," he said, giving her a little squeeze. "We were up before dawn."

Naomi smirked. "Yeah. Get some rest, Emily. You look exhausted."

Then, hand in hand, the bride and groom walked the opposite way. Naomi still had the most amazing body she'd ever seen, and Em couldn't help the flash of envy she felt. Just once, just for one afternoon on the beach, she would've liked to have rocked a bathing suit. Okay, fine. She would've liked it for a weekend. A month. A few years.

And Kevin . . . He'd done it. He certainly wasn't fat anymore. He was the one percent—the perfectly beautiful people with perfectly beautiful bodies.

"You okay?" Jack asked.

"Yep." She stepped out from the comfort of his arm. "I appreciate the thought, Jack, but I really don't want to pretend to be a couple."

He looked at her for a long minute. "You sure?"

"Yeah. But thank you." She looked away from the kindness in his eyes and headed down the hallway.

Time for a very big glass of wine. Or two. They passed another hallway, and a familiar voice stopped Em in her tracks.

"Emmaline? Sweetheart!" It was Mom. "How are you? Are you crushed? Did you see Kevin? You were very brave to come."

"Of course you came, Emmaline. You're very strong, as I raised you to be," said Dad. There was a brief scramble as each parent tried to be the one to hug her first.

"Hi, Mom. Hi, Dad." She gave them simultaneous, one-armed hugs so as not to play favorites, then smiled at her sister.

"Emmaline!" Angela said, her eyes growing damp. "How wonderful to see you!"

Her sister managed to extricate her from their parents and gave her a hug. Then Dad had to give her another, extra-long hug to show that he was a better parent than Mom, which meant Mom had to hug her again and kiss her twice on the cheek.

"It's good to see you guys," Em said. She meant it, but there was no way she'd ever sound as nice and sincere as her sister. "This is my friend, Jack Holland."

"Jack, lovely to meet you," Angela said, shaking his hand warmly. Honestly, those nuns at the orphanage had done a fantastic job raising her.

"Oh! *This* is Jack?" Mom exclaimed. "What a surprise! I didn't—well, *we* didn't . . . ah . . ."

"What, Mom? I told you I was bringing someone."

"I just assumed this 'Jack' person—" Mom made quote marks with her fingers "—was actually 'Jacqueline.' Not that there's anything wrong with you, Jack."

"Very nice to meet you," Jack said, smiling at Em. He shook hands with her parents.

"Son, a pleasure," Dad said, to prove that he was way cooler than Mom.

"We were just going to have some dinner in the restaurant," Angela said. "It's very pretty. You have to join us, don't they, Mama? Papa?"

"Sounds great," Jack said, damn him. "Give us an hour, why don't you? We'll meet you there."

More hugs were exchanged until, finally, the three other Neals went off. When they were a sufficient distance away, Em looked at Jack. "What did I say about hiding in the room and drinking wine?" she asked. "I thought you were a winemaker. You were supposed to support that plan."

"They're your family. They love you." He picked up her suitcase, ignoring her attempts to grab it back. "You can have wine at dinner."

Emmaline couldn't have wine at dinner. No one could.

The resort restaurant—Sea of Tranquility—was beautiful, overlooking the Pacific. It also didn't serve alcohol. Where had *that* been on the website, huh? Rather hateful of them, really.

It had gotten chillier. There was a picturesque fire in a glass fireplace in the middle of the room and windows on three sides. Em, Jack and her family had a corner table; she thought Jack might've slipped the maître d' a twenty, but she was a little stupid with fatigue. Strangely beautiful candles, probably made out of wheatgrass and edamame, flickered, and, outside, a whip-poor-will started to sing.

Naomi and Kevin weren't in the restaurant, thank God. Em thought she recognized one of his

164

cousins, but no one called out a hello or stopped by the table, and she was deeply grateful. She'd see everyone tomorrow and Saturday—they'd been given a program of "Fun and Healthful Activities!" which included the mandatory water sports.

Saturday afternoon was the wedding itself.

She wondered how Kevin had felt, seeing her again. If they might have a real conversation, just the two of them, and maybe . . . maybe set some old feelings at rest. Maybe they could even manage to be friends again. Surely, somewhere in that beautiful sculpted body, a little bit of Old Kevin existed.

Dinner was a blurry, odd affair. Her parents were both talkers, but because they didn't speak to each other, it was as if there were two conversations going on at the same time, except for their sharp jabs at each other from time to time. Also, the combination of jet lag and stress was the equivalent to an Ambien and a baseball to the head.

The ranch only served gluten-free, vegan food, and while it wasn't awful, it also wasn't identifiable or filling.

Only Angela was normal, her usual charming self, laughing, laying her hand on Jack's arm from time to time, telling stories while Mom whispered questions to her about why Em had chosen to bring a man as her date.

"I'm straight, Mom," Emmaline told her for the fifth or sixth time.

"Not that there's anything wrong with that," she said, "but, Emmaline, you don't have to hide your sexuality from us. I'm very open-minded, even if your father isn't."

"I'm open-minded," Dad objected. "I think we all know exactly who's homophobic here. But, Emmaline, you never have to hide who you truly are from your old dad."

"I'm not hiding anything!" Em said. "I'm broadcasting my sexuality, okay? I like men. I've never kissed a woman, and I never want to."

"Too bad," Jack murmured, earning a scowl. He was acting way too boyfriendy for her.

"Can we talk about something else?" she asked, pushing some mysterious food that began with a Z around her plate. "Ange, what's new in the world of the moon and stars?" She turned to Jack. "Angela's an astrophysicist. Just finished her PhD at Stanford."

"Emmaline, you're so sweet to ask, but my job is so boring compared to yours!" her sister said. "Tell me how things are going in beautiful Manningsport. Have you had any interesting calls lately?"

"Oh, sure," she said. "Um, a four-year-old got a blueberry stuck in his nose, and I helped with that . . ." Okay, it had been more fun than it sounded. Little Flynn Maloney had been quite thrilled with the attention and rightfully proud of the effort it had taken to wedge the berry up so high. "Well, the other day, I had to unhandcuff a guy from his bed. His wife had dropped the key in the chocolate sauce and thought she might've swallowed—oh, uh, never mind, actually."

The frisky couple in question had been Prudence and Carl Vanderbeek. Jack's sister and husband. *Whoopsy.*

"Sounds like something my sister and Carl would do," he said.

"Bingo."

He smiled.

He smiled.

Oh, he *smiled.*

Yep, that was some *mighty* good mojo. His eyes were unbelievably pretty, and that smile was balm for the battered soul. His eyes crinkled at the corners, too! Damn and blast, Jack Holland's face was just . . . it was just . . .

"You two make a lovely couple," Angela said.

"No! No, no. We're just friends," Em said, jerking her gaze away from Jack.

"We play hockey together," Jack added. "She has the best wrist shot on the team." He put his arm around the back of her chair, doing that boyfriendy thing again. "But she looks pretty exhausted, so if you don't mind, we'll get back to our rooms."

"Of course! A well-rested body is the foundation

of good mental health," Dad said, leaping up to hug her. "You're wonderful, sweetheart. Daddy loves you very much."

"Love you, too, Daddy," she said.

"And I love you just as much. If not more," Mom added.

"Good to know. Ange? You want to chime in?"

Angela laughed. "And I love you more than these two combined, plus infinity."

Emmaline smiled, hugged her sister and mom, and she and Jack headed back to their rooms.

"What a nice family," he said.

Not the word she'd use, but they were hers, and she did love them. "Thanks. They liked you a lot."

"Everyone does." He grinned, taking away any conceit that might've been associated with the smile. After all, it was true. What was not to like? To love? Who wouldn't want to rub up against him and—

"You want to hang out or something?" he asked.

"Um . . . I should get to bed. I mean, do you?"

He hesitated. "No. I'm pretty whipped, too."

"In the morning, if you walk down to the beach, you might see some otters. They're really cute."

"I'll keep a lookout."

"There's a hot yoga class at five-thirty," she said. "It's on our schedule of events."

"I'll pretend I didn't hear that," he answered, sliding his keycard into the slot. "Sleep well, Emmaline."

She went into her room, as well. Double-locked the door. Washed up, got in her jammies and got into bed. Very comfortable. She flapped her arms and legs as if making a snow angel. Big bed. Plenty of room for Sarge. She wondered how he was doing. Shelayne, who had an unhealthy love of dogs, had him for the weekend. Em would be lucky if she got her puppy back, given how Shelayne had promised to spoil him.

Yep. Big bed. Very big. Very comfy.

Crap. She was wired. Exhausted but wired.

She closed her eyes and tried to relax. Pictured being on the ocean in a gently drifting boat. (Why was she drifting? What if she got caught on the Gulf Stream and ended up like Pi, minus the tiger? Or even worse, with the tiger?) Pictured the blue, blue ocean. (Note to self: warn Jack to check the shark report before he went swimming. Then again, the water would only be about sixty degrees. Then again, he was from the Finger Lakes. He knew cold water. And then again, maybe he wouldn't want to go swimming because of the rescue, but she kind of did, except that she'd have to wear a wet suit, and whose ass looked good in a wet suit? Naomi's and no one else's, that's whose.)

"Okay, this isn't working," she said aloud, flinging back the covers. Time for a little fresh air.

She went out onto the balcony, which was teeny but adorable, red trumpet vine curling up through the post. A small iron table, two tiny chairs. She breathed in the cool salty air. Maybe she'd have coffee out here in the morning. But wait . . . no. The ranch was also caffeine-free. Horrible place.

She glanced over at Jack's balcony, which was identical to hers. He'd left the slider open, and his curtain fluttered out in the breeze. She hoped he'd enjoy the weekend, being out of Manningsport in the land of sunshine and ocean. He really was an awfully good guy.

The lawns of Rancho de la Luna spread out before her, dark and green. The whip-poor-will called again, lonely in the quiet. The breeze was jasmine scented, a fragrance Em well remembered from her childhood, and she thought she could catch the sound of the gentle Pacific lapping at the sandy shore. Or maybe those were cars down on the Pacific Coast Highway. Either way, Rancho de la Luna certainly had a prime location. God only knew what this wedding would cost. The place itself had to be top dollar, let alone the food, band, flowers and activities.

Em's wedding was going to have been in her parents' house. Mom and Dad had worked side by side in silence each weekend for a year, getting the yard ready. Dad had even built a trellised archway, an adorably crooked little structure.

Boo-hoo-hoo. There were worse things in the world than being jilted by a fiancé. She knew that. She'd made a nice life for herself in

Manningsport. Loved her job. Loved her boss, loved Carol, even loved the dopey Everett. She had friends. She had a dog.

It was just that feeling of being alone. Coming home to an empty, dark house night after night. Week after week after month of not finding anyone she could picture spending a lifetime with.

Seemed like Kevin had been the love of her life. Old Kevin, that was.

She sighed and looked at her watch. She'd been awake for an hour already. Well, the Kindle hadn't been invented for nothing. "Elmore Leonard, here we come," she muttered.

She jumped at the sound of a thud from Jack's room. A really loud thud. "Jack? You okay?" she called.

He didn't answer.

"Jack?"

Emmaline went back inside. A door joined their rooms, and she knocked. "Jack? You okay?"

Nada.

Then there was another crash and some glass breaking.

The door was locked. "Jack! Open the door, buddy."

She didn't hear any movement inside.

She knocked again, more loudly this time. "Jack, it's Emmaline. Open up, okay?"

Five seconds, and no answer.

Okay. Time for some police work.

He had Josh Deiner by the arm now, and he was pulling him up. And really, this wasn't so hard after all; why had he been dreading going down here? It wasn't even cold, which was weird, because Anderson Cooper was on the shore narrating the action, and he kept saying how cold it was.

The car was deeper than Jack remembered, but that was okay, because it was warm and there were sea otters and the Deiner kid was even smiling a little, as if this was almost a joke between him and Jack. He wouldn't open his eyes, though. The other boys had. They'd swum as gracefully as the otters, but Josh was pretending to be unconscious, probably because he wanted to be an actor. Jack knew that because Anderson Cooper had said so.

Then all the sea otters darted away, like fish do when the shark is coming.

But it was cold, all of a sudden, and Jack looked up. Maybe he shouldn't have swum so far down, because the surface was far, far away. Weird that he could hold his breath this long. Actually, he couldn't, could he?

Suddenly, his lungs felt like chunks of coal, and it was getting dark; *oh, shit,* the ice was closing over them, a solid ceiling of ice blocking out the purple and red sunset, and Jack heard it close, it closed with a crash like glass, and he really, really needed to breathe now. He looked at Josh, and Josh's eyes were open now, and he was smiling, but it wasn't a nice smile. He grabbed Jack's arm and started sinking, pulling Jack down because Josh was already dead and furious that Jack hadn't saved him, and he wasn't going to be dead alone. Jack tried to pull free, tried to hit Josh in the face, but his arms were too heavy and slow, so he pinned the boy against the car—

"Jack! Jack! You're okay. You're dreaming, that's all."

There was a woman here. Underneath him.

"Hi," she said. "Wake up, buddy."

Right. Emmaline. He was gripping her wrists, the sheets twisted around him, and had her half pinned. The small lamp on the desk had been turned on.

He jerked back, releasing her wrists. "I'm sorry," he said, and his voice was hoarse. He ran a hand through his hair and found that it was sweaty. *He* was sweaty, in fact. All of him.

"Want a drink of water?" she asked, oddly calm for a woman who'd just been grabbed by a naked sweaty man.

Oh, yeah. He was naked, too. He always slept that way.

She didn't wait for an answer, just got up and went into the bathroom. He sat against the headboard and straightened the covers. Looked around, his breath still coming hard.

Actually, he had a glass of water somewhere. *Ah.* There it was, shattered on the floor, alongside the lamp.

Fourth time this week he'd had the same dream, more or less. The sea otters had been new.

"How did you get in here?" he asked when she came back in the room.

"I did knock," she said, handing him the glass. "You didn't answer, so I climbed onto your balcony. Very cat burglar of me. By the way, you should lock your doors at night."

"Figured the odds of an intruder would be low."

"Not low enough," she said with a grin. She bent down and picked up the lamp, turned it on, then started picking up the pieces of glass.

"I'll get that," he said.

"You stay in that bed," she said. "I bet you sleep naked as a frog, and I don't want a show just now."

He would've made a joke, except Josh's face was still burned in his mind, that unforgiving, ruthless smile.

Emmaline put the fragments of the glass on the table. "Do you have nightmares a lot?" she asked.

"No. Not really."

"Sounded like a doozy."

"I don't remember what it was about."

She gave him a look as if she knew he was lying. Better that than having her go all Dr. Freud on him.

He should be over this by now. The accident had taken place twenty days ago. Three of the kids were as right as rain.

Josh Deiner was holding his own.

If you could call a coma holding your own.

"Move over," she said, and he did.

She sat next to him, on top of the covers, and took one of the many pillows the hotel provided, holding it on her lap. Looked at him. Pushed her hair off her face. It was a utilitarian gesture—*hair is obscuring vision: fix.* So different from Hadley's sex-kitteny moves.

But Emmaline had something going on nonetheless. Her hair was dark and thick, and she had on sock-monkey pajama bottoms and a tank top. Nice rack. He tried not to notice.

He sensed he was about to be lectured on the importance of getting counseling, maybe something on post-traumatic stress disorder, or a pat on the shoulder and a reminder that all four kids would've drowned without him, not just Josh, and even Josh was *holding his own,* and he couldn't beat himself up.

"Want some chocolate?" she asked. "I'm starving."

Without waiting, she got up, unlocked the door that apparently connected their rooms—Jack had hardly noticed it—and came back a second later with a Hershey bar. With almonds, no less. She plunked herself down next to him and unwrapped the candy bar. "I brought a stash. Don't tell on me, or they'll make me do sit-ups or something." She broke the bar in half and handed him his chunk.

He took a bite of the chocolate. Hadn't had one of these in a long time. "So why did you say yes to this wedding, Emmaline?" he asked. Yes. Talk about something other than him.

She shrugged. "Stupid pride. Morbid curiosity, too." She took a bite of the Hershey bar. Her half was bigger, and it made him like her more for some reason. "You know. Is your ex really over you? Are you really over him?" She shot him a glance. "You must know what that's like."

"Not really."

"Does it bother you, having Hadley back in town?"

He finished his half (his third, really). "I'd rather she wasn't, but she is."

"Does she want to get back together?"

"Yeah."

She nodded. "Think you'll give her a chance?"

"No. Would you give Kevin another chance?" he asked.

She finished her candy bar and licked the wrapper, and Jack felt a jolt straight to his groin.

"I probably would," she said. "The Kevin I fell in love with would be worth a second chance, blah blah, who cares." She was quiet a second.

"But he's New Kevin now. I guess people change. Right?"

"I don't know."

"Did Hadley?"

Maybe it was the dim light and the late hour or the intimacy of sharing a candy bar, or just to think about something else, but Jack found himself answering. "She probably didn't," he said. "But I saw what I wanted to see."

"Men are stupid that way," Emmaline concurred, and, much to his surprise, he laughed.

"How are women stupid, then?"

"They go to their ex-fiancé's wedding, hoping for something that will probably never happen."

"And what would you like to happen? For him to leave the trainer and beg you to take him back?"

"That's fun to picture," she admitted. "But no. I guess just some kind of . . . apology, maybe?" She blushed.

Funny. She wasn't bothered by him lying on top of her or the fact that he was indeed naked as a frog under the covers, or the fact that he'd been thrashing around breaking things. But she blushed admitting all she wanted was a simple "I'm sorry."

"What does he have to be sorry for?" Jack asked.

She wadded up the candy wrapper and tossed it neatly into the wastebasket. "Three pointer."

Another shrug. "I don't know. Nothing. The comment in *People*, maybe."

"What comment in *People*?"

"God, Jack, with three sisters, I figured you'd be up on town gossip."

"They're white noise as far as I'm concerned."

Another blush. "He said I was unsupportive."

"That's it?"

"Well, I wasn't unsupportive, Jack! I *was* supportive! I was 1950s girdle supportive."

"I'm getting that you were very supportive," he said, biting down on a smile. "Supportive of what, again?"

"God. You're a terrible date. Of him losing 150 pounds."

"Really. Well, good for him. So it changed him, did it?"

"Yeah. Old Kevin was pretty fantastic. New Kevin is a self-obsessed idiot." She gave him an assessing, coplike look, one he recognized from Levi. "You okay now?"

Jack felt his smile turn to wood. "I'm fine. Thank you. Sorry I woke you."

She shrugged. "I was awake anyway." She stood up. "Hope you sleep better the rest of the night, Jack."

"I'd walk you to the door, except I'm naked as a frog."

She smiled over her shoulder and unlocked the door that connected their rooms. "Call me if you need me." Her tone was matter-of-fact and not unfriendly.

She didn't lock the door behind her.

Jack considered that.

It had been a long time since he'd slept with a woman.

Emmaline smelled nice. She didn't talk too much. She didn't ask those stupid date questions, like what was his ideal evening and did he see himself with kids in five years. She didn't seem to be assessing him for genetic potential of her future children, and she hadn't flirted with him once. She didn't ask questions about the accident.

Him being naked as a frog hadn't had any effect on her.

She was simply . . . *nice.* Well, no, that wasn't the right word.

She was easy to be with. She was honest. He liked the edge she had to her and the tolerant affection she had for her family, so clear and yet meted out with eye rolls and snarky comments.

She smelled good.

She had a spectacular ass.

Her upper lip was a little fuller than her bottom lip, and he wondered what it would be like to kiss her.

And if he had her in bed with him, he'd have something to think about other than the Deiner kid.

Chapter Nine

Emmaline decided to embrace her California roots the next morning and go for a run on the beach trail.

It was early. She was still on East Coast time, and she figured she'd be safe. Also, running had always been her thing. She wasn't fast and she didn't go terribly far, but there was something about the simple action of running—you didn't have to be good at it to have it work. That and a kickboxing class kept her in shape for her job. If she stopped eating like a college football player, she'd probably slim down a bit. Be a size eight, maybe. But the time she'd spent with Kevin when he was losing weight had made her hate dieting in all its forms. Besides, Ben & Jerry's would fold without her.

Em had never really had an issue with her figure. Overall, she liked how she looked. She was tall and big-boned and strong.

But around people like Naomi, she felt grotesque. Colleen O'Rourke was also gorgeous and slim and perfect, but there was a difference. Every time Emmaline had ever seen Naomi, she was in some sort of pose that emphasized her perfectly muscled arms or flat stomach. Colleen, by comparison, was normal. Also, Naomi *wanted* people to feel crappy about how they looked. It was her job to prey on people and make them think they needed her to direct their every move.

Sure had worked on Kevin.

Kevin, who had once told Emmaline that every morning when he woke up next to her, he wondered what he'd done to get so lucky.

"Snap out of it, Neal," she said to herself. She pulled on her running shorts, sports bra and Body by Ben & Jerry's T-shirt, then pulled on her Nikes and headed out.

No one else was around. The hot yoga people were not in sight, thank you, baby Jesus. A bleary-eyed waiter gave her a perfunctory smile as he set out a tea station. *Dang. That's right. No caffeine.* Hard to believe people paid money to stay here.

That being said, it *was* beautiful. Em ran down the trail toward the Pacific. Coreopsis was in bloom in bright yellow clumps amid the silvery sagebrush, cheerful little beacons in the semi-gloom.

At the top of the cliff, she stopped.

The sky was still deep blue, but a line of pink cracked the horizon. There were a few cars racing down, but she could hear the ocean, and her hair fluttered in the breeze.

She didn't miss much about SoCal, but she did miss this view. She started running again. No music today—she wanted to hear the birds. The trail was wide and twisting, flanked by the bushy foliage of the area. It was cool this morning, maybe fifty degrees.

It had been kind of nice, sitting with Jack last night, even if he was in the throes of PTSD. He'd have an easier time if he'd acknowledge it. She wasn't the child of psychologists for nothing; her bookcase back home had quite a few books on stress and trauma and people's reactions. She figured it would help with the high-intensity calls that she might have to go on as a police officer.

A coyote ran across the trail in front of her, a scrawny little thing compared with the beasts they had back home.

She glanced at her watch. Twenty minutes in one direction, twenty minutes back . . . That'd be about four miles altogether (oh, fine, it was closer to three). Who cared? Any activity would absolutely justify a trip into town for some jelly donuts at Nance's Coffee Shop, if it was still in business, please God.

When she hit the twenty-minute mark, she turned around, inspired by the thought of donuts. Then she heard footsteps behind her.

Kevin. A shirtless Kevin, no less.

"Hey, Emmaline!" he said, and damn if the sound of his voice—that friendly, lovely voice—didn't make her heart jump.

"Hey, Kevin. How are you?"

"Great!" He stopped and wiped his forehead with his forearm.

He was shirtless. Had she mentioned that? Oh, yes. All that perfectly perfect perfection had an impact. He looked like a feature in *Men's Health* or some porno website. Heck, if men in pornos looked like that, she just might start watching.

"How'd you sleep?" he asked, and it was such a normal question.

"Good! Good. You?"

"Great." He smiled. "Want to walk back? I usually like to run at least twelve miles, but it'd be nice to catch up with you. Hear what you've been up to."

"Sure." Her heart was jackhammering.

"So how far did you run this morning?"

"Oh, um . . . just a couple miles."

"Well, you can make up for it later. We're doing a half marathon tomorrow before the wedding."

"Fun."

"Did I tell you Naomi's on the short list to be on *The Biggest Loser*?" he said.

"No, Kevin. You haven't told me anything. We haven't talked in three years, remember?" And, man, that would *really* suck, having to see Naomi's face on TV, snarling at sobbing contestants.

"True enough," he said mildly. "Well, you know Naomi—she'd be the best. She has an audition on the thirteenth."

183

"Good luck to her."

"Luck has nothing to do with it, Emmaline. It's all about work and goals. You set goals and commit to them."

One upside of being dumped—didn't have to hear those stupid sayings anymore. She could also point out that he'd committed to marrying her and hadn't stayed loyal to that. Then again, water under the bridge.

"I'm sorry," he said, surprising her. "I sound like a jerk." He stopped for a second, bent down and picked a small yellow flower. Handed it to her with that boyish grin she remembered so well. "How have you been, Emmaline? I've missed you." His eyes were kind.

Oh, no.

It was a glimpse of Old Kevin. The sweet, thoughtful guy she'd adored for so long.

The stutter twitched in its sleep.

She took a deep breath and thought in a British accent.

"Fine, really. I'm good."

"Your mom says you're a cop?"

"Mmm-hmm."

"And you like the work?"

"I do. It's very—" *Intimate,* she wanted to say, but the *I* sound got stuck tight.

The stutter opened its eyes.

Better to say nothing than to mangle a word. She tipped her head as if searching for the right word.

"Rewarding, I'd imagine," Kevin suggested.

"Yes. Exactly."

"And your boyfriend, what does he do?"

Correcting Kevin would require more words than she was willing to risk. "He's a winemaker," she said. There. A complete sentence, no mangling anywhere. Three entire words. Five syllables.

"Really? I don't drink anymore, but that's a very cool profession." He stopped, turning to look at her. She'd forgotten how ridiculously lush his eyelashes were. "Em, I have to admit, I've thought about you so much over the past three years."

She cut him a sharp glance. Was it coming? The apology? More?

"I was worried about you. You seemed so . . . broken."

A cold fist of fury clenched in her stomach. *Really?* she wanted to say. *Broken, as in "heart-broken"? And why would that be? Because you jilted me two months before our wedding? Because you left me for some exercise-addicted shrew and told the world I sabotaged you when in fact I loved you with all my heart for seventeen years? Why on earth would you worry?*

"I wasn't sure you'd ever get over me," he said, reaching out to tuck some hair behind her ear.

She jerked back. "Well, somehow I managed. They dropped the suicide watch a while ago."

He gave her a sad smile, and she remembered it

well. The commiseration smile, back when he was fat and she was a stutterer, the "yeah, I know what that's like" smile, and somehow that was the worst thing of all. How dare he feel sorry for her? How dare he worry about her? How dare he bring back her stutter when she really should be past this, goddamn it?

"I'm glad," Kevin said. "I hope you and your guy will be as happy as Nay and I are." *Nay. How gross.* "Are things serious?"

"Yep. In fact, we're engaged."

Oh, shit and whiskey. Not smart. Not smart at all.

But it was kind of great to see Kevin's mouth drop open. The stutter, too, was shocked and retreated to a corner to regroup.

"You are?" Kevin asked. His cheeks mottled with color, and he glanced down at her left hand. "Where's your ring?"

"It's being resized." *Well, well, well.* Seemed like she was a pretty excellent liar. The things you never knew you could do until you had to.

"I'm happy for you."

He sounded anything but.

Guess Kevin had gotten a good bit of satisfaction, thinking about her mooning over him (which she had), staying home every Friday night (okay, yes, she did that a lot), feeling like no one would ever fall for her again. (Fine! She had those thoughts, all of them!)

Even so, this walk had just become a lot more enjoyable.

"So when are you getting married?" he asked.

"We haven't set a date yet."

"Well. Uh . . . this is great, Emmaline."

"Thanks," she said. "Listen, I think I'll run the rest of the way, okay? See you later."

Because satisfaction aside, she had to tell Jack. Pronto.

"Sure. I'll see you back at the ranch. You're playing some of the couples games with us later, right?" He smiled, but it wasn't the sweet Old Kevin smile from before. "Wait till you see Naomi in a bikini. That'll get you motivated to lose some weight."

Oooh. War had been declared.

"Not everyone is fixated on physical appearance," she said sweetly. "Some people put more emphasis on kindness, loyalty and decency."

"Yeah. I used to tell myself the same thing when I was fat. Off you go. Burn those calories. Hey, I'll race you."

Jack was shaving when the police tried to bust down the door.

Correction. When Officer Neal tried to bust down the door, dressed in running shorts and a T-shirt, drenched in sweat and blowing like a steam train. "Have we been invaded?" he asked, opening up. "Aliens? Meteors? What's—" She pushed past him, ignoring the fact that he was wearing only a towel. "Why don't you come in?"

With a sigh—*women*—he went back into the bathroom and continued shaving. She followed, flipped down the lid of the toilet and sat herself down. "We're engaged," she panted.

"Make yourself at ho—what?"

"I'm sorry. I know I said I didn't want the whole pretend boyfriend thing, but I told Kevin we're engaged."

"Then I demand conjugal rights."

"Shut up, Jack."

"Is that any way to talk to your fiancé?" He rinsed the razor and continued shaving.

"He was being so nice. He even picked me a flower."

"Bastard."

"Exactly! Oh, you're being sarcastic. Save it, pal. Anyway, he was very sweet. Then he was all condescending, and then I said something about us being engaged. Just let it ride, okay?"

"And your family?"

"Shit." She closed her eyes. "My parents are pathologically incapable of keeping a secret. I can't tell them. I'll call them after we leave this hellhole."

Another set of frenzied knocking broke the quiet, this time on what sounded like Emmaline's door.

"Emmaline?" said her mother. "Open up! Why

did you keep this from us? Are you sure it isn't a mistake?"

"Oh, the tangled web we weave," he said. "Better open the door, Pooh Bear. And give me a second to get dressed, okay?"

She finally noticed. Her face went red. She glanced away from him, then back at his torso, and Jack smiled. "We have a lifetime to explore each other," he said. "Now open the door before they get a battering ram."

"I hate lying," she muttered.

"Your other option is to come clean with Kevin."

"I don't hate lying *that* much." Then she went through the adjoining door into her room and greeted her family.

Jack finished shaving, rinsed his face and pulled on jeans and a T-shirt. Doting fiancé, check. Hey. Women did things like this. Hadn't Colleen O'Rourke asked him to pretend to be her boyfriend? Or was that Shelayne Schanta? Whatever. Women got squirrelly around their exes. It was a known fact.

"I knew it!" Angela crowed when Jack joined them. "Jack! You devil!"

Emmaline's father shook Jack's hand vigorously. "Welcome to the family."

Her mom looked puzzled. "Emmaline, are you . . . I was so sure you were—" Angela gave her a gentle nudge. "Well," she amended. "This is very happy news." She gave Em an awkward hug—awkward because Em looked as relaxed as a concrete wall.

"Do you have a ring?" Angela asked.

"Tell them about the ring, sweetheart," Jack said.

"Oh, yeah. It's nice. Very, um, pretty. It's being resized."

"What kind of cut? Emerald? Cushion? Solitaire?" Angela asked.

"Sort of round," Em mumbled.

"Why do you have two rooms?" Mrs. Neal asked, glancing around.

Jack lifted an eyebrow. He'd let Em handle this one.

"I . . . Jack has . . . a medical . . . condition. He . . . he can't, uh . . ."

"Shy bladder?" her father suggested. "Don't worry. I'm the same way."

Emmaline looked as uncomfortable as if she were giving birth to a large bad-tempered porcupine. "It's just more spacious this way. Space is good. We like space."

"The final frontier," Jack murmured.

"Exactly," she said. "So. Who's doing all those stupid couples activities today?"

"You *said* you were just friends," Mrs. Neal said. "I try so hard to establish an intimate mother-daughter bond with you, Emmaline, but you've kept this entire relationship from me."

"I suspected," her father said, nodding. "I

picked up on something in her tone the last time we talked."

"No, you didn't!" her mother spat. "You thought she was gay, too."

Jack's new fiancée looked pained. She started to answer, stopped, then said, "I have to make a phone call. I just remembered."

"Coward," he whispered as she bolted past, closing the door to his room. Then she came back immediately, grabbed her phone and went back, slamming the door.

"This must've happened fast," Em's mother said. "Why the rush?"

"Well, we didn't want to waste time," Jack said. "You know."

There was a collective gasp.

Oops.

"Is Emmaline pregnant?" Angela whispered.

Jack grimaced. "I'll, uh, let her answer that."

"Emmaline!" her mother shouted. "Are you pregnant?"

She burst back into the room. "No! What did you tell them? I'm not pregnant!"

"I misspoke," Jack said. "She's not pregnant. Definitely not."

"You *are!* Aren't you?" Angela crowed. "Oh, hooray! I'm going to be an auntie!"

An eon of muttered lying later, the Neals left, firmly convinced that Em had a bun in the oven.

"How could you do that?" Emmaline wailed. "Honestly, Jack! I'm gonna have to pee on a stick before they'll believe I'm not preggers, and my mother will want to be right there when I do, so thank you for that."

"Well, I'm sorry," he said. "It's all a little blurry, seeing that I only learned we were engaged thirty seconds before."

"Exactly! I'd think it'd take a little longer to conceive."

"Then let's get right on that."

"In your dreams, Jack. And knock it off, by the way."

"Don't we have somewhere to be right now?" he asked.

She flung herself into the chair. "Yes. Couples volleyball starts in ten minutes."

"I can't wait," he said.

She got up and started yanking drawers open. "And to top it all off, I have to wear a bathing suit. God hates me today."

With that, she went into the bathroom and closed the door.

Which was too bad. Now that they were engaged, Jack felt he at least deserved to see her naked.

It wasn't couples volleyball, Jack soon learned as they walked to the pool. It was couples chicken. Well, it was called something else, something crunchy and fake sounding, like Partnership Water

Celebration, but it was chicken. The pool was a vast, turquoise thing shaped like a shamrock, waterfall on one side, an organic kale smoothie bar on the other. Several very fit couples were shrieking and laughing and flexing, looking like a commercial.

Beside him, Emmaline groaned. She was wearing what looked to be a white parachute. He'd seen burkas that revealed more skin.

It was a shame they weren't going to swim in the ocean. Apparently, the ocean was too cold without a wet suit (Californians had clearly never swum in Keuka in May, the way Jack did every year).

At the memory of cold lake water, his heart began to thud. He stopped abruptly, and Emmaline, walking beside him, stopped, too. "Jack? You okay?"

Now his breathing was funny, shaking in and out of his chest. His heart felt the size of a cantaloupe. Something was wrong; he might be having a heart attack—

Then Em was towing him to a lounge chair and pushing him in it. He grabbed her wrist. "Nice and easy," she said, sitting so they were face-to-face. "Slow down your breathing, big guy." She reached out with her free hand and pushed some hair off his forehead. "Nice and slow."

He was supposed to be looking after her this weekend. Not the other way around.

"The weather's amazing today, isn't it?" she said. "Say what you will about Southern California, we have great weather."

She smelled like sunscreen. Also, she had freckles. He'd never noticed that before.

"I thought we could take a drive later on. It would be good to get away from here for a little while. Not that I'm having a terrible time or anything." She smiled a little. Twisted her hand so he wasn't gripping her wrist anymore, but left her hand in his. "There's a great donut place not far from here. Well, there was. I hope it's still in business. I'll buy you a sugar—"

He leaned forward and kissed her, and her mouth opened in surprise. Her lips were soft, and that was enough. That was all he needed. Her soft, pretty mouth, and her hair, hot from the sunshine, under his hand as he cupped the back of her head.

The panic attack drifted to the back of his brain. The breeze fluttered her hair against his face, and he smoothed it away, still kissing her, which he should probably stop. And he would. Eventually.

She did it for him. Pulled back a few inches and didn't look at him. Pressed her lips together.

"I'm sorry," he said quietly.

"No. That's . . . It's fine."

Colleen O'Rourke—well, Colleen Campbell now—was suddenly at their side. Jack hadn't seen her yet—they'd been on different flights out here—but she was an old friend of the bride or something. "Holy Saint Patrick, were you two just kissing?" she asked.

"Leave them alone, Coll," said her twin.

"Hey, Connor," Jack said. "What are you doing here?"

"Penance." He sighed and looked at his sister. "I'm her babysitter."

"He's my date," Colleen said at the same time.

"Colleen and Connor," boomed a voice. "Please report to the pool immediately." *Ah. The bride had a bullhorn. Nice touch.*

"Good God," Connor muttered.

"Lucas couldn't come," Colleen said. "Believe it or not, Con wasn't my first choice. But Lucas's niece had an appendectomy, so he had to go to Chicago yesterday, and he forced Connor to come with me, because I'm a delicate flower, Jack, as you may have heard, and also percolating a baby." She paused for breath. "You guys playing chicken? Con and I are a team."

"This is horrifying," Connor said. "I can't believe I have to do this. I don't even like hugging you."

"Oh, stop. It's a piggyback ride. It won't kill you."

"It might, the way you're eating these days."

"Colleen and Connor, report to poolside immediately."

"Can you believe her? I didn't like her in

college, and I don't like her now." Colleen looked up at Em. "Are you guys playing?"

Emmaline, who hadn't said boo, cleared her throat. "We thought it was volleyball. By the way, Jack and I are pretend engaged."

Connor gave him a look, and Jack shrugged. Colleen clapped her hands. "I told you—you should've just committed to that plan to start with. Come on, Connor. Naomi's summoning me. God, I wish Lucas was here!"

"You're not the only one," Connor said.

"Well, believe me, I didn't want to be here with my grumpy-ass brother—oh, and by the way, Connor, you should've said yes to coming to this with Emmaline, because then you wouldn't be here with your sister as your date."

"I'm not your date. I'm your keeper," Connor said.

"Emily and Jack, report to poolside immediately," boomed the bride. *What was that term? Bridezilla? Yeah. That worked.*

"Well, shit." Colleen sighed. "Come on, Connor. Prepare to fight to the death. Your death, of course. You have to save me and my unborn child."

"This is so wrong," Connor said, but he obeyed, and off they went.

Jack looked at Emmaline, who was still not looking at him. "Sorry about the kiss."

"No, no. It's . . . whatever."

"Thank you, by the way."

She looked at him abruptly. "What for?"

Her eyes were blue. Dark blue.

"Talking me down," he said. "Letting me kiss you."

She blushed. Made a weird snorting noise. "It was a huge sacrifice, Jack. I mean, have you looked in the mirror? You're hideous. Hey, did I tell you I'm going to be a crisis negotiator? Well, sort of. I mean, I'm taking a class when we get back home. You know. Hostage situations. Suicidal people. So it was good practice. Not that you're taking any hostages, or, uh . . . never mind. It's fine. We're good."

She was nervous. It was kind of cute.

"Ready to play chicken?"

"No."

"Come on. It'll be fun. Take that thing off and let's get going."

"I should never have come to this wedding," she said.

"You're a cop. Be brave."

"Bite me."

"That's my girl."

Her blush deepened. Then she scowled at him, grumbled a little more and yanked the burka over her head.

Hello.

Now why the hell would she be worried about wearing a bathing suit when she looked like that?

She had long legs, a *really* nice ass and an amazing rack that was on fantastic display, and whoever made that suit should be given a Nobel prize in engineering, because wow.

Emmaline wasn't lean by any stretch of the imagination, but Jack always kind of liked that. She looked like a woman, not a prepubescent girl. The kind of woman who'd feel soft and sturdy at the same time.

Let's find out, his brain told him.

"What are you looking at?" she growled.

He looked away. "My grandmother has that same bathing suit," he said. "Try a bikini next time."

"Right. I'll also try setting myself on fire, since it would be just as fun. Bad enough that I'm here in the Land of Plastic People."

"Emily and Jack, get over here now!" boomed the bride.

"I'm getting you a bikini," he said, standing up. "Now that we're engaged."

"Let's just get this over with. I apologize in advance for any herniated discs."

"Relax. Be happy. We're engaged and possibly expecting a baby." He took her hand and headed for the pool.

The thought of going into the water didn't bother him. A pool wasn't a lake. There was no chance of a car accident here. Everyone would be fine.

The bride put down her bullhorn. "About time,"

she said, scanning Emmaline up and down.

To her credit, Em ignored her and dived neatly into the deep end of the pool, then surfaced, looking as if she wanted to be banged silly.

Okay, Jack, enough of that. The poor kid is going through a tough time. Also, that may be transference on your part.

He dived in, too, the cool water sliding over his head. No problems. Good. He was a navy man, after all. He couldn't be afraid of the water. And he wasn't. Here was proof.

He swam over to Emmaline. "Mount up, Pooh Bear," he said.

"This is the stupidest thing I've ever done in my life."

He seemed to be looking at her breasts again. Being in the water only made them look more . . . buoyant. "You're rocking this suit," he said.

"Yeah, yeah, you're gorgeous yourself. And where does a winemaker get washboard abs, by the way?"

Nice of her to notice. "I'm a Greek god, remember?"

"I resent the fact that you remember that." But she smiled a little nonetheless.

There was a splash from the deep end. "Oh, gosh golly!" Colleen called. "We lost. Con, let's get something to eat. What do you say? I'm starving."

Jack turned to Emmaline and smiled. "Upsy-daisy, Pooh."

Emmaline was not happy.

The miracle bathing suit was constricting her stomach to the point of Scarlett O'Hara's corset, and she was having difficulty breathing.

The Ta-Ta Ta-Dahs were in place, and while she was sure she never wanted to meet the weird, breast-obsessed, Mommy-didn't-nurse-me person who'd come up with them, she had to give him credit. The girls looked quite ambitious.

Jack kept looking, which might've been gratifying, were it not for (a) the look was fake, and (b) the two cold fake raw chicken cutlets felt just as disgusting as one might think.

And now she had to climb on Jack's shoulders. Hopefully, he wouldn't cry out in agony and crumple.

However, those shoulders looked pretty sturdy to her. In fact, all of him looked . . . so . . . He was . . . What was the question again?

Because even in this crowd, where wedding guests seemed to have been chosen from the modeling lineup for Abercrombie & Fitch, Jack stood out. Not only was he ridiculously handsome, he was working-man delicious. He wasn't ripped and chiseled (or waxed, thank heavens) . . . but he was, well, hell, kind of perfect.

While Kevin and the other guys looked like what they were—gym addicts—Jack just looked

strong. He had broad shoulders that would soon be put to the test under her weight. A flat stomach that rippled with muscle. Arms that got their definition from lifting barrels (or whatever his job required him to lift, but picturing him hefting wooden barrels was quite satisfying). There was a happy trail from his navel to the waistband of his trunks, and—

"Emily and Jack! Can you please get going here!"

"Ready?" Jack said, and before she knew it, he ducked underwater and—oh, boy—between her legs. Then he stood up and she was teetering on his shoulders, and how did her stomach look? Was the miracle suit all it promised to be?

She grabbed on to his forehead so she wouldn't fall.

"You good up there?" he asked.

"Yep! Very good," she chirped. So, *so* good. Lawdy, the Bitter Betrayeds were going to hear about this! Maybe she'd even get a tattoo on each thigh—*Jack Holland's head was here.*

There was a DJ set up by the smoothie bar, and the theme song to *Jaws* started playing.

"We're in it to win it!" Naomi bellowed, clambering on top of Kevin's shoulders. Two other couples were also in this gladiator match, and both women were quite gorgeous, too, except not *quite* as beautiful as Naomi. Both wore string bikinis, as did the bride.

Sigh. No, no! None of that! You will not feel like an ugly duckling, she told herself firmly. *You have a 93 percent accuracy rate for head shots with your Smith & Wesson. You can pick up all three Cabrera triplets at once. You rock.*

"Let's take a dive like Colleen and Connor did," she suggested to Jack, somewhat concerned about squashing his vertebrae. "We can go get donuts instead."

"No way," he said. "We're in it to win it, too."

The rules were simple—knock the other couples down. They were in a part of the pool where the water was about chest deep, and each couple had their own quadrant to defend. Hopefully, no one would fall and hit their heads, because if any blood got in the water, Em was pretty sure Naomi would go into a feeding frenzy. Even now, she was flashing a sharklike grin. The music didn't help.

Em suspected she was about to have her leg bitten off.

"Do we have a strategy here?" Em asked. Jack's wet hair tickled her thighs.

He looked up, the motion of his head making her squeak with lust. His beautiful blue eyes crinkled with a smile. "Hold on," he said.

"On your mark!" Naomi bellowed. "Get set! Go!"

There was a sloshing noise as all the couples charged the center. The DJ turned up the music. *Duh-duh . . . duh-duh . . . duh-duh-duh-duh.*

Jack reached couple number one, a redheaded woman on top of a very beautiful man. "Hi," Em said.

"Hi."

"Um . . ." Emmaline reached out with one hand and gave the woman a gentle push.

She went down like a narcoleptic kitten. Then again, she probably weighed as much as fog.

"Sorry!" Em said, guilt flashing immediately.

"No, no. Don't worry," she said. Was it Em's imagination, or did the woman look relieved?

"Incoming," Jack said, turning around. Couple number two didn't wait; the man took a dive before Emmaline even touched the woman.

"Oh, come on, Randy!" Naomi bellowed.

"Yeah, come on!" Kevin echoed.

It dawned on Emmaline that no one wanted to compete with the happy couple. Indeed, Naomi seemed a little ticked that the other two couples were already swimming for the stairs.

"How badly do you want to win?" Jack murmured.

"I don't really care."

"Well, I do." With that, Jack surged forward, and Em gave a little shriek. *Oh.* This was almost sexy time. Would it be wrong to ask him to do that again? Because the feeling of his head against her—

Then Kevin and Naomi were right in front of them. Naomi's savagely beautiful face was right in front of her in what Em could only describe as a snarl. "Don't mean to scare you," the trainer said, "but Kevin and I have never lost. Right, Kevster, babe?"

"Right, babe," he answered obediently.

"Neither have we," Jack said.

"Well, you're about to," Naomi said. "The only difference between 'try' and 'triumph' is a little 'umph.' "

"You deserve to lose for that alone, Naomi." There was a smile in Jack's voice.

"I never lose," she said. Then her hands were on Em's shoulders, and she shoved, hard.

Em locked her feet around Jack's back to keep from falling—she might've been choking him to death with her thighs, but you know what? She didn't care all of a sudden. All she wanted was for Naomi to lose at *something,* and she leaned in, grappling with Naomi. And really, this was idiotic. Why not just put Naomi in the Hunger Games and let her kill everyone else, but damn it, Emmaline was not going to lose.

Even so, she couldn't help but admire Naomi's gorgeous shoulders.

Then Jack stepped to the side, possibly because he was desperate to breathe, and Em leaned forward, using his momentum, and pushed. Hard. Naomi wavered, and Em imagined her as a threat to those adorable Cabrera kids and pushed again. She wasn't a badass cop for nothing.

There was a splash as both Naomi and Kevin fell.

"That wasn't fair!" Naomi shouted, smacking the water with her fist. "You can't use your body weight like that."

"Yeah," Kevin said, a sulk in his voice. "Obviously, you weigh a lot more than Nay does."

"What am I supposed to use?" Em asked. "A sword? My crossbow?"

"Shake hands, kids," Jack said. "Remember, humble in victory, gracious in defeat." He grinned up at her. "I feel very humble, don't you?"

Uh-oh.

She was having . . . feelings. That smile. Those eyes. The fact that he hadn't once complained about how heavy she was.

Then he dumped her, and she was under the water. She surfaced, pushing the hair out of her face. "Thank you, mighty steed," she said. "That was more fun than I thought it would be."

He was still smiling. Then his eyes dropped to her chest, and his smile faltered. "Uh . . . Em, you seem to be . . . deflating."

She looked at her boobage. "Shit."

One breast was plumped up and coconut shaped, same as when she'd left her room earlier.

The other was normal.

Which meant . . .

Panicking, she looked around. Where was it? Where was it? Maybe it just slipped . . . She

205

groped herself, patted her stomach to see if it had slid . . . no. It wasn't there.

Where was her Ta-Ta Ta-Dah?

"Uh . . . is that what you're looking for?" Jack whispered.

Kevin and Naomi were talking in low voices, still in the pool, Naomi hissing, Kevin apologetic. And there on his beautiful shoulder blade, like a giant leech, was the Ta-Ta Ta-Dah.

"What the hell is that?" Jack whispered.

A seagull cried out, circling over the pool, then hovered. Em knew that pose. That was the "I see dinner" pose.

She lunged. Jack lunged. The seagull dived, snatched the breast booster off Kevin's shoulder, causing him to scream in surprise, which would've made Emmaline laugh if her Ta-Ta Ta-Dah wasn't in the seagull's beak. But it was too heavy for the poor thing. The bird's head wobbled; it opened its beak and the silicone slab fell with a splat back in the pool.

She dived for it, but Jack was faster. He grabbed it and turned to her.

"What the hell was that?" Naomi asked.

It might be time to commit suicide.

Jack surfaced next to Emmaline.

"Is this raw chicken?" he whispered.

"Sh! No! Give it to me!"

"You guys cheated," Naomi said.

"How is there cheating in Partnership Water

Celebration?" Jack called. "Don't fuss, kids. Drinks are on us." He turned back to Em. "Here," he said more quietly, giving it to Emmaline. "I'm so glad I'm not a woman."

"I want a rematch!" Naomi demanded.

Em grabbed the disgusting, slimy boob enhancer (that had just been in a seagull's beak). Should she put it back? Or leave it? If the bird had any diseases (avian flu, for example), would the chlorine in the pool water kill off the germs?

"Well?" Jack said. "You gonna put that back, or shall I?" He lifted an eyebrow.

"Very funny."

"All right, at least let me . . . here." He pulled her a few steps away and hugged her. "Go for it. You can tell me later why you're wearing raw chicken."

"It's not chicken. It makes . . . never mind." She slid the offending object back under her breast.

Couldn't help noticing how it felt to be pressed up close to Jack. Wet. Warm. Slippery.

"I was wondering how the girls defied gravity like that," he murmured. She could feel his voice rumble in his chest as she adjusted her suit.

"Don't make fun of me," she ordered. "This is a stressful weekend."

He pulled back a little and looked down at her. A drop of water slid down his neck and pooled against his collarbone, and Em suddenly really, really wanted to lick it.

"Just for the record, you don't need any enhancing," he said, and her knees buckled a little. His eyes crinkled, and he kissed her forehead.

Crap on a cracker. She was falling for this guy.

"Thanks," she said briskly, and then, because the mortification of Jack—and possibly everyone else—knowing what she'd stuck in her bathing suit was settling over her, she swam to the stairs and got out of the pool.

Chapter Ten

"My kingdom for a cheeseburger," Colleen murmured.

"You said it, sister," Em answered.

The rehearsal "dinner" consisted of a raw vegetable buffet. Drinks were decaffeinated green tea (hot or iced), mint tea, nonfat soy milk, water and cranberry juice, the real kind that made your entire body pucker. Emmaline had a raging headache, probably due to a frightening lack of caffeine, carbs and ice cream in her diet for the past twenty-four hours.

The first thing she would do when she got home, after loving up Sarge, of course, would be to take him to O'Rourke's—Sarge was theoretically a police dog in training—and order the nachos grande and two of the biggest burgers they had. One for each of them.

Her stomach growled.

"Where's Jack?" Colleen asked, putting some kale on her plate.

"I think he's sleeping," Em answered. She'd knocked on his door, but there'd been no answer. Maybe the jet lag had caught up with him. Maybe he was walking on the beach. Maybe he was in traction after the chicken game. Maybe he just needed a break from this dopey weekend.

She hoped he wasn't . . . well, suffering. That lost look that came across his face just killed her.

"Back to the bridesminions' table." Colleen sighed. "See you later."

Right. She and Jack had been assigned to a table of Russian-speaking older people. Naomi's relatives from Irkutsk, if Em had understood correctly, based on the map the sole English speaker had drawn on a napkin. A great-aunt or grandmother was filling her purse with cucumber sticks. One old man was asleep. Another kept looking at her boobs (even un-Ta-Dahed, they looked pretty nice in this dress, Em thought), but otherwise, they just talked among themselves. Em smiled at them occasionally to show she was one of the nice Americans. Only the boob-looker smiled back, and he was missing two teeth.

Angela, Mom and Dad were seated with Kevin's

parents; Angela had very loyally offered to sit with Em, but Mrs. Bates (who had once quite loved Emmaline, if memory served) had almost given birth to a Komodo dragon at the suggestion. Em assured her that it'd be fine back here in Siberia, and the truth was, she was relieved not to have to make conversation.

Kevin and Naomi sat at a tiny table for two under a spotlight.

They really did look in love.

"Okay, folks, time to burn off some calories and dance!" the DJ barked. Yes, heaven forbid those ten or twelve calories from dinner be allowed to simply rest. The Black-Eyed Peas came booming from the speakers.

Any minute, Em suspected, Kevin and Naomi would do a choreographed dance to their special song.

The song she and Kevin were going to dance to at their wedding was "Unforgettable" by Nat King Cole. Em still couldn't hear it without a small brain bleed.

"Naomi and Kevin wanted you all to have one of these as a party favor," said a little girl who was holding a basket. Please, God, it was full of bottles of Jack Daniel's.

But no.

The little girl held out something all too familiar. *People* magazine, "Half Their Size" edition.

On the cover was a picture of Kevin holding up

a pair of his enormous pants. Pants that Emmaline had bought him, since he'd hated shopping for himself back then. Probably loved it now.

The Russian relatives opened the magazine. Em slid hers into her purse. She could burn it later. Not that it would help. She had the damn thing memorized.

Page forty-seven. The usual stuff about how Kevin had struggled with food all his life, his blood pressure issues, his prediabetes. And then the killer blow:

"I was living with someone who wasn't supportive," says Bates. "She sabotaged my efforts, always buying food that fueled my addiction. Then I met Naomi, and I realized I had to leave that other relationship. She was just too unsupportive."

Naomi Norman, Kevin's trainer and soon-to-be wife, chimes in. "The people we surround ourselves with make a huge difference in our lives," she says, laying her hand on Kevin's now-sculpted arm. "I believe in Kevin and support all his dreams and goals. He's the most remarkable person I've ever met."

Gack.

Also, ouch. And now, everyone was poring over their magazines, dazzled with Kevin's weight loss. Maybe tomorrow, rather than just walk out to the altar, New Kevin would burst through a picture of

Old Kevin, like they did on *The Biggest Loser.*

Though there weren't as many friends from college as Em had expected, a few people knew who she was, and looks were shot her way. At least the Russians didn't appear to care; they were looking at pictures of whatever red-carpet event had been covered in the same issue.

My kingdom for a really strong martini, Em thought. She smiled at the Russians, then checked her phone. Angela had just texted her. This is the tackiest wedding I've ever been to. I plan to burn my magazine in a dramatic pyre and eat ice cream as I do.

Em looked over at her sister and smiled.

Faith had also texted her, asking how things were going. So had Shelayne and Allison. Shelayne had sent a picture of Sarge sleeping on her bed (under the covers), and Em smiled. It would be so, so good to get back home.

Jack still wasn't here. She'd go check on him. A great excuse to leave.

Just then, the DJ tapped his mike. "Ladies and gentlemen, please give it up for Naomi and Kevin in their last dance as single people!" The jolly beat of a familiar song came over the speakers. Bruno Mars, of course. "I Think I Wanna Marry You."

How adorable.

There were shrieks and screams and giggles, and then, yes, the choreographed dance.

Kevin always had been a good dancer.

"Mind if I sit here?" a woman asked. She was about Em's age. "I'm Trisha."

"Emmaline. Have a seat."

"I just needed to take a break from dancing. Feeling a little light-headed."

"You're probably hungry."

Trisha laughed. "Yeah, the food here isn't exactly filling. But I could lose a few pounds anyway. How do you know the bride and groom?"

"I went to college with Kevin." Definitely the safest answer.

"Oh, yeah? I work with him now. I had a huge crush on him. Can't blame me, right? The guy is gorgeous."

"That he is." How very well adjusted Emmaline was! She'd have to give herself a sticker. Perhaps a run to a package store was also in order.

Trisha settled back and watched the dancing. "Guess what I heard?"

"What's that?"

"Kevin's old fiancée is here. She's stalking him. I guess she can't get over him and did all this hateful stuff."

"Really. Like what?"

"Said all these vicious things to Naomi. Tried to sabotage Kevin's weight loss." She pointed to the nearest *People.* "It's right in there. Sad that she was so threatened. Hey, you must've known him when he was heavier, right? Isn't his transforma-tion amazing?"

"It is. I'm the fiancée, by the way."

It was kinda fun watching Trisha's face rearrange itself.

"And I was invited. No stalking necessary, though I do have a dead squirrel in my suitcase for tomorrow." Em smiled sweetly. "Want to come back to my room and see it? It's pretty."

Trisha fled.

"Having fun, Pooh Bear?"

"Jack! How are you?"

"Fine. Why didn't you wake me up?"

"I knocked. Figured you were sleeping."

"Well, you should've knocked harder. I'm here for a reason, after all." He scowled, and his blue, blue eyes were troubled.

Bet that nap hadn't been exactly peaceful.

"Have you talked to Levi, by any chance?" he asked.

"Yeah, I checked in a couple hours ago."

Jack looked at the dancing couples. "Did he happen to mention Josh Deiner?"

Em's heart squeezed. "Actually, yes. He said Josh is . . . hanging in there." She was paraphrasing. "No change" was what Levi had said.

Something flickered through Jack's eyes. "Any improvement?" he said, and there was so much packed into those two words.

It would've been so easy to say something hopeful and vague, like *some positive signs* or *no reason not to be hopeful.* But she couldn't lie.

"No. But no decline, either."

Whatever had just flickered went out.

Her parents emerged from the crowd. "Emmaline," Mom said. "Are you feeling all right? I heard there was a fight in the pool. Should you be doing that, in your condition?"

"There was no fighting," she answered, suppressing a sigh. "And there's no condition."

"Jack!" Dad boomed. "Very glad you're here! Shall we discuss future plans, son?" Now that Dad thought she was straight, he was moving right into doting father-in-law.

"We were just about to take a walk, guys," Emmaline said. "We'll catch up with you tomorrow, okay?"

"That sounds very wise," Mom said. "It can't be easy for you, seeing Kevin moving on."

"Thanks for the vote of confidence, Ma."

"Honey, I just *care.* Is that so wrong? That I care?"

"Spending intimate time together is the foundation of a strong relationship," Dad said. "Which is why your *mother* and I didn't work out. She was too busy with her career."

"Me? Your *father* was the one who was obsessed with his patients, Emmaline. As I'm sure you remember. Jack, don't make that mistake with my daughter."

"No, no, I won't," Jack said. "She's . . . she's just great."

"You make a very nice couple," Mom said, and her voice was oddly wistful. "Maybe we can go dress shopping together this time."

Okay, time to cut bait. Even if they were Dr. and Dr. Dysfunctional, her parents were good people. They loved her in their weird way, and Em's stomach was twisting at lying to them (or twisting because of the kale salad).

Em would come clean on Monday. Sunday, even. The very second she got out of this place.

"When will you come home? We need to make plans for the wedding," Mom said.

"Um . . . soon. We're gonna take that walk right now. Bye!" Emmaline forced a smile and rather awkwardly groped for Jack's hand, got his wrist and practically dragged him from the dining room.

"Slow down, Seabiscuit," he said. "What's the matter?"

"I have to get out of here or I'm going to tell the truth."

"If you want to tell, do it," he said. "It's fine either way. You want to leave? We can go home. Whatever you want."

"You're not helping."

He smiled. "Before we go anywhere, let's stop by my room first. I have contraband."

"Tell me you brought wine."

"Of course I brought wine. I'm a winemaker."

"Angels bless you, Jack Holland. Though you might've mentioned this yesterday."

He grinned, and she felt it down to her toes.

Fifteen minutes later, they were down on the beach. It was cold enough for a blanket, which Jack had thoughtfully provided. Two, in fact. One for the sand, one that he wrapped around her shoulders, as her dress wasn't doing much for her warmth.

Very romantic indeed.

She would have to be careful, she thought, taking a grateful sip of the wine. It was a well-known fact that Jack was like this with everyone, and half the women of Manningsport would eat a live puppy for a night with this guy. She couldn't read into anything.

Not even that kiss. That had been a way for him to get out of a bad moment. That was all. He'd even apologized for it.

The waves lapped at the shore, gentle at the moment. There was no wind, and the moon was rising, making the sand look like snow.

"How old were you when your parents adopted Angela?" he asked.

"Fourteen," she said. The wine was good, mellow and smooth and whatever other adjectives winemakers liked to use. "I went to live in Manningsport, and Mom and Dad didn't like the empty nest, so they went to Ethiopia and adopted Angela."

"Was that weird?"

"It was . . . surprising."

"You and she seem really close."

"Well, she's great, as you probably saw. Beautiful, smart, talented. She did some modeling in college and donated it all to the orphanage that took care of her. She's about as nice as they come. It's hard not to like her."

"You're nice, too, you know."

She snorted.

"I take it back," Jack said. "Do your folks still live out here?"

"They moved to Palo Alto to be closer to Angela. She's doing research at Stanford."

"Research in what?"

"Something about the evolution of stars in the ancient universe," Em said.

"Cool."

"You know, you could always ask her out, Jack. I'm sure she'd say yes." Imagine their babies. Beautiful to the thousandth power.

"I don't want to ask her out. I'm a science geek, that's all. You jealous?"

"Yes. Aflame with jealousy." She took another sip of wine. "Seriously, you could ask her out."

"I'm here with you."

The words sounded *amazing*. The urge to lay spread out like a starfish and pull Jack onto her . . . *Wow. Very strong.*

He nudged her with his shoulder. "So how do you like my wine?"

"Nice. So grapey."

He gave a beleaguered sigh. "Troglodyte."

"I take it I've just been insulted with that big word."

"It's our best pinot noir in ten years, Emmaline. Don't chug it like it's Pepsi. Take a second to smell it." She obeyed. "Blackberry, currant, clove and leather," he said.

"Oh, yeah. Leather. Mmm-hmm. Getting leather, sure." She sniffed again. "I'm really more of a beer person."

"That's it. We're done. Give me back your engagement ring and tell your dad not to worry about the dowry." He smiled.

He should really stop doing that. Every time he did, she became a little more of the Bitter Betrayeds' cliché—get dumped, make Jack Holland be your date for a dreaded event, fall half in love with him, return home never to go out with him again.

"What year did you graduate high school?" he asked.

"I was a year ahead of Faith."

"Really?" He turned to look at her. God, he was just *beautiful*. The salt air had made his hair curl a little, as if he needed something extra to make him more appealing. "Why'd you move?"

He'd kissed her today. Largely to distract himself from a panic attack, but he'd kissed her, and it had been a soft, gentle, amazing kiss that made her throb with . . . with something she hadn't felt in a long, long time.

Tenderness.

And lust, yes. No sense in pretending otherwise. It had taken all her self-control not to climb right onto his lap and take a bite, he was so delicious.

"None of my business. Sorry," Jack said.

Oh, right, he'd asked a question. "I was bullied."

This was usually when the response was, "Really? You? You're so tough/badass/scary, Em," and Em would either agree or change the subject. Not that she brought it up much.

"Must've been pretty bad if you had to move to get away from it," he said, looking out at the ocean.

"Yeah."

"Kids can be such little shits."

"I won't disagree."

"Why'd they bully you?"

"I stuttered."

He looked at her again, then put his arm around her. He was warm and solid, and, for a second, she felt the prick of tears in her eyes. *Don't get carried away here,* a little voice warned her.

"Also, Kevin went to boarding school in Connecticut. And he was . . . We were very close."

Kevin's kindness had been an antidote to the casual, razor-sharp cruelty of her meaner classmates. And even worse, the kids who didn't instigate but just stood by, pretending not to hear, unwilling to take a chance on a nobody like Emmaline.

What doesn't kill you makes you stronger. How was that for a T-shirt?

"It must've been tough, not being able to speak your mind," Jack said.

"Yep. It was." She cleared her throat, took another sip of wine. "I had this imaginary friend. Horatio."

"Horatio?"

"My parents read a lot of Shakespeare. Sue me."

"So what was Horatio like?"

She slipped off her sandals and dug her feet into the cool sand. "Well, he was very loyal, of course. I'd psychically tell him everything I couldn't get out, and he thought I was very smart and funny."

"You *are* very funny and smart. You also have a wicked hip check." He gave her another grin. "I had an imaginary friend, too."

"Really?"

"Yeah. But mine had a cool name, unlike poor Horatio."

"Listen, bub. Horatio is incredibly cool."

"Mine was named Otis."

"Otis is not a cool name, Jack. It's sad that you think so. I'm very sorry to tell you this, but Horatio wins this round."

"Says you."

"Did Otis serve a purpose?"

"Absolutely. Whenever I got into trouble, I'd tell my parents that Otis had done it. And that he talked to me at night. Totally freaked out my sisters. They thought either our house was haunted or I was possessed."

"And are you?"

He laughed, and the sound caused her stomach to pull in a wonderful, warm ache. "I don't think so. Not anymore, at any rate."

"Emmaline?" came a woman's voice. "Oh, my God! Is it really you?"

Em looked up. "Uh . . . hi!"

The woman, who was thin as a whippet and had very long hair, gave her a disbelieving look. "You don't remember me?" She swept some hair around to the front and began stroking the ends.

"I'm sorry. The light isn't very good here."

"It's me! Lyric! Lyric Adams? We went to school together!"

Oh, yes. Em finished her wine and got to her feet. She remembered Lyric, all right. The meanest of the mean kids. "Hi."

"Wow! You look . . . uh, great!" Lyric said.

"And you look very, uh, good," Emmaline said. Lyric had had a little work done, as the saying went. Or, more precisely, a lot. Weirdly inflated lips—the famous trout pout—huge breasts exploding out of her tiny, underfed rib cage and a much thinner nose than she'd sported as a kid.

"I know!" Lyric said, her voice taking on a different tone. "I work out with this amazing trainer? And Pilates four times a week. No gluten, no meat, no dairy, plus these cleanses? You should try them! Wheatgrass and fish oil. Amazing."

"I'll have to pass," Em said.

"OMG! You don't stutter anymore! I barely recognize your voice. Remember how bad you sounded? 'H-h-hi, I'm Eh-eh-eh-maline.' It took you forever to get a sentence out!" She laughed merrily, her mouth barely moving, courtesy of whatever toxin she'd had injected.

"This is my friend Jack," Emmaline said, trying to ignore the burn in her cheeks. Lyric had been a piranha at age twelve. No reason to think she'd gotten any nicer.

Jack stood up. "Jack Holland," he said, putting his arm around Emmaline. "Em's fiancé."

"Hi!" Lyric said. "I'm Lyric, Lyric Adams-Rabinowitz. And yes, my father is *that* Travis Adams. I'm an old friend of Em's."

"Doesn't sound like it," Jack said.

The comment went right over Lyric's head. "So you probably heard what I'm up to these days," she said. "My baby clothing line? Totally adorbs. Beyoncé's daughter? She wore one of my outfits. And North West? Same. Can you even believe it? So, are you guys visiting? Wait, wait, oh, my God! You're here for Kevin and Naomi's wedding, aren't you? Oh, my God! So am I!"

Em's toes dug into the sand. Kevin had been bullied by Lyric, too, and, yes, he and Naomi had moved back to Malibu, but still. The idea that Lyric had been forgiven was . . . wrong, somehow. Em's teeth ached, which meant she was clenching her jaw again.

Lyric was still talking. "My husband? You can meet him. Not to brag, but he's a real estate mobile, and he made eight figures last year."

"I think you meant mogul," Jack said.

"Excuse me?"

"Mogul. You said *mobile*. You meant mogul, as in tycoon. Not mobile, as in something that can be moved. I'm guessing your mobile didn't marry you for your beautiful mind."

Emmaline bit down on a smile.

"Whatever. So you and Kevin were together for a long time, right, Emmaline? This must be so hard for you."

"We were together for a long time, yes."

"And what do you do now?"

"I'm a cop."

"You *are?* Why?"

"To protect and serve the good people of Manningsport, New York."

"Oops! My phone's ringing! Gotta go. S-s-see you t-t-tomorrow!" Another whinnying laugh, and Lyric cantered away.

"Holy shit," Jack said, sounding almost surprised.

"Yeah. She was kind of doomed from the start. Thanks for sticking up for me, by the way."

"You're welcome." He was quiet for a minute, then asked, "You okay, seeing her again?"

Em shrugged. "Sure."

"You should tell her off."

"I know her type. It wouldn't do any good. I'd tell her how miserable she made me, and she'd tell me how much her shoes cost."

"There was a kid in my class who made fun of Faith once," Jack said. "She had a seizure at church, and he did an impression of her. I beat the living snot out of him, right there at Sunday school." He paused. "Too bad I wasn't your brother."

I have no interest in you being my brother, Jack. "Well, we should get back."

"Whatever you say, Officer Neal."

His phone chirped, and he took it from his pocket. She saw the name *Hadley* on the screen.

"So how is it *really,* having your wife back in town?" she asked.

"Ex-wife," he said.

"Right. And how is it?"

"It's fine." His tone, which had been warm and edged with a smile for most of the night, was cool and formal. She understood. The topic was off-limits.

Then again, Emmaline was a police officer, and cops liked answers.

"You still love her?"

"I'd rather not talk about Hadley."

Yes, in other words.

They picked up the blankets and headed back up the hill to the ranch.

She'd do well to remember he was here as a favor. Jack, like a lot of men, loved a woman in distress. While Em appreciated that, she didn't like being in distress (though she was aware that this whole ridiculous wedding was distress inducing).

His ex-wife, the tiny and beautiful and vulnerable Hadley . . . she'd be *dying* to be rescued. Em would bet her front teeth (which had once been knocked out in a hockey match and had been very expensive to fix) that Hadley had put a great deal of thought and strategy into her return to Manningsport and would need to be rescued. Often.

Besides, Em wasn't the type to fight for a man. She'd tried that once and lost.

Not that Jack was even interested in her. That kiss had been a coping strategy and nothing else.

The walk back to Rancho de la Luna was quiet.

In thirty-six hours, she'd be on her way home. Hopefully, there'd be a crime spree in Manningsport, and she could go back to doing what she knew how to do.

Chapter Eleven

So here's the thing.

If you're going to your ex-fiancé's wedding, and he's marrying a woman who has twice been featured on the cover of *Fitness* magazine, you do *try* to look good. You do strange and exotic things like blow-dry your hair, even without the magic goop from Sicily, and when it comes out looking as if you've electrocuted yourself, you pounce upon a maid and beg her to find you something— anything—you can use, the end result of which is an industrial-size can of Aqua Net and hair that might shatter if you hit your head. You wrestle yourself into Spanx, hating yourself for caving to the societal pressures of this type of under- garment. You attempt makeup, then get mascara in the white of your eye, then try for ten minutes to get it out, then end up looking like you've been crying all night. You push your innocent feet into heels that look like something invented by the Holy Roman Inquisitor. You put the raw chicken breasts back in your bra.

And you put on a dress that makes you feel like you're trying way too hard.

Which, of course, you are.

Emmaline looked in the mirror.

She looked weird.

There was a knock on the door. "You ready?" Jack called.

Em sighed, grabbed her purse and opened the door. "Hey. You look—Have you been crying?" he asked.

"No. I had something in my eye. I *did.* Don't look at me that way."

"We can skip this," Jack said. "Go get a nice juicy cheeseburger."

"Get thee behind me, Satan," she said. "We can't skip this. As for cheeseburgers, we can go to an In-N-Out on the way to the airport in just twenty-two and a half short hours."

Jack smiled.

"You look very handsome, by the way," she said, then felt her cheeks flush. But he did. He had on a gray suit and a white shirt, and that smile could launch a thousand ships.

"And you look beautiful," he said. She managed not to snort. He offered her arm, and she took it, abruptly and overwhelmingly glad that Faith had asked him to be her date.

They were almost the last ones to the wedding, which was held on the lawn that stretched to the cliff edge. Rows of white chairs festooned with pink roses and yards of white fabric faced the ocean, where a justice of the peace waited in a snazzy red dress. A string quartet was assembled near the front. Her parents gave her a wave, and Angela made the shape of a heart with her hands.

If it felt as if everyone was looking at her, they probably weren't.

Besides, they all thought she was engaged to the man next to her.

The string quartet started playing something slow and lovely. Bach, maybe, and the first of the six bridesmaids came down the aisle. All were clad in pale pink sheath dresses and holding white calla lily bouquets. Colleen went past, the prettiest of them all, and rolled her eyes at Em and Jack, then resumed smiling demurely. She was too nice to behave badly, after all. And maybe she had fond memories of Naomi, no matter how loyal she'd been to Em.

Then came the adorable flower girls, four of them, dressed in white tulle with pink sashes, scattering rose petals.

And then there was the bride herself, unescorted, though her dad was here somewhere. Based on what Em knew of Naomi, she'd want to make sure every eye was on her and her alone. Naomi stood there a moment for dramatic effect, waiting for the bridesmaids to fall into place (or start doing burpees, maybe). They did, and the musicians stopped for a moment.

If you didn't look into her glittering red, Smaug-like eyes, Naomi made a beautiful bride.

There was that *body,* perfectly showcased in a

low-cut, low-backed wedding gown that swirled around her, clinging in all the right spots (everywhere, in other words), elegant and really hot at the same time. Naomi's skin was lightly tanned, her hair pulled up in a stark bun, and her jewelry was a single fat pearl on a thin gold chain, tiny pearls in her ears.

Very classy.

Then the music started, and Emmaline made a startled noise, then tried not to let her eye twitch. Found herself wishing a severe case of anal fissures on Kevin, because *please.*

The song was "Largo," from the winter section of Vivaldi's *Four Seasons.*

Emmaline knew this because Kevin had chosen that very piece for Em to walk down the aisle to. He'd said it was the most beautiful music he'd ever heard, and he wanted to hear it play as the most beautiful woman became his wife.

Would it be wrong to dry heave right now?

Naomi started down the aisle, slowly, smoothly. Frickin' beaming at her guests, seeming to make eye contact with every single person there. Except Emmaline, of course. Her eyes slid right over Em, seeing and not seeing.

Why the hell had Em been invited? Why the hell had she come?

Emmaline looked at the groom, who was staring in a tearful, happy daze at Naomi. New Kevin looked different from her Kevin, and that helped.

But his eyes were the same. And while of course Em had known for quite some time that Kevin wouldn't be looking at *her* with wonder and love and joy as she walked down the aisle, she'd managed not to picture those big dark eyes looking at someone else, either.

Funny how that worked. Denial, she believed it was called. Mom and Dad would be happy to spend several hours analyzing this for her later, should she mention it.

This felt more like a funeral than a wedding. Maybe that was why she was here—to understand that Old Kevin, *her* Kevin, was truly dead now, New Kevin flexing on top of his grave.

Her shoes hurt. *Yes.* Think about that. Maybe she'd have a blister. She almost hoped so.

Naomi handed her bouquet to her maid of honor and reached for Kevin, and the guests sat down. There was a buzzing sound in Emmaline's ears.

Then Jack leaned over and whispered, very, very softly, "I hate weddings."

He kissed her temple, looking, she imagined, exactly like a fiancé who couldn't wait to be at his own nuptials.

Without turning her head, she cut her eyes to him. "Knock it off," she whispered as one of the bridesminions fluffed Naomi's dress. "You're giving my parents false hope."

"You started it."

"And stop whispering into my hair. You might

chip a tooth, I've got so much crap sprayed in there."

"I know," he whispered, sending a shiver down her side. "You smell like ethanol. I can feel my brain cells dying. You wearing those chicken cutlets today? Because the girls are looking fantastic."

"Shut up, Jack." Her face was hot.

"Is that any way to talk to the man you supposedly love?" Another kiss to her temple, a wink at her mother.

"You'd make a wonderful prostitute," she whispered. His eyes were a distracting, magnificent blue.

"I get that a lot." His mouth pulled up on one side, and the knot in Em's stomach loosened a little bit.

"Good afternoon," said the justice of the peace, and six minutes later, Kevin and Naomi were husband and wife.

At the very farthest table from the bride and groom, the mysterious Russians were cheerfully passing around a bottle of homemade vodka. And Em had thought she was being punished by being seated here! The contraband booze tasted like death, but Em added a healthy glug to her unsweetened, locally grown, fair trade, organic, farm-to-table cranberry juice (which also tasted like death), improving both beverages probably

because her taste buds were committing suicide. Still, it was a very jolly table, more so with every passing minute.

"Your hair ees very beautiful," said Uncle Vlad, the boob-starer from yesterday. He reached out to touch it, winced and withdrew his hand.

"It's breakable," Em said. "But thank you."

Uncle Vlad put his arm around her neck and hugged her, then refilled her glass, *God bless him*.

Jack apparently had learned Russian in the navy and was chatting away, and it was good, it was fine, because for one, it was a stressful day. And for two, this flirty light stuff he was doing with her . . . it wasn't her thing. He kept putting his arm around her and murmuring compliments. It was making her very itchy and scratchy. And tingly.

"How you doing?" he murmured. *See?* The tingle turned into a nearly painful buzz.

"I'm good! Really good! Yes. *Da*." The one Russian word she knew. Well, that and vodka. *Yes, vodka!* What more did she really need?

"Go easy on that drink," he advised. "That has to be around one hundred proof."

"Roger that, Captain," she said. *Hmm*. Perhaps it had already taken effect.

She took a bite of the brussels sprout soufflé covered in faux cheese, shuddered and washed it down with another slug of cranberry vodka drink, which was becoming increasingly delicious.

"Ladies and gentlemen," came the voice of the DJ, "please turn your attention to the dance floor, where Mr. and Mrs. Norman-Bates will have their first dance as husband and wife."

"They're really hyphenating, huh?" Jack said.

But Em wasn't paying attention, because once again, a familiar song was starting up.

"Unforgettable" by good old Nat King Cole.

So Kevin wasn't that original. Big deal.

There went the last of the cranberry vodka. What were those drinks called? Cape Codders? Those Cape Codders knew what they were doing. Emmaline should visit posthaste. Have some clam chowder and drink some Cape Codders. Maybe meet some nice fisherman like, like . . . like Phil on *Deadliest Catch.* Wait. Wasn't he dead? Okay, then. It would have to be Sig.

Kevin and Naomi were very good dancers, all spinny and coordinated and stuff. Smiling, too. Very happy-looking.

Had Kevin really been so miserable when they were together? There had been times when he'd brood, but who didn't brood once in a while? He had seemed to love her so *much.* How did that—

Stop thinking about this, the sober part of her brain ordered.

Angela waved to her, a sympathetic smile on her beautiful face.

The song ended; Em applauded dutifully. Cake-cutting time, maybe a dance with her dad, then

beddy-bye. She was almost home free. And when she got back, she'd send Jack a big case of . . . well, something . . . and thank him for being the best sport ever.

There wasn't even dessert to look forward to. Naomi had announced with great pride that, like the dinner, the cake was gluten-, dairy- and sugar-free. Brown rice cake with prunes. She wasn't even kidding. The icing had beet juice in it. Beet juice, for the love of God!

"And now the bride and groom would like to invite their wedding guests to share a special memory of the two of them."

"Oh, fun," Jack murmured. The Russians muttered darkly, and the vodka was again passed around. Em smiled and shook her head, but Uncle Vlad ignored her and filled her glass halfway.

"Don't drink that," Jack advised. "I'm getting liver failure just looking at it."

"I may need it," Em said. "To share my super-special memories."

"If I said let's make new memories, would you hit me?"

"I would. Yes. And don't forget, I brought my gun."

He smiled. That was something, that smile. "Show-off."

The best man, someone Em had never met, was first to share. "The second I saw them together," he said, "I knew it was the real thing. I mean,

Naomi was *screaming* at him not to quit. And Kevin, he's benching like three hundred as it was. Right, bro? Anyways, it's times like that when you really know you've got a winner, dude —can I just say?"

"Beautiful story," Jack murmured. "And loosen up, okay? We're in love. Stop grinding your teeth."

"Right. Got it."

She unclenched her jaw and cracked her knuckles. Maybe she could flirt back if she gave it a shot. Then again, it was just that kind of thing that had her believing she was a fantastic dancer last year at the Bitter Betrayeds' Christmas party. The footage from Shelayne's phone had proved otherwise.

The special memories sharing was more of the same. The marathon when Kevin had to crawl across the finish line just after he lost control of his bowels. The difficult time when Naomi had ruptured her Achilles tendon and could only run seven miles a day. The hilarious time when they were doing an Ironman race and Naomi's bike had crashed, her shoulder dislocated, and God bless her! She'd just rammed it back into place on a convenient tree, got back on the bike and caught up to Kevin, who of course hadn't stopped because it was "emotionally important" for him to give this race his all, and of course Naomi understood and supported this.

"I don't know," Em murmured. "I think I'd want

someone to stop and call an ambulance for me."

"I would do that," Jack said. "And I'd tell the paramedics to give you extra painkillers."

"And to think I didn't want to get married." *Aha!* She *could* flirt!

He winked. Her knees quivered.

Then came Colleen's turn. She tried gamely to pass, but Naomi was grinning ferociously, so Coll took the mike and sighed. "Well, Kevin and Naomi . . . um, near, far, wherever you are, I believe the heart will go on." She handed the microphone back to the DJ and stole a mysterious lump of something from Connor's plate.

Connor was not spared the microphone, either. "Good luck," he said.

The DJ reclaimed the mike and headed for the back of the room. "Who else would like to share? You, miss?"

More vodka? Yes, I'd love some, she thought, snagging the bottle from the weird uncle, who smiled approvingly at her cutlet-enhanced breasts.

Even worse, her mother popped into an empty chair at their table. "How are you? Don't repress your grief. Let it out, honey. And why are you drinking? Isn't it bad for the baby?"

"Hi, Mom. How are you? There's no baby."

"Enjoying your dinner, Dr. Neal?" Jack asked, and Mom murmured that yes, she was, then turned to look back at Em.

Her mother's eyes were worried. That was the

sucker punch. Mom meant well. She tried. Em knew she was loved, despite her parents being pretty clueless . . . when it came to her, anyway. They were better with Angela.

"I'm so glad you have Jack," Mom whispered. "Even though I was upset that you didn't want to share that with me earlier, I'm glad. It was so hard to see you heartbroken."

Shit. Lying sucked. She looked away from her mom.

The DJ was at their table. "Do you have a special memory of Naomi and Kevin?" the DJ asked the tiny shrunken Russian grandmother.

"*Kogda uzhin?*" the grandmother said.

"When is dinner," Jack translated into Em's stiff hair. "Poor thing doesn't realize this *was* dinner."

"Great!" the DJ said, handing the microphone to the boob-watching uncle. "And you?"

"Many years ago, when I come to United States," Uncle Vlad began, "I say, here is country of opportunity and money! Ha-ha! And my little niece, she is living dream! *Za vas*, Naomi!" He tossed back a shot.

"Excellent!" the DJ said. "And you, sir!" He shoved the mike into Jack's hand.

"Well, I don't know either Kevin or Naomi that well," he said, "but I can only hope they're as happy as Emmaline and I are."

Mom beamed. Squeezed Jack's arm.

Em took a deep breath. "We're not really

engaged, Mom," she said. "I lied about that. I'm sorry."

Jack closed his eyes.

There was a collective murmur.

Ah. Seemed like the microphone might've picked that up. Shit and vodka, her luck really sucked these days.

"I knew that," Mom said hastily. "It's fine. I've always known you're gay, honey. Are you really pregnant, though? Is Jack the father, or was it artificial insem—"

"Nope. Not pregnant. And still not gay."

"Okay!" chortled the DJ, looking slightly panic-stricken. "Uh, would you care to share a special memory?"

Why not? Emmaline took the mike, stood up with hardly a wobble and looked toward the head table.

Kevin sat with his arm around Naomi, but he was leaning forward slightly, his head tilted a little to one side. Was that sympathy in his eyes? Understanding?

"Right," she said. "Um, I guess everyone knows that Kevin and I used to be together. We were . . . we were friends. Right from when we first met in eighth grade. Right, Kevin?"

He smiled in response. The Old Kevin smile.

The vodka whispered that not only was she an amazing dancer, but Kevin was finally listening, too. For the first time in years, maybe for the first time since he'd met Naomi. All of a sudden, it seemed as if that lovely, sensitive boy was here again.

God, she'd loved him back then.

"When I knew Kevin, he was—" *the kindest, funniest person I'd ever met.*

But no. Her words slammed to a halt. Her tongue was behind her teeth, trying to make the *th* sound, but nothing was happening. Her throat muscles seized and lurched, but nothing happened.

The stutter.

It rose up and wrapped its hot bony fingers around her vocal cords, strangling her words. No sounds came out now. Nothing. Now, she'd just be the stuttering, maybe-gay, not-engaged, not-pregnant former fiancée who was so pathetic that she'd come to this Wedding of the Damned.

"He w-was—He w-was th-the m-mo—"

Kevin looked away. Naomi smirked. Of course she did. It was her resting expression. And Lyric Adams, who was sitting a few tables away with a much older man, had her phone out, her thumbs flying away as she snickered.

Jack took her free hand.

She took it back. She didn't want pity. Hell to the no power.

Think British, she commanded herself. *Think Harry Potter or Tom Barlow or Colin Firth or—*

"Okay!" the DJ said, taking the microphone back and moving to another table. "How about you, mother of the bride? You *must* want to share a special memory!"

Emmaline sat down.

"You okay?" Jack asked.

"You lied to us?" Mom asked. "Emmaline, this is just . . . just . . . It's practically pathological! Why on earth would you—"

"Dr. Neal," Jack said, "I think you understand that Emmaline is in a tough—"

"No, Jack. M-Mom, I'm sorry. I r-r-really am." Her heart sank as the words struggled to get out. She pictured the stutter leaning against a doorway, wheezing its dry, whispery laugh. *Hahaha. Got you again.*

"I think you need time to process your feelings," Mom said, a world of hurt in her voice. "See you later."

Who could blame her?

Finally, the speeches were done, though she'd stopped listening. The music started again, and Em sat there like a lump.

Jack took her hand. "Let's dance," he said, and she complied. Angela was fending off the best man, but she shot Em a sweet smile, flawlessly conveying camaraderie and humor with no disappointment or blame whatsoever. Somehow, it made her feel worse.

It was a slow song, something by John Mayer, and Jack pulled her close. It might've been sexy, if she hadn't felt like a slab of oak.

"Hang in there," he murmured against her hair. His chin made a crackling sound as it broke through some of the hair spray. She would've answered if she wasn't terrified of either stuttering or crying.

"I have to say, I'm a little disappointed you called off our engagement," he said, looking down at her with a smile. "I was hoping for a bachelor party at a strip club."

Thank you, Jack, for being a perfect date and the nicest guy in the world and also gorgeous. Thanks for not making me feel worse than I already do. Instead, she just tried to smile and shifted her eyes to his shoulder. He held her a little closer, and she had to bite her lip hard.

By tomorrow night, she'd be home again in her snug little house, with her good puppy and her excellent job. Levi wouldn't ask how the wedding was because he wasn't that kind of boss, and Em would ask Everett if he wanted her to cover a couple of his shifts, which he always did. She'd meet with her at-risk teenagers and go to her crisis negotiations class and have a night with the Bitter Betrayeds and by then, she'd have had time to spin this weekend into a good story.

Then her dad tapped him on the shoulder. "Mind if I dance with my firstborn?" he asked.

"Not at all, sir," Jack said, stepping aside.

So she danced with her father, breathing in his comforting Dad-smell.

"You must be experiencing some powerful feelings right now," he said.

"Mmm," she managed, hating the stutter even more because it made her unable to talk to her father, who did love her in his weird psychoanalyst way. He kissed her forehead, and Em swallowed and gave him a squeeze.

The slow song ended. "I'd better go dance with Angela," Dad said. "That best man isn't taking the hint." Em nodded, kissed him on the cheek and watched him go.

She'd have to come back and visit her parents to make up for lying to them. She'd call them tomorrow. Angela, too.

Jack didn't seem to be nearby, or at their table in the back, and people were giving her those embarrassed sliding glances. She grabbed her purse and walked out of the ballroom, smiling at whoever made eye contact (not that many) and grabbed the nearest parking attendant. She wasn't about to drive, not after two (or possibly three) zillion-proof vodka drinks. "I need a favor," she said, handing him a hundred-dollar bill. "Would you drive me into town?"

"Sure," he said, pocketing the bill. "Where do want to go?"

"You know Nance's diner?"

He smiled. "I absolutely do. You hungry?"

She folded her arms. "You have no idea."

Chapter Twelvee

Jack could swear he smelled bacon.

He was back in his room; Em had ditched him at the wedding, leaving him to hear about Naomi's grandmother's colonoscopy last year, which sounded even more horrific in Russian. All those guttural sounds.

He was a little worried. Emmaline hadn't answered when he knocked. Hadn't responded to his text, either. She wouldn't have driven; she was a cop and knew better than most that drinking and driving didn't go together.

As Josh Deiner would now understand, if he wasn't brain-dead.

For a second, Jack could swear he felt the lake water close over his head. The car seemed so far away, lying there on the bottom of the lake. All that cold and darkness.

No. No, thanks. He dragged his mind from the memory of that cold, that grim darkness. He was here in California, where it was now fully dark, a half-moon rising over the Pacific. Fifty-five degrees, maybe. If there was a reason to live in California, it was the weather. And San Francisco, a place Jack had visited a few times. Also, California wine country. Flippin' gorgeous.

Good. He was thinking about other things. He packed his stuff, since they had an early flight, and changed out of his suit into jeans and a T-shirt.

His phone chirped. Mrs. Johnson, of all people, texting him. Jackie, dear, you are terribly missed. When are you leaving California and coming home? Your father longs to see you.

He had several other texts, too. All three sisters, wondering how the wedding was going. One from Ned, asking if he wanted to go out for a beer, then another saying he forgot he was away. Two from Abby, asking for help with a chemistry project when he got back. One from Goggy that said WJY sek to DDjk. Goggy had just gotten a smart-phone and, much to the chagrin of the entire family, complained about the tiny keys and had yet to understand AutoCorrect. That or she'd just had a stroke.

There were five texts and two phone calls from Hadley.

He answered Abby and Mrs. J., told Goggy to stop trying to text until Ned showed her how and ignored Hadley.

He really wished she'd leave town. Honor had told him that she'd moved into the Opera House apartment building. That wasn't a good sign.

He heard a sound from Emmaline's room. So she was in there after all.

That had been hard, seeing her flail today. Not being able to make her feel better.

He knocked on the door that separated their rooms. "I hear you, Neal. Open up or I'm calling the front desk and telling them you're a suicide risk."

"Don't bug me, Jack." She sounded irritable.

"Aren't we supposed to be in love?"

"Not anymore. I outed us."

"Yeah, why'd you do that? Twelve hours more, and you'd have been home free."

"I don't like lying."

"Can you open the door? This is stupid."

"No. I'm very busy."

"I smell bacon. Now open up and share, or I'll call Naomi to break the door down."

She opened the door, and the smell of bacon was much stronger.

Well, her hair looked better, anyway, out of that weird bun thing. She'd showered, and her hair was damp. She smelled good, clean and citrusy. But the skin under her eyes was faintly pink.

She'd been crying.

A surprisingly strong feeling flooded his chest. Emmaline didn't seem like the type to cry. Ever.

She wore pajama bottoms and a tank top, and there was a smear of brown on her cheek. In her hand was a giant bag of Skittles, and on the table behind her were several white bags, an enormous slab of cake and a bottle of wine.

She folded her arms under her chest and glared at him.

"You ate meat without me? This is the thanks I get?" he asked.

"I could use some time alone, Jack."

"I think you've had plenty of time alone."

She huffed. "Come in, then. There's half a cheeseburger left."

"Have you been crying?" he asked.

"No."

"Liar. You have frosting on your teeth, by the way." He picked up the half cheeseburger and took a bite. It was fantastic, by far the best thing he'd eaten since he got there.

She flopped into the chair and grabbed a chunk of cake. "I'm eating my emotions. Show some respect."

"And what emotions are those, Officer Neal?"

"Irritation, embarrassment, frustration, jealousy, envy, gluttony . . . How many do you need?"

Jack finished the burger and broke off a chunk of the cake slab. Incredible. It didn't seem fair that they'd been eating root vegetables and mist when there was food like this around. He poured some wine and looked at the label. A midcoast zinfandel. Took a sip. Not bad with beef and chocolate, actually.

"You're not really jealous, are you?" he asked. "Not to criticize your taste in men, but he seems like an asshole, Em."

"He wasn't always." She took a rather savage bite of cake and gnashed away.

"What were you going to say?" Jack asked. "When the DJ gave you the microphone?"

"I don't know," she said, swallowing. "That he wasn't *always* an asshole. That he was good and funny and kind until he cheated on me with that . . . that . . . that hideous beautiful mannequin with the abs of steel."

Jack nodded. "How much of that homemade vodka did you have?"

"Oh, shut up. I'm not drunk. Unfortunately, I might add."

"You know, my wife cheated on me, too."

"Yeah, Jack, everyone knows that story." She winced. "I mean, thanks for sharing. It's just that your sisters talk a lot. Well, Prudence talks a lot. Faith and Honor have never said boo. But it was the best town gossip there for a while. I mean, not best. Just the most interesting. Shit. I'll stop now."

"I'd appreciate that. Deeply."

"Is there something appropriate I'm supposed to say? Like, 'Sorry your marriage went down in flames' or something?"

He smiled, unable to stop himself. "You tell me. Maybe they should make a line of cards for people like us. 'Sorry your fiancé turned out to be a dick.' "

She laughed, choking a little, then took a slug of wine and stretched out her legs so her feet rested on the bed next to him. "How long did it take you to get over what's-her-name? Blanche DuBois?"

248

"Let's talk about you," he suggested.

"Still a pulsating wound, then?"

"No. It's just that we're at your ex's wedding, and if there's a raw, pulsating wound, it's you." His lovely date gave him the finger. "Come on, Em. How are you doing?"

"I'm just great, Jack. I'm a stuttering, lying, not-pregnant lesbian who puts raw chicken in her bra."

He grinned. "I can't tell you how many boxes that checks."

"Shut up." But she smiled as she said it. And it was kind of refreshing that she didn't want to talk.

Her foot was propped up on the bed next to him, and he put his hand on it. Cute foot. Very clean and nice. Smooth skin.

Try not to think about that, Jack, the nobler part of his brain advised. *We don't sleep with heartbroken women.*

"Is your heart broken?" he heard himself ask.

She made a face. "No. Not really. It was three years ago."

"I remember."

"You do?"

"Yeah. You were moving in, and I helped you carry some boxes."

"No, I remember. I just didn't think you did. I bet you were an Eagle Scout."

"As a matter of fact, I was. We're trained to help damsels in distress."

"If you ever call me that again, I'll kick you in the soft parts."

She had no idea how appealing she was.

He poured her some more wine. She might have said she didn't know anything about wine, but she knew how to taste it, holding it in her mouth a second before swallowing, then licking her lips afterward. Even the way she held the glass said so, close to her breast, the red a deep contrast to the white of her—

Ah. She was speaking.

"Old Kevin . . . he was a peach. He was so *nice,* Jack. You have no idea. But that guy is gone, and I'm the only one who seemed to notice or care, and for some reason, that makes me feel really, really sad."

"Sure," he murmured, making sure he was looking at her face.

"All the things I loved about him . . . they seem dead now."

"So this was something of a funeral," Jack said.

Something flickered through her eyes. "Yes."

His hand slid up to her ankle and rested there. "I'm sorry, then."

She cleared her throat. "You know what sucks?" she asked. "I bought into the whole looks thing. I wore high heels and bought Spanx and I tried to look like *them.* The beautiful people. And the thing is, I like myself just fine. I'm tough, I'm strong, but get me next to someone like Naomi, and I stick raw chicken under my boobs and hope that Kevin will say something nice to me. And, of course, he didn't. So I sold my soul a little, and for nothing."

She looked at the painting on the wall and, very subtly, ran a finger under her eye.

Because she was crying. Not a lot, but, yep, those were tears.

Which was intolerable.

She took another bite of cake and didn't look at him.

"You know," he said gently, "we men don't really pick you women because of your looks."

"What does that mean?" she snapped. "Are you saying that Naomi has a stupendous body *and* a better personality?"

"Calm down, Simba. I'm saying that looks aren't as important as you seem to think."

"Said the Greek god."

Jack smiled. "Besides, you're very pretty."

"Don't make me shoot you, Jack. Go back to 'You have a great sense of humor.' "

"I never said that. Let's not get carried away." She didn't smile back.

Jack stood up and reached out for her hand. "Come on. Let me show you something."

He tugged her up and led her to the mirror. Turned on the light.

Emmaline flinched. "Damn. How did I get chocolate there?" She looked down at her shirt and rubbed a spot of chocolate over her heart.

"Look," he said.

"At the stain?"

"No, Emmaline. Look at yourself."

"I'd rather not do this, Jack."

"Don't be such a baby. Look. See what everyone else sees."

He stood behind her and pulled her hair back from her face.

"You probably do have a great sense of humor," he murmured, breathing in the sweet smell of her shampoo. "And you're very competent at hand-cuffing people, I'm sure. But you're also beautiful."

She rolled her eyes.

"Except when you do that," he added. "Stop being so grumpy and take a compliment."

"Where's that Taser when I need it?"

"Shush. Look at yourself."

His hands were on her shoulders now, and her skin was as smooth as silk. Women and their secret weapons. Yes, the breasts and lips and ear-lobes were all ridiculously appealing, and then they went and threw in silky skin and the smell of oranges and honey.

Without quite meaning to, Jack slid his hands down her arms to her hands, and back up again to her neck. Her long dark hair was sweet and damp between his fingers.

"Are you putting the moves on me, Jack

Holland?" she asked, her voice brisk. She didn't move, he noted.

He could see the pulse beating in her throat. "Your eyes are—"

"Normal."

"Stop interrupting. Your eyes are very pretty."

She shut them. "What color are they, Jack?"

"Dark blue."

She scowled and opened them.

"Your nose is perfect and adorable."

"Yeah. Perfect noses. So hot."

"Shush." Her ass was pressed right against his pelvis, and if he leaned in a little closer, he could—"Beautiful mouth. Made for kissing."

"Does that line work?"

"I don't know. I've never tried it." He smiled at her in the mirror, and her cheeks flushed. "You have perfect skin."

"Talk to me in two weeks when I have my—"

"You know, you suck at taking a compliment. Say thank you."

"Thank you, Jack, for slinging the bullshit. Is there any more cake?"

She *was* beautiful, and the longer he looked, the more beautiful she became. Her neck was long and smooth, her shoulders were strong and firm, her breasts were, well, breasts, and a very nice set at that, and there was a very appealing fullness to her hips.

He folded his arms over her chest and pulled

her a little closer. Her eyes widened, and her pink lips parted.

He turned his head to breathe in her smell and felt her shiver. She didn't pull away.

That skin smelled so sweet. He dropped a kiss on her bare shoulder. Smooth as water.

Emmaline inhaled, her breath shaky.

Another kiss, this one closer to her neck.

What are you doing? a small voice asked, but it was faint, drowned out by the hard, deep pulse that was thudding through his body. She tasted as good as she smelled.

"You should . . . I should . . . We probably shouldn't . . ." she breathed, but then his hand was wandering over her ribs to the fullness of her breast, which was soft and perfect, no push-up bra or raw chicken required.

A small sound came from Emmaline's throat, and Jack took that as invitation to turn her to face him. "I think we should," he said, and he kissed her, that sweet, full mouth, opening beneath his. He pushed his tongue against hers, tasting chocolate, and that thudding pulse surged hard and fast.

He backed her against the wall and leaned in hard against her, all that softness and good smells, that mouth. He didn't want to stop kissing her, because she was a drug and he was addicted, and he was throbbing now. He pulled her hands over her head and held them there, still kissing her mouth, her neck, the softness of her breasts against his chest making him drunk. She wasn't protesting. In fact, little sweet sounds were coming from her throat, and he could swear he felt her skin get hotter under his mouth, because he was kissing his way down her neck, scraping her skin with his teeth, because Emmaline Neal was edibly delicious.

Then suddenly, she pulled her hands free and grabbed his shirt in her fists and yanked, sliding her hands up his ribs, then unbuttoning his shirt in hard, jerky movements as he worshipped her neck, one hand covering the firm weight of her breast. Then he pulled her shirt off and, God, he was so greedy for her, urgent and hungry. And damn, he wanted to erase everything else from her mind except him, and them. The two of them.

She was fumbling at his belt, and, without breaking the kiss, he turned her and pushed her onto the bed, falling with her, on top of her. A few more tugs, and their clothes were off.

She was soft and strong and Jack wasn't even thinking anymore. There was only Emmaline and the taste of chocolate, and her beautiful, solid, silken body underneath his.

Emmaline woke up at 2:16 a.m.; Jack sprawled on top of her. From the slow, steady sound of his breathing, he was asleep. Slowly, she extricated herself and tiptoed into the bathroom, closed the door and turned on the light.

And there she was, wanton woman.

Holy shit.

Her hair was tangled, her lips puffy. Her legs felt weak and shaky, and certain parts were quite pleased at having had some attention, the first in a very, very long time.

Oh, and she was stark naked—had she mentioned that? Also, nearly dead. Cause of death: orgasm.

Not a bad way to go. No, sir, not bad at all.

And looky here. Her reflection showed a shit-eating grin, she believed it was called, and it lightened her face, which she knew was usually serious.

Kinda sorta forgot how great shagging could feel.

There was a mass of thoughts waiting to be unleashed—protests and winces and admonitions and some serious lecturing, but at the moment, she seemed to be quite taken with her reflection.

She felt beautiful. Jack had said it, a few times. It wasn't as if she didn't like how she looked. She had a good enough face. She liked being strong. She never really thought about beautiful.

Until now.

"Emmaline?"

She jumped. "Coming." She pulled on the Rancho de la Luna bathrobe and tied it closed, then got a glass of water and went back into the room.

He was gorgeous. The moonlight, which had been specially ordered for the wedding, flooded the room with white light, casting Jack's face in shadows and angles. His mouth was proof of a higher power, it was so perfectly shaped, and when he smiled, God was just showing off. The blue, blue eyes. His hands. Had she mentioned his big, strong hands, slightly rough from the farming work he did? Had she mentioned just what kinds of squeaky sounds those hands could get from her?

Ah. She seemed to be in the throes of sappy gazing. Clearing her throat, she looked down at the rumpled sheets. "Hungry?" she asked.

"Starving." He reached out and, very slowly, pulled the tie of her robe.

"There's still some cake," she whispered.

"I wasn't talking about cake," he said, his voice deep and rumbly, and her girl parts gave a hot, sudden throb. "But now that you mention it . . ." And with one quick move, he had her on his lap, robe open, and proceeded to feed her bites of cake in exchange for kisses. He took his time, sliding his hands over her as if he'd never touched a woman before, licking chocolate off her lips, and damn if it didn't work.

Very well.

Very well indeed.

Chapter Thirteen

You know that expression, the cold light of day?

Yeah.

For the first few seconds that Emmaline pried her left eye open, she wasn't sure why she was suddenly filled with dread. Hangover? No, no, she didn't feel terrible at all. In fact, she felt pretty . . .

And then she remembered, and regret and ruination rained down around her.

Shit and grilled cheese.

She'd slept with Jack. *Slept with* in all connotations, because not only had they had sex, he was dead asleep next to her.

She bolted out of bed, then, abruptly aware that she was naked, grabbed the bedspread and wrapped it around her.

"What's the matter? What's wrong? Who's dead?" Jack blurted, lurching upright. His hair was adorably mussed, and the muscles of his arms slid and bunched and—

"Nothing's wrong. Nothing." She looked away from the golden glory that was her bedmate. "It's—I have to pack. It's late. We have to leave in half an hour. We overslept."

"Emmaline—"

"Move it, Jack. Go pack."

Nice, said her brain. *Very tender.*

"I'm already packed," he said, narrowing his eyes at her.

"Well, *I* have to pack, so git."

"You can't pack in front of me?"

"No, I can't. So go shower and shave and eat something. Get out. I—I have to brush my teeth." *And put on clothes. Fast.*

She hustled to the bathroom, grabbing her suitcase on the way.

This. Had been. A mistake.

Pity fu—Okay, not that. Too ugly a term. Courtesy copulation, is that better? Yep. Jack Holland, god of Manningsport, had done her because she'd been in the throes of the most pathetic moment of all pathetic moments. Jilted single woman, desperate to feel attractive, drinks homemade vodka with Russians and overdoses on Skittles.

Well, maybe the homemade vodka and Skittles were unique, but otherwise, no.

All those thoughts that Emmaline had ignored in the loo last night were making themselves heard now in a very bossy and disappointed tone. Things about sleeping with someone for the sake of sleeping with someone. About going easy on vodka and wine. So what if the resort stocked condoms in the night table drawer? That wasn't carte blanche to go cartwheeling through Horny Land, was it? No. It was not.

She yanked her hair into a ponytail, took a marine-fast shower and pulled on her clothes with angry jerks.

Stupid, slutty, stupid. And wrong. She had used Jack for sex. Oh, sure, he didn't hate it—he was a guy, and it was sex. But here was a man dealing with some serious issues back home, not to mention an ex-wife looking for a reconciliation. He'd come here out of the goodness of his heart, and Em had done something that made her cringe.

She made him feel sorry for her.

A knock sounded on the door, and Em jumped. "What?" she demanded.

"Open the door and talk to me."

She opened the door. "Yeah. Listen. Last night was . . . thank you. Job well done." Automatically, she reached for her gun.

"You gonna shoot me?" he asked.

"Oh. Sorry." She put it back in the suitcase.

"Why do you even have that?"

"Because I'm a law enforcement officer, and I can bring it if I want to." She closed her eyes briefly. "We really do have to hurry."

"You can give me two minutes. Are you freaking out because we slept together?"

"As a matter of fact, yes. Bad idea, fun time. Just . . ." A frustrated growl came from her throat. "It's just I don't want a relationship right now."

"Fine. That'll be four hundred dollars, then."

"Don't sell yourself short. You were worth at least a thousand."

"Wow."

She winced. "Jack, look, I'm sorry. You're a nice guy."

"I'm so tired of people saying that."

"Okay, you're not. You're horrible."

His mouth tugged on one side, and Em's uterus responded in kind. Slut. She was a slut.

She stuffed her hands in the pockets of her shorts. "I imagine that you, being a very nice though horrible guy, want to be chivalrous and ask me out because your image of yourself doesn't have one-night stands. Plus, you have sisters and a niece you wouldn't want them to have a one-nighter with someone. I can't say that I'm the one-night-stand kind myself. But let's not go there. Let's just chock this up to a very brief vacation fling and never speak of it again, okay?"

"No. Not okay."

"You don't want a relationship right now. You have stuff. And things."

"Don't we all have stuff and things?"

"Yes, we do. But you never asked me out before. You're only here because I was desperate, and you wanted to get away from Manningsport. Also, you're invested in your ex-wife."

"You really know everything, don't you?"

"Am I wrong?"

At that moment, his phone chimed.

"Bet that's her," Em said. "How many times has she texted or called you this weekend?"

His face hardened. "A few."

"A few? More than a dozen?"

He didn't answer. So it was *way* more than a dozen.

"Let me see your phone," Em said.

"No."

"Chicken."

"Fine." He handed it over, and Em took it.

"What a surprise," she said. "It *is* from Hadley. 'Just taking a bubble bath, drinking Blue Heron wine, missing you. The bubbles are sliding down my—' "

He grabbed the phone back. "Point taken," he said. "She's a little . . . intense."

"Is that code for crazy?"

"Maybe I like crazy," he answered, reaching out and taking something from her hair. A Skittle.

"Then get back together with her."

"That will never happen. She was mean to my cat."

"Look. We should go. Thanks for the shag. I really do appreciate your . . . attention."

He looked at her a minute longer, his eyes beautiful and unreadable, and just as she was about to apologize and maybe ask to start over, he said, "Yeah, you're probably right," and went into his room, closing the door behind him.

It was for the best.

She wondered if he slept with all the women who asked him to weddings and reunions, then squelched the thought. That wasn't fair. Also, if it was true, so what? He was single; he was straight. Women threw themselves at him. If he caught them, as he'd caught her last night, who could blame him?

Part of the Bitter Betrayeds' speculation on Jack Holland was that he'd married Hadley because he wanted someone different. He'd never been serious with anyone local, and it hadn't gone unnoticed. His wife *had* been different, all right—as out of place, beautiful and useless as a butterfly in a February snowstorm.

But he had loved her. Em had seen them together. She knew what love looked like.

Em hurled her toothbrush into the suitcase.

Theoretically, she wanted to find someone. She definitely didn't want to be a Bitter Betrayed forever. And sure, this wedding had brought up stuff. And things. Maybe she wasn't ready for a relationship. Maybe she needed more time to get over the guy she'd loved for half her life.

Maybe, too, she was just chicken.

Couldn't get your heart broken if you didn't fall in love.

Chapter Fourteen

Five days after they got back from sunny California, Jack was sitting in the hospital parking lot once again. Twice, he'd gone into the lobby. He thought about what he would say to the Deiners. Debated over bribing a nurse. Jeremy Lyon was the Deiners' family doctor, and he'd once been engaged to Faith . . . Surely that meant he owed Jack a little insider information, right?

Okay, not that.

If he could just see Josh, then . . . then . . . then what? He could apologize? Did he really think Josh would wake up from his coma and say, "Hey, thanks for pulling me out! You're the best! No worries, man—I'm doing great!"

Jack sighed, his breath fogging the windshield.

It was as if Malibu had never happened. There was a foot of snow on the ground, it was fourteen degrees out, Josh Deiner was neither better nor worse and his family had just filed a lawsuit against Jack, saying that as an EMT, Jack should've recognized that Josh's needs were greater than the other boys'. They were also suing the town for not having a better guardrail in place and for not having a faster response time to the 911 call.

Not that they could win, Jack's lawyer had assured him. Josh had been doing sixty-four miles an hour in a thirty-five-mile-an-hour zone. Without Jack, the kid would certainly have died. No, this was just a grieving family lashing out in whatever direction they could.

Unfortunately, it did cause a collective gasp among the good people of Manningsport, and, once more, Jack was the topic of conversation. It was enough to make Jack wish Prudence and Carl would get caught for public indecency again.

And then there was Hadley.

Jack had glimpsed her the first night he'd been home. He'd been driving back from the hospital again and had to stop at the intersection on the green, where an ice-carving demonstration was taking place. Several dozen people stood bundled up in parkas and boots, watching Carlos Mendez carve a wolf out of a massive chunk of ice. Jack caught a glimpse of some of his family, and for a second thought about joining them.

But there were Sam Miller's parents, and rather than have them hug him and choke up with gratitude once again, he stayed in his truck.

Then he saw Hadley. She had a bag of groceries in her arms, and she was standing on the street, just outside the crowd. A few people streamed past her, and there was such a look of yearning on her face, such loneliness, that Jack almost called out to her.

She had no one in this town who cared about her. Except him. He did care; he just didn't want to get involved again. But he didn't want her to be shunned, or lonely, or miserable.

Fortunately, she went on her way, up the steps to the Opera House, and Jack continued home.

Unfortunately, he saw her again the next night, when she dropped off some dinner (bought from the caterer who had just opened in town) and stood shivering on his doorstep until he let her in. Just into the foyer, and only for six minutes till he told her she had to leave.

Speaking of difficult women, he was a little . . . mad at Emmaline.

Jack wasn't used to being rejected by women. In fact, he had the opposite problem. There was the time Shelayne Schanta hid in the back of his truck like a serial killer. The time Shannon Murphy wrote her college essay on being in love with an older man (him), resulting in two extraordinarily furious parents threatening to castrate him, despite the fact that his interaction with Shannon had been limited to robbing her of a home run last spring during a baseball game. There was the time Lorena Creech Iskin cornered him at O'Rourke's and told him in vivid detail about her husband's erectile dysfunction and how all she needed was fifteen minutes of his time.

So being thanked for a good time and sent on his way . . . That was new.

On Wednesday night, they'd had a hockey game. He'd said, "Hi, Emmaline," and she'd said, "Hey, guys." That was it. She didn't even hip check him.

He started as someone knocked on his truck's window. He rolled it down. "Hey, Abby."

"Hi, Uncle Jack." Abby volunteered at the hospital. "Guess you're wondering about Josh, huh?"

"Yeah."

"I don't know anything. Even if I did, I couldn't tell you."

"I know. But thanks."

She reached in and patted his shoulder. About a year ago, Josh Deiner had gotten Abby drunk. He'd been one of those kids who was too spoiled, too indulged, always bored, always looking for trouble.

Didn't look like he was going to be able to atone for any of that.

"You need a ride, Abs?" he asked.

"No, no, I've got Mom's car. You know what I found in it last week?"

"Do I want to?"

"No, but I feel like someone should share my pain, and you could use a distraction. You ready?" She paused for effect. "A riding crop."

"Please tell me she's taken up horseback riding."

"She has not."

"You're a cruel child, Abby."

She grinned. "Have a great day, Uncle Jack. Get out of here. Go do something with people your own age."

He watched to make sure she got to her car okay, and that it started, and then tailed her back to town to make sure she didn't speed or break any traffic laws (or careen into a telephone pole or a lake).

She didn't. Turned onto Old Farm Road with no problems.

But his breathing was getting shallow and fast, and he recognized the signs.

He couldn't go home. Not that his cat was bad company, but he needed humans. O'Rourke's it was.

"Hey, Jack!" said Colleen and Connor in unison as he came through the door. He nodded, figured he'd sit at the bar, maybe hang out with Lucas, who was there, as well. If things were slow, Connor might come out and have a beer with him.

Prudence, dressed much like he was in a flannel shirt and jeans, approached. "Hey, Useless!" she said, smacking his shoulder. "How's it hanging? Guess what? I'm officially in menopause. The results came back today."

"I'm thrilled for you."

"Oh, bite me. It's horrible, Jack. I want to climb Carl one minute, then slowly choke the life out of him the next. Speaking of Carl, do you happen to have any spurs?"

"No, Pru. Believe it or not, no."

"Damn. I back-ordered some, but they're still not here."

Out of the corner of his eye, Jack saw a table of women. One of them was studiously holding a beer to the side of her face.

She didn't even want to be spotted, in other words.

"Catch you in a little while, Pru," he said, walking over to the ladies—Shelayne Schanta, Allison Whitaker, Grace Knapton and Jeanette O'Rourke.

And Emmaline.

"Hello, ladies. Mind if I sit down?"

"Jack!" four of the five of them cried, moving their chairs to make room for him. "How are you, you look so handsome, want a drink, sit next to me, how was the wedding, have you eaten?"

One of them didn't say anything.

"Hi, Em," he said.

"Jack."

"You want to go out sometime? Grab dinner? Catch a movie?"

She gave him a dark look.

The rest of the women fell silent. "I'm game if she's not, Jack," Shelayne said.

"So am I," Allison said. "Just in case you're looking for an older woman with two not-terrible children."

"I'll go out with you, Jack," said Hannah

O'Rourke, coming up with a tray full of peachy-pink drinks.

"Me, too," said Colleen's mother. "Though I am dating Ronnie Petrosinsky on and off."

"The Chicken King?" Grace asked, naming Ronnie's franchise. "I just love their Mm-Mm Maple Glazed."

"How about it, Emmaline?" Jack asked.

"I'm very busy," she said. "But thanks just the same."

"That's too bad." He looked steadily at his prey, who was staring determinedly at the jukebox over Allison's shoulder. "Because I had a great time in California. Especially that last night."

Her eyes jerked back to his. "Good! I'm glad. Good for you. That's great. I have to run. Sarge needs walking. Nice seeing you, Jack. Bye, girls."

"You seriously don't want to go out with him?" Mrs. O'Rourke said.

"I'll walk you out," he said, following her.

"Together again!" Colleen called. "So cute. Coulda called it. Did call it, in fact."

"Stop harassing the customers, Colleen," Connor called from the kitchen.

Emmaline was already outside.

"Em. Hang on," he called, catching up to her. "Why won't you go out with me?"

"Is your ego bruised?" she asked.

"A little."

She smothered a smile. "You're really nice, Jack,

and you're not exactly the Elephant Man, but I don't think this is a good idea."

"I just want to have dinner."

She took a breath and held it, clearly on the fence. "Just dinner, Emmaline," he said. "Please."

Her eyes went a little soft and wide.

Score.

But then she looked over his shoulder, and her cop face reappeared.

"Have dinner with your wife. Here she is. Take care." With that, she turned and walked away, her feet crunching on the snow.

"Well, hey, stranger!" Hadley said. "How are you, Jack?"

And so, not wanting to be a jerk, he held the door for Hadley, took off her coat when she turned her back and gave her his hand as she truggled to sit on a stool.

Then, rather than getting webbed into a conversation with his too-beautiful ex-wife, he opted for the company of his cat and walked across the street to where his truck was parked.

There was a note on the windshield, on bright pink paper.

"You better watch yourself," it read. Laser-printed, not handwritten.

He glanced back at O'Rourke's. Was this a warning from Hadley, something to do with his interest in Emmaline? She seemed to be talking to someone.

Might be from Mr. or Mrs. Deiner. But they'd been camped out at the hospital around the clock. *You better watch yourself.*

The pink paper watered down the threat of the words.

Might not be a threat after all. Or it might have been meant for someone else; half the people in this town drove gray pickup trucks. It was just a note, anyway. Not a big deal.

He could feel the water slicing into his scalp as he went under. His chest burned from the lack of air.

By the time the flashback was over, Jack's flannel shirt was damp with cold sweat. He started up his truck and headed for home, his throat raw from the cold, cold air.

Two days later, Jack, his father and Pops were at work. It should've been easy, but for some reason, everything Jack did seemed wrong today. He bumped against a barrel, spilling his coffee. Missed what Dad had just said. Stepped on Pops's foot.

"You okay, son?" Dad asked.

"Yeah," he answered. "Not enough coffee, that's all." Except he'd had three cups.

The three Holland men had always been close. First of all, it was them against what seemed like dozens of women. . . . Mom, back in the day, the three girls coming and going with their girlfriends, then Mrs. Johnson. When talk turned to periods or squabbles over who used whose hair goop, the three men would slip off to talk about baseball or vines.

When Jack was in the navy, Dad called twice a week, checking in, the gentle constant in Jack's life. Both Pops and Dad assured him he had no obligation to return to Blue Heron, and Dad only wanted him there if it was what Jack wanted. It was. The family, the farm, the wine . . . It was everything Jack had ever wanted. He was the eighth generation of Hollands on this land.

But since the accident, he couldn't seem to get back in the groove.

Today, they were racking a small vat of cabernet out in one of the big barns. Racking was the process of siphoning the wine off the sediment into a clean vat in preparation for bottling. As soon as Jack pulled the bung, though, Pops looked up. "Something's off," he said. The old guy had a nose like a bloodhound. "It's over-oxidized."

Jack grabbed a glass and filled it halfway with the wine.

It was too brown, and Pops was right. It didn't smell right.

"Did you add the Campden tablets last time?" Dad asked.

"I thought I did," Jack said. The tablets kept microbes from forming in the wine. They'd just racked this barrel for the first time three weeks ago.

"Well, don't worry, son," Dad said as Pops pried the head off the barrel to dump it. "Happens to everyone."

"I'm really sorry," Jack said.

"Smells like your grandmother's perfume," Pops said, winking at Jack. "Speaking of the old bag, I should get back."

"That's my mother you're talking about," Dad said mildly.

"And the love of my life. Just don't tell her I said that." Pops smiled and ambled off to his battered old truck.

"Let's get rid of this," Jack said.

"It can wait till tomorrow," Dad said. "So how are things, son?"

"Good. Fine." Dad waited. "A little tense," he admitted.

"I ran into Hadley the other day."

"Yeah. She's like a dog with a bone."

"Any chance of you two getting back together?"

"No."

Dad tapped another barrel and started siphoning that one. "This is better," he said, filling a glass. "Smell that. It's beautiful."

Jack obliged. This batch was fine, no oxidization, a nice jammy aroma. He took a sip and felt his shoulders drop a notch.

He'd never screwed up a batch of wine before.

Wine making was all about science and luck, but mostly about science, and he prided himself on the quality of wine that came out of Blue Heron. He'd grown up watching his father and grandfather make wine, and he had two hefty degrees that said he should know better than to forget something as basic as sulfites.

"Anyway, I was just wondering about Hadley," Dad said, not quite meeting his eyes. "She was very, ah, forthcoming with me. Said she'd made a terrible mistake with you, but she'd grown up and learned her lesson and hoped that we'd be supportive if you decided to reconcile."

"There's no reconciliation," Jack said.

"You sure? Because if you were over it, we could be, too."

"Mrs. Johnson will never be over it," Jack said, forcing a grin.

Dad smiled. "No, maybe not her. But the rest of us would follow your lead, Jack. If that's what you wanted."

"It's not." He put his glass down. "And I sure am sorry about this barrel."

His father gave him a long look. "Jack, maybe you need some time off."

"I just took some, Dad."

"If you need more, just say the word. You've been through a tough time." He gave Jack a slightly awkward hug. "I love you. We all do." He pulled back and cleared his throat. "You want to come for dinner? Mrs. Johnson would sure love that."

"Dad, you two are coming up on your first anniversary. Aren't you allowed to call her Hyacinth yet?" Jack asked.

"Sometimes," Dad admitted with a sheepish grin.

"I'll take a rain check on dinner. You go home. I'll finish this up." He took the siphon from his father. "And thanks, Dad."

His father squeezed his shoulder, then left to go home to his bride.

Odd to feel jealous of your own father for having a wife to go home to. As for doing something fun . . . There wasn't a lot of fun to be had in the middle of winter here in Manningsport.

"Hallo, Jack." His British brother-in-law came into the barn. "Just saw your grandfather. He said I'd find you here."

"Hey, Tom. What's up?"

"I got an email today from Dr. Didier, the high school principal. You know her?"

"Only a little," Jack said. "I've seen her at the gym a few times."

"Right. A bit terrifying, isn't she?" Tom grinned. "At any rate, they've got a group of at-risk kids. The usual lot—hoodlums and the like—and she's looking for a chemistry tutor. I help out with math from time to time."

"Did Honor tell you to ask me?"

"Spot-on, mate. She said it might be good for you."

Honor. Always trying to run the world (and succeeding much of the time, he'd admit). But the thought of being around teenagers other than his niece and maybe Charlie, Tom's stepson, gave him pause.

They'd all know Josh Deiner.

"Levi's deputy runs the program. Emmaline Neal. You two are friends, aren't you?"

Jack looked up. "Yes. We are."

"I'm surprised she didn't ask you herself."

Jack wasn't. "I'll talk to her."

"Brilliant. Thanks, mate!" Tom clapped him on the shoulder and went off, whistling.

Emmaline peered at the faux hostage taker. "What did she do that made you mad?" she asked.

"She took the last Twinkie. Those were for my apocalypse shelter. Now what will I have for dessert?"

"Atta girl, Shirley," said Jamie, the badass instructor. "Sounds crazy, class, but I swear, you can't make this shit up."

Em tried not to smile, but damn! This sure beat out Consciousness and Form in Eighteenth-Century England, which she'd had to take her junior year. (She'd gotten a B–. She was fairly sure she'd be getting an A in Crisis Negotiations). Jamie, who was a negotiator with the state police in Buffalo, was filled with stories, curses and good advice. "Em, what's your response to Crazy-Pants here?"

"Stole your Twinkies, huh? That's not good," she said. "I love them. Thought I'd tear my hair out when they stopped making them. Good thing they're back on the shelves, right?"

"She's establishing empathy, people, and creating a bond between herself and the hostage taker. Keep it up, Neal!"

"You know, I can get you some more Twinkies," Emmaline said. "I can bring them inside and we can talk."

"I can't risk that," Shirley said. "There are zombies everywhere." The rest of the class snorted.

"That's okay," Em said. "I'm really fast. And I don't want you to go without Twinkies."

"Fantastic, kids," Jamie said. "We have to call it a day, but good job, everyone! Your homework is to read chapters four through six and deal with your in-laws without losing your cool. Think you can handle that?"

"If ever there was a time to barricade myself in a room with a gun," muttered Ingrid, a cop from Ithaca.

Jamie came over and leaned against Em's desk. "You're doing great in this class," she said. "You ever think about working for us?"

"I've only been a cop for nine months," she said.

"So? Think about it," she said. "There'd be more chances to climb the ladder than in your department."

That was true. Levi wasn't going anywhere.

The state police handled the big stuff for a town like Manningsport—if there was an actual hostage situation, for example, it'd be the job of the local police force to keep everyone calm until the staties got there and took over. Homicides, kidnappings, bank robberies—not that they were commonplace occurrences—were handed over to the big kids.

It was a thought. She wouldn't leave the Manningsport Police Department anytime soon, but maybe someday.

She radioed in when she was ten minutes from town, got a request from Everett to pick up donuts. Before the station had moved to the new emergency services building, it had been right on the town green, spitting distance from Lorelei's Sunrise Bakery. Everett had dropped ten pounds since the summer and much mourned the move.

Faith Cooper was inside, hands on her pregnant belly. "Hey, Faith," Emmaline said.

"Hi! How are you, Em? How was the wedding?"

"It was great. I, uh, I owe your brother something nice. He was a champ."

"Well, if you're giving out presents, don't forget me," Faith said with a smile. "It was my idea, after all. So he was a good date?"

"Very good." *So, so good.* The memory of Jack on top of her, kissing her, made her left knee buckle. But then it was Faith's turn at the counter, and so Emmaline was spared further conversation.

Didn't stop the thoughts from coming, though.

"Wipe your feet," Carol Robinson ordered Jack as he walked into the police station. She looked up. "Oh, it's you, Jack. How are you, sweetheart? Still feeling famous? How's the Deiner boy?"

"Hey, Mrs. Robinson," Jack said. He'd gone to school with one of her sons and had fond memories of her chocolate chip cookies. "You look beautiful in that color."

Carol beamed, her questions forgotten. "Call me Carol," she said. "Why are you still single, Jack? Oh, wait, I forgot. You got divorced. Do you want to marry my daughter?"

Levi emerged from his office and handed Carol some papers. "Stop matchmaking," he said to her. "Come on in, Jack."

Levi's office was tidy and bureaucratic-looking, except for rather a lot of pictures of Faith. And an ultrasound of the mini Cooper. "How's my sister?" Jack asked, always a little uncomfortable talking to the guy who slept with her. Curse of the brother.

"She's good. Another few weeks to go."

"You nervous?"

"Terrified." Levi smiled. He'd make a great father. Levi was one of those guys who was born to be a family man.

Jack sat down. "You heard anything about Josh?"

Levi's gaze dropped to his desk, then went back to Jack. "No change. I check in with his parents every night."

"That's good of you."

"Sorry to hear about the lawsuit against you."

Jack shrugged. "I understand." Couldn't blame them, either. *You left him for last. The one who needed you most . . .*

"So what can I do for you?" Levi asked.

"I'm here to see Emmaline, actually. Is she around?"

Levi started to answer, then stopped. His eyes narrowed. "Did you sleep with her?"

Guess he was a cop for good reason. Jack didn't answer.

"Be careful," Levi said. "She's like a sister to me."

"And my sister's like a sister to me."

Levi gave a begrudging nod. "Point taken. Em should be here soon. She was at a class in Penn Yan and has a thing tonight with her at-risk kids, but she said she'd stop by."

"That's what I wanted to talk to her about. The kids. Heard they need a chemistry tutor."

At that moment, Emmaline came in, tossed a

box of donuts on Everett's desk and said something that made him laugh.

A jolt went through Jack. Emmaline was in her uniform and wore a bulky jacket, a gun, a radio and a few other things on her belt. Her hair was pulled back into a tight bun, and her cheeks were pink from the cold.

And she was smiling.

Until she saw him, that was, and the smile dropped. "Hey, Chief."

"Deputy," Levi said. "How was the class?"

"It was fantastic. I get to taze someone next week."

"You and that Taser. Enjoy."

"I will." Her eyes flickered to him. "Jack. How are you?"

He stood up. "I'm fine. I'm here to see you, actually."

"Got a complaint to file?"

"No." He waited, and her cheeks got even redder.

"Didn't you two go to a wedding together?" Carol asked. "Are you dating? Levi, I'm leaving. It's almost five, and the neighbors are coming for dinner."

"Lucky neighbors," Jack said.

"Oh, you!" Carol, who was about a foot shorter than Jack, wrapped her arms around his waist and gave him a hug. "Come visit me sometime."

"Are you trying to seduce me, Mrs. Robinson?" Jack countered.

"I've thought about it," she said. "I might be a tiny bit old for you. Ask Emmaline instead. She'll go out with you."

"Is that true, Em?"

"In your dreams," Em said.

Damn, she was cute.

"I'm leaving, too," Levi said. "Jack, see you around." He left, holding the door for Carol. Everett was clicking through some pictures, his cheeks bulging with donuts.

Jack looked down at Emmaline, who was fidgeting with her jacket zipper. "Hi," he said.

"Hi." Tone not encouraging.

"I hear you need a chemistry tutor for your group of kids."

"How'd you know that?"

"Tom Barlow."

"Right." She folded her arms across her chest. "We do. You in?"

"Yep. You could've asked me yourself."

"We meet every Tuesday night in the church basement at Trinity Lutheran. If you can't make tonight, come by next—"

"I can make tonight."

She gave a nod. "Okay, I have to run home, change, walk my dog and eat something. See you there."

"Or I could come with you. Meet your dog." *Watch you change.* "Come on, Emmaline. I thought we were friends."

She didn't answer.

"Look," he said quietly. "The truth is, I like talking to you. I like being with you. My life is kind of a mess right now. I can't sleep, my ex-wife is hanging around and now I'm screwing up at work. So yeah, I have . . . issues. You were right. I'm not looking for a relationship, but I could really use a friend."

"Okay," she said almost before he finished. "I'm sorry if I was rude the other night. I can do friends."

"Thank you."

The blush flared again. "You won't thank me when you see what I have for dinner."

Okay, so this was . . . nice, Em thought as they left the police station. Her kids' group did need a science tutor. And if Jack wanted a friend, well, hell, she liked him, too. She could handle friendship. She'd love to be friends. Naked friends.

No, no, none of that, she cautioned herself.

Jack was looking for a distraction. He had just admitted he didn't want a relationship. Friends with clothes on, that's what they'd be.

They left the building, and Em broke into a run. Levi was crouched on the sidewalk, talking to someone on the ground. "Chief?" she said, drawing her radio. "Everything okay?"

Ah.

Hadley Boudreau was scenically arranged on the ground, her dress hiked up, just shy of slutty and just enough to show that she was wearing thigh-high stockings, the tops of which were lace. And really. It was eighteen degrees out. Full battalion makeup, perfectly applied. Em had never been able to pull off red lipstick, but Hadley sure knew what she was doing.

"Just trying to convince Ms. Boudreau to go to the hospital and get this checked out," Levi said, giving Em a significant look.

Em glanced over her shoulder at Jack. "I think this belongs to you," she said to him, then looked back at Scarlett O'Hara.

And like Scarlett, Hadley Boudreau had a way with men and a calculating look in her eye.

"I think my pride's hurt more than anything else, Chief Cooper. Jack, I was driving past and saw your truck, figured I'd catch you and then the next thing I knew, I'm ass over teakettles here on the ground."

"Imagine that," Jack said, his tone sawdust-dry. Good for him.

Hadley started to move, then pursed her cherry lips in pain.

Em tried not to roll her eyes. She wondered how long it had taken Hadley to arrange herself so just the right amount of thigh was showing. "Can you put any weight on it?" she asked.

"Oh, Chief!" Hadley said. "I heard you're married to Jack's sister! She's the sweetest thing. I always thought of her as a kindred spirit."

Em sure as hell hoped not, for Levi's sake. She clicked on her radio. "Gerard, get your lazy ass out here. We have a casualty in the parking lot."

"Roger that," Gerard said.

Hadley sliced a look Em's way. "I don't mean to inconvenience anyone," she said, an edge to her perfectly lovely husky voice.

"They're right here. No inconvenience at all," Emmaline said.

"I just need a hand up. Jack? I feel like an idiot already—don't make me lie here all the livelong day."

"Let's wait for the professionals," Jack said.

The door opened, and Gerard ambled out. Then, catching sight of a fallen and very beautiful female, he accelerated into a gallop. "What've we got here?" he asked, kneeling next to Hadley.

"Might need to be amputated," Emmaline said. Levi raised an eyebrow at her. *Right.* She was in uniform and was therefore required to be nice to idiots.

"I just need a little help," Hadley said. "I'm sure you're a wonderful paramedic, Mr. Chartier—" Gerard's name was stitched on his jacket "—but Jack and I used to be married. He can help me." Her tone was firm and friendly.

Jack sighed and went over. Emmaline followed. "Up you go," he said, offering his hand to his ex-wife.

"Maybe if you didn't wear three-inch heels in

the snow, you wouldn't trip," Emmaline observed.

"A lady always wears heels," she said, seizing Jack's hand. He pulled her up, and she collapsed against him. He caught her right on cue.

"Oh, dang," she said, tears filling her big brown eyes. She gave an awkward hop.

"That looks pretty bad," Gerard said. "Definitely a sprain, judging from the bruising. Let me take you to the hospital for an X-ray."

"No, no, it's just a sprain. Um . . . Jack, I hate to ask, but would you mind driving me home?"

"Yeah, Jack. Would you mind?" Emmaline echoed.

He gave her a look.

"Get an X-ray," Levi said.

"No, no, I'll just get on home and pop it up on some pillows. Ice, compression, elevation, right, Mr. Chartier?"

"Call me Gerard. And, yes, exactly," Gerard said, smiling at her like a proud teacher. The guy was such a flirt. "Throw in some Motrin and call it a day."

Well, Em had to give it to Hadley. Anyone could fake a fall in a parking lot. It took real commitment to actually injure yourself.

Hadley deigned to glance at her, and Em saw the gleam there. And Hadley knew she saw it, based on the twitch of lips. *Watch, listen and learn, Yankee. This is how it's done.*

"This is downright embarrassing," Hadley said,

"but I think you're gonna have to carry me to the car, Jack."

Jack sighed and picked her up.

Em had the impression there would be many more sprained ankles in Hadley's future. "Have fun," she said, starting for her car.

"Em, wait," Jack said. "I'll just be a few minutes."

"Oh, no, you should take care of Blanche DuBois here."

"It's Hadley," the other woman said sweetly.

"Em—" Jack began.

"I don't really want to have a conversation around the body in your arms," she said. "Have fun, kids."

Because the Opera House didn't have an elevator, Jack ended up carrying Hadley up the stairs.

"I really do appreciate this, Jack," she said as he set her down. She leaned against the door frame and got her keys out. "I guess I just forgot how dang slippery it gets around here. Oh, well." She smiled and opened the door. "Would you mind just coming in for a second? I did want to talk to you, after all. And maybe you could grab me an ice pack. I'm so sorry to inconvenience you. Really, Jack."

Right. If her ankle hadn't been bruised, he would've thought she'd staged the whole thing. It was right up her alley; she'd once confessed to him (while in bed) that she'd crashed her bike on purpose to get the attention of a football player in college.

She hobbled inside, and Jack closed his eyes for a minute, then followed. He couldn't just dump her here, as much as he might want to.

Sharon and Jim Stiles kept this apartment for people just like Hadley, folks who'd be in town for a few months at a time. Faith had rented it out when she'd first moved back from San Francisco, and Colleen's husband had stayed here over the summer when his uncle was sick. It was a cute little place, furnished and stocked with china and glasses and that sort of thing.

Way too easy for Hadley to make herself at home.

"It's so good to be back here," she said as he opened the freezer and grabbed a bag of peas, since she didn't seem to have an ice pack. "Frankie came up last weekend, and we were both real sorry you weren't around."

"I was away with Emmaline," he said.

Hadley jerked, then recovered. "Is that right," she murmured, sweeping her hair around to one side. She smiled as he handed her the peas. "Thank you, Jack. Um, would you mind getting a bandage? I think there's a first aid kit in the bathroom."

He said nothing but obeyed. The bathroom counter was laden with little baskets filled with bottles of perfume, makeup and other girlie stuff.

Looked like she was planning to stay awhile.

He grabbed the kit and a bottle of Motrin and went back to the living room. "Here you go. I have to run," he said.

"Do you think you could wrap my ankle?" she said. "I'm sorry, I just . . . I'm clumsy. As you could tell, I guess. I feel so stupid. Bad enough to be the town pariah. Now I'm the clumsy town pariah." Her expression was rueful.

"You're not a pariah," he said.

"If you say so. I've been getting dirty looks since I moved back."

Moved back. He didn't like the sound of that.

"Which I guess is what I deserve."

He sat down next to her, and she reached under her skirt and pulled off her stocking with a businesslike motion, which surprised him. He would've expected a striptease. Her skin was cold and smooth, the joint fairly swollen. He felt a pang of sympathy.

"Did you ever tell people why we split up?" she asked as he wrapped her ankle.

"They figured it out, Hadley."

"Jack," she began, her voice husky. "If I could undo what I did—"

"I appreciate the thought," he said. "There. You're all set."

"I know you're still hurt—"

"No, not anymore."

"But the thing is, I've learned so much. I was so young then."

"Not that young, Hadley."

"You're right. I was immature. I like to think I'm smarter now, at least smart enough to know you were the best thing that ever happened to me. And it wasn't all bad, was it? Here. Look what I brought."

She reached over and grabbed a book off the table. One of those photo albums you make online, and on the cover was a picture of the two of them in Central Park. "Remember?" she said. "We had so much fun that weekend. You took me skating at Rockefeller Center. And that dinner we had, at the place with the view of the Chrysler Building, and we laughed so hard? Remember that?"

"I do, Hadley. You're right. We had some happy times. I also remember the lying, the tantrums, the spending and the cheating."

"I'd make it up to you."

"You can't undo something like that," he said.

"But you could forgive me. And I am so sorry."

"You're forgiven. Doesn't mean I want to get back together, Hadley."

"I think you do. I think you're just angry. If you'd give me another chance, Jack, just one . . ."

Her eyes were full of tears. "Hadley," he said, putting his hand over hers. "Stop. I don't know why you're back, but I imagine some shit hit the fan somewhere in your life, and all of a sudden, life with me didn't seem so bad. But I've moved on."

Her eyes took on that stony look he remembered from when they disagreed. "Look at this picture," she said, pointing to a photo of him standing next to one of the carriage horses in Central Park. "Look how happy you are there. Just think about that, Jack. That's all I'm asking—if the happiest time in your life doesn't deserve a second chance. Because I'd do better. I swear it."

Their life together had had some movie-esque qualities to it, Jack admitted—their courtship, the choreographed, petal-strewn lovemaking, the dinners by candlelight, the way she could turn every move into something beautiful.

And in the past, when he'd remembered those times, he'd also remember her with Oliver.

"Rest that ankle," he said, and, with that, he got up and left.

Chapter Fifteen

When Jack and Hadley had returned from their honeymoon two and a half years ago, Jack had nine days before warning signs had started to flicker like broken neon lights.

Nine days.

Despite what she'd said about wanting to have a family as soon as possible, Hadley decided to stay on the Pill, which was fine. After all, she was the one who'd be pregnant and giving birth. It just wasn't what she'd been telling him or their families.

She also didn't want to work just yet; she just wanted to settle in first. Again, totally fine. She was living in a new town in a new part of the country. Of course she wanted to acclimate. Then, she said, she'd hang out a sign and start up her interior decorating business once more.

But now that the wedding was behind her and life started to settle into a routine, Hadley seemed a little . . . irritable. She was surprised there weren't more events like the Black-and-White Ball, and her interest in doing wine tastings and guiding tours for Blue Heron quickly faded.

She went to a garden club meeting but didn't

join, saying it wasn't for her. Joined the Art League, took two pottery classes and didn't go back. Honor asked her to help with the Manningsport Women's Club, which was organizing a tour of homes as a fund-raiser for local scholarships, but Hadley came back from that saying it made her sad, what passed for graciousness "here in the North."

"Don't be a snob, honey," Jack said, pouring her wine.

"Well, come on, babe," she returned. "You've been to Savannah. You know what I'm used to." Then she gave him a sheepish look. "Sorry. I'm just feeling a little out of sorts." Then she wandered off to her computer, calling him over to look at the Christmas decorating ideas she'd found online, even though it was still summertime.

She was alone in the house a lot. Pru and Honor invited her out a couple of times, but the sister Hadley most liked was Faith, and Faith was in California.

And then there was Lazarus, the cat who lived with Jack.

To say it was his cat would be a stretch; Jack fed him and housed him, and Lazarus allowed it. Occasionally, Laz would jump onto Jack's lap, knead his stomach for a few seconds, then make a hideous gacking sound and go off to parts unknown to murder and pillage the bird and rodent population. He was an ugly creature; tan with splotches of stripes, a shredded left ear and a crooked tail, wary of all humans except Jack.

When Jack first moved back to Manningsport, he'd been struck with a surprisingly strong yearning for his mother. He'd gone up to the family cemetery and sat there in the misting rain, a hard lump in his throat.

And then, from behind the gravestone of the first Holland who'd farmed this land, came a very small animal. It was battered and bleeding and matted to the point where Jack wasn't even sure what it was, but then it mewed.

Jack's mom had had a thing for cats. They'd always had a few, out in the barns, in the house. Kind of seemed like a sign from Mom, him finding a cat out here right when he'd been missing her. He wrapped it in his jacket and took it to the vet, who said he didn't think the kitten would make it. When he pulled through, Jack named him Lazarus.

Hadley hated Lazarus. Why, Jack had no idea, because Laz gave her a wide berth.

Hadley had a cat, too. Princess Anastasia was a fat, fluffy white Persian with startling green eyes and a fondness for shredding curtains, upholstery and human flesh. Princess jumped on the table, walked on the counters, crapped wherever she happened to be at the moment and shed large clots of white hair all over the house. In Savannah, she'd been ill-tempered and unaffectionate. But in New York, she became downright destructive . . . especially and ironically toward Hadley, ripping her clothes, vomiting in her shoes and scratching and biting her. Not just little scratches, either, but long bloody tears and actual puncture wounds that would make Hadley's hand or foot throb.

One night after such an attack, Jack grabbed the cat by the scruff and tossed her into the basement. "Jack!" Hadley yelped, clutching her bleeding hand. "She's just an innocent animal!"

However, Hadley had no such sympathy for Lazarus.

"Can't Prudence take him?" she asked one night. Her own cat was draped across her lap like road-kill, peaceful (until she decided to turn homicidal).

"He's not the problem cat here, babe," he said.

"I just think Princess Anastasia would be happier if that thing wasn't around, spooking her. Wouldn't you, Princess? You want that ugly ole thing to go live with Prudence?"

"Hadley. He's not going anywhere."

She stared at Lazarus, who was crouched under the coffee table, making his weird gacking sound. "He's disgusting, Jack."

"Hey," Jack said, grinning as he poured more wine for his bride. "I love that disgusting cat. He's got character. And, yes, he's ugly. But so am I, and you love me."

"Jack," she said. "You're gorgeous and you know it."

She kissed him then. But she didn't warm up to Lazarus.

One night about a month after they'd returned from their honeymoon, Hadley invited the whole clan for "a genuine Southern dinner." Honor, Pru, Carl, Ned and Abby, Dad, Mrs. Johnson, Goggy and Pops all arrived at once. Even Faith was home from San Francisco, and Jack was pouring the Half-Moon pinot gris they'd bottled four months ago.

"The house looks gorgeous," Faith said, and Hadley beamed.

She'd spent the whole day getting ready, setting the table with their wedding china, making place cards with her calligraphy pen, arranging flowers. Hadley had sworn she didn't want him to do anything for the dinner, and he'd been busy with some early harvesting, so he didn't know what she'd cooked. She fluttered around like a tiny bird, seeming even smaller standing by Jack's sturdy sisters.

They drank wine and chatted and all was fine and good until they sat down to eat. Hadley set down a crock and took off the lid.

"Southern chicken and dumplings!" she announced with pride.

Mrs. Johnson and Goggy both recoiled in unison. What was in the pot looked like lumpy glue.

"I'm starving, dear," Pops said. "Let's get eating! It's already six o'clock. I have to go to bed soon."

Hadley ladled out the dinner, which seemed to be a gelatinous goo with the occasional chunk of white meat thrown in. The dumplings were slimy, dense and slippery, and the chicken was chewy and tough, a far cry from what Jack remembered from when Mrs. Boudreau had made the same dish.

The Hollands didn't complain. They were Yankees; food was meant to nourish, not to enjoy, though their standards had risen during the Mrs. Johnson era (Mrs. J. was Jamaican and therefore believed in flavor).

"It's delicious, dear," Pops said. "Thank you for having us."

"You're always welcome here, Mr. Holland," she said, smiling and fluttering her eyelashes.

"Did you just bat your eyelashes?" Pru asked. "I've always wondered if that actually happened. I mean, you come across the phrase from time to time, but I don't think I've ever seen it live and in person. Carl, stop staring at her."

"You, too, old man," Goggy said, smacking Pops on the back of the head.

"Why can't I stare? She's beautiful. You're beautiful, sweetheart."

"Mr. Holland, you're the sweetest thing," she said. This got a snort from everyone related to

Pops. Hadley did have a way with men, and Jack had a soft spot for his grandfather. After all, the Holland men had to stick together, as Pops was fond of saying.

"So I'm thinking about redoing the house," she said sweetly, "and I'd love y'all's opinion."

"What do you mean, redo?" Mrs. Johnson asked sternly. "This house is perfect." Jack winked at her; he'd always been Mrs. J.'s favorite.

"I'm thinking it could do with a Southern woman's touch," she said. Pru laughed, then, realizing Hadley was dead serious, coughed to cover.

"Hadley, I forget. Are you an interior designer or an interior decorator?" Honor asked, taking a bite of slimy dumpling.

"What's the difference?" Abby asked.

Hadley didn't answer. She shot Jack a look he couldn't read and remained silent.

"An interior designer deals with how the space is used," Faith said when Hadley remained quiet. "Decorators deal with how it looks. Am I right, Hadley?"

"Um, yes. More or less. Excuse me, I have to check on something in the kitchen," Hadley said. She rose stiffly.

"Need help?" Jack asked.

"No, darlin'. You stay put."

She left the table. A second later, Jack heard their bedroom door close.

"Why is this gravy white, Jack?" Goggy asked. "Not that I'm criticizing, dear, but I'd be happy to teach her to cook."

"And *I* would also be happy to help her, Jackie dear," said Mrs. J., not to be outdone. "Jamaican cuisine is quite delicious."

"Is there any cheese?" Pops asked.

Jack got his grandfather cheese, then went down the hall to their room. "Babe? Everything okay?" he asked.

"Just fine," she said. She didn't spare him a glance, just returned to the table.

Shit. Fine equaled doom.

"How do you like life up north so far?" his father asked Hadley. "Hope you're not too home-sick, sweetheart."

"Oh, no, of course not," she said. "I just love y'all."

"Well, now. The feeling's mutual," he said. *Good old Dad.*

It was, in a lot of respects, a typical family dinner for the Hollands. Lots of talking, lots of wine, lots of laughter, a fair amount of bickering. They ate the meal, which, though bland and sticky, wasn't horrible. If Faith had made it, the teasing would've been merciless, but as Hadley was new to the family, no one said a word that wasn't complimentary.

Ned and Abby were ordered to clear the table, and Mrs. J. cut the grape pie she'd brought while she and Goggy argued over crust-making techniques. Three minutes later, when dessert had been decimated, Goggy announced that it was time for everyone to leave, and the family trooped out with thanks and kisses and hugs.

"See you tomorrow, guys," Jack said, closing the door. He smiled and turned to his wife. "So that went well."

Hadley jammed her fists onto her hips. "Are you crazy? Your family hates me! Your sisters are so mean! And your grandmother is so judgmental!"

Jack's mouth fell open. "Sweetheart, what are you talking about? No one hates you."

"That Faith, showing off like that! Spouting about how designers are better than decorators! And Prudence didn't even take off her work boots!"

"Was she supposed to?"

"What about your father, just sitting there, not saying boo! He hates me!"

"Calm down, sweetheart. Dad never talks much. He loves you."

"Mrs. Johnson is horrible!"

Okay, that was going too far. Mrs. J. was tireless and fierce and pretty damn wonderful. "Be careful," he said. "She's my first love."

"They hate me because I'm Southern."

"That's ridiculous," he said. "We won the Civil War. We're totally over it." She was not amused, shooting him a glare. "Come on, baby. Don't be

301

upset. Everyone wants you to feel welcome here. They were just trying to get to know you."

He drew her a bath. Lit candles. Poured her wine. Apologized if his family came on a little strong (which they did, but that was just how it was . . . which he'd assumed Hadley knew by now).

She took a sip of wine and sighed. "You know what? I'm just gonna lose myself in my work—that's what I'll do."

"That's great. Do you have a client?"

"Yes, silly. His name is Jack Holland. Now get in this here tub."

And just like that, her mood was better.

Hadley went crazy with the redecorating.

Jack's house was at the very top of the ridge, a good quarter mile up from the Old House, where his grandparents lived, and the New House, where Dad, Honor and Mrs. J. all resided. He'd been given the land when he turned thirty; Dad had similar parcels for the girls, but so far, none had done anything with them. Pru and Carl lived in a nice neighborhood on the other side of Manningsport, Honor lived with Dad and Faith was a Californian for the time being, though Jack suspected she'd move home soon enough.

But Jack had built his house two years before, after living in an Airstream trailer for six months to get the feel of the land, where the light hit at various times a day. He studied house plans from Frank Lloyd Wright and the Arts and Crafts era, then hired an architect to draw up plans.

The end result was an airy and open floor plan based around a huge stone fireplace with an exposed chimney. The floors were wide-planked cherry, the kitchen counters black soapstone. Two bedrooms upstairs for future kids, one down, as well as a home office. The basement contained a pool table and wine cellar. The house wasn't huge, but it had breathing space.

Most importantly, it blended seamlessly into the landscape, the most important thing to a Holland. The outside of the house was planked with cedar, with huge windows that overlooked the vineyard and Crooked Lake. On three sides, it was surrounded by a forest of maples, oaks and pine, so it was almost camouflaged. Faith had drawn him up a landscaping plan for a Christmas present, and he'd followed it.

The result was that Jack's house looked as if it had been there forever. It was modern yet traditional, too, and everyone who saw it was rather dazzled.

Except his wife. Oh, she'd cooed over it when she'd first seen it, but now that she'd lived there for a month, it was suddenly in sore need of "Southern charm." Which would've been fine if it had been the type of charm Jack had seen at her own childhood home, carefully chosen antiques and family photos, clean lines and high-end furnishings.

But no.

Throw pillows seemed to be her trademark. The couch was covered in them; it looked nice, but it was impossible to sit without moving at least three. Their bed had the two pillows they used for their heads, four additional pillows covered in something called *shams* and a dozen more pillows in various sizes and colors. There was a painstaking order to these pillows, one Jack could never quite figure out. Lazarus liked to hide in the sea of shapes and then leap out, scattering them, which irritated Hadley to no end.

She rearranged the furniture. Ordered a new couch, one that cost eight thousand dollars, without asking his opinion. Bought a rather hideous fan shaped like a peacock for the fireplace, which Jack had stacked with white birch logs until it got colder. She bought velvet curtains that blocked out the light. Little signs appeared everywhere, ordering him to "Live Fully, Love Deeply, Laugh Often" and reminding him that "We Are So Blessed!" In the kitchen, there now hung a chalkboard in the shape of a dancing reindeer that said "Only __ Days Till Christmas!" The sign that bothered him the most hung in the foyer—"Life isn't about waiting for the storms to pass. It's about learning to dance in the rain." He always felt as though he should apologize for that one.

After all, his people were Dutch Yankee Lutheran farmers. There would be no dancing in the rain.

But it was Hadley's house, too, now, so he moved aside the pillows and hoped her efforts would make her happy.

Then she asked if she could do some work for Blue Heron. When Jack said he'd ask Honor, Hadley sulked and said Honor was bossy and mean. And yeah, Honor *was* bossy, but not in a rude way. Just in the way that she had to be, because she was indeed the boss of the business end, and a damn good one. She certainly wasn't mean. She was maybe misunderstood, but when Jack tried to explain that, Hadley claimed he was taking his sister's side.

Honor said she'd love to have some help— proof that she wasn't at all mean. But by the end of Hadley's first day, Honor asked Jack to come by her office. She closed the door after him.

"Hadley's not going to work out," she said, getting straight to it.

"Shit," he said. "You sure? It's only been a day."

"I thought she could start out by picking merchandise for the gift shop, maybe rearranging some of the displays out there."

"That'd be great. She loves buying stuff. And rearranging." Just last night he'd caught his shin on the coffee table, which Hadley had moved for the fourth time.

"Well, she had other ideas." His sister fiddled with a pen.

"Like what?"

"She wanted to redo our logo and every label on every bottle we sell. Redesign the tasting room by getting rid of the bar and putting in Italian marble and tile flooring."

Italian marble? The tasting room (which had been voted one of the ten most beautiful tasting rooms in America by *Wine Spectator*) featured a long, curving bar made by Samuel Hastings, using wood from a tree that had fallen in a winter storm ten years back. Blue slate floors. Two stone fireplaces, post and beam construction, beautiful old Oriental rugs.

"She also thinks we should sheetrock the Cask Room, because the stone walls are—" Honor made quote marks with her fingers " '—down-right spine-chilling.' "

And the Cask Room was one of the best parts of the vineyard, an old stone cellar where the wine was aged in wooden barrels. Tourists loved it.

"I'd told her we were all set on those things, and she . . ." Honor paused. "Well, I think her feelings were hurt. You might want to bring her flowers."

Flowers didn't help. Hadley was seething, stating over and over that Honor hated her and didn't believe in her.

"Honey," he said, "you have to understand that

we all love Blue Heron. We don't want it to change. New ideas are great, but—"

"But you don't want new ideas!"

"Not an overhaul of everything, no. The tasting room is only a few years old."

"Well, it's ugly."

"Not according to our visitors," he said, his voice a little tight. He paused. "Honor knows what she's doing, babe. Maybe telling her to change everything on your first day wasn't the best idea."

"Fine. Take her side. You always do."

Her feelings of being persecuted baffled him. After all, his father called her sweetheart and always kissed her cheek and hugged her, Goggy beamed when Hadley made Jack show up at church each week, Pops told her she was the prettiest thing Manningsport had ever seen. Faith sent her emails and girlie gifts from San Francisco. Mrs. Johnson gave her the recipe for lemon pound cake, Jack's favorite dessert, which al-Qaeda wouldn't have been able to pry out of her. Pru invited them over and admired how good Hadley smelled, and Honor . . . well, okay, Honor didn't like her. But she never said anything that could even remotely be construed as impolite, not to Hadley, not to Jack.

Granted, the first year of marriage was the hardest, everyone said. And it wasn't all bad, not at all. There were moments when Jack couldn't believe he had a wife who literally skipped into his arms when he came home (sometimes) and who constantly told him how smart and handsome and wonderful he was. Who put her head on his shoulder and told him that all her dreams had come true the day she met him.

But Jack was learning that for every nice thing she said or did, he was expected to reciprocate in triplicate, and Hadley was definitely keeping score. One night, they went out to dinner to a really nice place in Corning, but Hadley barely spoke to him, becoming more and more sullen as the night went on, refusing to answer when he asked what was wrong. Finally, and only after they'd gotten home, she told him. He hadn't noticed that she was wearing a new black dress. When he pointed out that she owned quite a few black dresses (eight, to be precise, he counted later), she slammed the door so hard a picture fell off the wall.

She had an endless need to be complimented. If he said she looked pretty, she'd pout until he said *beautiful* or *gorgeous* or *sexy*. She'd ask if he noticed anything different about her, and God help him if he didn't guess it was a new perfume or a different shade of pink on her toenails, because she'd accuse him of taking her for granted. She loved gifts, and though he often brought flowers home, she'd make a pretend game of patting down his pockets to see if had anything else for her. The thing was, she meant it. Whatever he did get her, it wasn't enough, the one exception being her engagement ring. Even so, she was already hinting for an anniversary ring—a sapphire-and-diamond band that, according to the website she showed him, cost twenty-four thousand dollars.

Then again, there were days when she'd tell him a story full of dry humor and her musical laugh, and her eyes would dance, and he'd feel this almost painful pressure in his chest, because this was the way he'd always thought it could be. Sometimes she'd call him to say she just wanted to hear his voice. She might bake cookies and bring them down, still warm from the oven, for him and Dad and Pops.

And, certainly not least of all, their sex life was fantastic. Frequent, boisterous, interesting . . . planned . . . mapped out, really. Choreographed. By her. Hey, he wasn't complaining. It was just always a bit of a production.

In four months of marriage, not once had Jack just been able to go to bed at the end of the day and make love to his wife. Nor was he able to come home from work and kiss her and just take her to bed (or to the living room rug, or the couch and its many throw pillows). Morning sex was frowned upon. Lunchtime sex was okay, so long as he let her know a day or two in advance so she could get ready. Jack sort of thought that was his job, getting her ready, but . . . well. It was okay. Frequent and boisterous, those were good things.

Still, it might've been nice not to have to spend all that time lighting candles. Or scattering rose petals (he'd done that on their honeymoon, and now it was kind of a thing). Or playing certain music. Sometimes there was a theme to the night, and Jack would be asked to guess what that theme was.

These productions required a special wardrobe for Hadley, as well—new lingerie and red-soled high-heeled shoes, or skimpy little nighties, when all Jack really wanted was nudity.

While it was great that she put so much effort into that aspect of their marriage, it was a bit . . . much all the, uh, staging. And, yes, all the money.

"Is this a mistake?" he asked one night after he opened the AmEx bill. "Two grand at Bergdorf?"

"Nope. Not a mistake, sweetheart." She smiled at him, dimple flashing.

"When were you at Bergdorf Goodman?"

"I ordered something online," she said, not looking up from the game she was playing on the computer.

"And what did you order?"

"A pair of shoes."

"What else?"

"Nothing."

"One pair of shoes cost two grand? My God! Are you kidding me?"

"Don't raise your voice to me, Jack Holland!" she said. "And don't take the Lord's name in vain.

Yes. Two grand on one pair of shoes." She gave him a pretty little pout. "Don't you think I deserve nice things, baby?"

This is where fights began, Jack was well aware by now. Two *hundred* would've been a lot in Jack's book, unless they were those really good steel-toed leather work boots Pru had given him for Christmas last year. But two thousand? "Of course you deserve nice things. But you have dozens of pairs of shoes already. Two grand—"

"They're Christian Louboutin, babe! You sure didn't complain the other night." Another smile. Yes, the other night she'd done a very hot little striptease, leaving on only her trashy shoes. Even so, they weren't worth two grand.

He took a deep breath. "Honey. That's way, way too much."

"We have the money."

Jack folded his arms. "We don't have two grand to spend on one pair of highly impractical shoes, Hadley."

Well, that opened the door. She stomped her foot. Jack clearly didn't appreciate how hard she worked to make their home beautiful. How much effort she put into being attractive, because "that's what Southern women do, Jack, not like your sister, who looks like a man!"

Jack ran a hand through his hair. "Honey, you can't drive us into debt because you liked a pair of shoes."

"One pair, Jack! I think I deserve one pair of Christian Louboutin shoes!"

Except, he learned, she had four pairs.

They sat down that night and worked up a budget on how much discretionary spending money they had. She sulked.

It was obvious she'd had the wrong impression of just how much Jack earned. Yes, Blue Heron supported the family. Yes, Jack was a part owner and received a salary in addition to vineyard profits (most of which went back into the land or a savings account—farmers never took income for granted). She gave him the silent treatment for the rest of the night.

But the next morning, she apologized, said she'd been childish and kissed him sweetly. She baked a pie using one of Mrs. Johnson's recipes, and, after dinner, she called Faith and had a long giggle-filled chat.

They flew down to Savannah for a Southern Thanksgiving. Hadley was overjoyed to be with her family again, and they were happy to see both of them. He played Southern football (which was an awful lot like Northern football) with her dad and two brothers-in-law, both very good guys, as well as the kids and Frankie.

"You guys planning on having kids?" asked Beau, who was married to Rachel. The game had pretty much finished, and Jack was tossing a nephew in the air.

"Absolutely," Jack said.

"Might want to think that through," Frankie said, flopping on the grass. "Kids make things permanent. Right, ankle-biter?" she added, grabbing her niece around the waist.

"Now, Frankie," Hadley's dad said, shooting Jack an apologetic look. "Come on, kids—I smell ham and turkey. Your grandmother's worked too hard for us to be late to her table. Y'all get in there and wash up, now!"

Everyone went in, except Frankie and Jack.

"Sorry if I put my foot in it," she said. "You just seem like a real nice guy is all."

"What do you mean?" he asked.

"I mean, Jack," she said with a smack to his head, just like one of his own sisters, "Hadley's a handful. Gives us Southern chicks a bad name. Just be sure you know what you got there." She started in, then glanced over her shoulder. "By the way, I'm coming out to the family after dinner. Hope I can count on you not freaking. You knew I liked girls, right?"

"What? Oh, yeah." He was still digesting her words about Hadley.

Frankie's announcement wasn't exactly ground-breaking. Ruthie and Rachel stated that they'd known since Frankie was eleven, and Bill and Barb admitted that they had suspected but had hoped to be wrong, because it could carry some "difficult consequences."

"What are y'all talking about?" Frankie said fondly. "I'm a Yankee now. There's lots of us lesbians up north. We're all the rage." This got a laugh, and Bill came over and kissed his youngest and told her they all loved her no matter what.

"You'll look after her, won't you, Jack?" Barbara asked.

"Of course," Jack said. He liked Frankie a lot. "Not that she needs looking after, but we're just an hour away from Cornell."

"Jack and I are about ready to start a family," Hadley announced.

He looked at her in surprise. Since that first conversation after the honeymoon, the subject of kids hadn't been brought up. But the conversation turned to babies and pregnancy, and when Jack looked across the table at Frankie, she said nothing. Just cocked an eyebrow, and it dawned on Jack that maybe his wife was, in some weird way, trying to steal Frankie's thunder and turn the attention to her.

Hadley seemed a little blue at Christmastime, so Jack surprised her with a trip to Manhattan, earning a lot of happy shrieks and kisses (and the wrath of his grandmother and Mrs. J.). They saw a show, stayed in a nice hotel (though not in a suite this time), went skating at Rockefeller Center, Hadley clutching his arm and giggling as she wobbled and skidded.

Though she paused meaningfully in front of Tiffany's, Jack didn't take the bait; he'd already bought her some very nice earrings in Manningsport and arranged this trip. He wasn't about to break the budget just for a turquoise box. She didn't seem to mind, and took his hand as they walked down Fifth Avenue.

When they got back home, she seemed happier. The bumps in the road seemed to have smoothed out.

Then, in February, Jack stopped by the post office, which was one of Hadley's jobs. She had clearly defined ideas about what husbands should do and what wives should. It was a husband's job to empty the trash and clean up Lazarus's victims (and Princess Anastasia's hairballs); it was a wife's job to make the bed and pick movies. Husband shoveled the snow and scraped cars; wife went to the post office.

But Honor was expecting a package, and she asked him to swing by. He checked his own post office box while he was there.

Inside were three envelopes—one from Master-Card, two from Visa—addressed to John N. Holland IV.

Which was strange, since he only had one credit card, an American Express. He only used it when he had to, preferring to use cash whenever possible.

With a cold feeling in his stomach, he went out

to his truck and opened the envelopes, his breath frosting the air.

One bill was for $6,008.01, one for $8,772.15, and one for $4,533.98.

Almost twenty thousand dollars. At 24 percent interest, no less.

The charges went back as far as October . . . well after he and Hadley had the talk about the red-soled shoes that cost so much. They were from stores that Jack knew only by reputation. Tiffany's . . . he remembered how good a sport she was when they didn't stop in at Christmastime. Guess she could afford to be, since she'd already bought herself a little something. Henri Bendel. Neiman Marcus. Chanel, Coach, Prada, Armani.

Almost twenty thousand dollars on clothes, shoes and handbags.

Jack found that he was sweating.

After the flights back and forth from Savannah . . . after spending five months' salary on a Tiffany engagement ring and a diamond wedding band . . . after paying for the rehearsal dinner for seventy-five people . . . after the lavish honeymoon, the new couch, after Christmas in New York City, after all the crap she'd bought for the house . . . they simply couldn't afford this. Jack had never wanted for money, but this . . . this was twenty grand he just didn't have sitting around.

Worse than the money, though, was the lying.

She'd been *lying* to him for months.

Jaw locked hard, Jack drove home. She was there, sitting at the kitchen table, staring into space, idly stirring sugar into her tea. "Oh, hey, baby!" she said when he came in. "What are you doing home so early?"

He put the bills on the table in front of her. "Explain," he said tightly.

She was calm; he had to give her that. Stroked Princess Anastasia and said that, yes, she may have "overindulged," she shouldn't have kept that from him, but shopping had always been a hobby. She liked nice things; he knew that. She believed in buying quality. No need for him to have kittens.

He made her show him her purchases, and she sighed and complied. Some were right there in their closet, some in her jewelry box, some hidden in the attic.

Shoes galore. Seven new black dresses, each of which looked identical to the last. Four leather jackets. Five winter coats. More makeup than she could use in years. Special soaps and moisturizers and cleansers and creams. Belts and scarves and gloves. Perfume. An eight-ounce bottle of bubble bath that cost $179. "I thought Faith might like that for Christmas," she said unconvincingly.

"It's February."

"So? I like to shop all through the year."

"Hadley, we can't afford this!" he barked, and she folded her arms and stared at him patiently.

"Jack, we can. I know you're on the stingy side, but that wasn't how I was raised. Where I come from, a man takes care of his woman."

"By take care of you mean go into debt?"

"Fine. I did a little retail therapy."

"Maybe you should try the regular kind."

"That was uncalled for," she said. "You have no idea how lonely it is for me! You're at work all day long!"

"People who work for a living generally work all day long, Hadley."

"Well, you misled me, then! I thought you were—" She stopped abruptly.

"You thought I was what?"

Rich. That's what she'd thought. And he'd always thought he was—he paid his bills, owned a home, bought a new truck every 125,000 miles, didn't have debt (until now) and put a modest amount in the stock market and savings.

But he wasn't rich. Not by Hadley's standards, anyway.

She looked straight ahead. "I thought you'd value our time together more."

"How do I *not* value our time together, Hadley?"

"You always put your family first. You spend more time with your father than you do with me."

"I *work* with my father."

"That Mrs. Johnson growls at me any time I even look at her, and your sisters are horrible!"

"My sisters aren't horrible, Mrs. Johnson growls

at everyone and they're not the reason you spent twenty thousand dollars on clothes."

"You're overreacting. I'm sorry you don't think I'm worth it, after all I do to try to make you happy." There was a challenge in her eyes.

"This is practically hoarding, and it's money we don't have." He picked up a pair of long white gloves, the kind a woman would wear to . . . well, hell, he didn't know. "You forged my signature on three credit card applications, which is illegal, for one, and for two, means your own credit must be shot to hell. You're hiding things around the house because you know you shouldn't be spending so much. This is not how a responsible adult behaves."

She grew stony and wounded. She said she'd pay off the credit cards by taking on a few clients if money was all he cared about. Apparently, she'd misread him.

Jack loved his wife. He did.

Or you did before you got to know her so well, said a voice in his head, sounding a lot like Honor.

No. He did love her. But it was clear that she wasn't as straightforward as he'd thought when they first met. And it was also clear that she thought he was a wealthy vintner and not a guy who had to work for a living. Maybe this wasn't the life she thought she'd signed on for.

"Hadley, if you're not happy here," he began as gently as he could.

She jerked as if he'd hit her. "If I'm not happy, what?" she said, and suddenly her voice was shaking.

"Maybe we rushed into this. If you're not getting what you want—"

"Jack, no! Are you . . . do you want a *divorce?* Oh, my God!" She burst into tears, her hands over her face. "Please, Jack! I'm sorry! I'm so sorry! I'll return everything I can, but please don't leave me, Jack!"

He got up and put his arms around her. "Hadley, honey, it just seems like you expected something different," he said.

"Please give me another chance!" The sobs were tearing out of her.

He hadn't expected that.

He got a washcloth and wiped her face, held her tight, feeling like an absolute prick . . . and wondering how exactly that had happened. Poured her a hefty glass of wine, and another for himself, and assured her he didn't want a divorce.

And he didn't. He just wanted a better marriage.

The next day, Hadley wasn't home when he got back from Blue Heron. She came through the door a half an hour later, her face bright. "Guess who just got a job!" she said.

She was sorry about the credit cards. She would pay them off. He was right, she'd gone a little crazy, but now she had a job and all would be put right as rain.

Her job was clerking in the gift shop of Dandelion Hill, another winery on Keuka, run by Oliver Linton, a transplanted Wall Streeter who'd retired at the age of forty and bought a vineyard. Nice guy, as Jack knew from the wine association meetings and various events all the vineyards participated in. Oliver even took them out for dinner, and they reciprocated by inviting him up to the house one night, and it seemed that, finally, things were on the right track.

Jack was stunned at the relief he felt. Hadley had a job, a place to go every day, and it seemed like exactly what she needed. She laughed more and had more to say, funny little stories about the people she met or Dandelion Hill's grouchy shop manager. Things became more down to earth, more normal . . . happier.

It was almost liberating, her feet of clay. When they'd first met, she'd been perfect. Now she was real. Yes, yes, she spent too much money and played the victim when she felt defensive. But no one was perfect. She was happier now. She even started talking about kids.

"Jack, I have the best news!" Hadley said one night, bursting into the house, and his heart leaped. She was pregnant. It had to be. "Oliver wants me to redecorate! At last!"

Ah. Well, that was nice, too.

"What?" she said.

"I thought you might be pregnant."

321

Something flickered across her face. "Oh. No. Not yet. But it's still good news! Oliver wants me to redo the tasting room!"

Hadley threw herself into the job. Spent huge amounts of time on her laptop, talked about fabric choices and stool styles and glasses, all the stuff that Jack pretty much ignored at Blue Heron, as it fell under Honor's reign.

Oliver took to calling her in the evenings, and she'd apologize to Jack and then skip upstairs to the room she'd made into her office. She took even more care with her appearance, and when he teased her about it, she slapped his arm and said, "Jack! I'm not just a clerk anymore. I'm a decorator, baby. I have to look the part." Finally, she started making female friends, a couple of women who also worked at Dandelion Hill. Hadley joined their weekly book club, though they never seemed to read anything.

Jack hadn't seen her this happy since the wedding.

The only fly in the ointment was, oddly enough, sex. They just weren't doing it as much these days. "Oh, sugar, I'm sorry. I'm just exhausted," she explained. "And don't ask me why, because when there's news, mister, you'll be the first to hear it. I'm not one of those women who tells the whole wide world ten minutes after she conceives."

A baby. No, it was smart to be sure first, but Jack felt something huge move in his chest.

"Stop looking at me with that goofy face, Jack Holland," she said teasingly. "What did I just tell you?" Her phone rang, even though it was after nine. "Oh, dang it, it's Oliver, I swear that man cannot find his car keys without a flashlight and a blue heeler hound dog. Hello? Oliver, honest to goodness! I have no idea!" She smiled at Jack and left the room, still gabbing.

About two weeks after she hinted about the pregnancy, Jack decided to leave work early. He and Dad had been checking the tanks and doing some projections for the spring planting with Pru, but it was a quiet time of year. He stopped at the horrifyingly expensive gourmet market that had just opened, bought some filet mignon and cheese and asparagus. Allison and Charles Whitaker were there, too; they lived near Pru and came to Blue Heron all the time. "Making dinner for your bride?" Allison asked.

"I sure am," Jack said.

"Why don't you ever make me dinner?" she asked Charles, giving him a sharp elbow in the side. Her husband gave Jack a dark look and muttered something, and Jack left them, bickering in front of the beautiful, organic, locally-grown-and-prayed-over-by-the-monks-of-Saint-Benedict's vegetables.

Next, he swung by Laura Boothby's shop, flirted with her for a few minutes and got a bouquet of red roses. "Young love." Laura sighed. "You sicken me, Jack. But keep coming in, hon. You're good for business."

Last stop was the package store in town. Granted, he had a vast collection, but Hadley liked French champagne. Tonight, he wanted her to have something special, because since the big credit card debacle, she hadn't bought one thing that wasn't strictly necessary, and Jack was feeling a little miserly.

Also, they might have something to celebrate, in which case he'd put the champagne in the wine cellar and open it on their child's birthday. If she wasn't preggers, then hell. This would be her little treat. She was mighty cute when she was tipsy. (And mighty horny, too, so maybe Jack would finally get a little, because it had been a couple of weeks. An eternity, in other words.)

Pru was leaning against his truck when he came out. "Hey, Useless, our wine isn't good enough for you anymore?" she said, grabbing the bag from his hand and looking inside. "Ooh! Moët & Chandon White Star! Are you in trouble?"

"No, Prudence. I'm the best husband in the world."

"Gack. You're still a jerk in my eyes, little brother."

"I appreciate that. Give me back my champagne."

"Fine. I was going to invite you and Scarlett O'Hara to dinner, but I see you have other plans."

She smacked him on the shoulder and tromped off.

It was snowing pretty hard, and Jack felt about as happy as a man could get. Whistled on his way home. Nothing like being snowed in with a beautiful woman. He drove up the ridge to his house, the snow pleasantly muffling the sound of his tires, and turned off the engine.

There was Hadley's yellow VW Bug, covered with snow . . . Oliver must've sent her home early. And there was another car, too. One of her friends', maybe? He'd been telling her to invite the book club to their house so he could meet the famous nonreaders. Whoever it was, she'd have to leave soon, the way it was coming down now.

He gathered the bags and flowers in his arms and got out of his truck. For some reason, Jack stopped and brushed off the back of the strange car. It was a Mercedes.

Oliver had a Mercedes, if Jack remembered correctly. They must be talking about the redecoration.

Not that Dandelion Hill really needed a redesign. It was pretty spectacular . . . and newly renovated. Very sleek and modern and sophisticated.

Not something he could really see Hadley improving with throw pillows.

Funny how Jack had never thought of that before.

His stomach felt cold all of a sudden. But no, no, that was stupid. Oliver was her boss, and twelve or fifteen years older than she was. He was a good guy, and Hadley was happily married. Things had never been better. Pretty sexist of Jack, imagining something illicit going on. *Nah.* They'd be sitting at the kitchen table with fabric swatches or whatever.

He heard a little croak. It was Lazarus, waiting by the door.

His cat hated snow. He'd go out in rain and lightning and wind. Didn't mind the bitter cold or the muggy heat, but he hated snow. He held up his crooked front leg, shook his paw and made his little squeak of distress once more.

"Hey, pal," Jack said, setting down the grocery bags. The cat leaped into his arms. First time that had happened. He rubbed the cat's paws, wincing as he felt how cold and hard the little pads were. Lazarus had been outside for quite a while, it seemed. And the thing was, the cat would head-butt the door, scratch the glass and send up ungodly screeches if he didn't get let in the instant he wanted to.

And if Laz had given up, then he'd been at it awhile.

Jack opened the door and let the cat in, then picked up the groceries and flowers and followed.

The house was quiet.

Maybe they weren't there. Maybe they'd gone

down to Blue Heron to . . . to . . . look at the tasting room or something. Maybe Oliver had wanted to talk to Honor about some business.

It didn't explain why he felt sick.

He went into the kitchen. There was Hadley's black wool coat, lying on the floor.

And her red-soled shoes that cost so goddamn much, carelessly kicked off.

His chest felt like it was in a vise. A cold, metal vice.

His mind was oddly empty as he walked down the hall that led to the study, the half bath, the laundry room.

He could hear them now. There was moaning. Sighing. There was Hadley's voice. "Oh, my God, yes, yes, oh, God, yes!"

So much for taking the Lord's name in vain.

The door to their bedroom was open a crack. Jack pushed it open more, and yep. Hadley stood in the middle of their bedroom in a black push-up bra and thong. A buck-naked Oliver, complete with paunch, knelt in front of her, his fingers gripping her ass, making out with her belly button.

What was the protocol for this? Should he announce his presence? Yell? Leave? Beat the shit out of Oliver?

Hadley ran her fingers through Oliver's sparse hair. "Oh, Ollie! Oh, my!"

And then, sort of mercifully, Oliver opened his eyes and saw Jack there and reacted by hurling himself away from Hadley. He crawled around to the side of the bed—Jack's side—and grappled for his pants.

"Jack!" Hadley gasped, grabbing one of the throw pillows and holding it in front of her. "You're home early!"

He did drag Oliver outside and toss him in the snow. Naked. Threw his clothes after him. Hadley, wrapped in her bathrobe (her red silk bathrobe, one of her credit card splurges), followed Jack, hysterical, sobbing, accusing, excusing and begging all in the same breath. Then Jack went back in the bedroom and grabbed all the sheets and covers and asinine throw pillows and carried them outside, as well.

Oliver was gone by then. Hadley's hysteria didn't seem to be fading, though she'd had the presence of mind to clutch Princess Anastasia to her chest. The cat was writhing to get free, and Jack distantly hoped that the cat would get away and be devoured by a coyote, but then again, hey, it was an innocent animal, sort of. Mean as a snake, but he didn't really want it to die, of course not, but if it did, he wouldn't be shedding any tears.

Jack went into the cellar and found some lighter fluid and came back up. Hang on. He needed kindling. He went into the kitchen, ripped the "Happily Ever After Starts Here" sign off the wall. Grabbed "Keep Calm and Have Southern Charm," as well. And who could forget "Life isn't about waiting for the storms to pass. It's about learning to dance in the rain"? He tossed them on the sheets and pillows, then doused the whole mess, the whole unfaithful, cheating, disgusting mess, and lit it on fire, the heat making his face tighten.

"Jack?" Hadley said, her voice small.

"Get out," he said.

"You can't deny that you've been—"

"Get out."

"I know you want me to apolo—"

He turned to her, and she must've seen something in his face, because she shrank back and scurried into the house.

A few minutes later, Hadley dragged two suitcases and Princess Anastasia out to her car. The nasty cat scratched her hand, and Hadley jerked back, always surprised that the spoiled creature hated her. She turned to Jack, clutching her wounded hand like it had just been partially amputated.

"Jack, if you'd just—"

"Shut up, Hadley."

Her mouth dropped open. "There's no call to be rude."

"You've got to be kidding me. Get the hell out of here."

She finally did.

He watched her drive all the way down the road that led to Lake Shore, and, long after her little car disappeared up the road (toward Dandelion Hill, he couldn't help noticing), he stood in the falling snow, empty and stunned and furious all at once, the smell of lighter fluid thick in his throat.

Two days later, Hadley came up to talk. And here was where it got interesting.

Seemed as though maybe Oliver didn't want more than a little afternoon delight. Choosing her words very carefully, Hadley told Jack that she'd "been tempted" but had been just about to stop Oliver because she would "never risk their marriage" or "break a commandment."

"We're done, Hadley," he said.

She sat there for a minute, and her eyes filled with tears. Self-pity more than grief, he was sure. "Are you going to tell anyone why?" she whispered.

"I don't know." He hadn't yet. Not even his father, though Dad was aware that something was off. And hell. In a small town like this, there were no secrets. He wouldn't have to tell.

She moved in with Oliver. The rumor mill said he hadn't particularly wanted a live-in girlfriend, but she was there nonetheless.

A few weeks later, Bill Boudreau sent him a note saying he was very sorry to hear things weren't working out, and Jack remembered that conversation, that subtle warning Bill—and Frankie—had given him.

He'd always thought he was a pretty smart guy. An advanced degree in chemistry from an Ivy League school, right? But it seemed he was pretty fucking stupid just the same.

Hadley asked for ten grand in exchange for an uncontested divorce, and Jack paid it. One lump sum and nothing else. She made noise about laying claim to the house and her "investment" in it, but apparently her father talked her out of it. Throughout it all, she insisted that she hadn't been unfaithful, despite what Jack had seen, and his discovery that there was no book club . . . all those nights out when he'd been so happy his wife was making friends had been spent with Oliver.

New York state law said they had to be separated for six months before their divorce could be finalized, so Jack sat back and waited. Worked. Went home. Repeat.

One thing Hadley hadn't foreseen—cheating on Jack made her a pariah. The one time she and Oliver went into O'Rourke's, Colleen, who'd practically grown up in the Holland house, told them to get lost. When Hadley sputtered and gasped, Connor opened the door and told them they had three seconds to leave before he would ask Levi Cooper (also present) to escort them out. This was gleefully reported to Jack by

Prudence, who only belatedly heard him ask her not to tell him about it.

He couldn't avoid the gossip. Gerard Chartier, a firefighter-paramedic who saw Jack often on ambulance runs, told him that Oliver and Hadley were seen arguing at the antiques store. Honor said she'd run into Hadley, and she'd seemed absolutely manic, bouncing around the grocery store like a bee trying to get out of a car. At the Crooked Lake Spring Fling Wine Tasting, Oliver showed up to represent Dandelion Hill, but Hadley was nowhere in sight.

And then, three months after Hadley had left, on a night when the owl family had decided to serenade Jack as he sat on the deck with Lazarus, his phone rang.

It was Hadley, her voice a stunned whisper. "Jack, I don't know who else to call. I can't . . . I can't wake Oliver up. I'm not sure he's breathing."

He told her to call 911 and said he'd be right over.

It was three o'clock in the morning.

But Hadley didn't have anyone else. Frankie was an hour away at least.

So Jack went to Dandelion Hill and drove Hadley to the hospital, following the ambulance, then waiting in the relentless lights of the E.R. with his not-quite ex-wife. Got her a bottle of water from the vending machine, and when her cold hand slipped into his, he let it stay.

And when the doctor came out and said they'd done all they could, but unfortunately the patient didn't make it, he put his arms around Hadley and held her as she shook.

Oliver's parents came to town, heartbroken and furious at finding a gold digger living in their son's house; they kicked her out. She called him once more, her voice subdued and small, saying she didn't have any money (the ten grand must've slipped through her fingers like fog). Her father was furious with her, she couldn't ask her sisters for anything and all she was asking was if she could stay with him until after Oliver's funeral.

He said no. But he paid for her room and meals at the Black Swan B&B.

She came up to the house a few hours after the funeral to say goodbye and tell him she'd pay him back for the stay at the inn. Her face was white, her eyes too big and utterly terrified.

He almost wanted to take her in his arms and tell her it would be all right, that she could stay with him for a while.

Almost. It was disturbingly hard not to say the words.

Chapter Sixteen

"So how was the wedding, Officer Em?" Tamara asked as Emmaline walked into the basement of Trinity Lutheran Church.

"We're not going to talk about it," Emmaline said, smiling firmly at her at-risk teenagers.

"Sucked that bad, did it?" Dalton said.

"Pretty much, yes. Sarge, look! It's the kids! The kids are here to see you!" She unclipped her wagging, crooning pup and watched with a smile as the dog bolted for the teenagers, Squeaky Chicken firmly in his mouth.

One of the reasons Emmaline had gotten Sarge was for the kids. Also, because she was single and liked having someone to come home to, and also because she was a cop and could make little Sarge here into a police dog (or not, because he definitely lacked the *I'm a big scary dog* gene).

But for this purpose—for making four tough, bored, cynical potential dropouts tolerate her— her dog was perfect.

"So Cory, you got suspended again, huh?" she said, setting down the box of cookies she'd picked up at Lorelei's earlier that day.

"He told Dr. Didier that—"

"I already heard, Tamara. Cory? You were

already in trouble with Mrs. Greenley. Did you feel things getting to that snapping point?"

Cory shrugged. He'd been suspended today after suggesting that the principal of Mannings-port High was, in fact, a man. An ugly man at that, using some colorful words to describe just how ugly and just what evidence indicated Dr. Didier's masculinity, then threw Dr. Didier's paperweight in the trash—but he threw it hard. Like a baseball. The result was suspension.

"I'm guessing you did," Em said. "And we all have those moments, Cory, when we'd like to break something. But that's not acceptable."

"Unless you're an idiot," Tamara said, peeling blue nail polish from her thumb and eyeing the cookies.

"Bite me," Cory said. He took another cookie, put it in his teeth and let Sarge eat half of it, then chewed and swallowed the other half. Boys were so gross. Then again, Em had done the same thing the other night, so she was in no position to judge.

"So, Cory, what about your suspension?" she asked, trying to refocus them.

"Dude, you're gonna get expelled," said Dalton.

"You're the one who stole a car," Cory said.

"Yeah, but you're smart," said the other boy. "You could get a scholarship and everything. All I got is a life of crime to look forward to. Right, Officer Em?"

"Wrong, Dalton. Cory, he does have a point.

You could. But if you don't find a way to cope with your temper, it'll haunt you all your life."

"I know," Cory muttered. "But it's like I can't help it." He paused. "I was gonna throw that thing through the window, and at the last minute, I threw it in the trash instead."

Ah, progress. "Okay, so that was a step in the right direction. You made a less destructive choice."

"Maybe you'll get a sticker," Kelsey Byrd said.

Em kept talking. "Even little things like taking a deep, slow breath can help. Eat right, get enough fresh air. Those are clichés because they're true. Maybe you could join the boxing club."

"Or, like, listen to music?" Tamara suggested. "When my mom had my brother and he cried all the time, she'd go into the cellar and play Nine Inch Nails really loud and, like, dance. Badly, I might add. But she always felt better."

Cory gave a little smile.

"Four months till graduation, kids," Emmaline added. "You're almost there."

"Ooh, graduation," said Kelsey. "Like that makes a difference." She folded her arms and rested them on her pregnant belly. She had good reason to be bitter, Em guessed. Single motherhood was hard enough; single teenage motherhood was harder.

"Well, the thing is, it does make a difference," Emmaline said. "If you don't graduate or get a

GED, chances are you'll have to work longer and earn less. And by longer, I mean longer hours and more years. You want a nice car? A decent place to live? A job you like? It's going to be a lot easier if you stay in school."

"I wanna be on TV," Tamara said. "Like Ellen." She took a cookie and bit into it.

"Ellen graduated from high school, dumbass," Cory said. "How many days have you missed?"

"None of your business."

"It's my turn to hold Sarge," Kelsey said. "Come here, puppy." Her face softened beneath the harsh makeup.

Out of these four kids, Em was pretty sure that Tamara, Cory and Dalton had a decent chance. Cory's parents were doing all the right things for his temper issues, and they adored the kid. Tamara, too, had nice parents and average intelligence; she was just a late bloomer who liked getting attention by acting up. She'd probably go to a community college and figure out what she wanted to do a year or three down the road. Dalton was from a long line of petty criminals; both parents had served time. The kid had a good heart and charm, though, and was as cute as they came. If he could find something that interested him, he might do okay . . . She could see him in sales or advertising. Or as a grifter. Same thing, really.

Kelsey, though . . . Kelsey would be hard-pressed to break out. A baby on the way, her father dead, her mother one of Em's frequent calls for DUI and possession. They lived in a decrepit farmhouse on the edge of a field. Graying sheets hung in the windows for curtains, and there was a large hole in the roof. Kelsey was already heavily tattooed, seriously overweight and had those expander earrings and a pierced lip. She main-tained a D average, and that was through the generosity of her teachers.

The odds had never been in her favor.

"Kelsey, what was your week like?" Emmaline asked.

Just then the basement door opened, bringing in a blast of cold air.

"Who's that?" The girl pulled her head back like an offended duck.

It was Jack.

Huh. Emmaline hadn't expected him to show.

"Dude! It's him! The guy who pulled Sam and Garrett and everyone out of lake. Shit! Nice to meet you, man!" Dalton met Jack halfway and shook his hand. "You're, like, a hero or something!"

Jack's expression didn't change, but something went out in his eyes almost immediately at the mention of the accident. He glanced at her. "Sorry I'm late," he said, clearing his throat. "Hi, guys. I'm Jack Holland. Heard you need a chemistry tutor."

This was met with groans and a general exhausted sinking.

"Are you a teacher?" Tamara asked, scanning him up and down.

"Can you make crystal meth?" Dalton asked. "Like that dude on TV?"

"I probably could," Jack said, pulling up a chair next to Emmaline. "But I won't."

"Fair enough," Dalton said. "Just exploring your options, man. And if you need a Jesse for your Walter White, keep me in mind."

"How about a bomb?" Cory asked, sitting up with interest. "Could you make that?"

"Again, yes, I could, and, no, I won't."

"Poison gas cloud?"

"Poison gas, yes. Poison gas cloud? The kind that would float over a city and rain hellfire and brimstone down on people?"

"Yeah, totally!" Dalton said.

"Probably not."

"Well, what *can* you do, then?" Tamara asked.

"Make wine."

The kids rolled their eyes and slid deeper down in the folding metal chairs. Everyone made wine around here. How boring indeed.

"Chemists do a bunch of different things," Jack said. "And they're all really interesting. In organic chemistry, we work with carbon and carbon compounds. We can develop drugs, fertilizers, plastics. Inorganic chemists work with metals, electricity and minerals."

"Please stop him before I stab myself in the eye," Dalton said.

"And then we have analytic chemists, who identify materials and evaluate properties, and physical chemists, who—"

"You're losing them Jack," Emmaline said. "They're literally dying of boredom. Look at them, the poor babies. Dalton? Speak to me! Stay away from the light!"

Jack grinned. "I can also guarantee you an A on any chemistry test you have this year," he said. "And a B+ for physics and biology."

"Dude, we're all flunking out. Except Cory," said Dalton. "You might want to rethink your statement."

"The offer stands," Jack said. He looked down at Emmaline. "As does the offer for dinner," he added.

"Ooh, Officer Em! You got a boyfriend! You got a boyfriend!" Tamara crowed, doing a little dance in her chair, and for some reason, it delighted the kids (except Kelsey), who high-fived each other and made Sarge bark with excitement, then pee on the floor. Em got up to get the paper towels.

"I'm never gonna use chemistry," Kelsey said. "So I don't even care if I flunk."

"You ever hear of oxytocin?" Jack asked.

"My cousin's addicted to that," Tamara said somberly.

"That's oxycontin," Jack said with a smile.

"Oxytocin is an amino acid peptide. A hormone. They call it the love chemical."

"So?" Kelsey gave him a dead-eyed stare.

"So when you're further along in your pregnancy, more oxytocin receptors will be created in your uterine muscles. When the baby's big enough, your oxytocin level will rise, triggering labor, and will help your muscles contract so you can give birth."

"Gross," said Cory.

"No," Jack said. "Miraculous. Without the oxytocin, your muscles wouldn't be strong enough to push that baby out. But because of that chemical, you are. You'll be superhero strong." He smiled right into Kelsey's eyes. "Then, when you see your baby, that rush of oxytocin will help you bond. That's why they call it the love drug. And if you breast-feed, more oxytocin gets released, strengthening that bond. The maternal instinct is the strongest instinct in the world. Chemistry is definitely part of that."

"You should definitely breast-feed, Kelsey," Dalton said, wiggling his eyebrows. "I'll supervise."

"Shut up, Dalton," Em said.

Kelsey had a soft, rapt look on her face.

Em would bet no one had talked about Kelsey's pregnancy using words like *superhero* and *miraculous* and *love* and *bonding*.

"Cool," Kelsey breathed. Jack glanced at Em,

still smiling, and Emmaline felt . . . well, a little like Kelsey looked. Even if she was cleaning up dog pee.

She went to the kitchen, washed up and returned. "Dalton, it's your turn. How's your dad?"

"Still out on probation," Dalton said. "But he's getting itchy." He picked at his shoe. "Maybe you could swing by. I don't want him to do something stupid."

"You bet."

Jack was mostly quiet for the rest of the meeting, but it was different, having him there.

Em knew the kids were only there because they had to be; the alternative was being expelled. But she hoped she wasn't the typical adult, with too much authority and not enough understanding (like Levi), or one of the irritating kind who pretended to be their age and used words like *smexi* and *hater.* She wanted them to be able to count on her. They didn't have to like her, but she hoped they did.

It was eight o'clock before she knew it. "Pack it in, kids," she said.

"Show us your cop trick," Tamara said. The kids had been ridiculously thrilled last time when she'd radioed Dispatch for an audio check. Smartphones had replaced the wonder of walkie-talkies, it seemed.

"Shoot a bull's-eye into that clock," Dalton suggested.

"That would be illegal and get me fired," she said.

"Tase Dalton," Kelsey said.

"I can't. I can't tase anyone, alas," Emmaline said. "So unfair."

"Show us how to take down the bad guy," Cory suggested.

"Yeah!" Tamara said.

"I volunteer," Dalton said. "Don't be rough with me, Officer Em." He grinned like a naughty toddler.

"Inappropriate, young man," she said, borrowing a line from her boss. She glanced at Jack. "Do you mind helping me show the kids how to bring down an assailant?"

"Hell, no," he said.

She felt a warm buzz in her lady parts. She was about to touch him, and heck! She needed to get out more. "I might hurt you," she warned.

"You can try," he said.

"Oh, a challenge! How thrilling for little old me. Okay, kids, watch this. Jack, go ahead and grab me from behind."

"I was hoping you'd say that," he murmured.

"There are children present. Behave."

"I'm the bad guy. I'm not supposed to behave." He smiled.

She narrowed her eyes, then turned her back. Was her heart embarrassing itself by hammering a little too hard and fast? Why, yes, the idiot organ was.

The kids gathered around to watch.

"How should I grab you?" Jack asked.

"Any way you want," she said.

He bear-hugged her, eliciting a bark of joy and some laps of delirious excitement from Sarge, and Em really would've liked to just sit there and think happy thoughts and maybe press back a little bit and had she washed her hair today? Hopefully, it smelled good and not like garlic . . . Oh, where was she? She did a neat step- twist-push, and Jack was down on his knees and then flat on his face, and she had her knee in the small of his back and was hand-cuffing him.

Gosh, it was fun.

"Any questions?" Em asked, grinning at the kids.

"Yeah, Officer Em!" Tamara yelled. "You're such an awesome chick!"

"I turn eighteen in two months, Officer Em," Dalton added. "Just putting that out there."

Her dog loped over, licked Em's face and then bit Jack's ear. "Ow," he said.

"That's it for tonight, kids. I'll see you next week. And make sure you show up when you said you would for tutoring. Jack is not just here to look pretty."

She uncuffed her volunteer, and he got up. "Next time we use handcuffs, it's my turn," he said, his voice low and, uh, scrapey and velvety at the same time. She focused on putting the cuffs back on her belt and not blushing.

"See you, Officer Em," Cory said.

"You bet, honey. Stay out of trouble, okay?"

He muttered assent and left, hitching up his droopy pants. Kelsey followed, staring zombie-like at her phone, and Dalton and Tamara headed out, as well.

"You're really good with kids," Jack said.

"You, too. I'm surprised you and Hadley didn't have any."

"Why do you always bring her up?" He folded his arms and gave her a stony glare.

"Why is she always around? Why don't you tell her to take a flying—"

"This is America. She can live wherever she wants."

"I think you like having a stalker. How's her delicate little ankle?"

"Swollen and blue."

"You going over to carry her to bed? Tuck her in, read her a story?"

Jack didn't answer. Just kept looking at her, then raised an eyebrow with great effect. Em felt her cheeks flush.

"Sorry," she muttered.

Sarge flopped down on the floor and began gnawing on Jack's bootlace.

"Would you have dinner with me if Hadley wasn't around?" Jack asked.

"Would you *want* to have dinner with me if Hadley wasn't around?" she countered. "That's the real question."

"I'm guessing I would," he said, stepping closer. "I had a nice time with you in Malibu. I liked sleeping with you. I'd like to see more of you."

"Shit, Jack, knock it off."

He laughed. "What did I say?"

"Nothing! You're just hard to argue with."

"So don't argue." There it was again, that deep, velvety voice. "Just say yes." Em swallowed.

If she were honest, she'd say, "Here's the thing, Jack, I want a devoted husband and three extremely well-behaved but delightfully irrepressible children. You up for that? Because otherwise, let's skip dinner, since I'd probably fall in love with you in twenty, twenty-five minutes, then spend months resenting you for not feeling the same about me."

He reached out and touched her earlobe.

Good God. She was halfway to Planet Orgasm because he touched her ear. *Get a grip, Neal. You own adult toys for a reason.*

"Come on, Emmaline. Say you will."

Then again, who was she to tell him he didn't want to date her? Of course, he wasn't talking about dating, not really . . . it was just "dinner," which probably would lead to sexy time, and in this case, sexy time probably meant "I'd rather do you than have a flashback and also use you to make my ex-wife jealous" and that, friends, was where stupidity lay, but his finger *really* knew what it was doing, and who knew earlobes were directly connected to other parts of her anatomy?

His phone chimed with a text.

Em stepped back. "Bet I know who that is," she said. Her voice sounded normal, she was almost sure.

"Would you like to have dinner with me sometime, Emmaline?" he said.

"Check your phone."

"As soon as you answer, I will."

"Nah," she said. "I'd rather you take this first." *Da-da-ling.* "Ooh. Another one."

"You're tough," he said.

"Thank you."

He pulled his phone from his pocket, looked at it and put it back. "My sister."

"Which one?"

"Faith."

"Liar."

"Fine," he said. "You're right. It's Hadley."

"I bet she needs something, and you're the only one who can help."

"Well, I need something, too, and you're the only one who can help."

"See, that's just it, Jack. I don't think that's true."

"You have a terrible self-image."

"Wrong. But I can tell the difference between

someone who really likes me and someone who needs a distraction from—"

He was kissing her all of a sudden, and how the heck had she gotten against the wall? The clever man had backed her right against it, and holy bleep, Jack could *kiss*. His mouth was insistent and warm and his hand cupped her face, and she was kissing him back without even thinking about it, and her arms went around his lean waist, and whoops, yes, she might've been grabbing his ass, but come on, he was completely irresistible.

He pulled back a little, then kissed the corner of her mouth. Em was dimly aware that she was breathing hard.

Jack took her hand and put it over his heart; she felt the hard, solid thumping.

Damn, he was good.

"Please have dinner with me," he whispered.

"Okay." She cleared her throat.

"Saturday?"

"Okay."

He smiled. "I'll call you."

"Okay."

Not put off by her one-word vocabulary, he kissed her forehead and then walked off, just like that, leaving Emmaline shaky and flushed and . . . and worried.

It didn't look like she'd need twenty or twenty-five minutes to fall in love. It looked like she'd just needed that kiss.

Chapter Seventeen

"You need a thong, darlin'."

The statement was delivered by Allison as they stood over Em's pathetic wardrobe, the nicest piece being a cashmere sweater with a hole in the sleeve, courtesy of Sarge, who was surreptitiously trying to reclaim it. Allison's thumbs flew over her phone. "Yep. Caroline concurs with my professional opinion."

Was it wrong that Allison was consulting her child about slutty underwear? Granted, Caroline was on the elderly side of "child," but still. "Well, Jack's not going to see my underwear," she said.

"Sure, baby doll," Allison said. "They all say that."

"Who's they? Is Jack a slut? Tell me the truth."

"Hell, no! Maybe I could've gotten me a little some-some if he was. That being said, he was the best date I've ever had, and don't think I didn't call Charles to gloat about it."

"How is Charles?" Emmaline asked.

"Oh, fine. We're probably getting back together. He's given up the cookie jars. Don't tell anyone, though. I want to lord that over his little bald head the rest of our natural days together.

Anyway, back to you. Thong. Let's go. The bridal store has some real nice trashy underwear. Don't you make that face at me! I assure you, that ex-wife of his wore thongs all the time. Tramps like that give us Southern girls a bad name. And you're wearing a dress."

"This is not a dressy occasion."

"Shush, darlin'. You just let Auntie Allison do the thinking here."

And so it was that two hours later, Emmaline stood in her bedroom, cutting the tags off a pale pink lace bra-and-thong set from the bridal shop across the green. They were very pretty. And small. She put the bra on first. A little scratchy, but not too bad.

And then the thong.

This couldn't be . . . did women really . . . ? She must be wearing it wrong, because good God in heaven! It was horrible! Was the little string supposed to . . .

She took it off, went to her laptop and Google searched "how to wear a thong." No, she hadn't put it on wrong. She tried again.

Ow. Fantastic. This was just a twenty-five dollar version of a severe wedgie. She picked up her phone and called Allison. "Hey, Allison, I—"

"You'll get used to it," Allison said without bothering to say hello. "Takes a couple of weeks to adjust."

"Weeks? Are you kidding?"

"Gotta run. Some kid put a Lego Darth Vader up his nose, and I'm the doc on call tonight."

Okay, well, the thong was . . . horrible; there was no getting around that. But it did look nice. Better than the cotton panties with the orange and purple stripes (on sale, don't judge) and the rip in the side, purchased in the year I Can't Remember. And if she was going to sleep with Jack (*slow down there, girl,* warned the smarter, less slutty part of her brain), she felt he deserved better than orange and purple stripes. And rips. He deserved thongs and shoes with heels and Sicilian hair slime.

The fact that she'd already slept with Jack felt surreal. The moon had been shining that night, and the doors to the balcony had been flung open, and the ocean had lapped at the shores and all those other innuendo-laden metaphors. If he didn't refer to it, she'd pretty much think she'd made it all up in a post-wedding, homemade-vodka-induced fantasy.

But if they slept together *here,* in Manningsport, it'd be real.

She took a painful step toward the bathroom. *Crikey!* That hurt! How was she supposed to be able to walk, let alone sit?

She practice sat, made it halfway down, then jolted up, causing Sarge to run over to her, jump and cover her front with dog hair.

A half hour later, after slapping several yards of

tape over her front to remove German shepherd fur, Emmaline's doorbell rang. She hobbled to the door, and there he stood, the blond, the blue-eyed, the beautiful Jack Holland.

He had a bouquet of red tulips in his hand. "Hey," he said. "You look fantastic."

"Thanks." She took the bouquet, mentally counted the number of steps it would take to get to the kitchen and put the flowers in a vase and tossed them on the coffee table. "Where are we going? O'Rourke's?"

"Hugo's just opened for the season. I thought we'd walk there. It's nice out. Don't you want to put those in a vase? Your dog might eat them."

Indeed, Sarge was snuffling them right now.

She sighed. "Sure." Then, every step a reminder of heretofore ignored parts of her anatomy, she walked into the kitchen, grabbing the flowers on the way. Put them in a vase, stopping for a minute to touch the smooth, cool petals. Nice choice, tulips. Less cliché than roses. And she'd always liked how they felt.

She rubbed a bloom against her lip, breathing in the faint, peachy fragrance. Small wonder deer ate the blossoms right off every spring. She'd almost like to give it a try and see how they tasted.

Turning, she gave a little start. Jack was leaning in the doorway, hands in his pockets, a half smile on his face.

Something pulled in her chest.

"Ready?" he asked.

"You bet." She almost forgot her thong pain. He was that beautiful.

They didn't hold hands as they walked down the sidewalk, which was a shame. Maybe Jack could carry her and make her forget that her thong was trying to eviscerate her. Also, her left breast was incredibly itchy. She tried to rub it with her upper arm, which just made it worse. Wondered if she could subtly go at it with a fork once they sat down.

But they were almost there. (Just thirty or forty painful steps to go, and had she mentioned she was wearing heels? Not the sprain-inducing kind, but the kind that nevertheless made her feet throb.) Being a girl sucked.

Just as they got to Hugo's, however, Jack stopped in the foyer, and a curse slipped from his lips.

"Forget your wallet? Don't worry. I've got money."

"No. It's . . . uh . . ."

"Oh, my God! It's you! Honey, look—it's Jack Holland!"

Lori Baines charged. A murmur went up from the diners. Lori and Phil Baines were Garrett's parents. They owed Jack their son's life.

"Jack, it's so, so good to see you!" She hugged Jack tightly, her shoulders shaking with sobs.

"We're buying you dinner," said Phil, his voice

husky. "Whatever you want, on us. Please let us."

"Hey, guys," said Jessica Dunn, who worked there one or two nights a week. "Table for two?"

As for Jack himself, his face was on the gray side, but he was trying to smile as Lori showed him pictures on her phone.

"I'm not sure we're staying," Em murmured. "Sorry, Jess."

"No, he looks a little . . ."

"Yeah." Em put her hand on his arm. "Hey. They don't have anything gluten-free here," she said. "And you know how I am about gluten."

"My sister is the same way," Lori said. "And, Officer Neal, we never thanked you. You were wonderful that night, too."

"I'm glad everything turned out okay. For Garrett, I mean."

"Yes," Lori said, her eyes filling once more. "That poor Josh."

"Give Garrett our best, okay?" Em said. "We have to be going."

"But we wanted to buy you two dinner—" Phil began.

"That's so nice of you. Another time, maybe." Em smiled and took Jack's arm. "Have a great night."

He didn't say anything. Once outside, he started walking toward the green. Em had to hop-run to keep up, hobbled by her underwear.

He stopped at the first bench they came to and

sat down heavily, leaning forward with his head in his hands. Didn't look up when Em sat beside him, subtly trying to adjust the thong of pain.

"You okay?" she asked.

"Yep."

She waited. After a minute he ran his hands through his hair and looked at her. "Sorry."

"Nothing to be sorry about."

He sighed and sat back, closing his eyes.

She wanted to tell him how brave he'd been, tell him about the awe she felt at how he'd put his life on the line for those kids . . . and how he went back for Josh, even when the odds were so poor.

But she also knew he'd heard that a thousand times, if not more.

"People think when you rescue someone, it's the greatest thing ever," she said gently. "They never think about how scary it is, all the what-ifs that go through your head."

He opened his eyes, the intense blue still a shock to her. "Have you ever saved anyone?" he asked.

"Not yet. Not the way you did. I've pulled over a few drunk drivers. But otherwise, no."

"I really hate the hero worship," he said quietly. "I'm just a winemaker who was taking pictures of the sky that night. It doesn't get less heroic than that."

"What you did was extraordinary, Jack." She couldn't help herself.

"But it wasn't. Tell me you wouldn't have done the same thing if you'd been there. Anyone would've. My teenage niece would've. Faith would've. Her *dog* would've."

"But *you* did it. You were the one who was there, and you went in and pulled four kids out of a frigid lake, Jack. We might've tried, but I don't know anyone else who could've actually done it. And you . . . you didn't stop trying."

"Tell that to Josh Deiner. So much for extraordinary."

"He'd be dead without you."

He gave a bitter laugh. "From what I can tell, he's dying right now. Just slowly, in pieces, by inches."

"So should you have left him?"

"No," he said quietly. "I should've done better."

Her heart cracked. "You did your best."

"And it wasn't good enough." He looked at her a moment. "Well, this is cheerful, isn't it? Come on—let's get dinner." He grabbed her hand and hauled her to her feet. "You hungry?"

"We don't have to—"

"I'm starving. Let's go."

"Jack, what you're going through is—"

"I'm ordering the nachos. You know Connor will put salmon on them if you ask? Sounds disgusting, but it's fantastic." He towed her ruthlessly across the green, yanked open the door to the pub and became manically cheerful, kissing

Colleen on the cheek, shaking Lucas's hand. *And great.* There were Jack's dad and stepmother. "You guys know Emmaline, right?"

"Jack. Of course they know me." He was vibrating with energy. "Nice to see you again, Mr. Holland. Mrs. Holland." The Jamaican woman gave her a regal nod, and Em suspected she'd just won points for using Mrs. J.'s married name.

"You look very pretty tonight, dear," Jack's dad said. He had the same blue eyes as his son, and Em felt her cheeks warm with the compliment. "Well! We'll let you two kids get back to your date!"

"And we'll let you two get back to yours," Jack said. He took another minute to clap Gerard Chartier on the back and say hello to Lorelei.

Crikey. Emmaline was surprised he didn't fly around the room a few times, he had so much energy.

Finally, they made it to their table.

"Everything okay?" she asked as he sat down.

He sighed. "Please let's have a good time tonight," he said, looking her in the eye, giving her the full power of the blue. "I don't need a social worker. I need a friend."

Naked friends, she'd been thinking after that make-out session in the church basement. If they weren't going to be naked friends, she could've worn human underwear instead of this razor wire. "Friends it is," she said.

"I like you, Emmaline." He smiled, a wide,

adorable smile, and she had a flash of memory of Jack when he picked Faith up from some high school event, the college boy back to see his family, and how it made her wish she had a big brother.

They ordered the nachos and burgers and a bottle of wine that, Jack promised, would be perfect with dinner, a fresh, plummy pinot with hints of nutmeg and autumn leaves.

"If you say so," Em said, shifting. The thong was giving her a colonoscopy. She tried sitting on her hands. It didn't help. Crossed her legs—*yow! Bad idea, abort, abort!*

Jack frowned. "Is something wrong?"

"Other than your panic attack ten minutes ago?"

"No," he said, ignoring her comment. "With you. You've been walking funny, and you keep fidgeting."

"I'm fine," she said.

"Did you hurt yourself?"

"No, I'm fine."

"If you don't feel good, we can—"

"Jack, I'm *fine!* Okay? I'm better than you, Captain Avoidance." She shifted, wincing.

"You just did it again. You're like a long-tailed cat in a roomful of rocking chairs."

"What a quaint Southern phrase. Did you pick that expression up from your wife?"

"Her father, actually. What's wrong with you?"

"I'm wearing a thong, okay? It hurts."

Well, that stopped him. It also stopped the Saint Thomas vestry members, too, who were seated at the table next to their booth. Reverend Fisk gave her an appreciative wink, then redirected the rest of them back to their budget woes.

"A thong, huh?" Jack said.

"Yes. Enjoy the visual, because I'm never doing it again."

"If it's that uncomfortable, you can take it off." He grinned, the cheeky man.

"Sucks to be a girl, let me tell you."

"I'll have to take your word for it. But I'm glad you are."

A slow roll of squeezing warmth encompassed her stomach. Just then, Hannah set down their nachos, and Prudence Vanderbeek flopped into the seat next to Jack. "Hey, Useless! Hey, Em! Can I have some? I'm starving." She helped herself to a heavily laden chip and bit into it. "Are you guys on a date?"

"Just friends," Em said at the same time Jack said "Yes." Aha. So maybe the thong had been worth it after all.

"Ooh. I like the conflict," Pru said. "Keeps things lively. Enjoy all this friction when it's new, children, because when you've been married for a quarter of a century, you start having to be a little more creative in the boudoir, if you know what I mean."

"I don't want to know what you mean," Jack

said. "I'll pay you not to tell me what you mean."

"Em, ignore him," Pru said. "I can give you a lifetime's worth of tips."

"Do not take sex tips from my sister," he said. "Pru, get out of here, okay? You're ruining my game."

"You have no game," she said. "He's a sad, smelly bachelor, Emmaline. And have you seen his cat?" She shuddered. "You can do better." She took another slab of nachos, smacked Jack on the shoulder and left, her work boots thudding on the wooden floor.

"Deep down, she loves me," Jack said.

"I can tell."

He smiled. Em did, too, and for a second, they just looked at each other until she broke.

Damn. Dates were hard. It probably explained why she'd been on so few.

"You like being a cop, it seems," Jack said.

Good. Work. She loved talking about work. "Yes. Very much."

"Is Levi a good boss?"

"Will you tell him if I say yes?"

"Nah. Don't want him getting too full of himself."

"Me, neither," she said. "But he's a great boss. Is he a good brother-in-law?"

"Sure. Except that he's sleeping with my sister, I'm almost positive."

"Yes, Faith's tummy seems to indicate that."

Hannah brought them their burgers, ruffled Jack's hair (it seemed to be the law that if you were female, you had to touch Jack), and they were alone again.

And the thing was, it was nice. She was almost relaxed.

Except when she stopped to look at him for too long. Because, you know, he was just so . . . good-looking. Everything about him was perfect—his wide, lovely smile, his mouth (every time she thought about kissing, she nearly choked on her food). And his eyes . . . those sky-blue eyes were just the icing on a very fine cake.

Whereas she was okay. She was not unpleasant to look at. She also had a good smile, thanks to Dr. Warren's skill at replacing her front teeth. Her hair was behaving today, courtesy of the ingenious Sicilians.

She reminded herself to sit up straight, which exacerbated the thong issue. Tried to smile. Did smile. Tried to think of entertaining stories to tell him and came up empty.

Surely she had entertaining stories. Uh . . . yeah, she was almost sure she did, but could she tap into those right now? No. There was something about a cat, wasn't there? Oh, yeah, the cat story! That was a winner!

"So the other day, I was on a call, and—"

"Hi, guys!" It was Faith, rounder and prettier

than ever. "How are you?" She beamed, hands on her belly.

"Good," Emmaline said, ignoring Jack's groan. "You and Levi here for dinner?"

"No, I'm here with my sisters," she said. "We're spying on Jack."

"You better not be," he said.

"Pru says you have no game."

"Should I be more like her, then?"

"Please, God, no. You know what she told me the other day? She and Carl were watching a *Walking Dead* marathon, which of course put them in the mood for love, so—"

"Stop! Come on, Faith, you're as bad as she is."

Faith winked at Emmaline, and Em felt a warm rush of affection. She'd always liked Faith.

"Oh! The baby's kicking. Feel." She grabbed Em's hand and put it against her stomach, and sure enough, there was a mysterious roll and then another.

Wow.

There was a *baby* in there. Okay, obviously, there was a baby in there, but feeling the little thing move around . . . "That's really amazing," Em said, and her voice was husky.

"Faith, come on—leave them alone." Honor Holland came over and gave a rueful grin. "Sorry for the parade of sisters, Jack. How are you, Emmaline?"

"Just fine. Nice to see you."

"You, too. Come on, Faith. Your nachos just came out."

"Oh! Gotta go! Eating for two and all that."

"Honor, you're my favorite sister," Jack called as they left.

"What?" Faith said over her shoulder. "Who's making you godfather to her firstborn child?"

"I take it back, Honor. Faith is my favorite," he said. Honor waved.

"You have a very nice family," Emmaline said.

"They're okay," he said. "A little overwhelming, but they're pretty great."

Then his gaze jerked to the door.

Em looked, too.

Of course. Hadley had just come in, wrapped in a glamorous ivory coat and high caramel leather boots, a green-printed scarf tied in a complicated knot. Her hair was in a ponytail, making her look fresh and energetic. She took off her coat in a graceful swirl, revealing dark green leggings and a *really* adorable lacy top. Sophisticated yet fresh, casual yet elegant. Maybe Emmaline should take a photo and use it as a reference for how to dress for a date, because suddenly, her basic black dress felt both incredibly boring and pathetically ambitious at the same time.

She sighed. In another minute, Hadley was going to come over and say hello and make Emmaline feel like a gorilla who'd been allowed to dress up for the evening and play with the humans.

"So you had a story about a call?" Jack asked, looking back at Em.

"Do you want to go say hi to your wife?"

"Ex-wife, Emmaline, and no. Tell me about the call you went on." But his gaze drifted back toward Hadley, and he was frowning.

"You're frowning," she said.

"I'm irritated," he said.

"Sorry, Grumpy Cat."

"Not at you. We should've stayed at Hugo's."

"I'm sure she would've tracked you wherever you are. It's that computer chip she put in your neck." Emmaline took a nacho and waited for Hadley to float over and coo at Jack.

But much to her surprise, Hadley didn't come over. She did see them, gave a nod and a smile and took a seat at the bar. Not directly in Jack's line of vision, but not out of it, either.

Hmm. Suspicious. Even more suspicious, she took a book out of her bag.

Well, well, well. Hadley could read.

Then again, Em well knew the loneliness of the dinner table when night after night, it was just you and the quiet. Sometimes it was welcome. Sometimes it was not, and if ever there was a place to come when you felt lonely, this was the place.

Could be a coincidence that Hadley had shown up.

"So you have a cat?" Emmaline asked.

"I do," Jack said, returning his gaze to her. "Lazarus."

"Catchy."

"I found him when he was a kitten. Looked like he'd been attacked by something, all covered in blood, ear torn off, broken leg. I took him to the vet, and they didn't expect him to make it through the night, but he did."

His left hand was on the table. As was her right hand. Almost touching. She hadn't even noticed. Should she pull her hand away? Would it be even more obvious that she was nervous if she did?

He had big hands. Big, strong, masculine hands. Em swallowed.

Jack's little finger touched hers, just that smallest caress. A very slight smile tugged at his mouth, and happiness ballooned in her, warm and full.

He'd brought her flowers. He'd shaved. His little finger was making her feel wobbly, and if his little finger could do that, then what about an entire hand? What about his—

"Oh, no! No!"

Both Em and Jack looked over at Hadley, who had one hand over her mouth, the other clutching her phone to her precious little ear.

Damsel in distress, take two.

Emmaline sighed. "Go see what's wrong," she told her date.

"No," Jack said, though his eyes were on his ex. "If she needs me—"

"And she will."

"She can come over here."

Em rolled her eyes. "You're wasting time."

"Eat your burger."

Well, at least there was that. She took a bite— one of Connor's specials with caramelized, crispy onions and some kind of fabulous, gooey cheese —and waited.

Not for long. Hadley came over, tears spilling out of her Bambi-esque eyes.

"Jack, I—I'm so sorry to interrupt."

"What is it, Hadley?"

Yes, what indeed? What crisis would require Jack to carry her home this time? "Twist your ankle again?" Em asked.

"There's been a death in the family," Hadley whispered.

Crap. Em felt two inches tall. "I'm so sorry," she said and reached out her hand to hold Hadley's. The other woman gave a hitching sob.

"Oh, no. Who, Hadley?" Jack asked, standing up.

Hadley pulled her hand away from Em's, covered her face and broke down sobbing against Jack's chest. If she was saying actual words, Em couldn't make them out. She thought she made out the name Anna. What if Anna was a kid? Or Hadley's sister? Or grandmother or—

"I know she was twenty-three, but I guess I just . . . I just wasn't ready to lose her. Oh, Jack!"

Aw, shit. Twenty-three was *way* too young to lose someone. Poor Hadley! And why wasn't Jack being nicer? With a sigh, Jack put an arm around her shoulders, which made her burrow against him like a mole. "These things happen," he said.

Well, *that* wasn't very nice, especially coming from Jack.

"I just can't imagine life without her!" Hadley wept. People were staring openly now.

"Who's Anna?" Emmaline murmured.

"Her cat," Jack said. "Anastasia."

Em blinked.

For crying out loud.

"Twenty-three, huh?" she said. "That's amazing." Those nachos weren't going to eat themselves, so Em took some more. Hadley wasn't exactly going for stoic here. Em noted that her mascara was waterproof. Of course it was.

"She wasn't even sick," Hadley said. "This is such a shock!"

"I don't know. Twenty-three sounds like a ripe old age to me," Emmaline said. "It was probably just her time."

"It wasn't! It was not her time!" Hadley gave her a tragic, wounded (and possibly triumphant) look, then resumed clutching Jack's shirt. "She was so healthy. Remember, Jack?"

"But twenty-three," Emmaline said. "Quite,

quite old. This can't be that much of a surprise."

"It is!" Hadley said. "I'm shocked, I tell you! I wasn't prepared for this."

"No, why would you be? I mean, don't most pets live forever?"

Jack gave her a look. "I'm sorry about Anastasia," he said to his ex, trying to hold her at arm's length, but Teeny Tiny was apparently quite strong and she clutched him harder.

Em sighed, took another bite of her burger and wondered if it would be rude to check her phone to see the Rangers–Penguins score. In light of the fact that her date was being sobbed on by another woman, she didn't really care.

Several people had inched nearer—the vestry members making sympathetic clucks, Gerard Chartier, Victor and Lorena Iskin. "I had a cat who made it to nineteen," Lorena said in her booming voice. "It went under the radiator to die, and I didn't find him until the smell let me know where he was. Poor old Oscar."

Hadley cried harder.

"What's the life span of a cat, anyway?" Gerard Chartier asked.

"Maybe fifteen years," Victor Iskin said, who had many pets himself.

"Fifteen?" Em said, glancing up from her phone. (Rangers up by four, God bless 'em.) "Wow. Sounds like you got quite lucky there, Hadley."

"Well, I don't feel so lucky right now, do I?" the li'l ole bit of dandelion fluff snapped. There was a flinty look in her eye, and Emmaline squinted at her. Where was the steel magnolia thing when you needed it? Allison Whitaker would never sob in public like this.

"It's very sad," Victor said. "You could have her stuffed. I do taxidermy on the side, you know."

Teeny Tiny's sobbing escalated.

Em had had enough. "Okay, Jack, I'll see you around. My condolences, Hadley."

"If I'd've known she was near her time, I would've been there with her." Hadley wept. "Oh, Jack, she died without me! How could I have let that happen?"

"Calm down," he said. "Em, don't go."

"Thanks for the date. I had such a wonderful time." She made sure to give him a dead-eyed stare so he wouldn't miss the sarcasm.

"I'll come over later," he said.

"No, you won't," she said. "Stay here and comfort the grieving. I insist."

"Emmaline—"

She left.

To think she'd worn a thong for this.

Chapter Eighteen

Three days later, Jack woke up in a foul mood.

He'd walked Hadley home the other night, ignoring the fog of disapproval coming from his sisters and Mrs. J. as he left O'Rourke's. Between them, they'd texted him six times to weigh in.

Yeah, he was a sucker. But what else was he supposed to have done? Left Hadley there, sobbing her eyes out in a town where no one liked her? Driven an hour to Cornell and dumped her on Frankie's doorstep? Told her to just deal with it?

Princess Anastasia had been Hadley's beloved pet, no matter how satanic the cat's personality. Her seventh birthday present. And she truly was devastated. He knew that.

He left her apartment as soon as decently possible. Walked over to Emmaline's and stood there in front of her little house. There was a light on upstairs—her bedroom, maybe. The walls were painted green, and the ceiling slanted down. He could see some brick from the exposed chimney.

Bet her bed was messy and comfortable. Flannel sheets and soft old mattress, a couple of books on the night table. She seemed like the type to let the dog sleep with her.

He took out his phone and called her. It went right to voice mail. "Hey," he said. "I'm standing outside your house. I'm really sorry about tonight." He paused. "Give me a call, okay?"

She hadn't. Nope. He had the feeling she wasn't going to.

Which was too bad, because he liked being with her. She was an odd combination of tough chick and gooey caramel center. She scowled fiercely but wore a thong. Slapped on handcuffs but nuzzled a tulip. A hip check that could castrate a bull, but surprisingly soft and silky skin.

Well. His coffee was finished, and it was time to go to work. But first, he clicked on his computer, brought up the local newspaper's website and checked for news of Josh Deiner's death.

Not today. Not yet, anyway.

Lazarus gave his "feed me" screech, and Jack obeyed. Mrs. Johnson had chastised him for never coming over for breakfast anymore, and she had bribed him with an offer of a chocolate cake made just for him. It paid to be her favorite.

He grabbed his keys, mentally reviewing what had to be done today. Cask cleaning, which was good—mindless, hard work. Check the new Riesling vines with Pru, who was concerned that the heavier-than-average snowfall had hurt them. Talk to Dad about trying a new varietal of oak for their chard barrels.

Stop by the hospital and maybe run into the

371

Deiners coming or going. Maybe they'd tell him how Josh was. Let him see the kid, just for a minute.

The one who needed you most, and you left him for last.

Jack left the house, his movements deliberately exact. Locked the door and stopped for a minute.

The one who needed you most.

He stood there a minute, pushing away the memories of that night. Took a slow, deep breath of the cool, damp air. Fog hung heavy over Crooked Lake today, but up here, the pale March sunshine streamed in slices of gold. A crow called from the oak tree, then flew down and landed on a cedar post at the end of a row of vines.

Another breath, slower this time. There was the stone wall one of his ancestors had built and which Jack kept up, rambling alongside the field.

He opened the truck door, started to get in and froze.

There was a dead possum on the dashboard.

Possums under any circumstances are not attractive animals. But dead . . . and in Jack's truck . . . it was even uglier, its bald tail dangling, its mouth open in a too-wide rictus. Its neck was broken, judging from the sick angle.

There was no way a possum could've gotten into his truck. It didn't wander in through an open window, because there was no open window; it was early March, for the love of God, and it had been seventeen degrees last night.

Someone had put it there.

Later that day, Jack drove over to the police station and went inside. "Hi, Jack!" Carol said, hopping up for a hug. He obliged. "Are you here to see Emmaline? I heard your date didn't go so well."

"Is she here?"

"No," Carol answered. "She's taking a class for hostage negotiation. Not that we have many hostages around here."

The disappointment he felt was surprising. "Is Levi available?" he asked.

"Yes, he's in his office on the phone. Levi!" she yelled. "Jack's here and wants to talk to you when you're off the phone!"

"You're a great secretary," Jack observed.

"I'm an administrative assistant, smart-ass," she said. "And don't talk fresh to me. I changed your diapers when you were a baby."

"You say that to all the guys," he said.

"Come on in, Jack," Levi said from his office. "And, Carol, please try to master the intercom instead of yelling, okay?"

Carol rolled her eyes and sat back down, and Jack winked. He'd always loved Mrs. Robinson.

"What can I do for you?" Levi asked.

"This is . . . well, it's police business. Maybe. I don't know."

Levi sat behind his desk, and Jack sat down, too. "Go ahead," he said, picking up a pen.

"I don't know if I want to file a report or anything official," Jack said. "I found a dead possum in my truck this morning. Its neck was broken."

"Shit. What time?"

"About seven."

"And why didn't you call me right away?"

Jack shrugged. "It was dead. Its biting days were over."

"People don't usually find dead animals in their vehicles, Jack."

He ran a hand through his hair. "I know."

"What did you do with it?"

"I put on rubber gloves and put it in a garbage bag. It's in the back of my truck."

"And I bet you scrubbed that truck down, didn't you? And erased lots of fingerprints we might've been able to lift."

"You can check the door, but, yeah, I did. I don't want to make a big deal out of this. It's probably just kids." Poor "kids." They were blamed for so much.

Levi was quiet for a minute, doodling on a pad. "Anything else happen recently?"

"Someone left a note on my windshield. It said, 'You better watch yourself.' "

"Did you keep it?"

"No."

"You know, Jack, it's always frustrating when the taxpayers of Manningsport don't turn to their friendly neighborhood cop for help. Especially when that cop happens to be a member of their family."

"Yeah, yeah." He paused. "The notepaper was hot pink, if that helps."

"What would've really helped is if you didn't throw it away. Anything else you're not telling me?"

"There was another night when I came home and all the lights were on and the front door was open. I might've done that myself, though. I've been . . . forgetting things recently."

"That accident was bound to cause some stress. You doing all right otherwise? Any problems sleeping or anything?"

Nice to know Emmaline hadn't mentioned anything to her boss. For a second, he thought about telling Levi about the flashbacks and nightmares. But Levi was his brother-in-law, an expectant father, the police chief and combat veteran who probably had flashbacks of his own. Jack wasn't going to add to his load. "No, I'm good."

Levi stared at him. Jack stared back.

"Okay," Levi finally said. "Sounds to me like someone's mad at you, Jack. I'd like to talk to the Deiners."

"Absolutely not," Jack said. "No."

"Jack, they—"

"Their son is in a coma. I doubt very much that they have time to pick up roadkill and sneak it into my truck."

"Yeah. They haven't left his side, so I doubt it, too." Levi leaned back in his chair. "How about your ex-wife?"

The thought had crossed his mind. "The lights and the note on the windshield, maybe. But not the dead possum."

"You sure? Nothing makes people crazier than jealousy."

Jack paused. Hadley was a little . . . off; that was true. He couldn't see her doing this, though. "Doesn't seem like her style."

"I might ask her some questions just the same. Be smart, Jack. If something else happens, tell me. The dead animal in your truck—that ups the stakes a bit."

"Yeah." There was a picture of Faith on the bookcase behind Levi. "How's my sister?"

Levi's expression changed from stoic police chief to goofy-in-love. "She's great."

"Good. Can't wait to see my nephew." He stood up and shook Levi's hand. "Gotta go."

Emmaline still wasn't back.

Damn.

Chapter Nineteen

"Remember, this person is, for the time being, your friend," Jamie the badass instructor said. "Even if you hate what they're doing and wish you could kick them in the sac, for now, you *empathize,* you *listen,* you *mirror.*" She tapped the whiteboard to emphasize the words she'd written there. "Don't tell them that what they're doing is crazy or stupid. Don't deny what they're feeling. That's creating an argument, and you want them to feel they can trust you. Okay? Emmaline and Butch, you're up. Em, you're the tormented woman with your parents held at gunpoint. And . . . action."

Butch cleared his throat. He and Em were sitting in chairs at the front of the class, facing away from each other while Shirley and Gale pretended to be the cowering parents.

"So what's going on with you and your parents?" Butch asked.

"I hate them," Em said, winking at Shirley, who was her best bud in the class.

"Well, yeah, everyone hates their parents. I hate mine, too," Butch said.

"No, Butch," Jamie interrupted. "This isn't

about you. It's about Em and her shitty parents. Keep going."

"Okay," Butch said. "Uh . . . hate your parents, huh?"

"Yes," Em said. "They love my sister best." Might as well go for something close to home.

"Love your sister best, huh?"

"Yep."

"Why do you think that is?" Butch asked. Em could practically hear him sweating; he wasn't the best student in the group.

"Because she's just better. Prettier, smarter, nicer."

"She doesn't hold them hostage," Ingrid quipped.

"Keep going, Butch," Jamie said.

"So . . . uh . . . what should I say next?"

"How about some emotional labeling?" Jamie said. "Identify her feelings so she'll know you understand her situation."

"Right, right. Uh, so you're really pissed, right?"

Em tried not to smile. "Yeah, I'm pissed! That's why I tied up my parents and have this gun!" Role-playing was *fun*.

To be honest, there was a lot more psychological work in this field than Em had anticipated. Mirroring, empathy, active listening, behavioral change . . . For the first time in her life, she understood why her parents loved their jobs so much.

"Let me take over, Butch," Jamie said. She kicked Butch out of his chair and sat down. "So,

Em, you're feeling like it's not fair that your parents favor your sister."

"Exactly," Em said.

"That must be really frustrating. Note, class, that I'm labeling her feelings, not just echoing them, like Butchie was—no offense, Butch. But when I put a label on them, Em can see that I get it, and that I understand her. We're creating empathy here. Okay, Em, back to you. That must be frustrating."

"It is." Em felt a pang of guilt. "But I was no picnic, and my sister really is pretty great." Speaking of Flawless Angela . . . Em should give her a call.

"Sounds like you guys are close."

"Yeah. Pretty much. She's nice."

"What do you think she'd say about this situation?"

"She'd tell me not to do it." Jamie didn't respond, so Em kept talking. "She'd be upset. Devastated, really. She loves them a lot."

"See how I paused there, people?" Jamie said. "This isn't a rapid-fire police interrogation where you're trying to keep someone off balance to get them to tell the truth. Sometimes the pauses let your bad guy do some thinking, and their situation starts to sink in." She stood up. "And that, my friends, is all the time we have. Good job today."

On the way home, Levi radioed in and asked her to check on Alice McPhales, a sweet old lady struggling with dementia. She still lived on her own, but it was a matter of time before her son had to make some changes. She called the police at least three times a week, convinced she saw people creeping around her property, which was a farmhouse on the outskirts of town. Today she'd reported that someone had broken into her house. She called with this complaint a few times a month, so Em wasn't really worried.

Everett pulled up in his cruiser just as she did. "Slow day?" Em asked.

"I'll check the perimeter for intruders," Everett said, reaching for his gun.

"Keep that in the holster, dumbass," Emmaline said.

"Well, what am I supposed to do?" he asked. "I don't like going in there. It's too crowded."

"Everett . . . never mind. Knock yourself out and check the perimeter, but if you pull that gun out for anything less than an alien attack, I'm telling Levi."

Everett muttered and kicked some grass.

"Mrs. McPhales?" Emmaline called as she knocked.

The old lady opened the door a crack. "Where's Levi?" she asked.

"He's at the station. He asked me to come instead. I'm Emmaline Neal. Luanne Macomb's granddaughter. Remember? I'm a police officer, too."

"Oh, yes. Luanne. She's lovely! Such a good knitter! Tell her I said hello, won't you?"

"I'll do that, Mrs. McPhales." No point in reminding the old lady her friend was gone. "Can I come in and check things out?"

Mrs. McPhales's house was typical for an old person—too cluttered, too many little rugs that would make tripping easy. It was dark, too, since she had all the curtains drawn. "What seems to be missing, Mrs. McPhales?" she asked as she turned on a light.

"The gravy boat my grandmother gave me! I can't believe they took it!" The old lady began to cry. "It was so beautiful, and now it's gone. They must've come in when I was sleeping. I'll never feel safe here again, and my husband built this house. They've ruined it! They've *soiled* it!"

Em put her arm around her. "Why don't I make you a cup of tea?" she asked.

"I prefer coffee. But the . . . the . . . black box in the kitchen is broken."

"The coffeemaker?"

"Yes."

Em went into the kitchen. Dirty dishes were piled in the sink. The coffeemaker was unplugged. She plugged it back in and made coffee, and, while that was brewing, she filled the sink with hot water.

"You don't have to do that," Mrs. McPhales said.

"Oh, I don't mind. I like doing dishes. You can tell me where they go."

"Perimeter is clear," came Everett's voice over the radio.

"Imagine that," Em muttered. "Roger," she said back. "Why don't you head back, Ev?"

"Roger that, heading back to the station."

The cupboards were a mess—cereal boxes in with the glassware, an open jar of peanut butter in a colander. Em straightened up as best she could, then poured Alice some coffee. "So what does this gravy boat look like?" She took out her notebook so Mrs. McPhales wouldn't feel like Em was merely tolerating her.

Mrs. McPhales took a sip of her coffee. "What gravy boat?"

"The one your grandmother gave you."

"Oh, yes. It was white with pink flowers. It was very old. She brought it from England, and when I was little, she'd put it out at Christmas. I just loved seeing it on her table. It was so fancy and beautiful." She started to cry noiselessly, and Em's heart gave a tug. Her father's parents had died when she was little, Nana of a massive stroke or heart attack that took her while she was sleeping.

Em lived in Michigan at the time, and she remembered crumpling when her mom told her the news, and how wonderful Kevin had been, holding her close, the comforting smell of his shirt, the ever-present tang of his sweat, back when he carried so much extra weight.

Nana had been lucky. Old age wasn't so kind to most.

"Let me take a look around," she said, standing up.

"You won't find it! They took it. Those men, I wish they wouldn't come here!"

"Why don't I take a look around anyway? Make sure nothing else is missing." Em rested her hand on Mrs. McPhales's shoulder, and the old lady blinked up at her, her eyes still teary.

"Would you, dear? Oh, thank you!"

The gravy boat was in the bathroom, perched on the radiator. "Is this it?" Em asked, returning to the kitchen.

"You got it back! Oh, thank you, darling! Thank you! Oh, I just love you!" Em smiled, though she wasn't sure if Alice was talking to the gravy boat or to her.

After Em made Mrs. McPhales a sandwich and checked all the windows and locks for the old lady's peace of mind, she went out to her car and radioed Levi. "All clear here, Chief. But I think you should talk to her son about getting her into Rushing Creek, or maybe finding some live-in help. She's awfully isolated up here."

"Roger," he said. "Come on back to the station. I need you to do something."

"Roger that, big guy."

"It's Chief Cooper, thank you very much."

Em smiled as she clicked off. Levi took himself a little too seriously, but it was oddly endearing. He was a good boss and a better cop. Not that he needed to hear it from her—the townspeople worshipped the guy.

Em called her parents from the car. Pretending to hold them hostage and then seeing Mrs. McPhales so blue . . . well, heck. Her parents weren't getting any younger.

"Hi, Mom," she said when her mother picked up.

"Emmaline! Are you sick?"

"No. Just calling to say hi."

There was a pause. "Oh."

"So how are you?" Em asked.

"Fine. And you?"

"Good."

There was another pause. "Did you get those pictures I sent you from the wedding?" Mom asked.

Did she ever. "I sure did. Why would you send me pictures of Kevin and Naomi, Mom?"

"Why? Does it still bother you?"

"No, I just don't want to see them kissing."

"I thought some immersion therapy might help you get over him."

"I don't need help." *Except in talking to you, it seems.* "I'm really fine."

"Interesting that you choose that word to characterize yourself, darling."

Mom was in psychotherapy mode. Conversation

between the two of them had never been a strong point. Em tried again. "So guess what? I'm taking a crisis negotiations class, and it's got a lot of psychology in it."

"Really."

"Yeah." Emmaline waited for a question, using the pause technique. No question came. "I guess I can see why you like your work so much." *Rapport, anyone?*

Silence. Okay, so rapport was harder than it looked. "How's Dad?"

"I have no idea. Working."

"And Angela?"

"Wonderful."

Em sighed. Mom was like this sometimes, usually after a fight with Dad. "Okay, Mom, good talking to you."

"When are you coming home, Emmaline?"

Em caught her own grimace in the rearview mirror. "Um, maybe a weekend this summer?"

"I mean, when are you coming home for good, Emmaline? Your stint as a police officer has gone on long enough, don't you think?"

"It's a career, Mom. And I really like it."

"It seems to me that you're hiding from your real life."

"This is my real life."

"If Kevin is truly behind you and you've had closure, you can come home. I saw how miserable you were at the wedding."

"Well, Ma, first of all, you sold my home. And secondly, of course, the wedding was awkward. I—"

"Sweetheart, you're so smart. What about your degree? Don't you miss journalism? Surely you want to do something more meaningful than write out parking tickets."

Only a mother could stab so directly. Em made sure to keep her voice level. "My job *is* meaningful, Mom."

"You could be so much more."

"Thanks."

"Well, look at your sister! A doctorate in—"

"I know all about the PhD, Mom. I'm happy doing this."

"That's a shame."

Alice McPhales didn't think so. Her at-risk kids didn't think so (hopefully).

"Gotta go, Mom. I'm at the station."

She hung up and unclenched her jaw.

When Levi had first offered her the job, he'd made it clear that it would be 90 percent community service and 10 percent law enforcement. The occasional B and E, speeders and DUIs were about as dramatic as it got.

Well, hell, Jack's rescue. That had been dramatic (and terrifying, seeing him with ice in his hair, pushing on Josh Deiner's chest, the boys clustered around him in a knot of helpless terror).

But doing Mrs. McPhales's dishes and finding

her beloved gravy boat . . . There was a warm golden weight in her chest because of that.

"How was class?" Levi asked as she came in.

"Great," she said. "I love it."

"Good. I have another job for you."

"I'm free, Chief," Everett volunteered. "Is it dangerous?" Automatically, his hand went to his gun.

Levi gave Everett a long-suffering look. "No, Everett. I need Emmaline. And if I see you fondling that gun one more time this week, I'm taking it away."

"Roger that, Chief. No gun fondling. Yes, sir."

"Come into my office, Em."

She obeyed, snagging a cookie from Carol's desk. *Mmm. Oatmeal raisin.* "Take two," Carol said.

"Will you marry me?" Em said.

"Get in line," Carol retorted.

Levi sat behind his desk and folded his hands. "I need you to check on something. Seems like someone's got a grudge against Jack. Mostly mischief, but it's getting a little nasty. First, someone went into his house, turned on all the lights and left the doors and windows open."

"The Deiners?"

"I don't think it's them, since they're always at the hospital."

"His ex-wife, maybe?" She could kind of see Hadley doing something like that as a way to show Jack he needed her back . . . but no, Hadley seemed more the sort to go for the "rescue me" theme.

"Possibly," Levi said. "A week ago, he got a note on his windshield that said 'You better watch yourself.' Hot pink paper, laser-printed."

"Did he save it?"

"No."

Em made a disgusted noise. "Does no one watch *NCIS*?"

"I know. And then this morning, he found a dead possum in his truck. Neck broken."

Em jumped a little. "Shit."

"So." Levi looked at the wall. "I want you to go up to his place as a security detail."

"A security detail? What am I, the Secret Service?"

"Don't get fresh with me, young lady."

"I'm a year older than you, Levi. Do you really think he's in danger?"

"It's our job to make sure he's not." Levi picked up a pen and started fiddling with it. He didn't look at her.

"Chief," she said. "We have three people on this police force. You think a dead rodent means I should babysit Jack Holl—Oh, my God, you're matchmaking, aren't you?"

Levi sighed. "Faith made me do it."

"You gotta be kidding me."

"Still, I'm your boss. Please make sure Jack's tucked in tonight."

"Levi—"

"That's Chief Cooper, Officer Neal."

"Oh, don't get official on me!" She slumped back in her chair. "Okay, the broken neck thing is creepy."

"Yes."

"Can't Everett do it? You know how he likes to wander around with his hand on his gun."

"Yes, and he's going to shoot his foot off one day because of it." Levi sighed. "You have to admit, a dead possum in someone's truck is unusual. So get that look off your face and go up there and check on him. Check around his property. And maybe talk to his ex-wife. Faith said she was a little . . . unstable. If she deliberately sprained her ankle to get Jack's attention—"

"So you believe me now?"

"—who's to say she wouldn't pick up roadkill and put it in his truck? Especially if she's mad at him for dating you."

"He's not dating me. He keeps trying to date me, and—"

"Let's not talk about personal lives, shall we?"

"You're the one pimping me out here, Levi."

He crinkled his brow at her. Stared, patiently, slightly bored.

"Fine," she said. "I'll do it."

"Thank you so very much, Officer."

"Keep this in mind during my annual review."

"Will do." He allowed a faint smile, then waved her out of the office.

Em's first stop was the Opera House. She clomped up the stairs and knocked on the door of apartment 3-C. Hadley opened the door, a bright, expectant smile on her face that dropped like a lead hockey puck at the sight of Not Jack. "Hello, Miss Boudreau," Em said. "Mind if I come in and ask you a few questions?"

"Is Jack all right?" she breathed, peering around the door.

"Interesting you should ask. Any reason he wouldn't be?" Em asked, cocking an eyebrow.

"Um, I . . . I have no idea!" She flushed.

Guilty, Em thought. She waited.

"Well, do come in!" Hadley said. "Where are my manners?"

She was wearing a dress, a rose-colored sheath kind of thing that Em imagined would make her look as shapely as a pillow but on Hadley looked romantic and delicate. Her long blond hair was caught at the nape of her neck in the type of artless, casual ponytail that Em had never been able to master; her thick, not-straight, not-curly locks were the Houdini of hair and could only be forced into her regulation bun with a combination of the magic slime, a thick supermarket elastic once used to lump the broccoli together and seventeen bobby pins.

Suppressing a sigh—she wasn't supposed to care about this stuff anymore—she stepped into the dimly lit apartment. It had come furnished, Emmaline knew, but Hadley had put her mark on it. A vase of pink and purple tulips sat on the coffee table, and a soft ivory wrap was artfully draped on the arm of the sofa. Lots of throw pillows, a series of framed mirrors on the brick wall. Two or three candles filled the room with the scent of lavender, clogging Em's throat.

The whole room was set up for seduction.

Oh, and how cute. A giant wedding photo of Hadley and Jack sat on the bookcase, impossible to ignore. Em had to admit—Jack Holland in navy whites was a very nice sight. He and Hadley made a gorgeous couple; it couldn't be denied. Hadley was beautiful and radiant and tiny, and Jack . . . Jack looked incredibly happy.

Em forced her eyes away from the photo. A bottle of wine, nearly three quarters empty, sat on the counter. One glass. The cork and corkscrew were over by the sink, indicating that it had been opened recently.

A lot of wine for such a petite woman.

"What can I do for you, Officer?" Hadley asked.

"Jack found a dead possum in his truck today. Would you happen to know anything about that?"

"Really?" Her face lit up. "That's just awful! Was he upset? Should I call him? Does he need me?"

"Did you put it there?"

"Me? No!"

"And where were you last night?"

"I was here. Alone."

Jack wasn't even pressing charges. Maybe he knew it was his ex and didn't want her in trouble. "Is there anyone who can confirm that?" Em asked.

"Yes, as a matter of fact. I talked to my sister around ten. Frankie. Jack's very fond of her. He loves my family. Well, they're his family, too, of course."

"You didn't go anywhere?"

Hadley folded her arms. "I told you, I didn't do anything. You think I'd touch a dead animal? Do I strike you as that type?" She had a point. As much as Emmaline would love to arrest Hadley for criminal mischief, she really couldn't see her getting her perfect little manicured hands dirty. "After I talked to Frankie, I went straight to bed to get some beauty sleep. Maybe you should try it."

Emmaline indulged in a brief fantasy in which she slapped some cuffs on Teeny Tiny and Mirandized her. Put her in the holding cell. Happy thoughts.

"Do you always drink alone, Miss Boudreau?" Em asked, nodding at the wine bottle and glass.

"Well, being married to a winemaker certainly developed my appreciation for wine, Officer. But not always. Sometimes Jack and I have a glass together."

Em didn't take the bait. "Make sure you don't drink and drive."

"Oh, I'm perfectly sober. In fact, it sounds like Jack shouldn't be alone. I'll go on up and check in on him."

"No need, Miss Boudreau. The police have this covered."

Hadley scowled. "Well, I think Jack could use some company."

"Chief Cooper thinks so, too, which is why I'm going up there right now. I hope not to see any trespassers. Have a good night."

She left the Opera House and walked across the green, past O'Rourke's, which was already jumping, and down the street to her own little place. She needed to feed Sarge. Might as well bring Super-Pup, too, if she had to hang out at Jack's.

Sarge twirled in circles of joy when she came through the door, Squeaky Chicken clutched in his mouth. "Hi, handsome! Are you happy to see me? You are?" Indeed, Sarge was whimpering and crooning with joy. Em ruffled his sides with both hands and let him lick her face for a few minutes. "Who's a good boy? Huh? You are, buddy! Come on—out you go!"

While Sarge did his business in the backyard, Em took a look around.

It didn't glow with femininity the way Hadley's apartment did, that was for sure. But it was a happy space. There were a few pictures on the mantel; one of her and Angela, another of Levi pinning on her badge the day she'd graduated from the academy. Her and Nana one summer day long ago, both of them laughing, Em's two front teeth missing. The furniture was comfortable and sturdy (rather like herself). Lots of books in the built-in shelves. A beautiful Tiffany lamp that she'd splurged on at Presque Antiques on the green.

This house was where she'd spent the happiest times of her life, aside from those years with Kevin. This was more home than the place where she'd grown up, which was someone else's now, anyway. But it still gave her a pang, the ease with which her parents had sent their only child away for the bulk of every summer. They'd kept Angela close by their sides; even after the divorce, they were unable to split up because they might not see her as much.

Well. They had done Emmaline a favor. She'd been better off here.

"Come on, Sarge," she said, as her dog raced in through the doggy door. "We have guard duty tonight."

Chapter Twenty

Jack found that cooking had taken on greater importance since the accident, as it gave his mind something to think about. A science podcast was playing on his computer; another tool to keep his brain occupied.

Oddly enough, he wasn't really concerned about the possum in his truck. A teenager, he figured, probably one of Josh Deiner's friends. And if so, Jack sort of deserved it, didn't he?

His phone buzzed with an incoming text. Hadley. Great.

Heard about "incident" 2day. U ok???? Xoxox

Was it so hard to spell out the words? Text-style spelling would make Stephen Hawking seem idiotic. He opted not to answer.

That was a mistake. His phone buzzed again, vibrating on the counter.

Pls let me know ur ok.

Jack sighed.

U want 2 come over 4 dinner???

She had fast thumbs, he'd give her that.

I can come 2 c u if easier. :)

And now a smiley face, for the love of God.

Give me a call, ok???

No, thanks, he wouldn't.

Miss u!!!

Worried about u!!!

It was the emotional equivalent of nails on a chalkboard.

And now the phone was ringing. Three guesses as to who it was. He didn't bother picking up, but he did text her back. I'm fine. Nothing to worry about.

He thought about turning off his cell, but he didn't have a landline. And his grandfather had been looking a little gray lately. Jack had asked Jeremy Lyon to drop in on Pops, as the old man wouldn't go to the doctor without a gun to his head.

He added sausage to the garlic and onions he was sautéing. This would be a good dinner. Then again, food hadn't tasted like much these days. Oh, and there was Mrs. Johnson's chocolate cake for dessert. He picked up his phone and called her.

"Just wanted to thank you again for my cake," he said.

"Oh, Jackie, don't be silly! You know I love you best," Mrs. J. cooed.

"I do know that, and I lord it over my sisters whenever possible. And Dad." He smiled. "What are you guys doing tonight?"

"That's none of your business, Jack darling."

He shuddered. "You're right. Thanks again, Mrs. J."

Maybe he should get a dog. Lazarus wasn't much in the company department. As if determined to prove him wrong, the cat rubbed against Jack's ankle in a rare show of affection, then hissed and ran under the couch.

A knock came at the door, and Jack felt his jaw tighten. He turned off the stove and went to the door. If that was Hadley, he just might call the police.

It wasn't Hadley. It *was* the police, still in uniform. And the police officer's puppy, holding a stuffed animal in his mouth.

Jack felt himself smiling. "Hey," he said, opening the door. "How are you?"

"This is police business," she said, already blushing. "Levi made me come."

"I owe him one," Jack said. "Come in. I'm making dinner. You can stay."

"No, we're just, um, checking."

"For what? For dead possums?"

"Basically. Mind if I walk around your property?"

"Not at all. I'll come with you." He grabbed his jacket. "Hey, buddy," Jack said, bending down to pet the puppy, who wriggled in ecstasy, then whipped his toy—a chicken—back and forth. Lazarus darted out and ran under a bush, the better to spy on the dog. Jack stood up, catching the smell of Emmaline's shampoo.

Nice.

She had beautiful eyes. Cat-shaped and blue. Her mouth . . . He remembered that mouth. Hell, yeah. That was a good mouth. Perfect for kissing. Perfect for—

He realized he was staring and cleared his throat. "So what are you looking for?"

"Signs of a trespasser." She jammed her hands in her jacket pockets. "You shouldn't have wiped down the truck, by the way. Next time a crime is committed against you, please let the professionals do their jobs."

"Save it," he said. "Levi already lectured me."

"Is your driveway the only way up here?" she asked, starting off toward the stone wall that bordered the woods.

"No. You can drive up from the other side of the ridge and go through the Ellis property."

"Think you'd wake up if someone drove up your driveway?"

"Oh, yeah. It's gravel."

"Then I bet Possum Person came through the back way."

"Sounds about right."

The snow had melted during a brief warm spell, but the temperature had dropped back to the twenties last night. Their breath fogged in the sharp, clean air. Sarge snuffled behind them, off his leash, and Lazarus brought up the rear.

"How have you been?" Jack asked.

"Fine," she said. "Do you have any ideas who might leave a dead possum in your truck?"

"A couple of Josh's friends, maybe."

She nodded. "That's my best guess, too."

The light was fading, the sunset brilliant red on the horizon.

Same as the day the kids went into the lake.

The thought swelled in Jack's brain, blotting everything else out. The bottom of the car, so clear and foreign, sailing over his head. The thunk of the camera as he dropped it on the dock. The steely bite of the water over his head as he dived.

For a second, he couldn't breathe; he was looking up at the red-and-purple sky so far away. Josh wasn't budging, and Jack was out of air, and his vision was shutting down, and Josh was already dying. He was—

There was fur against his mouth, and a warm, wriggling body against his chest. Em had handed him the puppy.

"His paws are a little cold. Would you mind holding him?"

"Oh. Sure." Sarge was already joyfully licking his face and whining. "Easy, pal," Jack said. "We barely know each other." His voice was almost normal.

The dog made a mooing noise, then put his head on Jack's shoulder.

Emmaline was studiously not looking at them, holding the dog's toy chicken. It occurred to Jack that she'd given him the dog for a reason.

"Where'd you get this guy, anyway?" Jack asked.

"Bryce Campbell. He owns the animal shelter now. Hey, is that Jeremy's place over there?" She pointed to the Lyons Den, the nearest neighbor to Blue Heron, owned by Faith's former fiancée.

"Yeah."

"He's so nice. Maybe you could talk to him about your PTSD."

"I don't have PTSD."

"Were you aware that two minutes ago, you stopped in your tracks and didn't answer me till I handed you my dog?"

Shit. "Let's finish this up, okay? The perimeter check or whatever you're doing. Then you can stay for dinner."

She didn't answer, but as they got close to the house, she stopped at each window and looked at the ground. "Too bad there's no snow. And it's too cold for muddy prints," she said. "But maybe someone dropped a cigarette butt or something."

Sarge was snoring gently.

"I guess I'm done," Em said, seeming chagrined that she hadn't found anything incriminating.

"Good. When do you get off duty?"

"I'm on call tonight."

Just then her phone chimed. Jack's did, too. He checked it with his free hand—Levi's taking tonight's shift, so if Emmaline's there, why don't you have her stay for dinner? xox your favorite sister.

Em sighed.

"Everything okay?" Jack asked.

"Yeah."

"So if you're not working tonight, I guess you can stay for dinner."

She frowned. "Who says I'm not working?"

"Your boss's wife." He smiled. "Come on, Em. Stay. I could use the company. Stop scowling. I'm a good cook. And since you're off duty, you can have a glass of wine."

Jack Holland looked awfully good in the kitchen, Em thought. He caught her looking, and she jerked her gaze away.

"I visited your wife earlier," she said.

"I have no wife," he answered calmly, pouring her a glass of white. "Our unoaked Granite Chardonnay, so named because it comes from the field next to the family cemetery, and we felt funny about naming it Cemetery Chard. Vanilla and floral bouquet, clean mineral notes, a buttery finish that lingers on the palate. Why on earth would you go see Hadley?"

"To ask about that possum."

"You're just stirring the crazy pot, you know," he said. "The more attention you give her, the worse she gets." His fingers brushed hers as he handed her the glass, and a current ran up her arm.

She sat on the stool at the counter and took a sip of wine. "You like it?" he asked.

"It's not bad."

"Stab me in the heart, why don't you?"

"She seemed awfully thrilled that someone's stalking you."

Jack set down the spatula from whatever meaty, yummy thing he was stirring. "Emmaline, I don't want to talk about my ex-wife. Okay?"

"Sure. What are you cooking?"

"Sweet Italian sausage ragout in a creamy vodka sauce with broccoli rabe over penne. Here. Taste it." He held the wooden spoon to her mouth, and she obeyed.

Holy food orgasm. Spicy and creamy and sweet and frickin' unbelievable.

"You cook like this every night?" she asked.

His eyes were on her mouth. "I could if I had a reason."

She stopped chewing. Swallowed a bit hard.

Men like Jack should be careful about what they said. A lot could be read into a statement like that.

Then his cat made a sound like an old screen door, and Sarge dashed after him. "Want me to put the dog in the cellar?" she asked.

"No, it's fine. Lazarus can take care of himself." He got a spice out of the cupboard and added it to the frying pan.

She couldn't remember the last time a man had cooked for her. Well, cooked her a meal she actually wanted to eat. Those last few months with Kevin didn't count.

A fire crackled and popped in the big stone fireplace in the great room. Em got up and wandered around.

Jack had a few pictures here and there—one of Levi and Faith and Blue from last year, at their wedding. Em had gone to that one, and she remembered the photo being taken, people laughing as Blue kept nudging in between the couple. Another photo from a wedding she'd gone to, Tom and Honor's. This one was of Jack and Honor. *Nice.* Here was one of Jack and his father holding up a gold medal and a bottle of wine. Another Holland family portrait, but this one with Jack's mother in it. Prudence's wedding, young Jack tall and skinny and geeky-cute.

The bookcase was filled with biographies and

political thrillers, the typical man stuff when it came to reading. A couple dozen tomes on wine, as one would expect.

The windows showcased the Holland farmland, all the way down to Keuka.

Jack's furniture was beautiful—simple and functional, but with inlaid wood and graceful lines. "Where'd you get this?" she said, running her finger along a tall narrow table.

"I made it," he said.

Of course he made it. He saved children and made beautiful furniture and cooked and looked like a movie star.

"It was my first and last project," he said. "I almost cut off my finger with the miter saw." He grinned and held up a hand. "Nineteen stitches."

Oddly enough, it was nice to know.

"I got my front teeth knocked out in college," Em said. "Hockey. Five stitches."

"Oh, yeah? Are those teeth fake, then?"

"No. The miracles of modern medicine. The dentist put them right back in. It was gross. Lots of blood. I was extremely brave, of course."

"No scar?"

"No, I have a scar."

"Let me see."

The scar was just above her upper lip, a faint white line about half an inch long, barely noticeable. "It's there. Trust me."

He came out of the kitchen and stood in front

of her. Cupped her face in his hands and stared at her mouth.

Emmaline could feel her heartbeat, slow, rolling thumps.

His face was serious. Mouth perfect. She didn't even dare look at his eyes for fear that her knees would buckle.

"Oh, yeah," he whispered. "There it is." He ran his thumb over the scar, and Em sort of forgot how to breathe. Was it in-in-out? Or . . . oh, wow, those eyes—oops, she'd looked—were *so* beautiful. All of him was so—

Lazarus came tearing into the room, Sarge hot on his heels. The cat veered under a couch; Wonder Pup didn't steer that well and crashed into Em's legs.

Emmaline stepped back. Cleared her throat. She was still in uniform. It was probably against some rule to kiss in uniform.

"Sarge, go lie down," she ordered. The puppy gave her a reproachful look. "Do it," she said.

He obeyed, giving her a mournful eyebrow as only a German shepherd could.

A timer went off in the kitchen, and Jack went back behind the counter.

Fat snowflakes began falling from the sky.

It was utterly romantic here, even with the demonic sounds the cat was making from under the couch. "Is he okay?" Emmaline asked.

"Oh, sure. That's his normal."

Jack seemed irritatingly unaffected by her scar-touching. *Men. Such mysteries.* She sat back down at the counter and watched him stir and nudge and adjust the heat. Captain Seduction one minute, Chef Ramsay the next.

Em had always had a thing for Gordon Ramsay, now that she thought of it.

"Can I ask you a question, Jack?" she asked.

"Sure."

"Why me? There are a lot of women in this town who'd love to go out with you. Who fantasize about going out with you. Who'd run their grandmothers over with a tractor to go out with you. Why are you interested in me?"

"I don't know," he said. "I'm a guy. We don't think that hard. Is 'because you're good in bed' a sufficient answer?"

A surprised snort of laughter escaped. "Um, no."

He poured her more wine. Such nice manners. "I have a question for you, Officer. Why won't you go out with me? And don't give me that bullshit about me still having a thing for Hadley or having PTSD."

"You do have a thing for Hadley. And you're the poster child for PTSD."

"I'll pretend I didn't hear that and await your answer."

Em covered by taking a sip of her drink. It really was fantastic. She'd never paid much attention to wine descriptions—it was wine, how bad could it be?—but when Jack identified the flavors the way he did, she really could taste them. Guess it wasn't just blowing smoke after all.

"What if Hadley wasn't in town?" he asked when she failed to answer. "And what if those kids didn't . . . crash? Would you go out with me then?"

"Well, you were never interested before, so I'd have to say no."

"Maybe I could say *you* were the one who was never interested, whereas I always thought of you as the hot hockey chick."

Another snort. *Must stop doing that.* "You never asked me out."

"You never gave me the time of day."

"If you were pining for me, you hid it well."

He gave her a tolerant look. "I wasn't pining for you, Emmaline. I did think you were the hot hockey chick. We all do."

"Which explains why I've had two dates in three years."

"Maybe your sweet and gentle personality has something to do with that."

"Oh, bite me."

"I rest my case." He smiled. "You don't have to have a sweet and gentle attitude. You do have to at least smile once in a while. You're a tiny bit guarded—has anyone ever told you that?"

"No, as a matter of fact," she lied. She took another sip of wine. Make that a chug. "Then there are your looks." *Shut it, Em,* her brain advised.

"I'm hideous?"

"A little. I'm sorry to be the one to tell you." He smiled, and her mouth went dry. "No . . . you're . . . incredibly good-looking. It's a consideration."

He looked at her as if she were a complicated algebra equation. "So you're not interested in me because I'm incredibly good-looking, since your ex was also good-looking and he broke your heart."

"In addition to the other stuff. And drop that expression. It's not as dumb as it sounds."

"Good. Because it sounds very dumb."

"Well, it's not. It's very complicated and intelligent."

Or not. Maybe it *was* dumb. Maybe she should eat something before drinking any more wine.

She took another sip just the same. "Jack, I think you want to be with me because I'm here, because we've already done the deed and because you want a distraction from your troubles."

"All of those things are true. I also like you."

For some reason, those words scared the living bejesus out of her.

He liked her. She already loved him. It wasn't like she didn't know that already.

Crap.

This was exactly the kind of situation that led to

doom and despair, to whining to the Bitter Betrayeds, to crying in one's pillow, to that unutterably bleak knowledge that you loved someone who didn't love you back. Jack wanted a distraction. He liked her; that was it.

"I should go," she said, clearing her throat.

He turned off the stove and came around to her side of the soapstone counter, and Emmaline swiveled on her stool to keep him in sight. That was a mistake.

He braced his hands on either side of her and leaned forward. Oh, he smelled good. Like laundry detergent and wine and food and smoke.

"Don't go," he murmured.

Then he leaned in closer, and rubbed his cheek against hers, and she felt the scrape of five o'clock shadow, the heat from his body. His lips brushed her jaw, and her legs went weak and hot, and a nearly painful throbbing began in her girl parts.

"Jack," she managed.

"There's chocolate cake for dessert."

She swallowed. "Is that your idea of foreplay?"

"Yes," he whispered, kissing the spot where her jaw met her throat, so, so softly. "Is it working?"

She leaned back a little and looked into those clear, smiling blue eyes. "Yes," she heard herself say.

Then his mouth was on hers, soft and smiling, and she'd been an idiot, because for two weeks now, she'd been putting him off when she could have been kissing him instead. His hand went to her head and started tugging at her bun, which of course wouldn't come out without a crowbar and a map to the seventeen bobby pins, but no, nope, he was doing it, her hair was loosening, and then his fingers were sliding through it, and a few bobby pins pinged on the floor. His mouth was on her throat, causing flashes of heat to spark through her. Without her thinking about it, Em's hands slid up his ribs and onto his chest, feeling the solid, warm muscles shift and slide.

Then he pulled her into a standing position, holding her close, which was a good thing because she wasn't 100 percent sure her legs were working. She tugged his shirt out of his jeans, feeling the warm, velvety skin sliding over muscle.

She took off her utility belt—oops, should've thought of that before, didn't want to accidentally shoot the guy—and draped it over the chair.

Then Jack lifted her up (strong, really, she had to give him credit), and lay her down on the kitchen table and proceeded to unbutton her uniform shirt, brushing away her hands when she tried to help. He pulled off her boots, unbuttoned her pants and tugged them off, cleverly unhooked her bra and slid off her panties.

And then Jack Holland did her right then and there.

Who needed cake?

• • •

"This cake is fantastic," Em said a very pleasingly long time later.

She was curled up on his couch, wearing a pair of rubber ducky pajama bottoms (his, a gift from his niece, he said) and a Cornell sweatshirt, eating Mrs. Johnson's famous chocolate mocha cake.

Jack was watching her eat, a smile playing at the corner of his mouth, and she felt *quite* like a sex goddess. *Oh, yes.*

Yeah, yeah, she was a tramp; sue her. Like she was going to be able to resist Jack when he whispered things about how she tasted and smelled and felt, and all those things were very complimentary and she felt beautiful and strong and weak and cherished all at the same time.

She'd taken a shower in his glorious bathroom and spent a minute looking at herself, bedraggled hair, bee-stung lips, a possible love bite on her shoulder that she rather felt like photographing and posting to her Facebook page. *My hickey— with Jack Holland.* Her chest was still flushed and her skin looked creamy and, hells yes, she had it going *on.*

His bathroom was pretty amazing. There was a massive rectangular tub encased in a huge block of dark wood, the lip wide enough so a person could have a few plants or a glass of wine, a sandwich and a book and not have anything get wet. The shower was equally impressive, separate from the tub behind a glass brick wall. She combed her hair and put on the clothes he'd given her and padded to the kitchen, where, in case Jack wasn't already everything and a bag of chips, he'd sliced them each a huge piece of cake.

Dessert first. Finally, a man who understood her.

Sarge was asleep in front of the fire, and Lazarus sat on the mantel, looking very vulture-like as he gazed at the fat little puppy.

"Will your cat eat my dog?" she asked.

"He'll try." Jack sat next to her and took her feet onto his lap. "We're dating now, by the way."

"Well, that's—"

"Hush, woman. We're dating. Now finish your cake. I have plans for you. You'll need your strength."

And for once, Em didn't object.

Chapter Twenty-One

Turned out all Jack needed was a woman. At least, that was what it seemed like to him.

Granted, getting her had been as hard as catching an eel, but once he had her, he appreciated her wriggly properties. And he meant that with all the innuendo possible.

He really liked Emmaline Neal.

She was funny, she was smart, she was amazing in bed. Her dog was incredibly cute.

It was nice not being alone. On Saturday, they went cross-country skiing after their hockey game, the cold air and hard, bright sky making it a perfect day for it. Sarge came along, galumphing through the snow, trying to wrestle the poles out of Jack's hand. Then they came back to Jack's house, and he went down to the cellar to get a bottle of wine.

When he came up, it hit him.

This was what the house was supposed to look like. When he was married, it was too much, all those pillows and signs and clouds of perfume. Alone, it was on the barren side, looking more like a magazine shoot than a place where people lived.

But now it was kind of perfect. She'd brought a paperback novel, which was on the coffee table, as well as a comic book for him. . . . He'd confessed to a love of Superman growing up, and she found an old copy in Presque Antiques. Her knapsack sat on a kitchen chair, and her dog lay on his back, trying to woo Lazarus. There was a coffee cup on the table, and her jacket hung by the back door.

The woman herself was sprawled on his couch, not trying to look picturesque, the way Hadley always did . . . just relaxing. Or asleep, from the looks of it.

"So? I'm tired. You've worn me out," she said,

not opening her eyes. "And I'm not talking about skiing. I slept like the dead last night."

The image of Josh Deiner, cold and lifeless on the dock, slammed into him.

Emmaline sat up. "Shoot. Sorry about that. Poor choice of words."

"No worries."

She fiddled with the comic book, straightening it out. "Did you go to the hospital today?"

He had. He did every day, for some stupid reason. "You hungry?"

"How's Josh?"

"I don't know, Em. I'm not allowed to see him. You hungry or not?"

She didn't answer, but she stood up and took his hand. "You need to deal with this, you know," she said gently.

He took his hand back. "Look. I saved three kids. Almost four. That's a good thing. Don't make me a victim, Emmaline. I thought it was your parents who psychoanalyzed everything, not you. Now do you want dinner or not?"

His voice was hard.

"Sure," she said. "Why don't I cook?" And she got off the couch and went into the kitchen.

His phone buzzed with a text from Faith. Is Emmaline there? Don't blow it. Are you wearing something decent? Hint: clean clothes are nice.

Almost immediately, there was another text, this time from Honor. Don't come down for Top

Ten Tumors. I'll TiVo it. Hopefully you have better things to do. Like Emmaline.

And another, this one from Pru. The Coven must be together, deciding that nothing was more fun than tormenting their brother. Don't be afraid to experiment.

"Good God," he said. He tapped Faith's name to place a call.

"And who might this be?" she answered, and he could hear the noise of O'Rourke's in the background.

"Leave me alone, girls. I'm busy."

"Yay!" she said. "Jack's busy, girls!"

"You need any tips, we're here for you, brother!" Pru called, and Honor laughed.

He hung up, smiling begrudgingly.

Emmaline was leaning against the counter, staring at a pot.

Jack got up and went over to her. "I'm sorry I snapped at you," he said.

"It's okay." She gave him a quick smile, which made him feel worse.

He kissed her then, gently, then boosted her onto the counter and kissed her not so gently, and ignored the small voice in the back of his head that told him he might be using her.

That Thursday, Emmaline rounded up her kids. "We're going on a field trip," she said. "Try to contain your excitement." There were the expected

415

groans and complaints and excuses. "Oh, stop," she said. "It'll be fun. It's a sport. Exercise and healthy living, kids. The keys to a good life."

"Officer Em, we liked you," Cory said.

"Shush, children, and get into the squad car, and if you're very good, I'll put on the siren.

She drove them to Pettiman Rink, where she played hockey each week.

"I can't skate," Kelsey said. "I'm pregnant."

"Really?" Dalton said. "I couldn't tell."

"I hate you."

"It's not skating," Em said. "It's curling, and you'll love it."

"What's curling?" Kelsey asked.

"It's that thing with the rock and the brooms and the ice for losers who live in the Arctic circle and shit," Dalton said.

"Is he kidding?"

"No, that's about right," Emmaline said.

"My GPA is too low for me to be on a team," Tamara said proudly. "Nice try, though, Officer Em."

"This is a club, not a team. I just got permission from Dr. Didier for you all to join. Isn't that sunshiney and sparkly and wonderful?"

"What drugs are you on?" Dalton said. "And can I have some?"

Inside the rink were two other kids—Abby Vanderbeek and Charlie Kellogg. "Can we join, too?" Abby said listlessly. "My mother said I needed to be on a team sport, but I really think she just wants more grown-up time with my father."

"I'm so sorry," Tamara said.

"Yeah, of course you can join," Emmaline said. "Have you always loved curling, Charlie?"

"I don't even know what it is," he said. "I'm just keeping Abby company." He blushed.

"Aren't you guys cousins?" Cory asked.

"No. We're not related." His face went from blush to lava.

"Everyone's related in this town." Abby sighed. "I hear you're sleeping with my uncle, Emmaline. Will I be calling you Auntie soon?"

"Shut up, Abby," came a voice. "Hey, kids!"

Speak of the devil. Jack came over to Em and planted a quick kiss on her lips.

"Disgusting," Abby said. "Isn't it enough that my parents are home pretending to be Lord and Lady Crawley? Now my uncle is making googly eyes with the last cool adult in this town."

"I think it's beautiful, man," Dalton said. "You go, Jack."

"You guys are cute," Tamara said. "You gonna get married? Can we be in the wedding?"

"Enough, enough," Em said. "Here are the rules, more or less."

For the next ninety minutes, Emmaline let the kids go at it. The curling stone, a hefty, polished granite rock, was pushed from one end of the rink to the other, the kids furiously scrubbing the ice in front of it. Em didn't bother with technique; it was enough that the kids were doing something other than sitting around, complaining about life's injustices. Dalton kept running down the ice and sliding on his belly like an otter, and Charlie Kellogg and Abby seemed to have a dozen inside jokes, which was kind of nice.

Em went to the bleachers and sat, taking a couple of pictures of her kids (and sure, one or two of Jack). It was rare to see her kids in motion, and for once, they were all smiling.

Kelsey even got in on the action a little as the lead, the person who pushed the stone down the ice. She was six months along, which meant the baby would come right before graduation. She hadn't named a father yet and hadn't made a firm decision about adoption, either. Em was worried. If Kelsey didn't graduate . . .

"Yes, my brother!" Jack shouted, high-fiving Dalton. "We win!"

And speaking of worries, Jack was a little manic today. He had been since the other night, when she'd asked him about going to the hospital. That same night, he'd had a doozy of a nightmare, unable to wake up from it. She'd tried to soothe him, whispering that everyone was safe. But there were dark circles under his eyes.

He saw her looking and flashed her a smile that was too bright.

She'd tried to fix Kevin, too. Fix his ego, his

weight problem, protect him from mean people and his own negativity, and that had backfired miserably.

There was no reason to think she could fix Jack. She could be a distraction. She could be fun. She couldn't save anyone, and she shouldn't try.

"Excuse me," came a sweet voice, and Em tried not to twitch.

"Hadley. How are you?"

"I'm just wonderful, thank you," she said. "And how are you, Officer Neal?"

"Great." Though it was a balmy forty-five degrees today, Hadley wore a black wool coat with fur around the collar and a matching hat, looking like something out of a Russian fairy tale. Em was in uniform, as usual.

As if on cue, Hadley looked her up and down. "You're looking very . . . muscular today."

"Thank you."

"It was more of an observation than a compliment. But I guess up here, you women need to be strong, since y'all are much more likely to stay single."

"True," Emmaline said. "I *am* single and can open jars all by myself. That being said, I've never been divorced." *Never cheated on my husband, either.*

"Yes, I read *People* magazine," Hadley replied. "Well. Doesn't everyone?"

"Touché."

"I'm here to talk with Jack, actually, but I just *love* watching him move. Reminds me of just how graceful he is. And predatory, if you know what I mean."

Em rolled her eyes. Glanced at her watch. "Pack it in, kids," she called. "And Jack, there's someone to see you."

Jack came over, his face neutral at the sight of his ex. "What can I do for you, Hadley?" he asked, ever polite. *Irritating.*

"Jack, it's so good to see you!" she said, clasping her gloved hands in front of her. "You looked so handsome out there. Well, you always do, don't you? Now, guess who's in town? Frankie! She's dying to see you, Jack! Please say you'll come for dinner this time, please. You know how she's always adored you. Oh, my gosh, you know what she remembered today? The time the three of us went on the ole trolley tour and you and she were standing in front of that bakery, and y'all didn't even notice when—"

"Yeah, okay," he said. "What time?"

"How about cocktails at six o'clock? You know how Daddy instilled that in us." She beamed.

"Fine. See you later, then."

"Oh, hooray! See you later, baby!" Knowing to quit when she was ahead, Hadley practically skipped away.

"You two-timing Officer Em?" Dalton asked, sliding over.

"No," Jack said. "It's just dinner."

"Dude, are you crazy?" Dalton said. "It's not okay! Although, props, man. She's gorgeous."

"Em?" Jack asked. "You don't have a problem with that, do you?"

"It's fine," she said. It was not fine. And yet, she knew he was fond of his former sister-in-law. And it wasn't like they'd made plans that he'd just canceled. Nor did she want to be that kind of girlfriend who told him who he could see and who he couldn't, because, let's face it, those women were control freaks.

Still. Teeny Tiny wanted him to come for dinner, and he was going.

"Oh, you're screwed," Dalton said. "Sucks to be you, pal." He ran down the ice and slid once again.

"Is he right?" Jack asked. " 'Fine' does tend to signal doom when it's said like that."

Em glanced over his shoulder. "It's fine. I have to get the kids back."

"It's just that Frankie and I stayed friends."

"You don't have to explain."

"Shit. I've screwed the pooch here, haven't I?"

"No. You can have dinner with anyone you like. This is America. Life, liberty and dinner with your crazy ex-wife."

"I haven't seen Frankie in months."

"Jack, it's fine." She summoned a smile. "But you'll miss me."

He bent down and kissed her on the mouth. "You got that right."

Emmaline dropped the kids back at the church and then headed for home. Looked as though she'd have to cook tonight, alas. She unlocked her front door and went inside.

There were four suitcases in the living room, and sitting on the couch with Sarge on her lap was her sister.

"Angela!"

At the sound of her voice, Sarge leaped off Angela, grabbed Squeaky Chicken and began twirling in his love circles, whining around his toy.

"Oh, Emmaline, it's so good to see you! I'm so sorry I didn't call first!" Angela unfolded herself like an elegant flower and hugged Em tight, causing further joy from Sarge, who leaped against their legs, trying to get in on the action.

"It's great to see you," Em said. "What a surprise!"

Angela made a rueful face. "You'll have to forgive me," she said. "It was impulsive, I know."

"Is everything okay?"

"Oh, yes, yes, it's fine. It's just . . . well, I'm a bit at odds. Can I stay with you for a little while?"

"Sure," Em said. "It's your house, too. Nana left it to both of us. But what's going on?"

"I'm filling in for a colleague at Cornell," she said. "It was rather sudden, but frankly, the timing was perfect. You see, I just ended a relationship."

"You did? I didn't know you were seeing any- one."

"Yes. I wanted to tell you at the wedding, but it didn't seem the right time. It's been ending for a while, actually, but now it's official. And Mama and Papa . . . They've been circling. You know how it is when they sense you're troubled."

"Like vultures?"

Ange smiled. "I knew you'd understand perfectly."

"You can stay here as long as you like," Emmaline said, meaning it. "We'll finally live together."

Angela's eyes filled with tears. "And how lovely that will be. Also, Emmaline, I'll need your help telling Mama and Papa some news."

"What news is that?" Was she pregnant? They'd be thrilled. Hell, *Em* was thrilled at the very thought.

Her sister took a deep breath. "I'm gay."

Em's mouth fell open. "I, uh . . . wow. I didn't know that." She paused. "Will they be crushed that it's you and not me?" she asked, and much to her relief, Angela burst out laughing and hugged her. "Just promise me you'll have biological babies someday," Em added. "We don't want your gene pool to go to waste."

Chapter Twenty-Two

One of the things Jack remembered most about Hadley was she couldn't cook to save her life. From two flights below, he could smell smoke.

"It don't smell so good in here," Frankie said when she opened the door, using her good-ole-boy accent. "I may be staying with you tonight, Jack, 'cuz it may be that something crawled in that there oven and took its life. Or it could be Big Sister's version of pot roast. Best if we don't try to find out."

"Hey, Frankie," Jack said, giving her a hug. "Good to see you."

"You, too, big fella! We're going to O'Rourke's, if you don't mind. Hadley was trying to impress you by cooking, but I remember the burgers at O'Rourke's with a deep and abiding fondness, so I'm not at all sorry with this turn of events." She thudded down the hallway to get her coat.

Jack took a couple of steps into the apartment. There was a nearly empty bottle of Blue Heron Chardonnay on the counter. The wedding photo beamed out at him.

"Oh, Jack, I'm so embarrassed," Hadley said, coming out of the kitchen and untying her apron.

"I wanted us to have a nice family dinner, and I just do *not* know what happened."

There were tears in her eyes. One thing Hadley hated most of all was to look foolish in front of her sisters, those high-achieving, high-IQ women, and he felt a pang of sympathy for her.

"Well, it was really nice of you to try," he said.

She gave him a faint smile. "Thanks," she whispered. "Guess you know I was always something of a pretender to the throne when it came to cooking."

"Don't worry about it. Come on, ladies—off we go. Frankie, is that a new tattoo I see on your wrist?"

"Sure is, Jack." She pulled up her sleeve. " 'Conscientiously and with dignity.' Part of the vet's oath."

"I wish you wouldn't keep getting tattoos," Hadley said. "It's so un—"

"Unladylike? Oh, my Lord, don't you say that. You sound like Blanche Freakin' DuBois."

"Well, for someone who supposedly loves animals so much, you sure didn't show me much sympathy about Princess Anastasia, did you?" Hadley snapped.

"I sent a card. I called. Was I supposed to declare a national day of mourning? The cat was older than Methuselah, Hadley. And don't forget how she bit me on my ninth birthday. Still have the scar."

The sisters bickered and picked at each other with surprising fervor on the short walk across the green, making Jack slightly more grateful for his own sisters (not that they were perfect, God knew, especially with the number of texts and bits of romantic advice they'd been offering lately). But if ever there were two women with less in common, it was Frankie and Hadley.

O'Rourke's was mobbed. *Right.* It was Mardi Gras. Colleen wore a low-cut maternity dress, her belly more noticeable these days. That wasn't the only thing—the girls were on fine display, as usual, enhanced by pregnancy. Jack always thought pregnant women were beautiful, and Colleen had a lot going for her to begin with. Lucas was behind the bar, helping out. Colleen waved, then did a double take. "Oh, hey! Frankie, right?"

"You have a great memory," Frankie said. "Is that a love bump I see?"

"It most certainly is." Colleen put her hand on her stomach and beamed. "This Spanish pirate is my husband, Lucas Campbell."

"I'm actually a contractor," Lucas said, shaking Frankie's hand. "Nice to meet you. Hey, Jack. Hadley."

"I liked pirate better," Frankie said. "I'm Jack's ex-sister-in-law."

"I don't think Jack considers you an ex-anything," Hadley chirped.

"Let's see." Coll scanned the restaurant, then smiled knowingly. "You want to join Emmaline and her sister? They just sat down, and I bet they won't mind. Otherwise, it'll be about forty-five minutes."

"Oh, no, that's fine. We'll wait for a table," Hadley said.

"Sure, we'll join them," Jack said a bit too aggressively. "Sounds perfect."

Emmaline and Angela had been having a really nice time—well, Angela was the type who'd have a really nice time with anyone from Kim Jong-un to the Real Housewives of New Jersey, since there wasn't a mean bone in her body. But it was rare that the sisters ever got to do anything just the two of them . . . maybe twice, Em thought.

And, she admitted, it was awfully nice to have Angela confiding in her.

Angela had been in a relationship with a woman named Beatrice, but things hadn't been right for a while. When the chance came to teach astro-physics at Cornell for the rest of the semester, she jumped at it.

"I just couldn't face Mama and Papa," she said. "They're going to be shocked. They're not the most observant people in the world, for all that they're such involved parents," Angela said with a guilty smile.

"I know," Em murmured. "I think I've broken their hearts by being straight."

Angela laughed, then looked up. "Why, hello, Jack! How wonderful to see you again!"

Jack stood there with Colleen, Hadley and another woman, shorter and also quite pretty, with spiky hair and lots of piercings.

"You guys mind sharing a table?" Colleen asked, giving Em a wink. *Good old Colleen.* Em smiled back.

"Not at all, not at all," Angela said. "Please join us. Hello, I'm Angela Neal, Emmaline's sister."

"Frankie Boudreau. My sister Hadley here was married to Jack for a brief time."

Angela didn't bat an eyelash. "Hello, Hadley. What a pretty name! I'm Angela."

"Hi," Hadley said. She looked as if she smelled decaying animal.

"How do y'all know Jack?" Frankie asked.

"Em and I are dating," he said, claiming the chair next to Emmaline.

"You are?" Angela exclaimed. "Oh, hooray! I knew it was real. I could feel it." She sat back and beamed.

"Well, tonight just got more interesting, didn't it?" Frankie smiled and sat down across from Angela.

"So you need a bodyguard?" Em whispered as Jack sat next to her.

"You got that right," he murmured. "I owe you."

"Yes, you do," she said, taking a sip of her wine (apricot and grass with a hint of limestone . . . or maybe it was just grapey, but she was trying).

Hadley sat down across from Jack, slid her little pink cardigan off her shoulders to reveal a pink sleeveless dress. "This is so nice, being here again," she said, fluttering her lashes. "I always loved this little place. Jack and I had so many fun times here."

"Isn't it lovely?" Angela said. "Frankie, forgive me—I'm not from around here. Do you live in town?"

"I don't, but before I say another thing, I just gotta tell you how much I love your accent," Frankie said.

Angela laughed. "And I love yours, as well."

"Eastern Africa?"

"Oh, my goodness, yes! What an ear you have!"

"I spent a few weeks in Kenya on an animal preserve," Frankie said. "I'm finishing up my veterinarian degree at Cornell."

"How wonderful! I start teaching there next week. Relativity and astrophysics for Dr. Bering."

"That smelly old dog? I took his Searching the Solar System class just for fun, or so I thought. Well, I tell you, his students are in for a real treat when you walk through the door."

"Should I make her stop flirting?" Jack asked Em.

Em looked at her sister, who certainly didn't

seem to be suffering. "Nah. Ange can handle herself."

Hadley had a pinched look on her face. "Looks like our sisters are getting on like a house on fire," Emmaline said to her. "Sweet, isn't it?"

"Mmm," Hadley said, opening the menu.

Jack had his arm around the back of Em's chair. He gave the back of her arm a small caress, and her side broke out in goose bumps. When his eyes met hers, a hint of a smile warmed his eyes from January blue to Caribbean sky.

God. Listen to her. So much for warning herself not to get carried away.

But he shouldn't be looking at her like that in front of his ex-wife, no matter how much of a pain in the ass the woman was.

And Em knew what it was like to watch your ex with another woman.

"How are things with you, Hadley?" she surprised herself by asking.

Before Hadley could answer, Hannah O'Rourke swung by with a bottle of red and another of white. "For the hero of the Midwinter Miracle and his friends," she stated grandly. "Sent by Barb Nelson, who wouldn't mind interviewing you for the paper. She guessed the answer would be no but wants you to have the wine anyway."

Jack's eyes went flat. "She's right," he said. But he turned around, spotted Barb and waved. When he turned back, Em could feel him locking up. His arm was no longer around her chair.

As the evening unfolded, Frankie and Angela did most of the talking, each of them gifted at the art of conversation. Hadley said very little, though she laughed loudly whenever anything remotely funny was said. There was a "Look at me—I'm so much fun!" desperation to her, and while it was irritating, Em couldn't help feeling sorry for her. In this little circle of five, she was the odd man out.

"Have you had any decorating jobs lately, Hadley?" she asked as their dinners were brought out.

"No. As a matter of fact, I haven't," Hadley said tightly.

"Are you an interior decorator?" Angela asked. "How interesting!"

"Not according to my family," Hadley snapped. "Frankie'll be a vet before long—"

"You'll never guess where this hand was today, by the by," Frankie said. "In a cow's vajayjay. Mother and calf are both doing just fine."

"And as I was saying before my sister interrupted me, my sister Ruthie is a doctor, and Rachel's a state representative, and, as my daddy puts it, I like pretty things. No one understands or appreciates what I do."

Frankie rolled her eyes, and Jack sighed. Em concurred. Hadley was hard to take.

"I think it's a wonderful field," Angela said.

"What would life be like if we didn't all have our little refuges to come back to?"

"Emmaline and I went curling today with her high school kids," Jack began, and a storm flashed across Hadley's face at the change of subject.

"What's curling?" Frankie asked.

"Excuse me," came a rather slurred male voice. "I just had to tell you how beautiful you are."

"Oh, thank you!" said Hadley, looking up with a bright smile. "That's so sweet of you to say!"

"I wasn't talking to you."

Hadley's mouth dropped open in shock. And please, Em thought. Hadley was beautiful, yes, but *Angela* was breathtaking and otherworldly and dazzling. Em smiled at her sister, who lifted a flawless eyebrow. "He's talking to you, Emmaline," she said.

Em looked up. "You are?" Goofy-looking guy, that dorky, sculpted hair flip in the front. He was maybe twenty-five years old.

"Yeah." He smiled. "You're really . . . wow." He swayed a little.

"You driving tonight?" Em asked.

"Not if you'll take me home," he said, bracing his hands on the end of their table.

"Have I mentioned I'm a cop?" she said.

"Have I mentioned how hot that is?" he countered.

"She's with me, pal," Jack said. Hadley's lips disappeared.

"Oh, I *love* that," Frankie said. "I mean, I may like girls, Jack, but that was delicious, buddy."

"S'okay, dude," the guy said. "I getcha. But you, lady, are hot." He glanced at Frankie. "And you're not so bad, either."

"No driving, bub," Em said.

"Yes, Officer. Though I wouldn't object if you handcuffed me."

"Wow. I've never heard that one before," Em said.

Jack started to rise, but the guy grinned—he *was* pretty cute—and wove away.

Angela clapped in delight. "Oh, Emmaline, does that happen to you all the time?"

"Uh, no," she said with a grin. Only Angela could ask that with a straight face. "Excuse me, I just want to make sure he's really not driving."

"Yes, please do," Hadley said. "The poor man was so drunk he could barely see straight." She drained her wine and held her glass out for more.

Em paused. A talent was a talent, and Hadley had certainly mastered the art of the razor-sharp put-down.

She went over to the guy's table in the corner, where he was sitting with some friends about the same age. "Do we have a designated driver here?" she asked.

"That'd be me," one of the guys said, holding up his glass. "Seltzer water."

"Great. Just wanted to check and make sure the

Boy Wonder here wasn't driving. I'm a cop," she added, just in case.

"You followed me! I knew it!" Drunk Boy said. "You wanna step in the bathroom, have a good time?"

"No," Emmaline said. *Drunk people. Sigh.*

"Shut up, idiot," one of his friends said.

Em turned to leave, but suddenly she heard the scrape of a chair and there was a hand on her shoulder. She turned around fast. "Knock it off," she said firmly.

But the kid grabbed her and kissed her square on the mouth.

Now, nine months ago, Emmaline would've just kneed him in the nuts and left him whimpering on the floor. But now she was a cop, and rather than be accused of police brutality, she opted instead to push her index finger into his Adam's apple.

And it worked, of course; no one could kiss when his airway was being toyed with. Then all of a sudden, he was yanked back, and Jack had him against the wall with his arm on his throat, and the kid was wheezing and terrified.

The kid's friends surged, then stopped, not sure what to do. "Stay," she commanded. "Jack, knock it off." She put her hand on his shoulder.

The bar grew quiet, only the music from the jukebox playing.

"You okay?" Jack bit out.

"I'm fine," she said. "I'm even a little bored."

"Problem here?" asked Connor O'Rourke, wiping his hands on a dish towel. Lucas stood behind him, as well as half the fire department, ready to rumble.

"No," Em said. "Just a kid who can't hold his beer. Jack. Let him go."

He did (took him long enough), and his face was stony when he looked at her. A tiny muscle under his left eye twitched.

"Fuck you, mister," the drunk kid said.

"You guys are done here," Connor said to the youths. "Settle up and off you go."

Jack's jaw was still clenched, his eyes burning holes in the drunk kid, and, really, it was kind of hot. No one had ever been jealous over her before. Then again, it was also pretty over the top. "Let's go back to our table," she suggested, taking his arm and steering him away. He let her, though he grumbled most attractively. Em smiled.

Then there was a thunk, and Jack staggered forward. Em turned, and there was a rush of people and then Connor and Lucas and half the kid's friends had the idiot pinned against the wall.

Because Drunk Boy had just hit Jack over the head with a beer bottle, and Jack's blond hair was steeped with red.

"So let me get this straight," Levi said at the E.R. about an hour later. "My brother-in-law and deputy were brawling in a bar?"

435

Jack sighed. His head was throbbing, Hadley was yowling like Lazarus during a trip to the vet and he really didn't need all this . . . attention.

"Levi, drop the disapproving parent act," Emmaline said. "The kid coldcocked Jack."

Jack barely heard. Several floors above, Josh Deiner lay hooked up to his machines.

"Jack, why did the kid coldcock you?" Levi asked.

"Because he kissed me, and Jack was defending my pure and untainted honor," Emmaline said. *Ungratefully. Women. You never could win with them.*

Levi raised an eyebrow, then looked over at Hadley, who was still choking with sobs. Frankie sat next to her, reading a magazine. "And why is she here?" he asked.

Why indeed? Because Jack's ex-wife fed off attention like a vampire. Whatever happened to anyone happened to Hadley more. Just the fact that the shit-faced kid had hit on Emmaline had been guaranteed to make her crazy, so Jack wasn't surprised when she went the Route Hysterical moments later.

As soon as the drunken idiot coldcocked him, Hadley had started screaming like a banshee (speaking of a lack of sobriety), begging him to speak to her, even though he was standing with a dishcloth of ice against his head, handed to him by Colleen seconds after he was hit. But that wasn't enough for Hadley, and she'd actually crawled over to him as Frankie tried to pick her up off the floor.

Then Everett Field arrived, in uniform, puffing up with self-importance as he led the handcuffed kid away to the applause of the O'Rourke patrons. Pru and Carl had been at the bar, too, hidden in one of the back booths dressed in Star Trek uniforms, and Pru burst out laughing at the sight of her brother's blood, which was fairly typical.

Then Levi had come in, as well as Faith, and, against Jack's wishes, the ambulance was called, much to the delight of his fellow members on the Manningsport volunteer EMS squad.

He really just wanted to be home. With Emmaline.

As if picking up that thought, Hadley paused in her crying, glanced over and burst into renewed sobs.

"I have to interview her," Levi said, his forehead wrinkling.

"Sucks to be you," Em said.

"How much longer will this take?" Jack grumbled.

"They're busy tonight," Levi said. "Want me to call anyone? Your dad? Mrs. Johnson?"

"I'm sure your wife already has. If Pru didn't beat her to it." Privacy wasn't an ideal the Holland family held dear.

"Hello! I'm looking for John Noble Holland

the Fourth? Gorgeous name, right? Come on in!"
Jack stood up and walked toward a tiny Asian
woman who looked to be about fourteen years
old. "Hi! Nice to meet you. I'm Dr. Chu. Sorry for
the wait! It's totes crazy here tonight."

Hadley got up and tried to follow them in, but
Jack simply said, "No," which caused still-louder
crying.

"Will you pipe down?" Frankie said. "They're
gonna medicate you if you don't. Stop being such
an attention whore, Hadley. He's fine. And he's
not your concern anymore."

"I thought he was dead! Oh, Jack, if you'd
been—"

Mercifully, the doors swung shut behind him,
cutting off his ex-wife's wails.

The doctor, who couldn't have been more than
five feet tall, showed him into the exam room.
"Have a seat, Mr. Holland. We'll get you taken
care of lickety-split. Positive attitude, check!"

There was a knock, and Emmaline peeked in.
"Want company?" she asked.

"Sure."

"Are you his wife?" the doctor asked.

"No. Girlfriend." She blushed.

"Well, from the look of that gross and bloody
towel, Mr. Holland," the doctor said, "I think
you'll need some stitches. I love stitches. They're
my favorite! Has anyone ever told you you're
really handsome, Mr. Holland?"

Christ.

"Hey, is Jeremy Lyon on tonight?" Em asked. That's right. Jeremy took shifts here a few times a month.

Dr. Enthusiasm paused. "Um . . . yes?"

"He's a family friend. Mind if he sees Jack instead?"

The girl sighed. "Fine," she said, deflating. "I'll get him." She slouched away.

"Thanks," Jack said.

"Sure." Emmaline sat down on the edge of his bed, glanced at him, then back at her hands. "You okay?"

"Yeah."

"Thanks for . . . you know. Looking out for me." She stuffed her hands in her pockets. "It wasn't necessary."

Jack's irritation melted a bit. "You're welcome. I probably earned a kiss, don't you think?"

"Maybe."

"Definitely."

"I'll think about it."

He reached out and hooked a finger in the front of her sweater and pulled her to him, then kissed her. Em's hands went to his chest. Her mouth was so soft, a balm against this whole stupid night. "I really hated seeing that guy kiss you," Jack murmured against her mouth.

"I should hope so."

He kissed her again, and this time, his tongue

brushed hers, and she melted against him.

"Hey, Jack—Oh, my God, you two are together? Why am I always the last to know the good stuff?" Jeremy stood in the cubicle. "This is so nice! I only wish I could take credit for fixing you up. Hi, Emmaline, how are you?" He hugged her, then shook Jack's hand. "So you got hit on the head, huh? Not very smart of you, Jack."

"He turned his back on a drunken idiot," Em offered. Jeremy tsked and shook his head.

"Actually, *you* turned my back on a drunken idiot," Jack said.

"True. Sorry about that."

"Did you lose consciousness?" Jeremy asked, washing his hands.

"Nope."

"How's the pain?"

"Fine."

"You military types. So stoic." He looked at Jack's head, then opened a cabinet and took out a suture kit. "Gonna need a few stitches, bro. This will sting."

When Jeremy was done, Em said she'd check on Hadley and see if Levi needed anything else. "Other than the head wound, how are things?" Jeremy asked when she was gone.

"Good."

"Any sequelae from the rescue?"

Jack looked up sharply. "Like what?"

"Inner ear pain, balance issues." Jeremy paused, his eyes steady. "PTSD."

"No."

"This is confidential, of course, since I'm here as your doctor. PTSD would be things like nightmares, panic attacks, flashbacks."

"I know what it is, but I'm fine, Jeremy. Thanks."

"Okay. Glad to hear it." He signed a paper. "Ice, Tylenol if you need it, come to the office in a week for stitch removal." Jeremy smiled. "Good to see you, even under the circumstances."

"You, too, Jer." He gave Jeremy a manly hug. The guy was practically part of the family. As decent as they came, too.

Emmaline wasn't back yet, and Jack found himself going to the elevator. Got in, pushed the button. The elevator rose, and six seconds later, the doors opened to a sign.

"Fourth Floor, Intensive Care Unit. Please speak quietly."

The hall was quiet except for the beeping of machines and, farther down, the murmur from the nurses' station. The squeak of rubber-soled shoes. The hiss of a ventilator.

Room 401 had a whiteboard hanging on the door. *McGowan, H.* was written in green marker. Jack could see a bed and someone sleeping (or dead). Across the hall, 402, *Zaccharias, M.*, 403, *Blake, S.*, 404, *Humbert, L.*

Room 405, *Deiner, J.*

The door was open a few inches.

He shouldn't be here.

His heart was smashing in his chest, hurling itself against his ribs like that bobcat.

If he opened the door just a little more, he'd be able to see something. Josh's feet, maybe.

The image of Josh Deiner, sitting up in bed, texting on his phone or watching TV or eating Jell-O, came to him so fast and hard that Jack's knees nearly buckled.

"Can I help you?"

Jack jumped. He hadn't even heard the nurse behind him. "Jane MacGregor, APRN," her name tag said. Jack was aware suddenly that he was drenched in sweat.

"How's he doing?" Jack whispered.

Her face softened. "Are you a family member?"

"No."

"Then I can't discuss—"

"How dare you? Get out! Get out!"

Josh Deiner's mother stood in the doorway, her voice like breaking glass. "How dare you come here? Get away from my son!"

"Mrs. Deiner, I just wanted—"

"Get away from us!" she screamed, and shoes were squeaking on the floors and visitors' heads popped out of rooms. "He's here because of you! How dare you intrude like this!"

The nurse took Jack's arm and led him down the hall, and Jack thought he might fall; he wasn't sure his legs were working right. Maybe it was the hit on the head, but he was wrong, something was wrong, and *Josh, please, please don't die.*

The elevator doors opened, and there was Emmaline.

"There you are," she said.

"There's been a disturbance here," said the nurse. "Security's on their way up."

"Josh Deiner's room?" Em asked. "Jack here is the one who pulled him out of the lake."

"Oh, I see." The woman looked at Jack, her face kind. "I'm sorry, but I still have to ask you to leave."

"We're going," Em said. "You won't need Security. I'm Manningsport P.D."

"What you did was amazing, by the way," the nurse said softly. "I'm sorry about the Deiners." Then she walked back down the hall.

Jack could hear Mrs. Deiner sobbing, the loneliest, most heart-wrenching sound on earth . . . a mother mourning her only child.

Josh wasn't getting any better. Jack didn't need a doctor to tell him that.

"Let's go home, big guy," Emmaline said. She pushed the button for the elevator, and the doors opened.

When they closed behind them and the elevator started to move, Jack put his arms around her, held her close and didn't say anything.

When they reached the lobby, he let her go and saw that her eyes were wet.

"I'll tell Angela I'm staying at your place," she said, and that was all.

Chapter Twenty-Three

Emmaline was slurping down her third cup of coffee a few days later. It was her day off, and she and Angela had been up late the night before with the Bitter Betrayeds, who'd graciously accepted Angela as an honorary member, despite declaring her "too beautiful and too nice."

The group was full of news—Jeanette O'Rourke was going on a cruise with Ronnie Petrosinsky, the Chicken King. Allison was indeed going back to the irritatingly perfect Charles, who'd proven his love by sending her a gift-wrapped box of cookie jar fragments. Shelayne announced that she'd just been approved as an adoptive parent, and there were hugs and more Peach Sunrises and a bottle of champagne.

And lastly, Em was grilled on how Jack was in bed. Her silence had brought on some fierce (and very colorful) speculation.

"She's blushing," Grace had pointed out, coming in from the kitchen with a fresh pitcher of

Peach Sunrises. "You know what *that* means. Jack is a dirty, dirty boy." Coming from their senior citizen member, this had caused shrieks of laughter from the women.

"Maybe it's time you changed the name of your group," Angela had suggested. "None of you seems particularly bitter or betrayed."

That had given the rest of them pause.

"Call yourself the Sunrise Girls," Ange had suggested. "These cocktails are simply wonderful, Grace."

It was surely their best meeting yet. No one had mentioned the book they'd neglected to read, but that was never really the point.

Angela, of course, leaped out of bed that morning, completely unaffected by last night. Emmaline wasn't so lucky. Sarge was upstairs, having decided he loved Angela more, the faithless wretch, and was barking in excitement at whatever Angela was doing. Loudly, Em thought, wincing.

Ten minutes later, both of them craving chocolate, they walked to Lorelei's Sunrise Bakery. The smell of pastry sent out its siren call. "Oh!" Angela said. "Look at this. A bridal salon! Let's go in, Emmaline."

"Why?" Em said.

"I'm thinking you should try on dresses," she said. "For when you and Jack get married. I always hated that sad little dress you bought."

"It wasn't sad," Emmaline said.

"Please. It looked like you were going to a dance at the Elks Lodge circa 1983," Angela said. "No, this time, you must take me with you. I insist."

"How do you know what an Elks Lodge dance looks like? Besides, I'm not getting married anytime soon."

"Please. He's crazy about you. He'll be popping the question in a matter of weeks."

Emmaline opened the door of the bakery and bumped squarely into the man himself.

"Jack! We were just talking about you," Angela said.

"Really." He gave Emmaline a look as if trying to place her.

"Jack, what do you think?" Angela said, her eyes twinkling. "Ivory or white? Which do you prefer?"

"Ignore her," Emmaline said.

Jack glanced across the street where a poufy dress shimmered in the window of Happily Ever After. He didn't smile. "Would you like to have dinner with my family tonight?"

Angela gave a muffled squeal, and Em shot her a filthy look. "Uh . . ."

"You'd be welcome, too, Angela," Jack said.

"Oh, no! No, thank you for including me, Jack. You're terribly sweet, but no, I have to be at Cornell this evening." She gave Emmaline a sly smile. "In fact, look at the time! I should go. Always lovely to see you, Jack." She strode away, waving at someone inside the antiques store.

"I wasn't shopping for a wedding dress," she said, immediately regretting it.

"Do you want to come for dinner?" he repeated.

She squinted at him. "You sure you want me there?"

"Why would I ask you if I didn't?"

"I don't know."

"Six o'clock at Honor and Tom's. I can pick you up if you want." He looked at his watch.

"No, that's fine. Jack, are you okay?"

"I'm great. I have to run. See you tonight."

Somehow, Emmaline had forgotten just how many Hollands there were.

The driveway was filled with cars, and Blue, Faith's giant golden retriever, raced up to her door. Sarge yipped wildly, his tail whacking Em in the head.

Honor had called her earlier to invite her to dinner personally and told her to bring her dog, since who didn't love puppies? She said her own little dog could use some socializing.

The Hollands' big white house was a landmark in Manningsport. Em had never been inside before, and it was a little imposing. Made her glad she'd dressed in a skirt.

She clipped on Sarge's leash, got out and let her

dog wriggle in ecstasy as Blue sniffed him over. Then she grabbed the flowers she'd brought— gerbera daisies—and with a deep breath, went up to the front door and knocked.

No one answered, though the door practically shook from noise inside. She knocked again. Nothing. Opened the door and peeked in.

The place was mobbed.

"Emmaline! Welcome," said Honor, bustling over. "Oh, these are gorgeous! Thank you."

"Thanks for having me. Are you sure you don't want me to leave Sarge in the car?"

"We all love dogs—don't worry." She bent over to pet Sarge, who sat and wagged his tail. "Hello, handsome! Are you here to teach Spike some manners?" She unclipped the leash and smiled.

A tiny Yorkie came skittering over and growled at Sarge, causing the much larger puppy to collapse in delight and roll over in the acknowledgment that, yes, the Yorkie was boss and could do whatever it wanted.

"Best friends forever," Honor said with a smile. "Come on in. It's chaos, but that's who we are. I'll hang up the leash and put these in some water." She took the flowers and walked off, leaving Em alone.

The periwinkle-blue living room was big and gracious, filled with tasteful furniture, built-in bookshelves and a gorgeous white marble fire-place. Jack and his father were in deep conversation there, each holding a glass of wine in their left hands. Easy to see where Jack got his looks. The older Mr. Holland, Jack's grandfather, stood listening while eating a chunk of cheese the size of a smartphone. The grandmother speculated why on earth Honor had painted the living room *this* shade of blue when she herself preferred *pale* blue, then segued into how Abby should beware of white vans, because that's what kid-nappers drove.

Em edged toward Jack, overhearing Mrs. Johnson lecturing Tom Barlow on his curry-making technique. Pru and Carl Vanderbeek were arguing over something, Pru doing some magnificent eye rolling. Their son, Ned, was talking with Charlie Kellogg, and Levi stood in the corner, watching as Abby pressed her hands against Faith's belly.

The noise level made Emmaline's eyes throb.

"Hi."

She jumped a little. "Hey, Jack."

He didn't kiss her. "Guys, you all know Emmaline, right?" he asked.

"Hey, girl," Prudence said. "What are you doing here? Did Jack invite you? Wow. He hasn't done that since he brought the Southern belle home. Is there news? You guys engaged or knocked up or something?"

"Jack," said his grandmother, "you should try marriage again. Your grandfather won't be around forever, you know. Don't you want him to have more great-grandchildren? This one has nice breeding hips."

"Goggy!" Faith yelped.

"What? You do, too. Don't worry."

"Leave them alone, guys," Honor said. "Sorry, Emmaline."

"No, no," Em said, feeling slightly sweaty. "Breeding hips are . . . good. Thank you, Mrs. Holland."

"Hallo, Em," Tom said, giving her a kiss on the cheek. "What would you like to drink?"

A lot, Em thought. "Oh, wine is great," she said.

"Brilliant. Be right back."

The three dogs raced through the living room, then up the stairs, then down the stairs. Em seemed to be the only one who thought this was perhaps a bit rowdy. Then again, her family dinners consisted of carefully modulated voices swapping bitter insults disguised in psychobabble, compliments from Angela and grunts from herself. Topics of discussion included self-actualization, repressed memories and why Emmaline was wasting her life, with a side of martinis.

Rowdy dogs weren't so bad at all by comparison.

"It's ten after six, Honor, sweetheart," said old Mr. Holland. "Can we eat? What are we, Europeans or something?"

"I'm so glad you're dating my loser uncle," Abby said, bouncing over to Em's side. "Also, would you mind taking me to the firing range? I want to learn how to kill a man."

"Just kiss him," Ned advised. "He'd die of horror."

"Shut *up,* Ned! Levi, did you know that Ned drove to Geneva on Sunday to see your sister?"

"We're just friends!" Ned said. "Stop glaring at me, Levi. If you hurt me, Faith will be heartbroken."

"Oh, I don't know," Faith said. "I only love you about half the time as it is."

"I'm starving," the grandfather complained. "Can we get this show on the road?"

Levi and Em were the last to go into the dining room, as Jack was pressed into service in the kitchen. "Is it always like this?" Em whispered.

"Yeah," Levi said. "You'll get interrogated over dinner, by the way. Same thing happened to me the first time I came for dinner, and to Tom last spring. Don't worry. They're good people."

"I'm sweating like a farm animal."

"I remember the feeling. Hang in there, Deputy. Think of it as a hostage situation, except you're the hostage this time." He gave her a half smile.

"Thanks, Chief," she said. "You're not so bad sometimes."

"My God. I'm having that engraved."

"I take it back."

They crowded around the table, and Honor, Tom, Mrs. Johnson and Jack emerged from the kitchen laden with platters and dishes. The noise level increased as the food was passed and described and argued over, and before Emmaline managed to sit down, old Mr. Holland and Charlie were taking seconds.

"So, Emmaline, dear," said Mrs. Johnson. "Tell us about your family."

"Oh, uh . . . well, it's just my parents and sister and me. Angela. She was adopted when I was fourteen."

"So you were an only child until then?"

"That's right."

"Lucky," said Ned and Abby in unison. Charlie snickered.

"And are you close with your parents?" Mrs. Holland asked.

"Oh, sure," she lied.

"Do I know them?" Mrs. Holland asked.

"No, but you might remember my grandmother. Luanne Macomb, my mother's mother? She lived on Water Street, where I live now. I used to spend summers with her, and then I came to live with her when I was in high school."

"Why would you leave your parents?" Mrs. Johnson asked, a fierce frown on her face.

"Mom, will you send *me* to live somewhere for the rest of high school so I don't have to see Ned all the time?" Abby asked.

"Do it, Mom," Ned added.

"Didn't you go there to play sometimes, Faithie?" Jack's father asked.

"Yep. Em's grandmother would have a few of us down in the summer. She made the best brownies." Faith smiled in fond remembrance.

"So where did you grow up?" Mrs. Johnson asked.

"Southern California," she said.

"Oh, how horrible," Mrs. Holland murmured. "Well, I guess you can't help it."

"It's actually quite beautiful out there, Goggy," Faith said.

"Do you see your parents a lot?" Mrs. Holland asked.

"Leave the girl alone!" old Mr. Holland said. "She hasn't taken one bite of food."

True. It'd be nice if Jack jumped in here and called off the dogs, but he didn't seem to be listening.

"I visit a few times a year, Mrs. Holland," Emmaline said.

"Call me Goggy."

Do I have to? Em thought. "Goggy it is, then."

"Good! Since we're going to be family," the old woman added slyly.

"Stop it, Goggy," Honor said.

"Charlie, tell everyone about your match the other day," Tom said, winking at Emmaline from across the table. "Emmaline, our boy here is becoming quite the boxer."

● ● ●

A thousand or so hours later, Emmaline thanked Honor and Tom once again and led Sarge out into the rain, which felt blissfully cold on her hot face. Jack followed.

The subject of marriage had been broached nine times tonight. Hints about babies, eleven. Goggy (that name!) had expressed her hope that Emmaline and Jack wouldn't "live in sin"; Pops had countered with the opposite opinion. Abby unsubtly requested more cousins. Pru showed Em a website for sex toys called KinkyKitties, making Abby, Ned and Charlie go into fits of horror and hysterics.

It felt like someone had taken sandpaper to her brain.

Jack had barely said a word. And while she didn't want to be a weenie, it would've been nice if her . . . her . . . her *boyfriend,* curse the stupid word, had come to her aid once or twice tonight. She had to wonder why he'd even invited her in the first place.

She put Sarge in the car; the dog was limp with exhaustion at the moment, though that would change the second she started the engine. The rain was harder now, soaking her hair.

"So that was fun," Jack said.

She looked at him. He was serious. "Fun? That was fun? That wasn't fun, Jack."

He frowned. "It wasn't?"

"Right, right, you weren't exactly present, were you? Well, I'm glad you had a good time."

"Didn't you? Everyone really likes you." His phone buzzed, and he looked at it.

"Everyone? Even you? Because you didn't speak to me the entire time."

He looked as if he had no clue what she was talking about. "I didn't?"

"Well, let's recap," she said. "I think you said 'Hi' and . . . and that was it. Meanwhile, your grandmother was asking about how long my mother was in labor with me, Mrs. Johnson asked how many kids I thought I'd like to have, then actually wrote down the answer, and your niece wants me to teach her to shoot to kill."

"That sounds about right. How many?"

"How many what?'

"How many kids?"

"I told her eighteen. Possibly twenty."

A faint smile crossed his face. "Want to come back to my place?" he asked.

She blinked. *Men.* "Jack, why are we dating?"

"I have no idea."

Then he kissed her, the two of them standing there in the rain. His mouth was gentle and soft, his body warm against the cool night. Em was torn between the desire to smack him and . . . and . . . and to just keep kissing him, because his hands were cradling her head and her arms were around his waist and he knew what he was doing. Yes, indeed, his mouth moving, lips soft and smooth in contrast to the scrape of his razor stubble. "We're together," he murmured against her mouth. "Get used to it."

She stepped back and sucked in a breath of damp, cold air. "You're very unpredictable, Jack."

"In all the best ways. Come up to my place and I'll show you." He grinned, and it was like the sun coming out, causing a flare of warmth in her chest. That smile made her legs hot and wobbly. Made her think of blue-eyed babies, eighteen of them. Okay, fine, maybe not eighteen, but a few, anyway.

Being that he was Jack Holland, he got into his truck and started it, completely confident that she'd follow.

And being that she was rapidly becoming one of those swoony, lovesick females, she did.

Men were confusing.

But you know what? She had a sister, and while Angela might be gay, she was also the smartest person on the continent. She pulled out her cell and hit her sister's number. "How did it go?" Angela asked by way of greeting.

"Um . . . I have no idea. He's happy now. Barely spoke during dinner. I've been told I have breeder's hips. We're going back to his place."

Ange laughed merrily. "Time to rock his world?"

"I don't know."

"Well, if I may be so forward, Emmaline," Angela began.

"I was hoping you would be." She started up the long winding lane that led to Jack's house.

"Maybe you need to be a little less . . . careful? A little more heartfelt? Because I sense that you have very deep feelings for Jack, and perhaps it's time he knew. He brought you home to his family . . . maybe he needs a sign from you, too."

"Like what?"

"That's where I can't really help. But you'll know. You will. I'm heading back now. Would you like me to walk Sarge?"

"No, he's with me. But thanks, Angela. Thanks."

"See you tomorrow, darling."

Em drove up Jack's long driveway and sat there for a second. Lights went on inside the house, and a warm sensation washed over her. The house was beautiful. The man who owned it was beautiful, and he was waiting for her. And Angela was right. Time to rock his world.

"Come on, puppy," she said to her dog, wiping off his paws with the towel she kept in the car for just such a purpose. She carried him inside the mudroom and set him down, then took off her coat and hung it on a hook. Lazarus came to investigate, croaked at Sarge, earning a tail wag and a wary head lick, which the cat endured before skittering off.

Jack was lighting a fire as she entered the living room.

We're together now. Get used to it.

So this wasn't just for sex or a distraction or a human shield for Hadley. Maybe this was real.

The warmth in her chest seemed to expand.

His phone buzzed on the table next to her.

"Probably one of my sisters," he said, adding a log. He stood up and came over, looked at the phone. "Yep. I should sell a few off. You want a glass of wine?"

"Sure." She'd barely had any at dinner.

"I have a nice bottle in the cellar. Be right back." He kissed the top of her head and went downstairs. He hadn't said boo at his family's, but he was making up for it now. She could live with that. She wasn't perfect, either.

Sarge went over to the fireplace, turned in a circle five times, then curled up. Lazarus approached, warily, then lay down near the puppy's head.

Aw. They liked each other.

Jack's phone buzzed again. And again. In fact, it was vibrating right to the edge of the table. Without thinking, Em picked it up before it fell.

And then, before she could even make a case against it, she looked at the screen.

Pru: We like her, Useless. Are you guys naked already? Don't let her see those ugly-ass pajamas Honor bought you for Christmas. In fact, burn those.

Faith: You should've talked more tonight, dummy. She looked like a deer in the headlights. Tell her she doesn't have breeder hips even if that will come in handy later. Takes one to know one.

Goggy: Wermww ri&ght cmlwlr?.

Honor: She took that like a champ. Tom & I both approve. Charlie too.

Hadley: Jack, I need 2 speak 2 U asap. We belong 2gther. Pls. call asap. I no u still love me. We can work this out!!!

Goggy: qhy ro$(ia we flt rgis

Okay. Jack's grandmother appeared to be drunk. But, no, Abby had complained about getting seventeen texts from her that day alone.

Hadley's text—not so nice. The woman really needed to get a clue or some counseling, stat.

But Em was glad Jack's sisters liked her, which she already knew, more or less. And Jack liked her, and she liked him, way too much . . . or maybe the right amount. Maybe it was time to go for it. And if she wanted to prove something tonight, a constantly buzzing phone wasn't going to help.

Maybe she'd just mute it for a little while. It was after ten. She slid the switch over. *There.*

She and Jack had been together for a few weeks now. And, yes, she'd been wary, given her own romantic past and Jack's ex-wife being around, not to mention the emotional maelstrom surrounding the accident.

But tonight, she wouldn't be.

He came back upstairs, and Emmaline stood up.

"So was tonight really awful?" he asked, setting the bottle on the counter.

Rather than answer, she went over to him, wrapped her arms around his neck and kissed him for all she was worth. Hot, wet, demanding, 100 percent slutty kissing.

Jack didn't waste time. He grabbed her breeder hips and boosted her up on the counter, and Em pulled him close, feeling him hard and solid and hot against her. She slid her hands under his shirt, over his lean stomach, his lightly furred chest, and tugged his shirt off over his head, then let her hands wander down his back, kissing him again, pulling his hips harder against her.

Jeans, unfastened.

Then she scooched off the counter, pulled off her sweater, unhooked her skirt and let it fall to the floor. Jack's eyes lowered and a very gratifying noise came from his throat right before he unhooked her bra, and then she was kissing his neck, his hot, beautiful neck, and bit down on his collarbone. And then the smooth, cool tile of the kitchen floor was against her back, and Jack was on top of her, hard and heavy and hot, while his mouth burned heat on all the best spots until she wriggled free and returned the favor.

So yeah.

Wary no more.

Not when you were doing it on the kitchen floor.

The animals, bless their furry little hearts, stayed sound asleep, despite the noise.

Chapter Twenty-Four

Jack Holland was a happy man. For now, anyway.

After the kitchen floor encounter—which, by the way, *yes*—he'd led Emmaline into the master bathroom, turned on the bath taps and made out with her while the tub filled. Left her to get in while he uncorked the wine and brought them each a glass. Then he got in with her, pulling her back against his chest, so, so glad he'd gone for the big tub when he built the house.

The only sound was the water sloshing if either of them moved and the rain beating against the windows. The puppy came in and tried to drink out of the tub, making them both laugh, and if there was a better sound than Emmaline laughing, Jack didn't know what it was.

Her skin was creamy and soft, and her body was

solid and strong and perfect. After a little while, she couldn't help notice that he was noticing, and she turned around to face him and they did it right there in the tub.

Come to think of it, Jack *did* know what sound was better than Emmaline laughing. It was her saying his name in a breathy, almost startled voice, and it made him feel incredible to make her feel so good.

Then he took her to bed and pulled her against him, her dark hair against his jaw, her hand over his heart. She was asleep within seconds, but Jack just lay there, feeling something he hadn't felt in a while now.

Peace.

His marriage had been tumultuous, Jack never knowing which version of Hadley he'd be coming home to at the end of the day. The brief periods of happiness had been built on what he thought he knew, like judging a wine on its color and clarity, only to find it had turned to vinegar. After he'd walked in on Hadley and Oliver came that edgy, angry sense of failure—and loneliness.

And then, since the boys had gone into the water, his mind had been like a river after a savage flood, all sorts of sharp, dangerous things sliding under the current, sharp and unseen, sometimes rushing past, sometimes slamming into him without warning.

But now there was something else blanketing

that, and for the first time in a very long while, Jack felt at peace.

He wouldn't have guessed the potty-mouthed hockey-playing cop would've been the right one for him.

He'd have been wrong.

Lazarus jumped up on the bed, and, after a second, Jack heard the cat's rusty purr. From Emmaline's side, no less. Even his feral cat liked her.

He wasn't aware that he'd fallen asleep until he heard a noise. A thudding.

Thunder?

No.

Someone was at the door.

The clock read 2:37 a.m.

He slid out of bed, pulled on his pants and went to the front door. It was Pru.

It couldn't be good.

"I've been calling for forty-five minutes, Useless!" she barked. "Pops had a heart attack. Hurry up, Jack! It's not good."

Adrenaline shot through his arms and legs. He grabbed a sweatshirt from a hook and pulled it on, ran to get his wallet and keys. And phone.

Sixteen missed calls. A screen full of texts. Why the hell hadn't he heard?

"Is everything okay?"

Em stood there, wearing his bathrobe, hair tangled.

"Our grandfather's in the hospital," Pru said. "Heart attack."

"Oh, no! Can I do anything?"

"My phone was off," Jack said tightly.

Her hand flew over her mouth. "Jack, I'm so sorry. I muted it before . . ."

Jesus H. Christ. That was something that Hadley would do. Not Emmaline. "We have to go," he said. "I'll call you later."

He didn't have time to discuss it.

His grandfather was dying, and he hadn't even known.

Everyone was at the hospital, sitting grimly in the waiting room of the E.R. Goggy was flanked by Honor and Faith; Abby was sobbing quietly in Ned's arms; Carl, Levi, Charlie and Tom stood off to one side. Mrs. J. had her arm around Dad.

Jack went right to Goggy and knelt in front of her chair. "Oh, Jack," she said, and hugged him.

"We don't know anything right now," Honor murmured. "Jeremy's still with him."

Apparently, Pops had awakened with chest pain radiating into his left arm. He'd been unable to talk, and Goggy didn't waste time, just pressed the emergency button that all apartments at Rushing Creek had and shoved a baby aspirin in her husband's mouth. The facility had its own ambulance service, and they'd gotten him to the hospital in fewer than fifteen minutes. Goggy also called Jeremy, who was Pops's regular doctor, and Jer was with the cardiologist now.

"Sounds like you did everything right," Jack told his grandmother. "Just like always."

"We only just started liking each other last year." She wept against his neck, and Jack hugged her closer.

"Now, now," Jack murmured, his throat tight. "You know what he told me the other day? He said you were the love of his life."

Goggy tried to smile. "Of course I am. Who else would put up with him?"

"Hey, guys," Jeremy said from the hallway. "He's stable for now. Elizabeth, he wants to see you in a minute. John, could you come with me?"

Dad looked at him, and Jack went with him, putting his arm around his father's shoulders as they walked down the hall.

Usually, his sisters would make disgruntled comments about sexism in the family and call Jack the little prince. The fact that they didn't was horrible.

No one lives forever, of course. That wasn't exactly news, but it was still shocking when that universal truth hit home.

Pops was easy to dismiss as a joking, bickering old man, but that was just the surface. John Noble Holland, Jr., had a deep love of his family and land, the work ethic of a Spartan and a sentimental streak that he did his best to keep hidden. But he got choked up every time he saw Jack in his navy whites. He put flowers on all the graves in the Holland family cemetery on the anniversaries of their deaths and each April before the blessing of the crops. His eyes filled when Faith and Levi told everyone about the baby. Last year, when Goggy had almost died in a house fire, the fear of losing his wife had practically felled him.

Jeremy stopped outside a room and signaled them to go in.

Pops was gray, an oxygen mask over his face. If not for the beeping of the heart monitor, Jack would've assumed he was dead.

"We're here, Dad," his father said, taking the old man's hand. His eyes were full of tears.

"Hey, Pops," Jack said.

Pops's eyes fluttered open. He gestured weakly to his face, and Jeremy leaned over and took the mask off. "Proud of you," he whispered, looking at Dad, then Jack. "So proud of my boys."

Then his eyes closed again, and the beeping of the monitor slowed.

Chapter Twenty-Five

To say that Emmaline was writhing in guilt would not have been an exaggeration.

Shit. How could she have decided to mute

Jack's phone? Without even asking him? For the tenth time that morning, she scrubbed a hand over her face.

She was still at his house, though she had to go to work in half an hour. But she'd stayed, hoping to see him first. The coffeemaker was set up, and she'd even baked somewhere around 4:00 a.m.—an almond coffee cake, her grandmother's recipe, and one of the few things Em could bake from memory. She'd imagined Jack coming home and telling her his grandpa was okay, what a night, had she baked, all was certainly forgiven, no worries on the phone thing.

But he didn't come home, and he didn't call or text, either, and she didn't dare interrupt. She wasn't family, after all.

The rain had turned to snow at some point, the fat, heavy, discouraging snow of late winter, not enough to be a real storm, more than enough to be depressing.

Sarge erupted into excitable barks, and Emmaline jolted from the table where she was sitting. Sarge's tail wagged and he whined and pawed at the floor-to-ceiling window.

It was Hadley, walking up Jack's driveway, wearing a shiny black raincoat.

Super.

Emmaline opened the door just as the other woman knocked. "Surprise!" Hadley said, opening the raincoat.

467

She was wearing a fire-engine-red bustier and tiny scrap of panties.

"Hi there," Em said. "Nice underwear." That was a perfect body, all right. Em guessed her thigh and Hadley's waist had about the same circumference.

"Where's Jack? I need to talk to him. Right now."

Uh-oh.

Hadley was drunk.

Her eye makeup was smeared, and while she didn't quite look like Heath Ledger as the Joker, it was close. Her red, red lipstick had been crookedly applied, and the usually smooth and perfect blond hair was matted in the back. Despite the cold, she wasn't wearing stockings. Or sensible shoes . . . those had to be four-inch heels, and her feet were nearly blue.

"Come in," Emmaline said. "Jack's not here."

"Well, I was already at Blue Heron, and no one's there, so don't you lie to me! I wanna see him! He's my husband, after all!"

"Not anymore he's not," Em said. She wasn't about to tell Hadley about poor Mr. Holland. She'd end up going to the hospital, and Em didn't think Jack would want that one bit.

But you know what? This was good practice for crisis negotiations. Half the calls they got were because someone was under the influence. First rule of negotiations: establish rapport. "Come on in, Hadley. Those shoes are amazing, but your feet must be freezing."

"I don't hafta do what you say," Hadley slurred.

"No, of course not. But are you sure? It's nice and warm in here. There's coffee."

"Take a bite of my pink . . . Southern . . . ass." She poked a finger against Em's chest with each of the last three words.

Em smothered a smile. Hard to commit to active listening and empathy with a statement like that. "You must be pretty frustrated," she said.

"Go to hell. Where's Jack?"

"He's not here. I promise."

"Are you two sleeping together?"

Ruh-roh. Emmaline paused.

"No!" Hadley shrieked, guessing the answer. "How dare you steal my husband, you Yankee slut!"

Clearly, stating the obvious wasn't going to help here. Em opened the door wider. "Hadley, come on inside and we can talk. You, uh, you have a point."

"No! You're not the boss of me! And if I can't have Jack, then I may as well go off and die!" She burst into noisy sobs.

For the love of the baby Jesus. "Hadley. Let's have some coffee, and you can, um, see Lazarus. Right? You must miss him. You're a cat person, right?"

"I hate that animal! I hate him! Jack! Jack! I

need you! If you don't come out right now, I swear I'm gonna make you sorry!"

With that, she picked up a rock and threw it at the house, and it was like she was channeling Derek Jeter firing to first base, because there was a smash as a window broke.

Clearly, that hadn't been planned, because Hadley's mouth dropped open. She cut her wide eyes to Emmaline. "Oopsy," she said, then bolted, wobbling crazily in her ridiculous shoes. Instead of down the driveway toward the road, she ran into the woods.

This was just great. With a curse, Em ran after her. This was *not* how she wanted to spend her morning, and God forbid Jack come up the driveway to see his girlfriend (who'd turned off his phone to make sure their shagging wouldn't be interrupted, preventing him from being with his family during a crisis) chasing his ex-wife (who was drunk off her pink Southern ass and nearly naked).

For a drunk, Hadley was fast. "Hadley!" Em yelled. "Knock it off! You're going to hurt yourself!"

Or freeze to death. It was raw today. Hadley's coat flapped like awkward wings. And what was that about making Jack sorry, huh? Aside from breaking his window, that was?

Jack didn't need this. Not with Mr. Holland in the hospital, very, very sick . . . or even dead. "Hadley. Please stop."

She turned around and gave Emmaline the finger.

Nice. A branch slapped Em across the forehead and tangled in her hair, and she growled with irritation.

She caught up to Hadley as the smaller woman tried to climb over a rock wall. Hadley saw her coming, bent over and picked up a handful of something, then turned and shoved it in Em's face.

Dirt and snow. *Gross.*

Em grabbed her hand, twisted it behind her back and yanked her back against her. "Knock it off," she said, spitting out some frozen moss. "Or I'm arresting you for drunk and disorderly."

"Jack! Jack!" Hadley shrieked, struggling.

So. Getting a drunken, surprisingly strong woman out of the woods wasn't easy. "Can you just walk, please?" she said as Hadley writhed. "I really don't want to have to carry you." She got kicked in the shin as an answer. Branches snapped underfoot, and a squirrel followed them from the tree branches, laughing at the idiocy. Some of the snow Hadley had shoved at her had slid down Em's shirt (of course), and there was a cold, wet lump sitting on her chest like a third breast.

Five minutes later, Emmaline had Hadley handcuffed and locked in the back of the cruiser, where Hadley was sobbing. At least she couldn't hurt herself (or the car) if she was cuffed, and she'd done more than enough to earn it. There were a few leaves in Hadley's tangled hair and raccoon eyes from where her mascara had melted.

Em leaned against the cruiser, breathing hard. She wasn't much better off than her passenger. Her forehead stung, and her shin throbbed.

Okay, first things first. "I'll be right back," she told her passenger.

Emmaline went inside to the bedroom with the broken window and picked up the glass, then closed the door so too much heat (and the cat) wouldn't get out. Debated on calling Levi, and then decided he didn't need to hear about this just yet. He had other things on his mind.

She went back outside, opened the door of the cruiser for Sarge and got behind the wheel. "Is your sister still in town?" she asked.

"No! I've got no one and nowhere to go!"

"Have you always depended on the kindness of strangers?"

"As a matter of fact, yes!"

Okay, Blanche DuBois. Em stifled an eye roll.

She'd take Hadley to the station, because she didn't have time to babysit her at her apartment. She was the officer on call today. Hadley could just sit tight in the holding cell and sober up.

Em rubbed a spot on her jaw where Hadley's head had slammed into her.

It was going to be a long day.

Ten minutes later, they were at the station.

"You must be freezing! Isn't she freezing?" Carol Robinson asked when Emmaline brought Hadley in. Though Emmaline had tied Hadley's coat closed, it barely cleared her ass. Also, Hadley had refused to put on her shoes. "Isn't that Jack Holland's wife?"

"Ex-wife," Emmaline said tightly. "Everett, unlock the cell for me."

Hadley arched her back as they walked down the hall, still trying to get away. "Don't! Not in there! Please! Not that! I can't stand that!"

"It's not exactly a pit in the ground, Hadley," she said as Everett opened the holding cell door. "You'll just stay here for a little while. There's a blanket on the bed. Get warmed up, okay?" She uncuffed her, gave her a gentle push in and closed the cell door. "I'll bring you something to wear."

"Please! Please don't lock me up!" Hadley pressed a fist to her mouth and sobbed like she'd just seen *The Notebook* for the first time. Ev was staring at Hadley's outfit (or lack thereof), his mouth hanging open. Em smacked him on the head. "Ev. Come on!"

"Right, right, sorry," Everett said. "What happened to you? You look awful. You're all dirty."

"Emmaline, you're filthy," Carol pointed out.

"Yes, I know." Em went to her locker, where she kept a clean uniform as well as a pair of yoga pants and a MPD sweatshirt. She pulled the latter two out and handed them to Carol. "Bring these to

Meryl Streep, okay? And ask her if she's hungry."

"Is Meryl Streep here?" Everett asked.

Emmaline closed her eyes. "No, Ev. I meant Hadley. The woman in the cell."

Carol went back down the hall, and a second later, Hadley bellowed, "These are way! Too! Big!" followed by more sobbing. When Carol returned, she was trying hard not to giggle. "She wants to know if she gets a phone call," she said.

"She can have one when she sobers up a little." Em tried to be professional; Hadley was in custody and a guest of the town now, not just Jack's ex-wife.

But it was hard to know if she was treating Hadley like she'd treat anyone else, because maybe she was being *too* nice. Hadley had driven under the influence; somewhere during her rant on the way to the station, she'd admitted that, and her car was parked half on Blue Heron's lawn, half on the driveway. She'd thrown a rock through a window, which constituted criminal mischief. Drunk and disorderly. Menacing a police officer, more or less.

What would Levi do?

Em thought he'd do pretty much what she'd already done. Give her time to cool down, then deliver a stern lecture, name-drop some of the charges that could be leveled against her and tell her to grow up.

Yeah. All in all, Em was pretty sure she'd done a good job.

She washed up and changed into her uniform, brushed her hair and put it in its customary bun. Took a few deep breaths and left the locker room.

"Levi called," Carol said. "John Holland, the old one, had a heart attack, and he's being admitted, so he'll be at the hospital with Faith."

"How's Mr. Holland doing?" Emmaline asked.

"He didn't really say. Maybe you should ask Jack."

"Yeah. Anything else?"

"Yep." Carol handed her a few messages, then sat back down at her desk.

Typical stuff for a weekday. Mrs. McPhales thought she saw a trespasser. Someone saw a stray dog or possibly a coyote in their backyard. A speeder past Phyllis Nebbins's house. The Knoxes' free-range chickens were causing traffic danger. Dalton hadn't shown up for school.

Em checked her phone.

Nothing from Jack.

"Okay, I'll go out on these calls. Everett, keep an eye on Hadley, okay?"

"You bet," he said, going back to his computer. She heard the Angry Birds music, gave him a look and left.

When Emmaline got back to the station a couple of hours later, Everett met her at the door. "We

475

might have a problem," he said. "I just checked on Hadley, and she's not too good."

"Shit." She ran down the hall to the holding cell.

Hadley was sitting on the floor, practically drowning in Em's clothes. She was rocking and whimpering, and the smell of vomit was unmistakable. "Hadley?" Em said, going into the cell. "You okay?"

"Please let me out," she whispered, seeming completely different from before.

"Yeah, sure. You feeling all right now?"

"Can I make a phone call?" She was shaking.

"Absolutely." Emmaline led her out of the cell and into the station proper. "We're not charging you with anything. Not yet, anyway. I just wanted you to be safe. You were pretty . . . wild before. Do you remember that?"

She nodded. Em sat her at the desk and handed her the receiver. "Just dial nine to get an outside line," she said. Then she took a few steps away so as not to eavesdrop.

This wasn't good.

"What happened?" Carol asked.

"She threw up. I don't know what else. She's a lot quieter now. Everett, were you watching her?"

"Uh, yeah! Yeah, I was. I mean, when she settled down, I was kinda glad, you know?"

"When did you check on her last?"

He looked at the clock and winced. "An hour ago, maybe?"

Great. So Hadley could've been sitting in puke for an hour.

There was a hard pit in her stomach. This wasn't going to end well.

"Can I get you anything?" Emmaline asked Hadley when she hung up. "Some water, maybe?"

Hadley shook her head and just folded her hands in front of her.

"Do you need the bathroom? Want to get cleaned up?"

"No, thank you." Her voice was a whisper.

The minutes ticked by. Em tried to take care of some paperwork, but dread was settling over her like a cold, damp fog.

Then the door opened. "Jack," Hadley whispered. She stood up and wobbled into his arms, looking more like an orphan than the irate prostitute she resembled earlier. Her feet were bare. *Damn.* Em should've given her socks. Hadley was shaking like a leaf, all of her, right down to her toes.

For once, Emmaline didn't think she was faking.

"Emmaline, what the hell happened here?" Jack asked, his voice hard.

"She was drinking, Jack. She showed up at your house, and—"

"So you *arrested* her?"

As if they sensed a scene brewing, the four paid members of the Manningsport Fire Department, as well as Shannon and Kelly Murphy, who were training to become EMTs, wandered over. "Hey, Jack, how's your grandfather?" Gerard asked.

"Not good," Jack said. "Emmaline? You gonna explain this?"

Em glanced at the Murphy girls, who grimaced in sympathy. "I didn't actually charge her. I just put her in the holding cell."

"She's claustrophobic, Emmaline!"

Shit on rye. "I didn't know that."

"You couldn't tell? Take a look at her."

Em ran a hand over her head. "No one likes going in the drunk tank, Jack."

"She was screaming and crying," Carol said, most unhelpfully. Sounded a lot like police brutality, the way Carol put it.

"Well, she was screaming from the time she got to your house," Em said.

"So you arrested her," Jack said, his mouth tight. "She said you chased her and handcuffed and locked her in a cell. Really, Em? Because she was *upset?*"

"No! It was because she was . . . I thought she was a danger to herself. And possibly others. She was very aggressive. She—"

"You probably outweigh her by forty pounds, Em. You couldn't handle that?"

The stutter opened its skeleton eyes.

"I was acting in my capacity as a police officer," Emmaline said stiffly.

"Sounds like you were acting like a jealous

bully," he said, his voice calm and flat, and the words actually made her head jerk back.

Oh, God. Was he right? Her stomach curled in on itself. Hadley looked so small and ruined and . . . vulnerable. Her face was white. A person couldn't fake that.

"Jack," Everett began.

"I don't have time for this," Jack said tightly. "My grandfather is at death's door, and I have to get back to the hospital. But now I have to take care of her, because look at her! She's a wreck. Thanks, Emmaline."

"J-J-Jack, I d-d-didn't—" Her voice stopped cold.

The stutter, her old enemy, laughed and squeezed.

"I have to go," Jack said.

Then he opened the door, looked at Hadley's feet and scooped her into his arms so she wouldn't have to walk barefoot to the truck.

Chapter Twenty-Six

The good news was, Pops was still alive.

The bad news was everything else.

The past few days had passed in a tense blur of bad coffee and worse sleep. Jack went to the hospital, always careful to check the corridor for Mr. and Mrs. Deiner, not wanting to cause them any further upset than he had already. When he'd finally returned home late that first night, he'd found a broken window in the yellow room upstairs.

He'd taped a sheet of plastic over it, the silence of his house pressing down on him, grateful for Lazarus's weird little croaks. Then he lay down on the couch and fell asleep, his phone on the coffee table set on the highest volume, and woke around five o'clock, his cat sleeping on his chest.

There was a coffee cake on the counter, and the coffeepot was set up and ready to go.

That would've been Emmaline's work.

He felt a pang of guilt, but goddamn it, he was tired of feeling guilty. The woman had turned off his phone. He didn't have a landline. She knew that. What if Pops hadn't made it? What if she'd taken away his chance to say goodbye to his funny, crusty old grandfather?

Em had no right to decide when he could get calls. None.

Yeah, okay, taken by itself, it wasn't that big a deal. She hadn't known Pops was going to have a heart attack.

But what about arresting Hadley? Had all that really been necessary? Jack was well aware that his ex-wife was a drama queen, but she'd been genuinely traumatized, and when Jack saw her there in the oversize clothes, tears streaming out of her eyes, he . . . Ah, screw it. Jack didn't know what. But he couldn't just leave her there.

He'd driven her from the police station to her place at the Opera House, called Frankie and asked her to come. While Hadley was in the shower, he made her a grilled cheese sandwich and then waited till Frankie arrived. Hadley was pale and didn't seem to want to talk. She seemed, in fact, embarrassed. And something more, too. Whatever it was, Jack just wanted to get back to his grandfather, and the second Frankie arrived, he got back in his truck and returned to the hospital.

Since then, he'd been swamped with family responsibilities. Dad was quite a softy, as everyone knew, and Jack spent as much time as he could with him, the two younger John Hollands keeping vigil over the eldest. Jack also made sure to check on the business end of Blue Heron, Honor's domain, to make sure his sister wasn't too swamped, but the ever-capable Jessica Dunn seemed to be holding down the fort just fine. He called Faith twice a day, because she was due momentarily, and he wanted to make sure she wasn't overdoing it, because she'd been staying with Goggy. He dropped by Pru's house to see how Abby was; she'd never lost anyone close to her.

Then he drove back to Blue Heron to filter the wine and check the sediment, because it was almost time to bottle and those things couldn't wait. He made his calls, stopped by Hadley's (she'd been doing a lot of sleeping, according to Frankie), then went back to the hospital, then home.

Three days after the heart attack, Pops went back to the apartment at Rushing Creek. He was now on Lipitor and Coumadin with instructions to stop eating cheese, ice cream, whole milk and "anything good," in his words. He was weaker, but Jeremy called him "ridiculously healthy" despite his horrifying cholesterol level. Jack checked in with him and Goggy every night, because, despite his grandmother's protestations, he was worried about her, too. Neither grandparent was young, and Pops's scare had reminded everyone of that.

And now, four days after Pops's heart attack, Jack found himself driving from the hospital to Emmaline's little house on Water Street. Dusk was falling, and the lake was cobalt, a fat moon rising over the ridge.

He had the feeling he owed her an apology.

Being wrong wasn't a feeling Jack was used to. His sisters liked to call him the prince, the son and heir, and there was some truth to that. He knew his father had wanted a son—Mom, too—and he wasn't named John Noble Holland IV for nothing. All his life, he'd tried to do the right thing. He'd been an A student, an Eagle Scout, as good a brother as he could manage, having the occasional tea party with Faith, teaching Honor to drive, babysitting for Pru and Carl when Ned was a baby. His mom had thought he was pretty damn perfect, and Dad didn't think it—he believed it with his whole heart.

In truth, Jack could think of two times he'd made a significant mistake. One, the time he'd jumped off the falls up near the ruins of the old stone barn and broken his arm. Two, marrying Hadley.

Calling Emmaline a bully . . . yeah, okay. That was number three.

"Can I see you a minute?" Emmaline asked, standing in the doorway of Levi's office. It was nearly quitting time.

"Sure. Come on in."

She did, closing the door behind her. Levi had heard about the incident with Hadley . . . and Jack's reaction. Of course he had. Carol had told him the second he walked through the door, and Gerard had come over five minutes later with the same gossip.

She opened her mouth to speak, then found that her throat was tight. Not with the stutter. With tears. The stutter had slunk back to its hole, though last night, when Angela had practically goose-stepped her to O'Rourke's, Em's heart had been thundering, positive someone was going to say "H-h-hi, Eh-Eh-Emmaline," same as they had back in the day.

No one did. But people knew, anyway. Colleen even sent drinks on the house.

"What can I do for you, Deputy?" Levi asked.

"How's Mr. Holland?" she asked, even though she already knew. Word was out that the old guy was back at Rushing Creek, complaining that he already missed the pretty cardiologist who'd taken care of him.

"He's fine," Levi said. "He's doing really well, actually."

"Good. And Faith?"

"Very ripe." His mouth tugged up.

"You'll make a great dad, Levi."

"Thanks." He kept looking at her—it was a trick of his, that patient stare—and she broke.

"I'm thinking I should quit."

"Quit what?"

"This job."

More staring, then, "Unacceptable, Deputy."

She swallowed. "I screwed up, Chief. With Hadley. I didn't handle the situation well, and things just escalated. I didn't check on her." She looked at her hands. Probably time to take off that old nail polish she'd put on for stupid Kevin's wedding. "Maybe I'm not a good cop," she said, her voice husky. "She was in crisis mode, and I didn't take care of her."

Levi sighed and sat back in his chair. "Listen," he said. "You're going to screw up from time to time on this job. It's impossible not to. You investigate a call where you know the guy is beating his wife, but you can't convince her to leave him. You cruise through a neighborhood, and you still miss the burglary." He tapped a pencil against his desk, not looking at her. "You give a kid a lecture and ticket him whenever you can, and he still crashes into the lake."

Ah, yes. Josh Deiner had had few brushes with the law.

"This doesn't make you a bad cop," Levi continued. "Hadley was drunk, you didn't know she'd freak out the way she did and you had police business to take care of. If anyone screwed up here, it's Everett. He knows the drill. He was supposed to check on her every fifteen minutes, and if I know him, he was playing on his phone."

"I just feel like I . . . overreacted." She swallowed. "Like maybe Jack was right. Maybe I did what I did because she's Jack's ex."

"Emmaline," Levi said in that overly patient voice he used when he was irritated. "Jack wasn't right. You're not a bully. You couldn't be. If anything, you were too easy on her. So shut up about quitting, because if you leave me alone with Everett, I will hunt you down." He smiled, and Em felt herself smiling back.

"Okay. Thanks, Chief."

"Good. Now I have to get to the store because Faith is out of ice cream. You're a good cop,

Emmaline. You're a very good cop. Are we done here?"

She sat there another minute.

"What?" Levi said.

"Nothing. Just . . . I love you, Levi."

"Get out."

"No, I'm serious. I love you. You're the best boss ever."

"You'll hate yourself in the morning." He gave her a smile. "You still mad at Jack?"

She scowled. "Who said I was mad at Jack?"

"You ate an entire box of donuts yesterday. You've traded in walking for stomping. You're mad at Jack."

"You're right. Jack was—Wait a second. Am I really so pathetic that you want to talk about my personal life?"

Levi lifted an eyebrow.

"God. I'm leaving. See you tomorrow, Chief."

Em waved to Everett, kissed Carol on her cute little head and got into her cruiser, feeling considerably better, at least on the work front. She drove home, went inside and was greeted by Sarge and Squeaky Chicken, who seemed to have lost an eye and half its beak. "Angela?" she called.

"Namaste," Ange called. "Doing yoga up here. Be down in twenty minutes."

Em took off her belt and hung it up, then pulled out her bun and went into the kitchen. Poured herself a glass of wine—Lyons Den, thank you very much; she was boycotting Blue Heron at the moment.

The phone rang, and without looking to see who it was, she answered, then immediately wished she hadn't when she heard the voice on the other end.

"Hi, Mom," she said. "Looking for Angela?" Sarge put Squeaky Chicken, soggy with drool, on her lap as a consolation prize.

"No, actually, I wanted to talk to you."

"Oh. That's, uh . . . that's nice." She pulled a face at her dog, who raised his eyebrows, as surprised as she was. "How are you?" She took a sip of wine. A big sip.

"Good. We're moving to your area."

Emmaline choked, sputtering wine on the phone, Squeaky Chicken and Sarge's head. "Excuse me?"

"With both you and Angela there, we may as well."

"And by 'your area,' what exactly are we talking about?"

"Manningsport."

Dear God, I'm ready. Hurl down that thunderbolt. Love, Emmaline.

Mom was talking about proximity and the maternal bond. The habit of affection as influenced by visual recognition of loved ones. Her extremely close relationship with Angela. The usual.

Not once during high school did Mom and Dad

mention moving here, to be closer not just to Emmaline, but to Nana, too.

Not once in the past three years that she'd made her life here had they ever talked about moving here. They'd barely visited. But they'd moved from Malibu to Palo Alto, sure. To be closer to Angela, and that hadn't bothered Em, not really.

But the fact that they were coming here, on her turf, to be closer to Angela . . . A sudden flare of anger burned in her stomach.

"Yeah, do what you want," she said. "I have to go. Someone's here."

Without saying goodbye, she hung up, then nearly fell out of the kitchen chair as someone knocked, as if she'd summoned them. Sarge galloped out of the kitchen, then hurled himself against the front door, and Em followed. "Down, killer," she said as he whined and wagged. "At least pretend to be fierce, okay? You're going to be a police dog someday, whether you like it or not."

She opened the door, and her stomach burned again.

Jack.

"Hi," he said.

"What can I do for you?" she asked. A little hard to play it frosty when her dog had wrapped both front paws around Jack's work boot and was chewing on the laces.

"Can I come in?"

"Why?"

"Emmaline. Come on."

"Fine."

He came into the foyer and glanced around. "Is Angela here?" he asked.

"She's upstairs doing yoga. Sarge, stop." Sarge did stop, froze right in place, then raced into the other room and returned with Squeaky Chicken, whipping his head from side to side. Not the most dignified backdrop in the world, but hey.

"How's your grandfather?" Emmaline asked.

"He's good. Doing well."

Yes, I know, because Levi told me, and Faith told me, but you didn't say squat, Jack. "Glad to hear it," she said.

"Thanks."

She tried pulling Levi's trick of staring and waiting.

It worked.

"Look," he said, running a hand through his hair, "I may have overreacted a little the other day. I was under a lot of stress."

"Mmm."

"Sorry."

She lifted an eyebrow.

Jack sighed, that "women are so difficult" sigh. Hell yeah, they were.

"Is that it?" she asked.

"Should there be more?"

"Nope. Have a good night." She opened the door again.

"Emmaline, wait. Can I come in and actually sit down? Have a conversation with you?"

"I don't think so, Jack."

"Why?"

Because you called me a bully when I was only trying to help you and that idiot you married. Because you made me feel stupid and mean and unimportant. Because having you chew me out in front of my coworkers made me feel like I was in middle school again. Because you brought my stutter back. That's why.

"Here's the thing," she began.

"I hate when women lead with that."

"Suck it up. Here's the thing. Jack." She folded her arms. "I told you this would happen."

"You told me what would happen?"

"This! This messy, upsetting thing between us."

"That's a nice way to describe it."

"Well, you're the one who hasn't spoken to me in four days."

"I've been busy the past four days! By the way, why would you turn off my phone without telling me, huh?"

"Perhaps you remember the reason, Jack? No? The kitchen floor mean anything to you? The bathtub? Nothing's coming back?" Sarge whipped her with Squeaky's leg. "Look. I shouldn't have done that. It was an impulse, and I *am* sorry about it, and I did apologize."

"Fine. I forgive you," he said.

"Gosh, how great. But the *thing* is, Jack," she said, her voice getting tighter, because of course he was a *man* and would try to hang this on details when the big picture was staring him right in the face.

"What is the *thing,* Emmaline?"

"The thing is that at first this was a fake relationship. Then you needed a distraction. Then you wanted fun. Then I fell in love with you."

Well, shit on a steak sandwich. She hadn't meant to say that.

Jack's mouth opened. Nana's grandfather clock ticked from the living room. Sarge growled and bit Squeaky on the head, getting a soft hiccupping sound.

Otherwise, nada. "Right," she said. "Moving along." She looked at the wallpaper pattern, the little white cherry blossoms against the brown backdrop, and tried not to cry.

"Emmaline—"

She'd give him this chance. This one microscopic chance to say he loved her, too.

He looked at the floor. "You don't mean that."

"Oh, shut up! Of course I do. You're Jack Holland. Everyone loves you." Tears stung her eyes. *Stupid, stupid, stupid Emmaline.* "And you're never going to feel that way for me, and you want to know why?"

"I sense a trap."

Now was not the time for jokes. "Because I'm never going to be that woman who needs saving. If I twist my ankle, I can tape it up all by myself. If my ancient pet dies, I won't wrap myself around you like a python." She glanced apologetically at Sarge. "Even though I'd be very sad, puppy."

"I don't—"

"And if I cheat on you and my lover dies, I won't need you to hold my hand in the hospital."

His head jerked back. "How did you hear about that?"

"Everyone's heard about that."

He didn't answer.

"So," she said, her face hot, "I guess I'm not your type. You get off on being a white knight, and I don't need one. Not everyone has to be in a relationship to feel good about themselves. Some people are better off on their own."

"Wow. Glad you figured that out."

"But *Hadley* will always need you. She's the damsel in distress, and you're her hero, and part of you gets off on that. And guess what? I hate that you've put me in this position. I told you we shouldn't have started this. I've already competed for a man's love, and I lost. I'm not doing it again."

"I don't want Hadley," he snapped.

"Then why is she still in town?"

He didn't answer.

"Because she'll always have some kind of crisis, and you can always rescue her and be the big hero."

"Stop saying that word!" he barked, and Em actually jumped, she was so surprised. "You think I'm a hero? Josh Deiner is dying a little more each day, literally rotting away on life support, because I'm *not* a hero. Because my best wasn't good enough. Because when the time came, I failed. You think Hadley on a bender makes up for that? Are you out of your mind?"

Sarge barked, thinking this was terribly exciting, and dropped Squeaky Chicken on Jack's shoe. Jack looked down.

"You know what?" he said, his voice quiet now. "This is fine. You're right. We should be done. I wasn't really looking for a relationship and neither were you. You just wanted a date for a wedding, and I pushed it, and I'm sorry, and that's fine. Take care."

He turned around and went into the foyer, just as Angela was coming downstairs, clad in black yoga pants and a yellow T-shirt. "Namaste, asshole," she said, the curse word sounding quite elegant with her accent. "Stop yelling at my sister."

"Yeah." With that, he opened the door and went down the steps.

Em followed him out. "Jack."

He stopped but didn't turn.

"I wish you'd see someone about that PTSD."

He didn't acknowledge her, just started walking down the street to his truck.

From the soot-colored sky, snowflakes, swollen and tired, began to fall.

Chapter Twenty-Seven

Em went back inside and sat on the couch, not chastising Sarge as he jumped up next to her and rolled on his belly for a scratch.

"First things first," Angela said. "I'm calling the Chicken King—they deliver, did you know that? —and making martinis, and then we're going to talk."

Then she put a box of tissues next to Emmaline. "There. Just in case you feel like having a little cry."

"Oh, I'm not the type," Emmaline said, then promptly burst into tears. *Yuck.* She hated crying; it was so hot and embarrassing and uncontrollable, and yet here she was, sobbing on her sister's shoulder while Sarge licked her tears.

A half hour later, the fattening and delicious chicken had been delivered and Angela was making a second batch of martinis and Emmaline was surrounded by tissues and a solemn-looking puppy. Sarge's left ear was turned inside out, and she fixed it, getting a hand lick in return. Dogs were the best.

Sisters, too.

Angela came back, pressed a cold martini glass into Emmaline's hand, then folded her super-model frame into Nana's rose-patterned chair. "I think you're right about him having a white-knight complex. Men. You should become a lesbian, Em. It's so much easier on this side."

"Said the woman who fled across the country to avoid her ex," Emmaline muttered.

"You have a point." She sipped, looking like Africa's answer to Audrey Hepburn. "I'm going to say this once, darling, and keep in mind that my IQ was measured at 158 when I was fifteen years old."

"Already throwing around your creds."

"If you have them, flaunt them. Have you considered that perhaps—only perhaps—that you might have let this go a bit easily?"

"What do you mean? Explain it for us imbeciles with IQs in the normal range."

"Well, Kevin broke your heart, the horrible man. You've avoided relationships since then."

"Not really. Not on purpose."

"Please. Don't insult my extremely high intelligence. As I was saying, now you've fallen for Jack, and at the first sign of his not being absolutely lovely and perfect, you jettison him from your life to avoid further distress."

"Did I tell you Mom and Dad want to move to Manningsport?"

"Nice try at changing the subject. Does any of what I say ring true?"

"Yeah, yeah." Emmaline blew her nose and had another slug of martini. "The thing is, Ange, I walked right into this. I knew he was kind of messed up, and I knew I'm not really his type, but I fell for him anyway."

"Of course you did. He's wonderful."

Another hot line of tears streaked down her face. "He made me stutter," she whispered. "When he got mad at me the other day, I stuttered in front of everyone."

"And did the world stop spinning? Did you get fired? Did everyone throw trash at you?"

Em rolled her eyes. They may have gotten stuck, but her face was rather numb—Angela made a mean martini—so she wasn't sure. "No, smart-ass." Another sip. "But it's a sign of weakness just the same."

"It's a sign that you care very much about how he feels, especially in regard to you. That's not weakness. That's being human."

Sarge put his cute little nose on her knee. Her baby dog was getting enormous. She gave him a bite of drumstick in exchange for the drool-covered Squeaky Chicken.

"Okay, enough lecturing," Angela announced.

"Let's watch *Titanic*. I have a terrible crush on Kate Winslet."

They put the movie on, and just as Jack first saw Rose on the rich-people deck, Emmaline said, "Angela?"

"Yes, darling?"

"I'm so glad my parents adopted you."

Then it was Angela's turn to cry.

The next morning, there was a cheerful note from Angela on the kitchen table saying she'd be at Cornell for two nights to do some intensive research, but if Em needed her to come home, she would come as fast as a bumblebee, or if Em wanted to come to Ithaca, that would be lovely, too.

Angela. She really was flawless. Except she was a horrible slob in the bathroom and something of a flirt, from what Em had seen.

It would actually be nice to be alone for a night or two. Angela's insight and brilliance made it a little hard for Em to know what to think.

She had the day off, and the sun was shining. Last night's snow squall had melted, and it might even hit forty-five today, according to the notoriously unreliable forecasters.

"Do you want to go for a run?" she asked Sarge, smiling as the dog immediately grabbed his hideous chicken and ran to the door. She got changed, tucked her phone into her running shorts pocket, leashed up Wonder Pup and set out. People called to her and waved, and a few folks in the Village stopped to admire Squeaky Chicken and pet the dog.

The air smelled like spring. Sure, there'd be the heartbreak storm in April, there always was, but for now, it was warm (for New York) and soft and smelled earthy, the sharp scent of shale cutting through. She ran out of town, settling into a pace, Sarge easily keeping up beside her. Past the blue-and-purple Victorian where the nice Murphy family lived, crocuses peeking up from their lawn, past the old school that was possibly being turned into a community center. Shelayne Schanta was in her yard on Buttermilk Road, scooping soggy leaves from a flower bed. "Any news on the adoption front?" Emmaline asked, stopping.

"Just passed the home visitation," Shelayne said, beaming.

"Fantastic! If you need a character reference, let me know, okay? Since I'm an upstanding citizen and officer of the law."

She continued running, her legs strong and sure, despite it being a few weeks since her last outing. Nice mindless running.

Kept her mind off Jack.

She might not be his girlfriend anymore, but she was still worried about him. Even if he was a lost cause.

When she got to Meering Falls, she stopped,

breathing hard. Sarge dropped Squeaky long enough to drink from the heavy stream of water.

She loved it here. Not just here at the base of the beautiful gorge, carved out by water and time, but here in Manningsport. In New York. The perfect weather and excessive wealth of Malibu had never felt right, and she said a silent prayer of thanks to Nana for taking her in, a heartsick fourteen-year-old who could barely get a sentence out.

Her phone rang, startling her. Given that she was a cop, you'd think that the phone wouldn't scare her half to death, but such was not the case. *Great. Mom again.* She briefly considered letting it go to voice mail, but after the incident with Jack's phone, she was a little wary of doing that. "Hi," she said.

"I know you think we love Angela more," Mom started, her voice prim, indicating hurt feelings.

Em closed her eyes and sighed.

"It's just that I never knew how to fix you. I hated seeing you struggle, and I couldn't help you, and if there was ever a worse feeling in the world than failing your only child, I don't know what it is, Emmaline. Please cut me some slack. I did my best, and I'm well aware it wasn't good enough."

"Mom, you didn't fail me. You *replaced* me."

"That's not true."

"You were more than happy to ditch me on

Nana, and then four months later, you have a new and improved daughter. How is that not replacing me?"

"You're the one who wanted to live with my mother. You were so much happier out there. How could I say no?"

"You could've at least pretended to miss me." Sarge lay down at her feet and sighed, biting down softly so Squeaky Chicken seemed to mew.

"I *did* miss you," her mother snapped. "But what good would it have done to tell you that when you were so obviously improving? I hated that fucking stutter. I wanted to kill it for all the trouble it gave you, and when you called home and it was so much easier for you to talk, I couldn't burst into tears and tell you that I slept in your bed, could I? How would that have helped?"

Emmaline paused. "Did you just drop the F-bomb, Mom?"

"Adopting Angela was a somewhat impulsive decision. I felt like a failure as a mother, so, yes, I tried again. If I'd have known it would hurt you, I wouldn't have done it."

"Can you give her back?" Em asked.

"What? No! Of course not."

"It was a joke. I actually love Angela, you know."

"Oh. Well. That's good."

The rushing of the falls was full and lovely. "I love you, too, Mom."

Nothing. There was no sound from the other end of the phone.

"Are you crying?" Emmaline asked.

"Yes."

"In a happy way?"

"Yes."

Emmaline found that she was smiling. "Come and visit, okay? Soon?"

"Okay," Mom said. There was a pause. "Emmie, I'm so sorry I couldn't help you with the stutter."

Em stroked her dog's soft fur. It had been a very, very long time since her mother had used that nickname. "It wasn't yours to fix, Mom," she said. "Besides, it built character."

Her mother laughed, then blew her nose. "It sure did. No one has more character than you."

"Not even Flawless Angela?" Em teased.

"Oh, her. She's so boringly flawless."

"Except she's pretty fabulous."

"Exactly. All right, I'll let you go." There was a pause. "Can I call you again tomorrow?" Mom asked.

"You can call me again tonight."

"Don't tell Angela I said she was boring. She's not."

"I know it was a joke, Mom. Don't worry."

When she hung up, she knew where she had to go. "Up and at 'em, Sarge," she said. "We have places to go, people to see."

•••

She brought flowers. Yellow tulips, because nothing seemed more cheerful than that.

They didn't work of course. Em realized that the second she knocked on the door of Room 405.

"Mrs. Deiner? It's me, Emmaline Neal. Officer Neal? I was on call the night of the accident."

Gloria Deiner looked up from where she sat at the side of the bed. "Oh. Hello." Her voice was flat and quiet.

The Deiners were not particularly popular in Manningsport. They'd moved here six or seven years ago, from what Emmaline had heard. Too rich, too showy. They'd bought a perfectly lovely farmhouse way up on the farming side of the lake, away from the vineyards where the Mennonite farms dotted the land, then torn it down, much to the heartbreak of the former owners. In its place was a garish McMansion with a five-car garage and eight bedrooms, eleven bathrooms, an indoor pool and an outdoor pool, just for the three of them.

From what Em knew (and had heard), Josh was the worst of the spoiled rich-kid cliché—drugs and drinking and sex and the insanely fast car. Trips to Vail and Turks and Caicos and London. His parents would pull him out of school for vacations, sometimes for weeks on end, then throw a hissy fit when he stayed back a grade. Nothing was too good for their boy, who deserved everything just because he'd been born.

Guess the Deiners were rethinking their child-rearing philosophy now.

But the fact that Gloria Deiner was here alone . . . That was just too sad. "Would you like some company?" Emmaline asked.

"Oh. All right."

The respirator breathed in . . . then out. In . . . then out. A beeping alarm of some kind went off in the next room, then stopped.

Em set the vase of flowers, which now looked obscenely happy, on the windowsill. It was the only arrangement there. She went over to the bed and looked down at Josh.

Oh. Oh.

He looked so small under all that equipment, the tubes and lines and swath of blankets. A downy beard sprung in patches on his face, and his eyes were open a slit but didn't move. His hands curled in toward his chest, which itself was sunken and thin. His hair was ragged and greasy, and he smelled of body odor and Ivory soap.

"Hi, Josh," she said, touching his hand. "It's Emmaline Neal. One of the cops in town."

"He can't hear you," Mrs. Deiner spat. "He's brain-dead. But I'm praying for a miracle." Her words were heavy with bitterness, as if she wanted Emmaline to start spouting facts and tell her to accept reality.

In . . . then out.

It was chilly in here. Em pulled up the blanket a

little bit. A *Star Wars* comforter, probably once much beloved. She swallowed. "Can I sit down?" she asked.

Mrs. Deiner shrugged, so Em sat.

"What was he like when he was little?" Em asked, and the woman's head jerked back in surprise.

"Why?"

"I don't know." She paused. "I was there that night. I guess I'd just like to hear about him."

The woman's face didn't change for a second; then it softened, and her eyes smiled with memory. "Oh," she said, and her voice was young again. "He was so beautiful. And mischievous!" She reached out to touch Josh's hand. "He had this laugh that let him get away with murder. Always running, always breaking things, but then he'd look at me with that smile, and I just couldn't be mad at him." Her voice cracked. "I just couldn't. I loved him so much. I still do." She started to cry. "My husband says we have to let him go, but I can't! How can I let my baby die? How do I stop being a mother?"

In a flash, Em knelt by Mrs. Deiner's side and hugged her. "I don't know," she said, her own voice shaking. "I don't know."

"The doctors say he's already gone," Gloria whispered, clutching Em's shirt. "My husband says the same thing." She looked at Emmaline. "Do you think he is?"

This was her chance to say the right thing. To

make all the difference to Gloria Deiner, whose son was surely dying. "I don't know," she repeated. "But whatever the right thing is, you'll know. You're his mother."

But Gloria just looked at her son, her face so full of sorrow that Em couldn't understand how she bore it. "Thank you for coming," she whispered. "I'd like to be alone now." She looked back at Em. "And thank you for talking to him. No one does that anymore."

Em hugged her again, but Mrs. Deiner was locked back into her vigil.

She was almost out of the room when Gloria's faint voice stopped her. "You were there that night?"

Em turned. "Yes. Chief Cooper and I. We . . . we took over for Jack Holland."

"Jack Holland." Her voice hardened. "We wouldn't be here if it hadn't been for Jack Holland."

No, Emmaline thought. *You'd be visiting a grave.*

"Jack left him for last," Gloria said in an odd lilting voice, as if she were trying to remember a song. "The one who needed him the most, and Jack left him for last. My baby was all alone."

The respirator breathed in and out, in and out.

"He wasn't alone," Em said very, very softly. "Jack was in the water the whole time."

But Gloria's head was turned to her son, and Em doubted that the grieving mother even heard.

Chapter Twenty-Eight

Jack knocked on the door of 3-C. A second later, Hadley opened the door. "Hey," she said. "Come on in."

She looked different. Younger and tired. And she wasn't beaming at the sight of him.

It had been a week since her incident at the police station, and while Jack had seen her every day, they hadn't really talked.

Today, they would.

"Can I get you anything? Coffee or water?"

"No, thanks," he said. "Sit down, Hadley."

She did, taking a throw pillow and holding it over her stomach. "This weather, huh? Crazy."

It hadn't been particularly crazy, not for western New York, anyway. Then again, people always talked about the weather when they were nervous.

"Hadley, it's time for you to move on," he said.

Her eyes filled. "I know."

He leaned back in his chair. "I'll take you back to Savannah, if you like."

"Why? Why would you do that for me, after all the trouble I caused?"

A good question. He shrugged. "I don't know. I

feel responsible for you. For us. For how our marriage didn't work."

"I cheated on you, Jack. I'm the one to blame for our divorce."

She'd never admitted that before. "People don't cheat for no reason," he said, looking out the window. "You weren't happy, so you looked elsewhere. I'm not excusing it, Hadley. But I understand. You were lonely and bored and wanted more attention than I could give." Than any human could give, he guessed.

"My parents barely spoke to me, they were so mad," she whispered. "They thought you were the best thing that ever happened to me."

"I don't agree," he said. "I think we were just . . . wrong for each other. No matter how it seemed at first."

A tear ran down her cheek.

If he'd listened a little more carefully to smart people like Honor and his grandparents, to Mrs. Johnson and Connor O'Rourke, he might have picked up on their subtle (and not-so-subtle) notes of caution. If he'd taken longer to get to know Hadley, had her spend more time here rather than one idyllic weekend, the truth would've come out. And the truth was, they'd both seen what they wanted to see and not what was actually there.

"Why'd you come back here, Hadley?"

She wiped her eyes. "It seemed like everyone

around me was married and having babies or a fabulous career or both, and you know what I was doing? Part-time clerk at Bed, Bath and Beyond. I was thirty years old with nothing and no one, divorced before our first anniversary. A failure."

He could've pointed out that there was no shame in hard work, or that she could've gone back to school for something else, but he knew from experience those words would fall on deaf ears. Hadley had always had a picture of how life was supposed to be, and anything less was just what she said. A failure.

Hadley swallowed. "When I saw you on the news, that handsome Anderson Cooper standing right there in front of the lake, and they were showing pictures of the vineyard and that photo of you from the website, and I thought, 'Hadley Boudreau, you blew it.' " She grabbed a tissue and blew her nose. "So I came up here to get back what we had."

"What we had wasn't that great, Hadley. We fought a lot."

"Made up a lot, too." She took a shaky breath. "Jack, is there any way you could forgive me and get past what I did? I do love you."

His heart gave an unwilling tug of sympathy. "No, you don't," he said gently. "You love the idea of me. Just like I loved the idea of you. And I forgave you a long time ago."

Until he said the words, he hadn't realized they were true.

"I'm so sorry for what I did, Jack," she whispered. "You deserved better."

Finally, a sincere apology, something she'd never offered before.

"Thanks." He stood up. "Get packed, okay? I'll call your folks."

That night, Em left O'Rourke's, where Lucas Campbell had graciously flirted with her for fifteen minutes, then been spelled by Jeremy Lyon and then Tom Barlow while Honor talked to Colleen. And to her surprise, Em flirted back, offering to give Lucas a demonstration on how handcuffs worked, fixing Jeremy's collar, telling Tom his accent made him unfairly attractive.

It was easy to flirt with nice men who were spoken for.

The night was clear, no moon yet, and the stars were bright and sharp over the lake. She'd take Sarge down to the park for his nighttime walk, then maybe give Angela a ring, see how things were going in Ithaca. Maybe call Mom, too, for that matter.

Maybe she'd drive up to Jack's.

No. Or yes?

She wasn't quite sure who had broken up with whom the other day. Either way, she wanted to see him. Just to check in, doing her civic duty, etc., etc. Maybe strip-search him. *Now, now. None of that,* she reminded herself. Except he was awfully good-looking, especially naked.

Maybe just talk to him, more calmly this time. Really see how he was doing, see if the shadows in those clear blue eyes had faded a little bit. Whether or not they were together, she did love him. Missed him horribly.

This was only the second time in her life she'd been in love.

That had to say something. She obviously wasn't the type to fall for every guy who gave her the time of day. But all those songs and books and movies were right. The sun shone brighter, flowers smelled sweeter, yada yada, it was true.

And Jack . . . hell. They didn't make guys like that every day. A man who loved his family, was good with children, who'd be the date for any lonely woman who needed one. Who'd jump into a frigid lake and save three lives, and only focus on the one who didn't make it.

She started down the street to her place, figuring she'd pop Wonder Pup in the car with her, then jerked to a halt.

Speak of the devil, there was Jack's truck, parked in front of the Opera House.

Em instinctively stepped into the doorway of Presque Antiques, the better to spy.

She didn't have to wait. Hadley came out a second or two later, looking gorgeous in her cream coat and high boots. Jack followed, carrying a suitcase.

"You got our tickets?" Hadley asked, her voice carrying easily across the tiny green.

"All done online," Jack said. "Savannah, here we come." He opened the door for Hadley and handed her in, ever the gentleman. Walked around to the driver's side, stowed the suitcase and got behind the wheel.

And off they went.

Emmaline swallowed hard. Pressed her lips together to keep from crying. She had to hand it to Hadley.

It's just that she hadn't really believed Jack would fall for her again. And though it had been years since Kevin had taken up with Naomi, Emmaline couldn't help the thought that roared to mind.

The beautiful woman won again.

Emmaline was with her at-risk kids the next day, trying to pay attention. But it was hard. Three of the four kids were being tutored by Jack, and every time his name was mentioned, it felt like someone had zapped her with the Taser. Kelsey was sullen, Dalton's ADD was enjoying a high spell—he was doing headstands. Cory was cleaning his nails with a Swiss Army knife, which Em was considering confiscating, and Tamara was texting.

"Why should I get detention for missing

school?" Kelsey said. "I'm pregnant. I deserve to miss school."

"Were you sick?" Em asked.

"No," Kelsey said as if it were the stupidest question in the world (which it might've been). "I just didn't want to go."

"They're discriminating against you. You should sue," said Dalton, flipping upright. "You got any more popcorn, Officer Em?"

"You ate it all," Emmaline said.

"Alyssa missed way more school than me, and you don't see Dr. Didier up her ass, do you?"

"Yeah, well, she's got a better reason than you," Tamara said without looking up from her phone.

"No, she doesn't!" Kelsey snapped. "I'm pulling off the miracle of life here. She's sad. Big deal."

"Who's Alyssa?" Emmaline asked.

"Josh Deiner's girlfriend," Tamara said. "And she's *totes* destroyed over this." Tamara paused. "We all were. Like, all of us girls? We were so crying and stuff. It was awful."

"Josh is an asshole," Cory said calmly.

"Yeah, well, he's dying, so does that make you happy?" Tamara asked.

"A little," Cory answered.

"Don't be like that, Cory," Em said.

"Honest, you mean?" Cory said. "He beat me up when I was a freshman."

Emmaline murmured something, but part of her was buzzing, humming with instinct. "What's

512

Alyssa's last name?" she asked.

After group got out, Emmaline drove to an upscale development on the west side of town. Come to think of it, this area had had a series of break-ins not too long ago. Josh Deiner himself had been the culprit, but being a juvie, only got community service.

She knocked on the door of 67 Barn Circle Road and waited. No cars in the driveway, no lights on inside except for one room upstairs. She knocked again.

After another long minute, she heard feet thumping on stairs, and the door opened. "What?"

"Alyssa?"

"Yeah?"

"I'm Officer Neal. Manningsport Police." She pointed to her badge. "Everything's okay, but I was wondering if I could talk to you."

"Are my parents all right?"

"Yep. I'm here to talk to you. Is it okay if I come in?"

The girls eyes were swollen from crying, and her brown hair was lank and flat. She wore pajama pants and a Manningsport High sweatshirt several sizes too big—Josh's, Em would bet.

Alyssa opened the door and padded into the living room, sat down and drew her knees to her chest.

"Are you here alone, honey?" Em asked.

"Yeah. My brother's in college. Did the school send you?"

"No, no. I just wanted to check in with you. You're Josh's girlfriend, aren't you?"

She burst into tears. Nodded.

Em wished she'd brought Sarge. He was good for this sort of thing. "It must be really hard," she murmured.

"I can't visit him anymore," Alyssa sobbed. "I just can't stand seeing him like that. I wish his mother would just pull the plug and let him die already."

Emmaline nodded. She grabbed a box of tissues from the end table and handed it to the girl, who snatched a tissue. Her nails were bitten past the quick. "Have you been going to school?" she asked. "Maybe it would help to be around some other friends."

Alyssa shook her head. "Everyone stares at me like I'm a freak. I just feel wrong all the time. My parents never liked him, and they're, like, relieved or something. I mean, they didn't say that, but I think they worried that Josh was going to turn me into a drug addict."

"You must feel really lonely."

Alyssa gave her a surprised look, as if she'd expected Emmaline to stick up for her parents. "I am. I miss him so much."

"Of course you do. I heard you guys were really in love."

"We were. Everyone thinks he was such a jerk, and, you know, he had his moments. He wasn't the easiest person in the world. But he could be so . . . so . . ." Her face crumpled again, and she grabbed another tissue.

"He had some nice qualities, too," Emmaline said.

Alyssa looked up, her eyes huge and wet. "Yeah. He did. Like, he never let me pay for anything. And I know it was his parents' money, but it was nice anyway. It felt really grown-up, having a boyfriend who didn't have to scrape around for change just to buy you coffee."

"Sure," Em said.

"And he was sweet. He really didn't mind hanging out and just doing nothing." She started to sob again. "I loved him. My mom says I have to get over this, but I can't."

"I had a boyfriend in high school," Em said, stretching the timeline just a bit. "When he moved away, I felt like I'd never be happy again, and my mom was not sympathetic. Not that it's the same situation for you. But I remember the feelings."

Alyssa nodded.

"Do you have any pictures of Josh?" she asked.

"Um, yeah. Of course. Want to see them?"

"I'd love to," Em said.

They went up the curving staircase to the girl's bedroom, which was unusually neat, the bed made, nothing on the bureaus except four gift bags, each tied with a different colored ribbon.

The buzzing in Em's knees intensified. "Is it your birthday?" she asked Alyssa.

"No. Um, I'm just clearing out some of my

stuff. Figured I'd give some jewelry away." She bit her nail, then stopped.

There was, however, a framed eight-by-ten picture of her and Josh in the middle of the desk, as well as a single sheet of notepaper.

Hot pink notepaper.

Alyssa slid that into a drawer, then handed her the photo.

Josh Deiner grinned out at her, blond and handsome, his arm around Alyssa. From the sound of it, he was a spoiled, entitled bully . . . but that wasn't really his fault. And now he'd never have the chance to be anything else. "You guys are gorgeous together," Em said.

"Were gorgeous," Alyssa corrected dully.

"This is a really pretty room. Do you have your own bathroom?"

"Um . . . yes?"

"Can I see it?" Because that tingling was getting stronger. The room was too neat, and those gift bags . . .

"No! Um, it's kind of messy."

"Oh, I don't care. Through here?" She put her hand on the doorknob, and Alyssa jumped.

"Please don't go in there," she said, covering Em's hand with her own.

Em looked at the girl. "Sweetheart, are you planning to hurt yourself?"

Alyssa bit her lip hard. Her eyes filled with tears once more. "I—yes."

Emmaline put her arms around her. "Oh, honey," she said. "Please don't. I know you feel alone right now, but you're not. I'll help you however I can."

Alyssa shook with sobs. "I'm just so tired of being sad." She wept. "I can't do it anymore."

"I know it feels that way. I really do. But it's not always going to be this bad." She kissed the top of the girl's head. "I promise."

Turned out Alyssa had swiped some sleeping pills from her aunt and was planning to swallow them that night. The pills were lined up on the bathroom counter, along with a bottle of wine. The pink paper on the desk was a note to her parents, and the gift bags on the bureau were her favorite pieces of jewelry for her two best friends and two cousins.

Em called Alyssa's parents and told them their daughter was safe, then explained the situation. Both of them screeched into the driveway within seconds of each other, raced through the door and hugged their daughter against them. Lots of tears. Alyssa had been seeing a psychologist, though she'd skipped her last two appointments, and because she was eighteen, the doctor hadn't been able to tell Mr. and Mrs. Pierson. They called the doctor and put Alyssa on with her, watching and wringing their hands. But the girl promised not to hurt herself and made an appointment to see her first thing in the morning. Her dad called Jeremy Lyon to see if he could prescribe an antidepressant.

By the time Em was preparing to go, Alyssa looked relieved, if exhausted, bundled up on the couch, sipping a cup of cocoa.

Mrs. Pierson walked her to the front door. "I can't thank you enough," she said, her hands still shaking. "We knew she was struggling, but we didn't know how bad it was."

"I'm glad she's getting help. It's not easy to get through something like this on your own."

"Officer Neal?" Alyssa said, appearing in the foyer.

"Honey, go sit down," her mother said. "You look as weak as a newborn kitten."

"This will just take a minute, Mom. Maybe you could make me a grilled cheese?"

"Of course, angel." She kissed her daughter on the cheek and went into the kitchen.

"What is it, honey?" Em asked.

"I, uh . . . I did some things to Jack Holland."

"I know."

Alyssa blinked. "You do?"

"The note, leaving his lights on, the possum?"

The girl flushed, and her eyes welled again. "I was just so . . . mad that he couldn't save Josh, too. Am I in trouble for that?"

"Of course not, honey."

"He might press charges and stuff."

"He won't. I can guarantee that. Now go sit down and let your mom take care of you."

"Thanks for coming over," Alyssa whispered, and much to Em's surprise, the girl hugged her. "Thanks for guessing."

When Em got to the car, she found that her heart was clattering like an old tractor. Her hands were shaking, and her face felt flushed. She couldn't tell if she was exhilarated or terrified or both.

What if she hadn't gone over? What if she hadn't asked to see the bathroom?

But she had. She'd listened to that prickling sense of warning, and Alyssa was going to be okay. She started the car and drove to the cow path by the old barn where the Manningsport police held their Memorial Day speed trap, turned off the engine and reached for her phone to call Jack.

Oh. Right. She couldn't do that anymore. She dumped him. Or he dumped her. Either way, he was with Hadley again.

Tonight, she'd saved a girl's life, and you know what? That mattered more. She called Levi. "Hi. It's Em," she said the second he answered. "I just left the Piersons' house." In a rush of blathering, she told him what happened.

Levi was quiet when she finally stopped talking. "Excellent job, Deputy," he said.

Emmaline smiled. Typical chief. "That's it?"

"Why? You want a gold sticker? You deserve

one. Write it up and we'll talk tomorrow. And Em . . ."

"Yeah?"

"Remember this. This was a good day."

"Thanks, Chief."

She called Jamie next, and her hostage instructor was thrilled. "I knew you had the stuff, Em! You have to come work for us. Think about it."

"I'm happy here. But thanks, Jamie. It means a lot."

She drove home, the adrenaline still pumping through her limbs. Too bad Angela was still in Ithaca—Em suspected she might be having dinner with Frankie Boudreau. She'd call her later, but for now, a nice glass of wine was called for. Slippers. Pajamas. A Gerard Butler movie.

A figure rose from one of the Adirondack chairs on her porch, and Em's hand went to her holster. Just before she drew, she realized who it was.

"Kevin. I almost shot you," she said calmly.

"Hi, Emmaline," he said, smiling. "How are you?"

Fifteen minutes later, Em was in her pajamas (screw Kevin, he'd seen her in worse), had a glass of wine in one hand and had poured Kevin a glass of water, since he was still alcohol-free, dairy-free, etc., etc. He was petting Sarge, who didn't seem to care that this was the man who'd once broken Mommy's heart and was mooing a love song as Kevin scratched his ears. Em planned to have a firm talk with her puppy later on.

"So what brings you to Manningsport?" she asked, sitting down.

"I have an Ironman in Buffalo," he said, smiling. Still had those damn beautiful eyes. Otherwise, the shock of his physical state was still, well, shocking. "Figured I'd come by and say hello."

"Hello."

"You like living here?" he asked. "In your grandmother's house?"

"I do. Why are you here, Kev? You and Naomi split up already?"

He laughed. "No, no. We're really happy."

"Great."

"How's Jason?"

"Who's Jason?"

"Your date? At the wedding? Your fake fiancé?"

"Jack. He's fine." She took a sip of wine. "So you didn't answer my question, Kev. Why would you come see me? Aside from your wedding, I haven't talked to you in three years."

He looked down at Sarge's head, which was resting on his knee as the faithless cur gazed up adoringly. "I'd like to apologize," he said.

"Go right ahead."

He gave a little snort of laughter. "You always were direct."

"One of the many things you said you loved about me."

"I did love you. I'm sorry I stopped."

Em took another largeish sip of her wine. Blue Heron. She'd run out of her Lyons Den stash, and this had been in the fridge. It was excellent. Steely and bright with notes of fairy's breath and sunrises. Whatever the case, it slid past the lump in her throat quite easily.

Kevin was just looking at her, a faint regretful smile on his face.

She put the glass down. "I'll never understand what happened with us. I mean, I'm over you—now—but I never could figure that out."

He nodded. "The thing is, Em . . . I hated myself. I couldn't think of anything except food and how disgusting I was. Everything else was fake, was just a very brief distraction from food and fat. I hated how fat I was, and I couldn't wait to eat again. When I started to lose the weight and rework my life, I . . ." He shrugged. "I hated you for loving the lazy, sad, pathetic person that I was."

"And you loved Naomi for hating you."

"Yeah. Ironic, huh?"

"So ironic. Well, thanks for coming by. What is it, two hours to Buffalo?"

He didn't move. "Not every love is meant to last."

"Do you have that on a T-shirt somewhere?"

522

He grinned, surprising her, and she felt an unwilling (and small) rush of affection for him. "I'm really sorry, Em," he said. "You'll always be my first love. I'll always be glad I knew you."

Her eyes stung.

That was a damn fine apology. Or a line from a Nicholas Sparks book. Or both. "Right back at you." She cleared her throat. "I wish you all the best, Kevin. I really do."

He took her hand. "And, Em . . . I'm sorry for what I said in the *People* article. You were never unsupportive. You were pretty great, in fact. And I wish you all the best, too."

She gave his hand a squeeze. "I don't know how I would've made it through eighth grade without you," she said. She might've been like Alyssa, in fact. But because of the love and acceptance Kevin gave her, she'd never had to find out.

She looked up, and, for a second, he looked like the boy she'd loved when she was so young, and her heart swelled. She and Alyssa both knew the might of first love, the huge, beautiful, terrible power it had.

And then the feeling was gone, and in its place was . . . nothing. Not in the bad way . . . in the way a room feels after you've tossed out the old furniture and put on a fresh coat of paint.

"I should go," Kevin said.

"It was good to see you." And even better to mean it.

She hugged him quickly at the door. "Give Naomi my best," she said, and she didn't even feel the urge to choke or roll her eyes.

"Will do."

"And good luck in the race."

"Thanks! It's a tough one, all right. But you know how it is. Excuses are for people who don't want it bad enough. Naomi says—"

"Drive safely!" she said and closed the door.

Sarge came over and licked her knee.

"That went well, don't you think?" she asked. "Me, too. And this, my friend, calls for some Ben & Jerry's. We can talk about your whorish ways later."

Chapter Twenty-Nine

Jack got back from Savannah just in time for dinner with Dad and Mrs. Johnson. "How was your trip, my darling boy?" Mrs. J. asked after he finished his third helping of roast pork, peas and salt potatoes, his favorite.

"It was okay," he said. "And it's done. That's the best part."

"How's her family?" Dad asked.

"They're great."

"I always liked them," he said.

"But not her," Mrs. J. said. "I told you, Jack,

that woman wasn't good enough for you, but you didn't listen to me, did you?"

"No, Mrs. J. And I should have. I'm sorry. Please can I have some pie?"

"In a moment, you ungrateful child." She folded her arms. "What's this nonsense I hear about you and Emmaline Neal?"

"Don't worry. That's over." His voice was casual, but the words caused an odd tightness in his chest. He and Emmaline hadn't been together very long, really. He shouldn't feel so . . . hollow.

Mrs. Johnson turned to the counter and cut him a piece of pie. "It being over is the nonsense to which I'm referring, Jackie." She put her hand on his shoulder, and Jack looked down. He was used to glossing over things where the Coven was concerned. Mrs. Johnson, though . . . she wasn't so easy to brush off.

"Hyacinth," Dad said, "could you give us a moment, sweetheart?"

"Of course, my darling. Jackie, listen to your father." She kissed Jack on the cheek, then left the kitchen. If Jack knew her (and he did) she'd eavesdrop.

"What's up?"

Dad gave him a long look. "I'm worried about you."

"You don't need to be," he said, too quickly. Somehow, his father's kind eyes made Jack feel a thousand times worse.

"I am, son. You seem lost."

Shit. Jack's throat tightened. "I'm doing okay."

Dad didn't speak right away, but when he did, his voice was soft. "When your mother died," he said, "there were days when I didn't know how I got from one place to the next. I'd be down in the barn and think, 'How did I get here? Did I eat breakfast? Did I drive here?' Sometimes I'd see my face in the mirror and I wouldn't even recognize myself."

Jack knew the feeling. He just didn't want his father—or anyone in his family—to lose sleep over him.

"So I see you these days, son, and I recognize that lost look." His father put his hand over Jack's. "I know you're hurting. We all do. I know it's not going to go away overnight, either. What happened with those kids was terrifying."

"I keep thinking," Jack said, and the words were hard to get out, "if I'd done something different, if I'd been even twenty or thirty seconds faster, or even ten, maybe . . ."

"You're only human. You did everything you could. You helped them. Those other boys would all be dead without you, Jack. You saved three lives that night. Those matter, too."

Jack nodded. Swallowed. He knew his father was right. Feeling that, though . . . believing it was harder.

"I want you to stop in at Honor's," Dad said.

"She has the name of a couple of therapists who specialize in PTSD. Will you do that?"

Jack nodded again. He stood up, and Dad did, too, and Jack hugged his father. Dad, who was as solid and enduring as an oak tree. "I don't want you to worry about me, Dad," he whispered.

"That's ridiculous," Dad murmured, hugging him back. "I'm your father. Mrs. J.'s your step-mother. Your sisters adore you, and you've always been here for us. Let us take care of you for once."

Honor had a list, of course, complete with phone numbers, emails and office hours. "Come on, brother," she said after she handed it to him. "Let's walk up to the cemetery." She clipped the leash on Spike, who bounced and pranced and bit Jack's boot.

The night was cool, but spring was coming. Tomorrow, Ned was planning to tap the trees so they could make maple syrup, and in another month, the Hollands would gather for the blessing of the crops. Pops was still with them, Faith and Levi's baby would be here, Tom and Honor were married now and Charlie was living with them full-time.

Josh would be dead by then, Jack guessed.

Honor opened the gate to the cemetery, and they sat on one of the benches. There were flowers on Mom's grave. There always were.

"You gonna lecture me, too?" Jack asked.

"I'm so good at it," Honor said, linking her arm through his.

"True." Her dog nuzzled its way into Jack's coat. "You and Tom seem happy."

"Thanks. We are."

"Charlie, too."

"He's pretty great." She leaned her head against his shoulder. "I was surprised you and Em broke up," she said. "She seemed kind of perfect for you."

An image of Emmaline coming through his door, a smile on her face, rolled over Jack like a truck. Her in the bathtub, up to her neck in suds. In the hotel room in Malibu, that smear of chocolate on her cheek. Laughing with her teenagers.

"I didn't really plan on this," he admitted. "It's not like it was with Hadley."

"Thank God," Honor said, her tone dry.

"If I ask you a question, will you tell the rest of the Coven?"

"It depends on how much you spend on my next birthday present." She nudged his arm. "No, of course I won't tell."

"How did you know with Tom?"

She didn't answer right away, which was good, because unlike his other two sisters, it meant she was actually thinking. Pru would say something about the raw animal attraction between her and Carl. Faith would say something dreamy and mushy.

528

Honor would tell him the truth.

"I guess it was pretty simple. I pictured what I wanted in the future, and he was it. His smile, his laugh, his voice. I couldn't see me with anyone else. We, um . . . we didn't have the most typical start, but when it came down to it, he was just . . . the one."

There had been a night with Emmaline . . . a completely unremarkable night at his house. He'd cooked dinner, and she told him about a call involving a squirrel that had somehow gotten into Barb Nelson's china cabinet, and the subsequent rubble the rodent caused. Jack had laughed long and hard when she told him how she had to trip Everett and take his gun so he wouldn't shoot the wee beastie, Barb snapping pictures for the newspaper. They'd watched a movie after dinner. Well, half a movie. Maybe a third, because they'd ended up doing it on the couch, Em's skin so soft, her eyes big and dark.

An unremarkable night, except it was perfect.

"I screwed up with her," Jack said. "I'm not sure how to fix that."

"Well, you're a guy. Of course you screwed up. It goes with the territory." She straightened up. "But you'll make things right." She stood up. "I have to get back to the house. *Tree Bark Man* is on, and I don't want to miss it. Why don't you come watch it with us?"

At that moment, his phone rang.

Jeremy Lyon. "Hey. What's up?" Jack asked.

"Can you get to the hospital?" Jeremy said. "Gloria Deiner wants to see you, and you should come now."

"On my way," he said, hanging up. "Sorry, Honor. I have to run. Another time, okay?"

"Everything all right?" she asked.

"I think so. I'll see you tomorrow."

The elevator doors opened to the fourth floor. Jeremy was right there, waiting, looking oddly official in his white doctor's coat. "Josh is winding down," he said without preamble. "His parents are going to take him off life support, and Gloria asked to see you."

"Okay."

"You ready for this, Jack?"

"No. But yes." In fact, his heart was pounding, and his T-shirt was damp with sweat.

Jeremy smiled sadly, gave his shoulder a squeeze and led the way down the dimly lit hallway. "Gloria? Jack's here," he said outside room 405.

There was a whispered exchange, and then Mr. Deiner came out. He nodded at Jack, his eyes wet, and went down the hall.

"Come in," Mrs. Deiner said.

"I'll go stay with Alan," Jeremy said. He lowered his voice. "Good luck."

Jack went in.

And there he was. For the first time in all these

weeks, Jack saw Josh Deiner, the boy whose life he didn't save.

What was left of Josh, that was. Weeks on a feeding tube, weeks of profound brain damage and respirators and muscle wasting had reduced Josh to near-skeletal proportions.

Jack looked at Mrs. Deiner, who was staring at her son. "Mrs. Deiner?"

She didn't look at him. "I thought you might want to see him," she said.

"Yes," Jack said, then cleared his throat. "Thank you."

"Then have a seat," she said. Her voice was oddly calm. "You can talk to him if you want. They say hearing is the last thing to go."

Jack sat on the hard wooden chair. Mrs. Deiner didn't say anything else. The rhythmic wheeze of the respirator counted the seconds.

It was hard to see past the medical equipment, and the spooky, half-closed eyes. The respirator obscured much of Josh's face. His hands curled inward, and his arms seemed too long, they were so thin.

But his eyelashes were long and blond, and he looked more like a child than the eighteen-year-old Jack had pulled from the lake. He had a freckle under his ear.

"I'm sorry," Jack whispered. "I'm so sorry." He put his hand over Josh's. The skin was cool and too smooth.

And then Jack bent his head and covered his mouth with one hand so Josh's mother wouldn't hear him crying. But the hot tears spilled out of his eyes, and even though it had been twenty years since Jack had cried, he couldn't now seem to stop. The best he could do was try to keep quiet, even as his shoulders shook.

This wasn't fair. It wasn't right.

"Was he scared?"

Jack straightened up and cleared his throat. "No," he said, his voice husky. "He was unconscious."

Mrs. Deiner adjusted the blanket, pulling it over Josh's sunken chest. She smoothed his hair back, her hand lingering for a minute on her son's forehead. "I don't want him to die," she said, then gave Jack an almost embarrassed smile. "Obviously." Her eyes filled. "Even if he stayed like this, I'd take care of him. I wouldn't mind. I'm his mother. That's what I'm supposed to do."

Jack nodded, unable to speak.

"But he's dying anyway. He never did listen to me." She stared at her son, petting his too-long hair. "I know you did your best, Jack," she said without looking up. "Thank you for trying."

Once again, Jack bent his head and gripped the cold metal bar of the bed hard.

And then Gloria Deiner came to his side of the bed and put her hand on Jack's shoulder. "You should go now," she said.

Jack nodded. He stood up, then kissed Josh on the forehead. He turned and hugged the boy's mother, felt her sob against him. Tears sliced down his face again. "I'm so sorry," he said once more.

"I know," she whispered. "Me, too."

Chapter Thirty

On an obscenely sunny day in the last week of winter, when it seemed impossible that the birds could be singing and the sky so pure and blue, Josh Deiner was buried.

The whole town turned out for his funeral. Em was on traffic duty and led the procession to the cemetery. She parked the cruiser outside the gates, leaving the lights flashing, and got out. Right behind her was the funeral home limo, and as Mr. and Mrs. Deiner got out, Em swallowed hard. Mr. Deiner was bent by the weight of his grief, bowed like an old tree that would fall in the next storm, and Gloria looked right through Em without a flicker of recognition, her face tight, lips trembling.

Em's chest ached with suppressed sobs.

The entire senior class was there, each kid holding a white rose. Alyssa Pierson walked past, flanked by her parents, tears streaming down her face. Mr. Pierson nodded to Em, and Em murmured a hello. Mrs. Pierson had called Em to tell her Alyssa was doing better, and, indeed, the girl looked less unkempt. Devastated, of course. Everyone was, because though Josh wasn't the best kid, it was an unavoidable, wrenching truth —today, two parents were burying their only child. Josh would never get to be more than a reckless kid who broke his parents' hearts, ruined their lives, leaving a legacy of "don't be like me."

Emmaline lifted her sunglasses and wiped her eyes.

There were the Hollands, and her heart ached even more.

Jack's blond hair shone in the sunlight. He wore sunglasses and a suit, easy to spot, since he was taller than most. Did the Deiners know he was here? Please, God, there wouldn't be another scene like the one at the hospital, when Mrs. Deiner had screamed at him. He was too far away for Em to tell if he had that awful haunted look in his eyes that she'd seen so many times these past couple of months. This funeral must be agonizing for him.

Levi stood next to him, maybe as a guard, handsome and solemn in his dress uniform. He said something, eliciting a nod from Jack. Faith was right there, as well, recognizable by her red hair and enormous belly, and she put her hand on her brother's arm. Any day now for her, and it was good, a new baby in that family. Something for Jack to smile about, because that smile was one of the best things in the world, and, God, Emmaline missed seeing it, missed it so much in that second that it was hard to breathe.

Reverend White began the prayers, and Em looked down. She could hear the muffled sobs of some of Josh's classmates.

"Em?" Everett's voice was a whisper over the radio. He was at the tail end of the funeral procession, which curved around the cemetery.

"Yeah?" she whispered back.

"This is so sad." It sounded like he might be crying.

"I know, buddy. Hang in there."

A short time later, the crowd began walking slowly back to their cars. A few people stopped at other graves, brushing off some leaves or bowing their heads in prayer. A little boy, maybe four years old, ran ahead of his parents, laughing. He grabbed a pinwheel off one grave, and his mother ran up to him and put it back, then knelt down for a lecture.

Was that what Josh had been like? His mom had said he'd been full of mischief, always naughty, but with a smile that let him get away with it. From now on, Gloria Deiner would have to look at other children, and Em knew she'd always compare them to her son, her lost boy.

"Hi, Emmaline."

Em started a little. "Hey, Jack," she whispered around the lump in her throat. "How are you?"

He took off his sunglasses, and, though he looked tired, his eyes were clear. "I'm doing okay. Better."

"Good. That's . . . that's good, Jack." She paused, her hand going to her Taser. Nervous habit. God, she was as bad as Everett. "It's nice of you to come today."

"I got to see him," he said.

"You did?"

He nodded. "You were right, Emmaline," he said, his voice low. "I haven't been . . . myself. I'm sorry you got caught in the middle of everything."

"It's okay. It's fine."

He looked at her a long minute, his eyes the same color as the bright March sky.

She wanted to ask him how it was, seeing Josh. What had changed Mrs. Deiner's mind. If it had been awful. If he was sleeping at all. If he was back with Hadley, and if he *was* with Hadley, she hoped the other woman was taking good care of him, because Jack . . . Jack was one of a kind.

Her radio blipped. "I have to go," she said, and her voice was husky. "Traffic duty." She paused. "It was good to see you."

"You, too."

And then, because she didn't want him to see

her cry, when other people had much better reason to be sad today than she did, she got into the cruiser and did her job.

A week after Josh's funeral, Emmaline was sitting in the police station, trying to show Everett how to correctly upload a report. It was the perfect time to teach Everett some basic computer skills. Mindless work. Levi had taken the day off, so it was just Emmaline, Ev and Carol, and no crime to keep them busy. Manningsport had been somber since Josh died—no speeders, no crime, no DUIs.

Em hadn't seen Jack. The other night, Angela asked if she wanted to go to O'Rourke's and Em said no, just in case Jack was there. She was glad he'd had some closure with Josh, glad he was doing better. But it didn't change the fact that she was in love with him, and he didn't feel the same way. *You're right,* he'd said. *We should be done. I wasn't really looking for a relationship and neither were you.*

Right.

"So what now?" Everett asked, dragging her back to the present.

"Just click Upload. Right there. No, not Escape! Great. Now you have to enter it again."

"How come you know more about this than I do?" Everett asked. "I've been working here longer."

"Because you have the IQ of a chicken," Carol said.

"Now, Carol," Em said. "Everett has many qualities."

The phone rang, and Carol pounced. "Manningsport Police Department, is this an emergency? . . . Oh, hi, Levi! . . . Really? Finally! I thought she'd never—okay, fine, don't yell at me. She's right here." Carol gave Em a long-suffering look. "Faith's in labor and Levi wants a police escort."

Em picked up the phone. "Faith's in labor and I want a police escort," Levi ordered. "Get your ass here now."

"On my way." She ran out to the parking lot and got into the cruiser. Lights and sirens, and it was exactly as much fun as it sounded. She sped into town, blipped at intersections and turned onto Levi and Faith's street. Their cute little bungalow was a few blocks off the green.

But apparently, word had gotten out, because the street was mobbed. John Holland's dilapidated red truck, Prudence's equally abused blue truck, Honor's white Prius, Jack's gray pickup. Further-more, Colleen was standing on the lawn with the Barretts, who lived next door, as well as Faith's grandparents and nephew and Levi's sister. "So Sarah, we should go out sometime," Ned was saying.

"My brother will make sure your body is never

found," Sarah Cooper answered. "But if you're willing to risk it, so am I."

"Need some crowd control?" Emmaline asked.

"Actually, yes," Colleen said. "There are a dozen people in there."

Just then, the front door banged open, and Levi appeared, Faith in his arms.

"Now that's hot," Colleen murmured. "I want Lucas to do that for me when my time comes."

Various and sundry Hollands streamed after them—Abby, Pru, Honor, Mrs. Johnson, Faith's dad.

Jack.

He was smiling, and Em felt it like she'd just stepped into a patch of sunlight.

Well. He wasn't smiling at her. She wrenched her eyes off him. She was on duty, after all. She was needed.

It didn't stop her stomach from tightening. She tried to ignore it. "You doing okay, Faith?" she asked, trotting next to Levi as he strode to the car.

"He's overreacting," Faith said. "But I do kind of want to push."

"Don't push!" Levi barked. "Do not push, honey. Please. No pushing. We have fifteen minutes to the hospital. You can make it."

"Have we thought about an ambulance?" Em asked.

"Gerard Chartier is not seeing my girl parts," Faith said firmly. "I can hold it in. Oh! Wow! This hurts! Hurry up, babe. Not you, baby. You, babe."

Jack opened the backseat of Faith's car, and Levi lowered her in. "I'm driving," Jack said. "Stay in the back with your wife." He looked at Emmaline. "You ready?"

"All set."

She got into the cruiser and let the siren rip. Glanced back from time to time to make sure Jack was behind her and slowed for intersections, making sure all was clear.

She wouldn't think about Jack. Not that way, not now.

But it did dawn on her that Hadley hadn't seemed to be among the crowd.

The trick was to go fast but not too fast, and basically to just clear the runway, so to speak. Jack had his hazards on, and it looked like a colorful presidential entourage, with all the Holland vehicles following him.

They made it to the hospital in twelve minutes instead of fifteen, and Em ran in to get a gurney. Crowded day, of course. Full moon. Shelayne was on duty, surveying the waiting room with a frown.

"Baby coming," Emmaline called. "Faith and Levi's."

"About time!" Shelayne said. Small towns. No secrets.

Emmaline ran out with the gurney and Levi put his wife on it. She was clinging to his hand, doing that *hee-hee-hoo-hoo* thing that couldn't possibly work. Probably just to distract the woman from the fact that she was in labor.

Jack fell into step next to her, one hand on the gurney. Em could smell his good Jack smell—grapes and laundry detergent and sun. He smoothed some hair off Faith's forehead, and the gesture made Em's throat tighten.

He was *such* a good guy.

They went through the automatic doors of the hospital, Levi murmuring to his wife. Behind them, the Holland clan followed, chattering like magpies.

A couple of kids were waiting to be seen, one of them running around with a paper airplane, the other holding gauze on his chin as he wiggled his front tooth. Crazy Matthias Pembry was talking animatedly to himself—time for a medication adjustment, no doubt. An old lady in a wheelchair was glaring at the runner, and a man clutched a bloody dishcloth to his ear.

"Are you a nurse?" he asked. "I seem to have torn off part of my ear." He held something up. *Ah. The ear.* A small trail of blood ran down his neck.

"That's nasty," Faith said.

"Step away from my wife," Levi said, not nicely. *So cute, men!*

"Oh, another contraction. God, I'm amazing. Look at me, talking through these. I rock."

"No ego problems here," Jack murmured.

"I really want to push," Faith said, a little breathlessly. "Can I push? Technically, we're at the hospital."

"Don't push yet," Emmaline said. "Shelayne? You want this baby born here, or shall we get moving?"

"Everyone's a critic," Shelayne said, coming over. "Hi, Faith. About time. You ready to meet the baby?"

"Good luck, guys," Em said. Suddenly, she was choked up. She punched Levi on the shoulder, and off they went, a chorus of "Good luck, Faithie!" and "We love you!" floating behind them.

"I still think I should be her birthing coach," Prudence said, flopping into a chair. "I've done this twice. Ned slid out like he was greased, all bloody and cute—"

"Mother. Cease," Ned said.

"I'm hungry," the grandfather said. "Who brought food?"

"Fred Norbertson?" a nurse called.

The man with the ear wound started forward, but his, um, fragment fell to the ground. He didn't notice.

"You forgot your ear," Em said. Abby dry heaved.

"Oh! Thanks." He picked it up and smiled at Emmaline, giving her a quick up-and-down scan.

The entrance doors opened, and Colleen came

in, sliding her phone into her bag. "The vigil begins! Connor's sending over sandwiches. Are we waiting here, or are we going upstairs to Maternity? How many of us are there?"

Time for Emmaline to go. She was the outsider here. "Good luck, Team Holland," she said with a self-conscious wave.

A chorus of goodbyes and thanks rose up from the ranks.

Her eyes stopped on Jack. "Bye," she said.

"Thank you, Emmaline," he said. He smiled. And that was it. For a second, she thought he was going to say something more.

He didn't.

The drive back to the station seemed long and lonely.

It was after five, so technically, she was off duty. Carol and Everett were gone, though Ev was on call tonight.

She tidied up the department kitchen and sat down at her desk. As she filled out a few reports, her mind kept going back to the hospital. She hoped everything would go okay. Nice, that whole mob there, waiting for news of the baby. Hard to imagine, being a part of that, when her own family was so small.

Speaking of her family, maybe Ange wanted to do something tonight. Go for a run with Sarge, maybe get some nachos at O'Rourke's afterward. She picked up the phone.

Then the station door opened, and Jack came in. Em stood up fast. "Is everything okay?"

"Yeah. Everything's fine."

"Did the baby come already?"

"I don't think so."

Em took a quick breath. "Then what are you doing here? You should be at the hospital."

"Would you want your brother there?" he asked. "I can go over later. When everyone's clean and not bloody." He put his hands in his pockets. "I came to see you."

"Oh." She sank back into her seat. "Um . . . hi."

"Hi." He smiled, just a little, his eyes crinkling before his mouth moved.

"How are you?" She swallowed.

"I'm fine. How are you?"

"I'm . . . That's . . . yeah . . . Good, I mean." So smooth.

Jack came closer. As in, right next to her desk. "I took Hadley back to Savannah. She won't be back. In case you didn't hear."

"I didn't. That's . . . that's great. I mean, it's great if you say it's great."

He looked at her hands, then back up at her. "Emmaline, I'm so sorry for what I said about you being a bully. You're not. You couldn't be if you tried."

"Right." Her voice was a whisper now. "Thank you."

"Also, I'm in love with you."

544

"Is that right. Wait. What did you say?" She felt her face flush, and her heart, God, it was humming-bird fast.

He smiled, a full-on, 100 percent smile, a smile so good she felt it in every molecule. "I love you, Em."

"But . . . I thought you weren't, uh, looking for a relationship." Her eyes seemed to be filling up.

"I wasn't. I seem to have found one anyway."

"Oh. I . . . that's . . . that's good."

"Glad you think so." He reached into his pocket. "I brought you a present."

He handed it to her, and she had to laugh, because it was a bag of Skittles. "Got any chocolate cake to go with that?" she asked.

"I do at home."

Home. Now that was a nice word. There was a whole future in that word. He took her hand and looked at it for a second. "I got you this, too," he said.

And then he dropped on one knee, and Em found that she was shaking, and this was *quite* a surprise. But holy bleep, Jack was *proposing.* Or he had just lost a contact.

Except he didn't wear contacts.

He looked up at her with those blue, blue eyes. "You're the best person I know, Emmaline Neal. Give me another chance. Marry me."

He had a ring. A *ring.* Good God, he had a ring.

"Okay," she whispered, and it came out in a

squeak, but it didn't matter, because he slid the ring on her finger, and then he stood up and was kissing her, his mouth warm and firm and smiling against hers.

"I love you," he said again.

"It's about time," she whispered.

Epilogue

Well, of *course* we're here at Jack and Emmaline's wedding! Where else would we be? What a beautiful day they got, too! The barn looks beautiful, doesn't it? It's a Holland family tradition to get married here. Faith did, and so did Honor, just last year, remember?

Hmm. The wedding party's a little big, but with Jack's family, how can you blame them? Look at the program. The groomsmen are his three brothers-in-law—Levi, Tom and Carl—and his nephew, Prudence's son. And Connor O'Rourke, they're old friends, of course. I see Emmaline made his sisters and niece bridesmaids. Doesn't Faith look wonderful, and with little Noah just a few months old. Good for her.

No, the maid of honor is Emmaline's sister. Gorgeous girl! We heard she modeled in college, and we believe it! She's practically a celebrity around here. No, no, don't fix her up with your grandson. She likes girls. She lives in their grandmother's house now, down on Water Street, and their parents just bought a place a little ways out of town. Well, of course Emmaline will be living at Jack's! Have you seen that place? It's stunning.

Oh, and look at this. She included the members of that book club that never reads anything. Grace Knapton isn't here . . . No, she got married! She lives in Hawaii now! You didn't hear? Well, she does. Dr. Whitaker's doing a reading; that's nice. There's Shelayne, that nice nurse from the E.R. who just adopted Kelsey Byrd's baby. I guess they have one of those "open arrangements" so Kelsey can come see the baby from time to time. Got to hand it to Emmaline; we never thought those kids would graduate, but they made it.

Colleen O'Rourke is about ready to pop, speaking of babies, and look at the way her husband looks at her. Isn't that sweet? Soon we'll have another baby in town. Practically a population boom!

Oh, I missed this. "Parents of the groom, John and Hyacinth Holland." Well, she deserves it, Mrs. Johnson does. Jack dotes on her. He's always been her favorite. I heard she made the wedding cake—wouldn't let Lorelei near it. And it's just so sweet that Jack asked his father to be the best man. John Holland's been blessed with those four kids of his.

Shh! The music's starting!

Well, now, look at Emmaline! She's *beautiful!* That dress is amazing. Nice to see her out of a uniform! Who knew she had such a gorgeous figure? Yes, she does play hockey—look at those shoulders. That's how she and Jack met, I heard. Turns out he always had a thing for her.

And look at Jack. Oh, what a smile! He looks so happy.

Kind of brings a tear to your eyes, doesn't it?

That's the kind of love you usually only see in your dreams.

Acknowledgments

Thanks to my wonderful agent, Maria Carvainis, and to Martha Guzman, Elizabeth Copps and Bryce Gold for all they do for me. At Harlequin, a thousand thanks to Susan Swinwood, Margaret Marbury, the unrivaled sales team and everyone else at the company who has a hand in my books. It's a joy to work with such nice people.

Thanks to Sarah Burningham at Little Bird Publicity and Kim Castillo at Author's Best Friend. You guys are the bomb diggety, and I'm so happy I get to work with you!

Thanks to the very wonderful Sayre Fulkerson of Fulkerson Winery, and to John Iszard, who's ever so nice and helpful; to Sergeant Jamie Carr Prosser, who tolerated all sorts of burning questions, such as "I need there to be a squirrel, a gun and blood . . . can you help me?" On the medical front, thanks again to Dr. Jeffrey Pinco.

Thanks to my lovely Plot Monkeys—Shaunee Cole, Jennifer Izkiewicz, Karen Pinco and Huntley Fitzpatrick. I love you guys!

For the use of their names this time around, thanks to Allison Whitaker, M.D., and Shelayne Schanta. Thanks to Peggy McKenzie for the lovely title of this book.

To my sister, Hilary, and my brother, Mike—you're both great, even if you did always make me sit in the middle of the backseat and I got carsick all the time. Thanks to Mom for making me Magic Cookie Bars, among other things, like raising me and stuff.

Thanks to Jill Shalvis for the many, many laughs we had while locked up in a hotel room. Love you, Shalvis! And thanks to my countless writer pals, most of whom I've met through Romance Writers of America, the loveliest and most generous writers' group in the world.

To my husband and kids—I love you more than words can say.

And to you, dear readers. Thank you for spending your time with this book. It's truly an honor.

Center Point Large Print
600 Brooks Road / PO Box 1
Thorndike, ME 04986-0001 USA

(207) 568-3717

US & Canada:
1 800 929-9108
www.centerpointlargeprint.com